PRIDE
and
PROTEST

PRIDE and PROTEST

NIKKI PAYNE

BERKLEY ROMANCE
New York

BERKLEY ROMANCE
Published by Berkley
An imprint of Penguin Random House LLC
penguinrandomhouse.com

Library of Congress Cataloging-in-Publication Data

Names: Payne, Nikki, 1982- author.
Title: Pride and protest / Nikki Payne.
Description: First edition. | New York : Berkley Romance, 2022.
Identifiers: LCCN 2022011892 (print) | LCCN 2022011893 (ebook) |
ISBN 9780593440940 (trade paperback) | ISBN 9780593440957 (ebook)
Subjects: LCGFT: Novels. | Romance fiction.
Classification: LCC PS3616.A976 P75 2022 (print) | LCC PS3616.A976 (ebook) |
DDC 813/.6—dc23/eng/20220419
LC record available at https://lccn.loc.gov/2022011892
LC ebook record available at https://lccn.loc.gov/2022011893

First Edition: November 2022

Printed in the United States of America
2nd Printing

Book design by Daniel Brount

To Charlene, my audience of one, the sister I chose

PRIDE
and
PROTEST

MAN SHORTAGE

A RED LIGHT BLIPPED ON THE TOP LEFT OF THE CON-
trol board. Liza B. had a caller. "Hello and good evening.
You are live with Liza B., the only DJ who gives a jam. Tell me
what's on your mind . . ."

The producer mouthed a name to her.

". . . Keisha?"

"Girl, we are in a man shortage. I'm broke! I can't be buying
my own steaks," a cheery woman's voice buzzed over Liza's headphones. Liza pressed a flashing orange button on the control
board and slid the dial all the way to the top. This was *her* pulpit.
Instead of airbrushed paintings of blond Jesus, posters of Afrobeat
stars, Punjabi crooners, K-pop idols, and reggaeton bad boys com-
peted for space on the cork wall of the small booth. Instead of
scripture, someone had graffitied MEGARADIO SUX on the table. Her
parishioners called in with their "confessions" and she gave them
the good word. She wasn't saving orphans in Soweto like she always imagined, but it was a *kind* of service to the community.

"It *is* a man drought, girl," Liza agreed. "What do you plan
to do about it?"

"You know those new buildings that they're putting up at Netherfield Court?"

"You mean the overpriced luxury apartments that will force us out of our neighborhood and change the fabric of DC forever?" Liza said.

"Um . . . yeah, those . . ." Keisha stammered. "Anyway, there are a lot of men working construction. I'm just going to walk past there in my shortest shorts!"

Liza remembered why she liked this job so much.

"So they can catcall you? Whoop and holler? What are *you* getting out of this deal?" Liza pressed.

"Do I need to spell it out, Alizé Bennett?" The woman dragged her whole government name out like an old boot. Being named after an alcoholic drink popular in the nineties was *not* a fact Liza wanted broadcast across the nation's capital. She had job applications floating around.

"That's Liza B. *Leesa* with a *Z* to you." She kept her name explanations ready. People saw a *Z* in your name and lost their damn minds. She could not count how many times she had been called "Lizard" with a straight face.

"Well, Liza B., I'm a woman. I have needs."

"Excuse *me*, I thought it's a kind of truth universally acknowledged that every broke woman wants a rich man, not just vitamin D!"

"Times are changing, honey," Keisha told her. "The construction company is having a get-together over at Netherfield. Will the radio station be there?"

"I have to pass," Liza said. She couldn't begrudge people for wanting to get fed and dance on someone else's dime. But she had her principles.

"Good! Maybe the rest of us will stand a chance without you and your sisters showing up looking snatched!"

"The world *still* ain't safe with *you* on the loose!" Liza pressed the button and said good night to Keisha. "You heard it right here, fellas. Come check Ms. Keisha out! She'll be dressed to kill at the Netherfield Gala. Remember to drink up their champagne, *not* their Kool-Aid. We're not selling this city to the highest bidder! Liza B. is out of here, folks! If I'm not in the studio, hit me up on the 'Gram. I'm giving out prizes to my thirty thousandth follower, and it could be you!"

Liza swiped the overhead mic away and twirled in her spinning chair. No matter what the future held for the radio station, if they let her go, she could take pride in what she'd done. Liza never meant to be a local personality. She'd taken this job three years ago out of sheer desperation and worked her way up to airtime. Slowly, listeners tripled under her voice. Booth G was cramped, overflowing with leftover radio station swag and advertising scripts for Busboys and Poets. The pay was on the low side of moderate, and not even an entire can of Febreze could get the sweaty smell of the sports jockey out of the seat. But it was home to Liza. People *listened* to her here. In Booth G, she was never a disappointment.

———

"DEYA IS THE ONLY CHILD OF MINE WHO STILL BOTHERS to come to church with me." Liza's mother, Beverly Bennett, slapped her heavy purse down on the rickety table. Liza raised her eyebrow but otherwise didn't stir. A saltshaker rolled off the table, and her older sister, Janae, absently caught it before it hit the peeling linoleum floor. Their apartment in Longbourne Gardens had had the same decorations, furniture, and even salt-shaker placement for twenty-seven years. Granny, Bev, and now Liza, sometimes her brother Maurice, Janae, and her baby sister, LeDeya, all called the sprawling three-bedroom apartment home. Bev kicked at the boxes in the hallway, a reminder of Liza's recent eviction from her own apartment.

"When you say 'church,' you still mean Operation Snatch-a-Pastor right?" Liza shifted her laptop and checked her email for the third time. She was supposed to be hearing from USAID about an international project manager position at a bank for women in Malawi. It had several things going for it: she could use her international studies degree and women's studies master's, she would have someplace to stay without fear of her rent rising above her ability to pay, and she would be thousands of miles away from her mother.

"Yes, Mother, what *was* the sermon about?" Janae chimed in, in a rare moment of fun at her mother's expense. Bev ignored Janae's tone and zeroed in on Liza.

"Liza, I want these boxes out of my hallway. This ain't the UPS Store." Bev pulled at her wig. The cascading platinum blond tresses shifted slightly to the left, then right. "What I *heard* in Bible study is that you were out there picketing for *the gays*," Bev informed her.

She made it sound like a Motown girl group. "Mom, you can just say 'gay,'" Liza said.

"Correct me again, and I'll correct your behind!" Bev spat out impatiently. "I don't want you involved in anything that's gonna ruin the family's reputation, you hear?"

Liza's mouth twisted sideways. "Mom, 'birthing the three prettiest daughters in Southeast' is not a reputation, it's an opinion."

"*Southeast*? My Janae was almost Miss DC—*the entire district*—for three years straight. And if you'd stop wearing those no-prescription granny glasses and put on a high heel every once in a while . . ." Bev didn't need to finish. This was a well-traveled conversational tributary that would eventually lead to her wailing that Liza didn't try hard enough—for a job, for a man, or for herself.

Janae sighed. "'Three-time runner-up' will be on my gravestone."

Bev eyed Liza again. "Your foolishness almost made me forget the good news. Where is your granny?" Bev stepped out of her shoes and handed them to LeDeya. "She's on the Longbourne Gardens Green Committee, and those nice little people next door at Netherfield Court invited all the gardeners to their groundbreaking gala."

Maurice sauntered into the front room then, dressed in a tan suit with a brown bow tie. He was going for a Nation of Islam look with none of the entanglements of having read any of the doctrine. He shook his locked hair out. At twenty-two, his face still flirted with handsomeness but never really settled there.

"Salutations, ladies," Maurice said.

"Maurice, you missed church," Liza said. "Momma, why didn't you wake Maurice up for church?"

They all knew why she didn't wake Maurice. Since he'd gotten back home from serving thirteen days for failure to pay traffic tickets, Maurice had been aggressively "woke." He went vegan for exactly six days, paid for an Arabic class he never showed up for, and kept calling women "*fe*-males" in a way that sounded a lot like "bitches."

"I think we should go to the gala," Bev said, ignoring Maurice entirely.

Liza closed her laptop slowly. "Momma, you cannot allow those developers to try to sweet-talk these senior citizens out of their apartments!" Liza stood up. "The only reason they want the seniors there is to scope them out. Longbourne Gardens is the last low-income complex in the area. My rent rose forty percent above what I paid before, and here *I* am living with you. Where are the poor supposed to live if they tear this down too?"

"Big sis is entirely correct . . ." Maurice piped in. Liza groaned. "This has its origins in African colonialism. The white man's need to colonize Black space is insatiable. That's why I see my dating of exclusively white women as reverse colonization. We need to rec—"

"Liza, do you hear that? *Maurice* is cosigning." LeDeya stomped her foot. "That should let you know how lame you're being right now. Why do you never want to have any fun?" LeDeya reached for Liza's laptop. At sixteen, she had already taken after their mother—all curves, height, big hair, and incredible nosiness. "Momma says those people over there are loaded—I'm talkin' Red Lobster rich."

Liza and Janae exchanged looks, but Maurice seemed to reconsider. LeDeya pressed on. "She just wants us to go to this little groundbreaking and be introduced to some people." LeDeya quickly tapped on Liza's laptop, then turned it around to show the evite in Liza's email like a *Price Is Right* model.

Liza lunged for her computer. "That only shows me you figured out my password again."

"There was nothing to figure out." LeDeya easily held the machine above her shorter sister's head. "It's *always* some lame variation of 'QWERTY123.'"

"Stop your snooping, Deya." Granny ambled into the living room from the back room. Her tennis shoes squeaked on the clear plastic runner supposedly protecting the grungy brown carpet. She wore a purple velour tracksuit with a polyester turban and large pearl earrings. She looked like she should pace around a neighborhood mall at all times or possibly tell fortunes in a storefront. "You too fast, girl." She eyed her youngest granddaughter. "You will not be introduced to any grown men—rich or broke."

LeDeya bent her head down, and she punched Liza in the arm before plopping herself on the sofa. She opened Liza's laptop again and began immediately scrolling through Instagram. Granny's word was like iron. In the ongoing saga between Liza and her mother, Granny was always saving Liza before total catastrophe struck.

"And you oughta listen to Liza every once in a while, Beverly," Granny continued. "She's the only one of you with some actual sense. Them people ain't nothing but vultures. Them fat cats want to know two things: what else they can tear down to make some money, and if we stupid enough to let 'em."

"Ma," Bev pleaded, "they're supposed to be all green and affordable. They have units set aside for the poor. Even Rosa Parks over here can't deny they're trying harder than those other guys."

"Okay, they want some good PR," Liza replied. "They want some poor Black people huddled around the microphone being thankful to their white saviors who are going to revitalize the community. And when they say 'revitalize,' they mean to take all the black and brown out of the décor," Liza said.

"Amen, sister," Maurice said. "But on second thought, this could be a chance to strike from within. Think of how uncomfortable it will make everyone there to see me, a hardened criminal raised by the streets—"

"Maurice, you were raised by your granny, and you didn't pay your parking tickets," Liza retorted.

Maurice looked taken aback, then shook his head in resignation. "That's the problem with sistas—they're too myopic. Can't see the long game."

"Oh Liza, USAID regrets to inform you they went with another candidate," LeDeya broke in.

Liza snatched her laptop away from her sister and slammed it closed with too much force. "Stay out of my email, Deya!" Heat crept up Liza's neck. It was the third no this month.

"It's funny that my daughter who finds fault with *everything and everybody* can't even find a job as a dog catcher or keep a man longer than a summer. Maybe look at your own self before you offer your famous opinions up?" Bev said. Her neck slid from side to side like an abacus bead.

Janae patted Liza gently while shooting a warning look at Bev. "Keep at it, Liza. You'll find your fit. As for the event, I think we can compromise. I think they want to build a community garden with the elders before the gala—no cameras. You know how Granny feels about gardening." Once Granny's eyes lit up, it was all but over. Bev smiled in triumph.

Liza was already deflating. "How do you know this?" It maddened her that her sweet-faced sister could convince people of something with such little effort, while Liza had been shouting all her life to no avail.

Janae unfolded a small flyer and handed it to her sister with a look. The subtext was clear. *Let Granny shine.* There were no World's Best Widows or Top Seamstress awards coming for her anytime soon.

African prints and gardening tools—two of Granny's obsessions—outlined the trim of the paper. "'Each one, teach one, Harambee,'" Liza mumbled under her breath. "'Developers and community members learn from each other! Let's build together! Join us for a community gardening event before the gala! Winner of the best home garden competition wins a trip to Philadelphia for Pemberley Development's fifty-year corporate anniversary.'"

The flyer was perfectly calibrated for the fifty-and-older set:

- Nebulous Pan-African language
- Magical Black mentors meet well-meaning white people
- Some distant promise of cash and travel

"Okay, *one* assistant writes a good flyer, and now they have permission to trample all over us?" Liza knew this was a lost cause, but she just had to be on record saying this was a *bad* idea. The battle against Netherfield Court was the only thing that was going right. It was the cause the community had *finally* rallied around her on, and with her recent eviction and looming job loss, she just wanted this *one* thing to go right.

Granny was already moving toward her overgrown jungle of a patio. "I suppose there are some things I *can* show these youngbloods . . ." Granny scratched the loose turban, shifting it comically to the side. "I guess I can go. But *just* to the gardening," she said, plucking a wilted leaf from the money tree she spoke to every morning.

LeDeya and Bev huffed, but Bev was the only one to speak. "Ma, how can you deny these girls the chance to meet men looking their best? Don't nobody wanna get all dirty gardening! Oh, my nerves!" Bev grabbed the worn fabric of the armchair. Her bracelets clinked and glittered. "You want these kids stuck in this apartment for the rest of their lives? Grown women and men sleeping two to a bedroom?" Her voice wavered. "You want them just like me. Trapped."

"These girls gotta get out of here with their minds, child, not their bodies." Granny huffed.

"When," Bev howled, "has that *ever* worked?"

Later, Liza sat alone in a darkened corner with her phone, still a little wounded by Janae siding with Bev, her thumbs tapping at her phone. The blank cursor bounced on her Instagram screen: It's #TFW Tuesday, hotties, you know what to do. I'll start us off! #TFW You feel completely alone in a room full of people.

ADVERSITY

From: HampdenR@PemDevCo.com
To: DFitz@PemDevCo.com
Subject: Acting CEO duties

The board would like to remind you again that it is currently not within your powers as acting CEO to amend or augment any existing portions of the budget. Rest assured, we are committed to the World Children's Organization as much as your mother was. But we will hold no further meetings about the budget.

You were absent from three groundbreaking ceremonies, and you also declined a golf invitation from a Virginia State senator very active in DC politics. The board would like to see you out in front for the company. You are a fresh face in development, and the board wants to capitalize on some of the excitement around you.

Best,
R.H.

Dorsey raised his arms to point at another graphic. When he looked down, he was horrified to see the deep half-moons of perspiration under his arms. It was fall in Philadelphia, so he couldn't blame the weather for the cold sweat drenching his body.

"I'm sorry, young man, what you're proposing is tantamount to theft," an older man grumbled.

"A tax on shareholders is what it is," another man said.

Dorsey ground his teeth. He was always "young man" when the board wanted to put him in his place. He found his sister's kind brown eyes. She silently mouthed the word "research."

Dorsey gulped an entire glass of water and exhaled. He was bombing this meeting. He knew it. His sister knew it. And the board knew it.

He pointed to the slide. "Companies with strong social performance also have strong financial performance."

"A positive association between charitable contributions and profits does not mean that giving serves a legitimate business purpose. Prosperous companies simply have more cash and highly valued shares, which makes it easier to give to charity," a woman countered. That comment got a lot of approving murmurs. Dorsey's chest tightened. Charitable giving should not be this controversial, but he had been locked in a battle of wills with the board for far too long, and they smelled blood in the water.

"Not always—" Dorsey began.

"Dorsey, we understand and appreciate you attempting to further your mother's philanthropic legacy. But an economic recovery is no time to increase spending. We were all shocked by your family's tragedy. But we must pull this company up, and we can't get sentimental about Pemberley's ultimate north star—

development," Hampden, a broom-bristle-mustached man said, his eyes a mix of pity and annoyance.

A cold-eyed woman shifted in her seat at the end of the table. "Do you have any *new* business? We'd like a report on the Netherfield properties."

That was it. He was shut down. He was acting CEO and had never felt the *acting* part more completely than he did right now. At thirty, he was too young to be taken seriously and too old to brush off. The board had been prepared to hold a nationwide search for a CEO when Gigi sounded the alarm and pushed him out in front, muscling their majority shares into a hammer and forcing the other shareholders' hands.

On cue, Gigi spoke, working her magic. "The CEO makes a valid point about the connection between strong philanthropic initiatives and economic success. Corporate giving programs can provide a competitive advantage when they are well designed and carefully executed, both of which I believe we've been capable of doing in the past," she said. "I mean, I'm just a business student here, but I think after we successfully launch Netherfield Court, we might be well-placed for federal development projects."

The room discussed the possibilities of federal contracting. The board members were seeing green, but Dorsey caught his sister's double meaning. *Give them Netherfield, and they will give you your philanthropy budget.*

The meeting adjourned early, though Dorsey, ever the realist, knew his presentation was likely already forgotten. Hampden came up to him and clasped his shoulder.

"We're more alike than you know, Dorsey. Your dad was a powerful personality, and your mother was a compassionate soul. I was there when he adopted every single one of you kids.

But you have to understand, his board is the same way—a *found* family handpicked by him for our skills. This meeting seemed harsh, but your father trusted us, and so should you."

Dorsey shook himself loose of the man's firm grip. "I trust you, Mr. Hampden, to maintain the same level of giving as we had just two years ago."

"I think coming from such *adversity* as you did, you'll always have a fighting spirit, and knowing that your father named your *younger* sister over you couldn't have been easy. But you have an opportunity here that only a handful of people in the world have. So let's just stay the course until she's ready to lead." Mr. Hampden tilted his head toward Gigi. "Make sure you're handing her a company in the best position it can be."

Dorsey had heard this many times over from his father's friends and family in the past year. It went like this:

- *The reminder that he had been plucked from obscurity out of the Philippines as a boy*
- *The subtle acknowledgment that he should be grateful for his position*
- *The even-gentler dig that he was not his father's choice to lead*

Not necessarily in that order, but always there.

"Mr. Hampden, I understand I am not anyone's idea of a natural heir to Pemberley Development. Instead of getting an MBA, I went into the Peace Corps. You read the *Wall Street Journal*, I read *The Atlantic*. I *understand* what that costs me. But right now, I *am* the CEO, and I want a larger budget for our key strategic philanthropic measures."

Gigi sidled up beside Dorsey, polished as ever. "Thank you

for your perspective, Mr. Hampden. We'll take it under consid-
eration." She nodded politely to the older man, and brother and
sister walked out of the boardroom in silence.

Gigi pressed the button for the elevator. "Datu, don't piss off
the board." She always called him his Tagalog surname when
she felt conspiratorial. He was born _____ Datu-Ramos. How
eager to get rid of him must his mother have been to not even
quickly scrawl a first name for him before she left him wrapped
in a soft T-shirt at an international orphanage. By nine years
old, he was just a surname and did not even know he was *without*
a first name until his first day in America. Unlike his sister, who
had known her Kenyan full and elaborate name her entire life.
The double standard, of course, was that she despised being
called Gheche.

"Gigi, I know I'm not a good surrogate, but I believe in this."
The doors closed behind them, and Gigi immediately took off
her high heels and put them in her enormous bag. She pulled out
a pair of simple Chuck Taylors and shoved them on, holding on
to her brother's arm for stability.

"You made brilliant points *and* had research to back it up.
They simply don't want to increase the budget because it risks
their own take-home. Your pitch was solid, bro. You just cannot
understand purely self-interested motivation." Gigi pulled off
her suit jacket and stuffed it into the bag as well.

When the doors peeled open, Dorsey and Gigi exited the
elevator nearly in perfect lockstep. Dorsey eyed an older woman
who had stopped to stare at them. Physically, they looked nothing alike. His sister's skin was the rich mahogany of the soil of
her native land, Kenya, while he had the umber complexion of his
native Philippine Islands. Her hair was a spun-cotton cloud of
tight brown coils, and his was a uniform curtain of bone-straight

ebony strands that he kept shoulder-length. Sure, they didn't look like siblings, but Gigi was his sister all the way down to their matching vintage Chucks and identical mannerisms. He'd grown accustomed to the looks they got and used to think it was purely racial. But as Gigi grew into womanhood, the looks had changed from confusion to something else—admiration. She had finally grown into her long features and had gone from gangly and bucktoothed to graceful and, well, slightly *less* bucktoothed. Braces could never *quite* conquer her prominent incisors.

He had also found himself suddenly the center of giggling girls' attention in high school when he shot up to an ostentatious six foot two. He had been a brooding teen, one of no less than ten adopted Asian children in his high school, and he was the only boy. They all actively avoided one another in school. It had somehow been lonelier to acknowledge the other kids' existence.

His recent breakup only proved what he'd known for a long time: he didn't fit anywhere. Even when he actually tried (and, god, how he *hated* trying), women really only wanted him to be someone else—to stay rich, of course, but to be some other fantasy they had. He had even watched *Spinster Island* for a girlfriend once—objectively the worst show on television. *That* was love, watching trashy reality TV for someone.

Why were there so *many* women if he was so terrible? He imagined the money helped. His older brother, Alexi, had had no problem keeping girlfriends. Pale as alabaster with sandy curls and piercing gray eyes, Alexi was rowdy and irreverent and had clashed with his parents about everything. They had lost him in the same devastating car accident that claimed their parents. Now the trio of siblings was down to two. Dorsey knew if Alexi were here, he would have much more vulgar words for Mr. Hampden and the board. Alexi had done everything boldly. What Dorsey called "thoughtful," Alexi would call "chickensheet" in his curled Slovenian accent. Now with his father and Alexi gone, and Gigi skilled but too young, Dorsey was suddenly the face of a development corporation. His family's legacy now rested on his shoulders.

"That wasn't too bad," Gigi said, bringing him back to the present. "If you give them Netherfield, they'll increase their CSR funds."

"Why can't they just keep the same rate they had in the past? Why do I have to beg for money that should have been set aside?" Dorsey asked.

"Sometimes to get what you want, play your cards a little closer to your vest. You're too rigid, D—"

"Don't say that. Don't call me rigid. I hate how much I'm expected to act. I hate how much time I waste being who I'm not!" Dorsey's voice tightened, and Gigi recoiled.

"Why do I have a feeling this is not all about the meeting? How's Rebecca?" Gigi nudged him toward a bistro, but Dorsey shook his head.

"Rebecca and I aren't together anymore."

"When did she break it off?"

"*I* broke it off." Dorsey couldn't hide his churlish tone. "Can't do the CEO and relationship thing."

"Dad did it for twenty-five years."

"All the ways I am not Dad could fill a book, Gigi."

Gigi turned to face him. "Why did you break it off for real?"

Dorsey started to double down, then gave up. It was hard to con his little sister. "She was DMing her ex. Called me an anxious bore and, I quote, 'acted like you're ashamed of me in public.'"

"You *are* weird about public stuff. Especially dancing and even holding hands. But how did you find out?" Gigi asked.

"It was the classic left-my-laptop-out situation," Dorsey told her. "I think she actually wanted me to see."

"Wow, four weeks. At least she was fun."

"About as fun as being hit by a bus."

"Well, we throw that party in DC next week. I have finals, but there are sure to be plenty of women there." Gigi paused. "You should really try for the board."

"If they want a show pony, Gigi, they need to increase the budget."

"They want to see that you're taking this position seriously. Win at Netherfield Court and they'll take the training wheels off, Dorsey, I'm sure of it. Why don't you bring David?"

Dorsey considered it. It could be a double whammy. David worked for their New York office, and he was the son of Robert Bradley, a board member and one of his father's oldest friends. It could work. People *loved* David. "I'll ask him," Dorsey agreed. "There is also some local discontent with the new buildings, and David may be a good person to smooth things out."

"I heard about that. Are you going to address it?" Gigi asked.

Dorsey summoned his Tesla. "God, no. I'm going to beef up security."

BABYLON

"YOU'RE LIVE WITH LIZA B., THE ONLY DJ WHO GIVES A jam. We have Tim from Anacostia on the line. What's on your mind, Tim?" Liza cooed.

"Hey, Liza, tell me you've heard about this party at Netherfield Court. My sisters are acting like the Super Bowl is in town."

"Oh, I heard about it all right. And I'm not mad at anybody trying to find love, but I agree that we have to look at the bigger picture here. They were foolish enough to give me a ticket, Tim, and you better believe I won't be there kissing frogs! These guys won't know what in the matcha-green-tea-latte hit 'em."

"Changed your tune since last week, eh?"

Liza straightened her shoulders. "You can do a lot of damage from inside the machine, Tim."

"Bob Marley said Babylon is everywhere."

"And we can fight it from anywhere," Liza finished. "Let me help set the mood. Download my playlist. I'm posting it . . . now. Feel my feels. Here's the first song on there."

Excitement pulsed through her. They would turn Booth G

into a shrine when she was gone. She adjusted her headphones and spoke into the microphone.

"The time is now. I know you've heard of a flash mob. Everyone gets together and spontaneously dances. At this Netherfield pity party, get ready for a flash protest! Show up, grab a sign, and smile for the world!"

"Liza, will you be bailing people out of the jail they all gonna throw our asses in for trespassing on a private event?" This caller was a tad peevish.

"I wonder if MLK wondered who would bail him out as he wrote his letters in a Birmingham jail?" Liza countered.

"You ain't no MLK, and I ain't going to jail so you can go viral."

"Yes, live comfortably, Caller Thirteen." Liza hung up the phone. "Many are called for the revolution, but few are chosen, folks. Meet me. Dare greatly." Liza had read this somewhere, and it seemed appropriate now.

LIZA LOOKED AT HER FACE IN THE MIRROR. TONIGHT WAS the groundbreaking gala, and she hardly recognized herself. "Deya, you're a magician. Where did my pores go? I did not know you were so good!" Liza's dark eyes sparkled. The liner and mascara brought out the doll-like roundness of her eyes. Her lips were full and deep red, and her eyebrows were perfectly arched. Her skin was a glowing warm brown that looked inviting and lush. LeDeya had a gift of transforming anyone into a beauty, including herself. Liza sometimes wondered if LeDeya had left any time to work on the inside when she took such pains to craft her own facade.

Liza *thought* she looked good . . . until she saw her older sister. Taller, sweeter, prettier, better—Janae was all "-er" than Liza.

"You are so . . . gorgeous," LeDeya and Liza said in unison. The word didn't seem right for what Janae looked like in her green pageant gown with her hair all swooped up in a classic roller set. She looked like Dorothy Dandridge in Technicolor.

"You guys are on the payroll." Janae blushed prettily. They all looked at one another for a moment and squealed. "Oh, Liza, I know how you feel about the politics of all of it, but I'm looking forward to the party. I just don't get to dress up like this anymore," Janae said.

"I know," Liza whined. A stab of guilt pinged at her side. "I thought I wouldn't want to go, but the more I saw you get ready, the more excited I became. I'm happy for you."

"Not just for me, Liza. *You* could meet someone too," Janae said.

Liza's mother had always had a powerful belief that a beautiful girl and a lonely, rich man were an instant recipe for love, and Janae shared their mother's penchant toward the fanciful. Liza thought it was endearing only when *she* wasn't one of the victims.

LeDeya snorted. "Fat chance. She's still got dirt under her fingernails from gardening with Granny at the Harambee. She is not trying to meet anyone." Her little sister's false eyelashes swooped up and down like feathered fans.

"Liza . . ." Janae said warily. "That's not dirt, that's marker." Janae folded her arms. "Whatever you're planning, I'm not saving you from Mom this time."

"What?" Liza said, trying to look innocent. "Janae, can you trust me for once? We'll just go to have fun." Liza looked away on the last part. They would only try to dissuade her if they knew.

"Go wash your hands, then," Janae scolded.

"You two are elitist swine," Liza said while the faucet water ran. "My man will love my dirty hands. 'I love a woman who can get filthy,' he'll say." She hugged herself tightly and gave the impression that dirty hands were groping her back. Her dress was one of Janae's early pageant dresses before she'd shot up three inches in six months, a black lace halter with a short, ruffled tulle bottom. It was backless, all the way to the base of her spine. It was a bold look to be sure. But she was too short to pull off a gown like her sisters, who had gotten their mom's height.

She was most proud of this hair, though. Liza's hair was in an immaculate twist-out that sat in rich brownish-red curls out to her shoulders. She had to immortalize it now before it turned into a ball of fur in ten minutes. When she pulled out her phone, her two sisters immediately went into a duck-face-hot-girl pose, and they must have snapped forty pictures between them.

"Off we go, Bennett sisters!" Liza said and snapped two more filtered pictures of her and her sisters.

"Are you going to post these on your Insta account?" LeDeya smiled into the camera.

"Not with those boobs out, I won't," Liza said.

LeDeya shrugged in her borrowed salmon taffeta gown. Even at sixteen, LeDeya filled out the chest much more than her sisters.

Janae pulled at the back of LeDeya's dress nervously. "I guess I let it out a little too much," she said while holding a sewing needle between her teeth. Liza laughed as LeDeya tugged, pulled, and protested against her oldest sister's modest revisions.

Liza scrolled to the best photo of all three of them and posted it with the hashtags #offtoBabylon #Bennett2winit.

Her feed exploded with exclamations and thumbs-up emojis. If her plan worked, she'd be a household name. Her followers were itching for a confrontation.

MERINO WOOL

From: DFitz@PemDevCo.com
To: Tom@TopSecurity.com

Just double-checking on the security parameters we set up for tonight. No one gets in with heavy coats, bandanas, signs, or weapons. I only plan to be there for the first 45 minutes. So let's make sure I have a detail in case people want to swarm me or pick my pockets.

D.F.

Dorsey Fitzgerald was in a terrible neighborhood. On purpose.

He leaned against the back doors of the Fort Stanton Rec Center. Tonight, he was supposed to be all smiles and graciousness. This was his first real showing as CEO, and he supposed CEOs had to do stuff like this all the time. He had struggled in business classes. His father wouldn't hear of him majoring in anything other than civil engineering. So he did what he always did—what was expected. He could see Longbourne Gardens from here—a battered condominium community next on his company's list to redevelop. He thought a vegan bakery and possibly a pet-grooming spa would do well there. They were the type of terrible trendy shops that signaled to old inhabitants: *You don't belong here anymore.* For the hundredth time, he asked himself if this was worth it. *Be smooth and smiling. Deliver Netherfield Court on a silver platter.*

He pulled a Treasurer cigarette from its slim gold package, then lit a match against the brick wall behind him and sucked his guilty pleasure down. Dorsey looked around at the liquor store and a church unironically named Our Lady of Perpetual Help sitting on opposite sides of the street, defiantly competing for the souls of the inhabitants. Cash-advance storefronts beamed neon **OPEN** signs that illuminated the cracked wet sidewalks like a vivid pulp detective movie. In his briefs, he was advised to engage in conversation about local curiosities, like that inexplicably giant chair on the corner of MLK. Apparently, it had held the title of World's Largest Chair for a brief period. If he had to talk about upholstery at all tonight, he wouldn't make it through the evening.

He saw her before she saw him. It took him a minute to be sure of what he was seeing—the image was so disjointed. A petite woman . . . naked? No, in a backless dress and some sort of large, furry hat on her head, hauling things out of a car. Yes . . . dragging what looked like picket signs out of a dark car.

Oh no. Not this shit.

"Where do you think you're going with those?"

At the sound of his voice, she stilled and the dark car sped away with a cartoonish rubber-to-pavement sound. The woman squared her shoulders and turned around. Upon seeing him, she visibly relaxed her shoulders and put one finger to her full lips, winking conspiratorially.

"Hey, brother, don't mind me." She hopped to the rec center's side door—not used to the heels, a tomboy playing at seductress. He then realized that the furry creature on her head was her hair. Dark coils defied gravity around her, like one of those eleventh-century frescos of monks with halos.

Here she comes, Our Lady of Perpetual Help.

The woman showed him the signs, which read, WE DIDN'T ASK 4 NO NETHERFIELD! and WE WILL NOT BE DISPLACED. She was actually proud of this kindergarten display of disagreement.

"Can you tell me which poster will look best with the Mayfair Instagram filter? Don't you think this has too much red?"

She *couldn't* know who he was. Dear god, she kept talking. She wanted in. And she was not above using her charms to get past him. The security he'd set up was an absolute joke.

"Do you want a picture with me?" she continued. "You can tag me. Trust me, it's gonna be great for your feed."

This woman sidled up next to him, her hair tickling his jaw. She made a peace sign and pushed out her hips in a pose he had seen too many times. Roasted coffee beans and some other nutty sweet smell curled around him. When his arm didn't lift to snap the photo, she nodded. "You're right, this is your place of employment. If they think you had something to do with this, you don't know where your next paycheck would come from." She put her hand to her heart. *"Solidaridad, hermano."* He would have laughed if he weren't so offended.

He got this a lot, actually. No one could ever guess his heritage, and he did not look like his parents *remotely*, so no one would assume he was the scion to the country's most profitable development firm. He was the brown-skinned Asian in the crowd of pale, patrician faces. At six foot two, he was freakishly tall for a Filipino, unfashionably dark for a Taiwanese, too vaguely Asian for his white American friends, and too socially awkward for the wealthy socialite set. His loving adoptive mother and father never seemed to notice how often their multicultural children were mistaken for the servants' children. His Kenyan sister, his Slovenian brother. No one was ever really sure how they all fit together, but they had, and before the accident, they had all been happy. Only two Fitzgeralds had escaped that car accident. And while he was grateful he and his little sister survived, Dorsey sometimes wished that someone other than him—someone more worthy of the title—could protect the family's interest.

People like this insipid woman with ridiculous hair did not see past his race to determine his position in society. Was he a busboy out for a smoke break to her? *The gall*. She put her hands on his forearms and frowned, appearing slightly surprised by the soft, buttery feel of the coat.

"So nice . . . What is this material?" she asked.

"Merino wool," he said coolly. "Hand-tailored." A wholly unnecessary comment, but he wanted her to take the bait. His responsibility was over, really. He had subtly told her he wasn't who she thought. To her credit, her smile did not waver. Her eyebrows knit together with the slightest tell of confusion.

She was probably the prettiest girl in her little neighborhood. Who in this sad-ass place could say no to *that* high beam smile? She *was* pretty, he allowed, but he had grown up with sun-kissed California girls, met Nigerian princesses, lounged on the beaches of Rio de Janeiro with Brazilian beauties, and bought items right off a model at Paris Fashion Week just to see her naked—so he could certainly handle DC pretty. So why were his nails digging into his palms? He was too wired. Perhaps he had smoked one too many.

When she saw that neither her Instagram barter nor flirting was working, she reached into her tiny purse and pulled out two crumpled ten-dollar bills.

The absolute nerve of this woman.

"I was saving this for the bar, but why don't you hold on to it? You didn't see me here," she said—and winked! This woman winked! What kind of used-car salesperson was she?

"Sure, lady." He took the twenty dollars and grinned. "Why don't you let me put your signs in the kitchen? I know a real good place."

"Oh, I couldn't . . ." the woman said, though he could already see that she was considering it.

"There is no way to hide them in the ballroom. You'll show your hand too soon. There's security everywhere," Dorsey offered sweetly.

"Really? I didn't see much . . ." the woman said, looking around. "The fools who set this up put security on the entrances, but not the exits. All you have to do is catch someone coming out." Of course this little hoodlum knew how to get around security.

"The person—er people who set this up are smarter than that. I'm kind of on the *inside* of this, so . . ."

The woman seemed to soften. "I guess you would know." She nodded slowly. "Okay, you're right . . . Actually, that's a better idea. I should have thought about how it would look on the inside." She patted his shoulder the way you would pat the haunches of an obedient pet.

Dorsey was nearly seething now. *I am a damn thirty-year-old man!*

"They can't be paying you much here." She looked into his eyes, all fake earnest, with the condescension that seemed to be the natural birthright of do-gooders. "But there are people out here who see your struggle." She touched his sleeve again.

When had he given her permission to touch him so? His cheeks burned. *A blush is a perfectly reasonable reaction to anger.*

"Oh, they give you such nice uniforms," she continued and rubbed his forearm again. "I just want you to know we're fighting for the rights of everyone in this community: Black, Latino, Asian, whatever." She held her hand out like a job interview candidate—all enthusiasm and fake bravado. "I'm Liza. You may already know my voice." She cleared her throat. "The only DJ who gives a jam?" When he didn't respond, she faltered slightly. "And are you *full-time* event staff? What do you do?"

This was his chance once again to set her straight. He let it pass.

"You mean besides co-conspiring with back-alley activists?" Dorsey quipped and was pleased to see her eyes sparkle. He rarely made jokes that landed. "What do *you* think I do?" he asked. *Why am I trying to prolong the conversation?*

"Um . . . audition as the villain in telenovelas?" Liza retorted.

Dorsey let out a genuine laugh at that, surprised by someone for the first time in . . . he didn't know how long.

"Sell vape pens out of your coat?" she continued.

Dorsey clutched his chest. "Ouch, you think I would vape?"

"I smell the remnants of a nasty habit. And you have a man bun."

"I smoke when I'm nervous. But I try not to make being nervous a habit." Why did this woman need a run-through of his insecurities five minutes into meeting? He touched the small bun at the back of his head. His stylist had convinced him this would be "dead sexy." She flashed him another smile—the charlatan. He could see her on the streets of Cairo, coaxing travelers into just one more follow-the-ball game. He was still surprised at the tiny jolt in his low belly.

"You have nothing to be afraid of. *I'm* the one who has to stand up to some old white dude—Dorsey Fitzwhateverthehell. It's truly terrifying to make people with money angry. One snap of his powerful fingers, and I'm poof! Gone!" Her arms flailed like a magician's.

"Oh." Dorsey's breath quickened. *Finally, some fun.* "Sounds pretty dangerous. How will you know when you've found him? Did you look him up?"

"Look at me." Liza leaned in close. At this angle, if he wanted to, he could see the soft rise of her breasts. But he didn't want to. He would *not* look down her bodice. He would not be one of those guys who ogled—

Shit.

He looked down her bodice.

"I'll know who he is because I can sniff out a self-entitled old-money asshole in three seconds flat. I'll just follow the trail of ass-kissers and hangers-on." She was actually swaggering. She was John Wayne with an excellent pair of breasts.

"Good strategy," was all Dorsey could say.

"I'll come find you in an hour. We're going to blow the lid off this place. Then you can take me out dancing." Her hips swayed inelegantly as she attempted a sexy saunter. She was *not* pulling off sky-high heels. But he watched her smooth back as she walked past him anyway. What would it feel like to grip that tiny waist, both hands on the small of her back, his thumbs resting on her tailbone? The back of her dress—all the way down to the V above her tailbone—disappeared into the ballroom, leaving him with nothing but her signs.

Thinking only of that cinnamon swath of skin, he'd almost pulled out his phone to search "Latin Dance Clubs in DC," when his smile faded. He didn't dance. He wasn't Latino. She *had* charmed him after all. It was so simple. He was astonished and angry at the same time.

The double doors hadn't even closed completely behind her before he set a match to the pile of wooden stakes and papers.

THE MONEY

LIZA WAS ELATED. SHE COULDN'T HAVE WORKED IT out any better. She had found an inside man. Poor guy, the way his eyes had lit up when he saw that money. *That will feed his family tonight.* From the look of his hard face, he had probably served some time and was paying his dues in low-wage jobs. He was Latino, maybe with some other heritage as well—either way, she was surprised at his immaculately tailored uniform. Extra lining material at the cuffs, merino wool, and wide seams to accommodate additional tailoring. God, those eyes, though—obsidian black as the night around him. That dark-eyed waiter could toss her around all night and never call her back, and Liza would *not* be mad.

Once inside, Liza wasn't particularly impressed by the ambiance and attendees. She saw her grandmother in her church finery, a green sateen tracksuit and a sparkling pillbox hat with a multicolored plume of feathers settled against her close-cut wig.

"You couldn't find *one* dress to wear, Momma?" Bev asked.

"I'll wear a dress to my funeral," Granny said.

Beverly was dressed to kill in a too-tight, bright yellow con-

tour bandage dress that showed her panty line, accessorized
with long gold-looking earrings, which were fooling no one. She
paired this outfit with white wedge espadrilles that only slightly
showed their age. Despite the festivities, though, she looked
worried. Liza sidled up next to her, and Bev rolled her eyes.

"These are all the same old fools from our neighborhood. I
know the look of a cheap suit," Bev said. Liza nodded in agreement. Granny was a seamstress, and since her hands had become
shakier over the years, a lot of the alteration work had gone to
Bev and the children.

Liza started to tell Bev about the excellent-quality waitstaff
suits but couldn't find another like the one she'd seen on the
Latino man. It was just the type of detail she and her family
liked to note. Liza knew what Bev was thinking—that she had
taken off work and had missed out on a shift for nothing. Guilt
gnawed at her for the twenty dollars she had just spent.

Liza had seen the inside of the Fort Stanton Rec Center gym-
nasium a hundred times. The place kept a sweaty smell that the
planners had attempted to choke into submission with hundreds of
floral bouquets. The rug was thick and intricately patterned with
red, gold, and black—no doubt rolled out of some dusty broom
closet. Liza's heels drove into the high pile with every step and
teetered this way and that. There was a wooden platform with
a DJ spinning nineties R and B. He sifted through crates of re-
cords, and Liza briefly wondered how anybody working with
these developers could have found this legit DJ. He was reading the room, changing vibes according to what people nodded
their heads to. He was currently in a Monica four-song set that
had Janae and LeDeya screaming into their forks. Liza might
actually cut a little rug tonight before she spoke truth to power.

A multicolored light show flashed on and off without the aid of any music, and the chairs were covered in white linen that reflected the lights. The overall effect was like everybody's cousin's wedding—you know, the cousin you're not really close to but you go because you heard there would be shrimp.

Whispers swelled in the corners of the ballroom. She saw a crowd hovering around a small group of people.

The money's here.

Beverly pushed her way into the throng, grabbing her most beautiful daughter along the way, and then—hastily, as if it were a last-minute decision—grabbed the wrist of her uselessly clever child as well.

"Let's see what we can fetch in the market," Liza said.

Janae laughed, then stopped abruptly as she was nearly thrown upon a man who *had* to be Dorsey Fitzgerald. Younger than she thought, though. Maybe she *should* have looked him up? Light eyes, light hair, and light smile. To Liza, this Dorsey looked like a boy in men's clothing. He had the bland charm of a local news anchor. She could see him giving them their traffic on the 12s. His smile turned goofy when his eyes met Janae's, and he stuttered and fumbled as he presented himself.

"I'm David. I'm very pleased to meet you."

Liza's brow wrinkled. *David? Not Dorsey?*

Janae did what she did best, which was sit and look bemused like a cartoon doe while David composed himself enough to talk to her.

And just like that, her mother had done it. She'd completed, on some level, exactly what she had set out to do. Even Liza could see that this David boy was falling all over himself to speak to her sister. Biology *would* win out when a pretty girl was put in the path of a rich young man.

"Excuse me, may we pass?" A woman failing miserably to

suppress her annoyance smiled tightly at Beverly. Same light hair. Same light eyes. While the features were warm on David, they looked glacial on her. At that moment, the DJ let out the first riff to "Electric Slide," and Beverly pretended not to hear the woman.

"We live next door to Netherfield," Bev said to David, cupping her hand over her mouth to amplify her voice. "You'll be seeing a lot of us! Do y'all know how to do the Electric Slide?" When the blond man's face turned up in a question, Beverly pounced. "Oh, you have got to let my Janae teach you. She can really cut it up!" Bev gently pushed them toward the dance floor.

"Will you teach me?" the man-boy asked. The color on his cheeks was high, and Janae bobbed her head in reply, hiding a giggle behind her hand.

Liza knew *that* giggle. That was the same nervous chortle Beverly had attempted to break Janae of before answering any serious pageant question. *Yes, Janae, who do you most admire?* Every time Janae would giggle and bring her hand to her face, Beverly would smack her knuckles with a ruler. As a result, Janae had the poise, composure, and delivery of a career politician. They all thought they would never see that hideous giggle again. Wonder of wonders, *Janae* was nervous. But men didn't make Janae nervous. It was always the other way around. Was it because he was so rich? In her pageant days, Janae would get inquiries from three to four such men a night, but none of them had made her giggle stupidly behind her hand. Liza's own little cynical heart warmed a bit. *My big sister is nervous.*

"Excuse me, can we get by?" It was a man's voice.

Liza whirled around. Smoky black eyes met hers.

Has it been an hour already?

"And you are?" Beverly was a little put out at the tone of the busboy.

"Dorsey. Dorsey Fitzgerald."

Liza looked up and froze.

Shit.

Was that a half smile she saw flit across his face?

That tricky asshole.

Her mouth flew open, and a kind of croaking sound escaped her throat. His eyes kept hers as if he wanted to bore this memory into her brain, then finally, mercifully, his eyes bounced away.

"Close your mouth, child. Are you tryna catch flies?" Beverly mumbled out of the side of her mouth and then snapped back to the waiter turned chief gentrifier. "Well, Dorsey, it's rude to sit out the Electric Slide." Her mother gripped Liza's shoulders, preparing to throw her toward the man, but Liza dug her heels into the deep pile of the carpet. "Let my Liza show you how we do it here in *Merydon*."

"Ma, I'm fine." Liza tried to squirm free. The entire neighborhood eyed them in expectation. The raucous room suddenly stilled.

"I'll pass," Dorsey yelled, just as the DJ scratched and transitioned into a new tune. The result was a hard refusal directed to Liza that everyone heard. She heard some low "Ohhhhs" in the background. Liza raised her chin and squared her shoulders, trying to awkwardly dance her way back into the crowd.

The DJ had the good sense to restart the music before Dorsey brushed past Liza's openmouthed mother. The icy woman with Dorsey attempted to hold in a guffaw. And Liza and Beverly were left there looking mortified in front of the crowd. Liza saw thumbs texting furiously and rolled her eyes. She had unintentionally invited the entire neighborhood to view her utter humiliation.

Beverly huffed, and her chest expanded to let in more air. *Uh-oh, she's about to let it rip.* Liza pulled her mother near the hors d'oeuvres table and stuffed her mouth with a crab-dip cracker.

"You see him trying to front on you? He looked at you like you was a dog. Now, I know you ain't no Janae, but what he did was just *out of line.*" Bev patted her daughter's back gently. "I saw you looking at him. He's kinda handsome, Chinese or not. Don't look nothing like the people he's with."

"Momma, there are so many things wrong with what you just said. But I appreciate what you meant. I'm fine." And she was. It didn't matter to her what men like that thought of her. She would always be a thorn in their side.

A short woman popped up behind Bev, and Liza brightened. Lucia Ochoa, or Chicho, was the most welcome face Liza had seen in days. Chicho was her neighbor, her best friend, and remarkably well-adjusted for someone who lived in her calamitous house. Chicho's mother and father were not the most stable of role models. Her six brothers and sisters had the good sense to get out of the house as soon as they were able. Her youngest sister had left at the tender age of thirteen. But when Chicho's mom had her youngest son, Fredo, Chicho had stayed for a little while to help with him "just until she got on her feet." But a little while had turned into four years.

"L, what's up on the plans?" Chicho raised her eyebrows at the last word. Liza realized she had stupidly left her picket signs with the last person she should have. "Do I have the wrong night?" Chicho's lips pressed together in concern.

"Liza, I know you are not trying to stir up any trouble here!" Beverly warned. "Look at your sister."

Liza saw Janae tilt her head in that funny way that always

made men stare. Liza had practiced that delicate tilt in the mirror for as long as she could remember, but she only ever looked like she had a crick in her neck. Her sister was enchanted by this boy. And after everything Janae had lost, she deserved an enchanting night. The guilt pricking her insides was warring with the embarrassment she would feel if she didn't pull off her pop-up protest. Not only that, but Granny was the belle of the horticulture ball after everyone went gaga over the state of her roses, so she and some professional gardeners were deep in conversation.

"Momma, you see the type of people we're dealing with? Janae could find a man ten times better than this guy." Liza pulled away, but her mother grabbed her arm and intertwined it with hers. From an onlooker's perspective, it didn't look hostile or painful at all. "Ma! Let me go."

"Don't you get upset over that Dorsey boy." Her mother's mind was back on matchmaking. "Men like that marry top models and have them sign ironclad prenups and divorce them once the *newness* wears off."

"Momma, please, I said I was fine. May I go now?"

When Bev released her daughter's elbow, Liza shot out like a racer. She didn't have time to be embarrassed about Dorsey's discourtesy, but the way she ran out of the ballroom was probably giving everyone that impression. *I don't care.* She had spent hours on this, and the signs were ready for prime time. Nearly every local and national news outlet was here today. It was now or never. Liza pushed open the double doors to see the charred remains of her signs.

IT'S ELECTRIC

DORSEY WATCHED LIZA MAKE A BEELINE TOWARD THE back door. He had never anticipated a woman's anger so excitedly in his life. He nearly followed her out the door. David had, of course, ditched him as soon as he saw a beautiful woman, so Dorsey was left making excruciating small talk with Jennifer Bradley, David's older sister. When they spoke, it was like someone had put two live mics too close to each other. She *had* to feel it too, and yet she tried so hard to connect with him. Dorsey knew her type. He and his brother had called these women Paper Dolls. Everything had to look good "on paper" for a woman like that to even look at you: schools, GPAs, social circles, parents. They were fixated on the optics. And once a Paper Doll had decided on you, there was little you could do to put her off.

"I'm so glad you sprang for extra security. I did not know this place would be so rough." Jennifer checked the time on her slim watch. Dorsey was staying longer than he said he would, but he just had to get another look at the woman's crestfallen face. *I want to stay—just to see the show.* He swilled the last bit of the terrible champagne, then looked down the plastic flute to see if he had been drugged.

I want to stay.

Wow.

The security guards chatted at the front entrance and weren't even checking invitations and IDs.

"Waste of money that security was. We would have done better putting David at the front."

"Dorsey, *we* are the most important people here. You look like you're waiting for the president to walk through that side door."

"Not exactly." Dorsey turned away from her.

"Oh, right. This thing could erupt in gang violence at any minute. Were we careful with gang affiliation and all of those things in the invites?"

"It's not like people RSVP with their gang affiliation, Jennifer." There was a long silence. Dorsey had nearly forgotten she was there until she spoke again.

"I know I didn't come from adversity like you, but that hardly makes you an inner-city scholar," Jennifer said. There was that phrase again: *come from adversity.* Code for *You are a stowaway on this luxury liner.*

Dorsey easily spotted David's blond hair in the crowd of elaborate braids, Afros, and church hats.

"David!" Dorsey greeted the young man with too much enthusiasm, eager to stop chatting with Jennifer.

At thirty, Dorsey was nearly three years David's senior, and on nights like this, he felt it. David bounced around the room, emanating joy, making people trust him when they should roll their eyes.

Dorsey had struggled so much to find his place in his parents' world, and places like Merrytown threatened that. Merrytown, which everyone stubbornly pronounced *Merydon*, was a laughable misnomer for the resentment, mistrust, and pride that haunted these few dark blocks of DC. It reminded him that this would be much closer to his actual life had he not gotten a golden ticket out of it. But his job tonight was to smile while he picked the pockets of the desperately poor. To make them at ease with their ultimate dislocation. The contrast with what his philanthropist mother would think of this and what his industrialist father would expect of him warred inside him. But in the end, his late father's expectations and the Fitzgerald family legacy always won out. His eyes wandered around the room. Where had that woman gone?

HE HAD BURNED THEM. THAT SON OF A BITCH HAD BURNED them all.

There was too much on the line. Her community was here, and they were—mostly because of her mouth—expecting a show. There had to be some way to salvage this.

She weaved her way out of the kitchen only to be nearly mowed down by a small orchestra. Teens from the local high school rushed past her, fixing reeds and fingering keys. Across the line of bustling students, she saw Dorsey Fitzgerald speaking in an animated voice with the only blond man in the room.

Dorsey was seriously attractive. So what? The sun rises in the east and sets in the west. They were just facts, not proof of his goodness. Looks had never been the most interesting thing about a man to Liza. She could cop to his appeal without liking his demeanor. She *was* an art history minor and prided herself on seeing beauty while still maintaining a critical eye.

Why am I comparing Dorsey to art?

Liza flowed with the trail of band members—she was short enough to blend in—and moved with the students until she was directly behind the two men, partially obscured by a sturdy white column.

". . . You have *got* to be kidding me. *Why* are you pretending with these people?" Dorsey asked.

"Oh, I'm *not* pretending. We can't just *take* and not give back, Fitzgerald, it's not sporting. People are scared. They've lived here all of their lives, now everything is changing," the man-boy said.

"This party is *not* giving back. I don't see how you can smile and shake hands—"

"Your sister said you'd be conflicted about this," David said. Liza didn't think he sounded conflicted at all, simply bored.

"I'm doing what I have to do."

"Then tell your face, man."

Dorsey nodded in begrudging agreement. "Well, I would smile too if I were dancing with the *only* beauty in this place."

"Now, that's not very generous. Her sister seems like a lovely woman."

"'Lovely woman' is how you describe someone with a pleasant personality, not a beauty. And that hair!" Dorsey chuckled to himself and held his hands out around his head. "David, do you forget I've kissed Ms. Venezuela?"

Liza gagged. *This dude is really feeling himself, and Mr. I-only-kiss-supermodels feels some kind of way about my hair? Typical Eurocentric beauty standards.*

David shook his head. "You are a snob, Fitzgerald."

"Don't give me those big baby blues. I am a realist. These girls are looking for their next meal ticket."

"The women at the country club are doing the same," David shot back. Dorsey was thoughtfully silent.

A student's tuba connected with Liza's backside then, and she jumped, thinking it was a fresh schoolboy. This, unfortunately, put her directly in the line of sight of Dorsey Fitzgerald. She smoothed her hair self-consciously.

Breathe.

She was making her way over to him before her brain registered the movement.

"It's called a twist-out," Liza offered, patting her coils once again. She was unsure why—with livelihoods on the line—she started her tirade by defending her hair, but she didn't want to lose momentum. Her voice was buoyant with false confidence. "And it's magnificent." She flashed her phone. "As of thirty minutes ago, it has its own hashtag." Liza looked down at her phone. "And I quote, 'On God, Liza's twist-out could solve world hunger.'"

David's face grew red, and he clearly had the decency to be embarrassed that Liza had overheard the uncharitable things Dorsey said. She could see David mentally recapping the conversation while Dorsey squinted at her hair. David rushed to her side.

"I'm David. You're Liza, right? Your sister is such a talented dancer." He rolled his head at the word *such* for emphasis.

"Yes, we all are." Liza's barb went over David's head, but Dorsey smirked and signaled for a server carrying plastic flutes of cheap champagne.

"And your hair," David continued, "*is* glorious. Please don't mind Fitzgerald." He leaned in closer. "He's not very sociable."

"Nonsociable does not equal culturally insensitive," Liza said with a huff, "and your friend can probably speak for himself." She plastered on her prettiest smile. *You've got bigger fish to fry tonight, girl. The entire neighborhood is watching. Don't ruin it all over hurt feelings.*

Dorsey took a long-stemmed glass from the server's tray and took a quick swig. He then dug into his jacket pocket and pulled out the two rumpled ten-dollar bills Liza had given him and *tipped* the server, whose eyes widened as he gave Dorsey another drink.

"Did you say something about cultural sensitivity?" Dorsey's eyes were a sharp indictment.

"You could have corrected me," Liza said. Her eyes followed the crumpled bills out of sight.

"You shouldn't have assumed," Dorsey said, looking down into his plastic flute and setting it on a nearby table like it was radioactive. He didn't even want it, the asshole. A theory bubbled up out of her rage.

"There are two types of people in the world: those who Electric Slide, and those who don't." Dorsey let out a snort, but Liza continued. "People who shy away from communal activities are rarely to be trusted."

David shook his head. "What if you just don't know the dance?"

"That's the thing about group dances—they're remarkably forgiving for the uninitiated. Bumbling through the steps is part of the dance," Liza asserted.

David laughed. "So those who *don't* partake?"

"Either (A) have an overinflated ego that makes them afraid of looking silly, or (B) hold the other parties in disdain," Liza said, not taking her eyes off Dorsey.

"What a ridiculous way to divide the world." Dorsey's dark eyes pinned her as he finally took Liza's bait. The inky orbs brought intensity to the smallest of his affectations. He had the kind of self-important face Liza could *never* imagine blowing out birthday candles or wearing a tiny green Saint Paddy's Day hat. In the ballroom's light, she could see now that she had made a grievous mistake confusing him with the waitstaff. That suit was *not* a rental, for one. His mannerisms were too cool, his speech too crisp.

Dorsey shook his head. "If someone does not want to dance, then maybe that's just the entire story. You don't have to invent some ego crisis."

"Look around, Mr. Man Bun. This is a dance party. Anyone here *not* dancing is here on nefarious business, in which case my earlier statement—part B—still stands." She put her hand on her hip—an old trick of her mother's when she needed to take up more space.

"So we've both made fun of each other's hair. Let's call it even." He patted his head, and a flush of pink spread across his cheeks.

"Even? For you, a man with that much power, to punch down? We will never be even."

Dorsey's eyes tightened around the corners. He turned to David. "Why don't you go find that pretty little lady you were dancing with"—Dorsey's gaze slipped back to hers—"and I'll finish up with this one?" He guided David's confused face away.

"This one?" Liza repeated. She noticed glances and murmurs. She had been standing with him too long, and people would talk. For the fortieth time in an hour, she regretted inviting all of Southeast to the gala. "No, we're not *even*, Dorsey, but let me tell you how we're going to get *even*. I'm calling the big boys: city council. They are going to be all over this cheap trick you guys are trying to pull. And don't think I won't have the equal-housing folks up your ass."

"We are revitalizing this neighborhood, inviting business, and paving sidewalks. There are a lot of benefits," Dorsey countered, but his enthusiasm seemed to sputter. Liza didn't even think *he* believed in the snake oil he was peddling.

"Who do you think is going to move into those fancy town houses, huh? The actual community members? Blacks? Latinos? No. The type of people who carry dogs in their purses and stand in line for vegan cupcakes!"

There was a small flick of Dorsey's eyelashes going up and down her frame, as if taking her in all over again. Dorsey put his hand over his mouth, honest-to-goodness looking like he was trying to hold in a laugh. *Is he that callous?* Liza pressed on anyway. He was gonna hear it all today.

"And you burned my signs!" Liza shouted. *"And"*—this was the most offensive by far—"you're not even a real Latino!" His shoulders shook gently, and Liza was so furious she was sure steam was coming out of her ears.

Just then, a perfectly shellacked news anchor, perhaps smelling blood in the water, signaled for the camera. And for a moment, Dorsey stood there frozen. She saw him collect his breath and plaster on a bright smile. He greeted the man with a firm hand on the shoulder.

"Do you mind if we get a few questions in while we wait for the festivities?" The anchor's eyes flicked over Liza in a kind of naked appraisal. She saw him do the mental calculus in his head—that a person like her couldn't be with a man like that. He was wondering if he needed to call security.

"No, not at all. I'd love to answer your questions," Dorsey said. He lifted his elbow to subtly signal for Liza to leave. Liza blinked prettily into the camera. She was sensing an opportunity.

"Should we get Jennifer Bradley, Mr. Fitzgerald?"

Jennifer must be the woman he came with, the icy blonde who was actually a part of his world. She looked like the villainous stepmother in every Disney movie Liza had watched as a child—the one who wanted to send the heroine off to boarding school as soon as she got her hot dad to fall in love with her.

"They are giving out door prizes to residents near the DJ booth," the reporter told her.

Am I hallucinating, or did I just see his fingers make the shoo motion?

When Jennifer approached, Liza could see that she looked excruciatingly ready to leave. She wore a lovely floor-length halter-top dress with minimal accessories, effortlessly elegant. Liza wondered if that was something they taught at whatever elite liberal arts college the woman had obviously attended. With Jennifer's hand resting comfortably on Dorsey's shoulder, their bodies close but not indecent, the reporter began the interview.

"Is this just the beginning of your redevelopment plans for Merrytown?" he asked, almost immediately forgetting Liza.

It was slowly sinking into Liza that she had lost. Whatever her plans were for tonight were being pushed aside just like she was. *Why do people like this always feel they can take advantage of the powerless with no consequences? Why does he not even give me the human decency of a greeting?* Wasn't she in the same world breathing the same air as him? *God, this is so unfair!* Dorsey's elbow nudged at her side, ever so slightly pushing her out of the frame. This was, as Liza would later recall it to her sisters, "The. Last. Effing. Straw."

Liza looked in her ridiculously tiny purse—not large enough to fit anything bigger than her lipstick—which gave her an idea.

She grabbed a thick white cloth napkin and scribbled furiously. When she was done, she held the large napkin up behind Dorsey Fitzgerald, photobombing his entire live interview. He spoke earnestly and gestured dynamically, never knowing what the whole world behind him saw scratched out in deep red lipstick:

NETHERFIELD MUST GO!
#SOUTHEASTGIVESAJAM

MR. MEME

Hi, all.

I have been forwarded all manner of memes involving the events of last night. Some of them lean toward the inappropriate. I can understand the novelty of such an event as this but would thank you all to cease all company forwards or/and communications regarding a certain napkin and unnamed protester.

BTW, Sharon, DFitz is my email. DFatz is your office gossip buddy. Let's not make this mistake again.

Dorsey clicked the link for what was at least the thirteenth time today. His DC offices were not so well-appointed as the ones in Philadelphia. The city had some weird ordinance against skyscrapers, so the brutalist, bureaucratic buildings stared you right in the face. The day did promise to produce some first-rate weather. As a child, he'd always loved to look at storms and stare the intensity down.

Now the weather was of a different sort. It swirled around him, but instead of wind and rain, it was made of gossamer, electricity, murmurs, and images. An *internet storm*. He had never been in a meme before; now he was in two. The "I'll pass" meme was less famous but cut Dorsey the deepest. He winced at the harshness of his tone. Every time he rewatched it, new little nuances came alive: her mother's protective frown, Liza's moment of genuine surprise and embarrassment, then the cool hardening of her face to indifference, and that perfect mouth turning down into a frown. In the other meme, she had photobombed his interview with Jennifer. A GIF of Liza holding out her protest napkin played on a loop with various phrases added to it. "When your ex shows up with his new girlfriend" was one of his favorites. Liza's curls bounced as she jostled the napkin. *Why did I make fun of her hair?* Now it was all he thought about.

Sure, it was intense now, but this curiosity would fizzle out like so many of his relationships.

"Rigid." "Cold." "Distant." These were the words people leveled at him when they were tired of pretending to like him because of his money. Some of his past romantic partners were what Gigi called energy vampires, so he always felt too *on* for them. Most of his relationships would fizzle out from pure exhaustion on his part.

But Liza—and god help him, he couldn't even have a thought without that woman finding her way in—Liza seemed a little like his best friend, Joseph. Dorsey didn't feel pressure to perform for her; he was *delighted* to. He had even teased her outside of the rec center. *What do you think I do?* It was more fun than most of his first dates, actually.

He met a lot of women through introductions from some well-meaning friend or his meddling sister. But it was hard to get over that hump of awkward emptiness that settled in just before the drinks came.

Then there was the money. People laughed louder at his jokes because of it. They nodded approvingly at his ideas, even when he was full of shit. It was confusing. You either bought into the false adoration and thought you were God's gift to women or became cynical about everyone's motives. He had been leaning too far in the cynical direction lately.

But Liza disliked him precisely because of his money, which he found . . . different. She had, in fact, liked him *better* when she thought he was the waitstaff and invited herself dancing with him.

You're not even a real Latino.

She had hurled it like the worst insult. Dorsey laughed again.

But his smile faltered at the memory of turning her down. He had been too hasty. He had been wrapped up in his anxiety and his need for everything to go perfectly and had only seen her as an irritant, a fly in the ointment. But now that the event was over, he faced the realization that he had publicly turned down the most provocative woman he'd ever encountered. Her beauty was not the heavy-handed type that knocked you over. No—her entire persona was like binge-watching true-crime documentaries. You tell yourself, *I'm only half-interested. I'll only watch the first half hour.* Next thing you know it's six a.m., you've overeaten, and you're still frantically pressing next episode.

His cell phone rang. Gigi.

"Hey, Mr. Meme."

Dorsey rolled his eyes. "Yes, Gigi. I know you're enjoying the hell out of this."

"Why are you so awkward?" Gigi teased. "I watched it again, and I saw you doing that thing with your hand like you're jingling keys. Chances are one hundred percent you were smoking like a chimney last night."

"Just one."

"Of your precious Treasurers, right?"

"Leave my ridiculous cigarettes alone."

"I still can't believe you know her."

"Who, Liza Bennett? Is she someone to know?"

Holy shit, am I cool?

"Have you ever read any of her stuff? She's sharp."

"No, I haven't," Dorsey lied. He couldn't give this shark even one drop of blood.

"You need to read more. And speaking of, I want to send you something."

Dorsey prickled with uneasiness. "What?"

"Some pages from an article I want to write. About my past." Gigi had always struggled with belonging, even more than he had. It had driven her to some extreme behaviors, including a few altercations with their adoptive parents she would later admit to regretting.

"Gigi, can't you just come out on Twitter like everybody else?" He paused for a beat. Oh. She was talking about the *other* thing. "I thought you wanted to lead this company. No one will let you near any boardroom if you write about all of that."

"Dorsey, I have a record. If that record would keep me from serving, it always would. Quiet or out loud." The pause was heavier than Dorsey liked.

"Don't you want to protect our parents' legacy?" Dorsey faltered. "I mean, we owe it to them to keep the Fitzgerald name—"

"Get real, *Datu*. No one sees you as a Fitzgerald." It felt like a hot slap in the face. "No one sees me as one either. I'm an African girl with the right last name."

"You *are* a Fitzgerald. Those labels—African, Black, whatever—don't define you."

"Tell that to everyone else. All my life I've been treated like some kind of museum exhibit. And the boys . . . the boys we grew up with don't want to date me."

"What do *you* care what boys want?" His sister had renounced men a long time ago.

"I did *then*. And I need to break free of that girl. She was so desperate to fit in."

"That doesn't mean you have to go to the extreme. You don't have to keep punishing yourself for Isaiah."

"Don't mention him. Unlike you, *I've* accepted what I've done and know it's a part of me. This is about me expressing myself. I had to pay consultants one thousand dollars a session to teach me how to fix my hair. I rely on a team of seven people to tell me which makeup shades go best with my skin. Copying everyone around me only works if you look like everyone around you."

It suddenly flashed through Dorsey's head that Liza would be the perfect person to talk to his sister. *It's called a twist-out, and it's magnificent.* But he had made fun of Liza's hair. Dorsey dropped his head in frustration. He wished he could take that damned night back.

Dorsey took in a ragged breath. "Look, I can't pretend to fully understand what it feels like to be in your shoes. But I beg you to think, before you write some tell-all about your life, who else it might affect."

"Yes, Datu. We all live in service of your image." Gigi hung up on him.

Nobody needed to know about all that dreadful business.

HALFWAY IN LOVE

MARLEY WAS A FREQUENT CALLER ON LIZA'S SHOW. Liza *normally* enjoyed her.

"Oh, you showed up last night, Liza B.! I mean, at first it was a little sad because you got dissed when you asked Crazy Rich Asian to dance. But photobombing Channel 4 was the best revenge!" Liza just now noticed how much Marley's voice grated on her nerves.

"Thank you. But photobombing Channel 4 had nothing to do with me wanting to dance." Liza tried to keep the bite out of her voice. "I was trying to bring attention to the crisis of affordability in our neighborhood." She didn't want to be seen as a woman scorned instead of an activist.

"Oh, come on, honey. Everyone in that room wanted a piece of that man. And he was wearing the hell out of that suit! I wish he would wear me like that—"

"The suit was . . . good." Liza was the last person to not give a good tailor their due. "But let's focus here. We struck a major public relations blow to their woke development image."

"Blow. Mm-hmm."

"Thank you for calling, Marley." Liza turned the next song's volume up as she turned the woman's sound down.

———

IT HAD ONLY BEEN A WEEK SINCE THE GALA, AND LIZA was still getting a lot of social media attention for her stunt. "Somebody saw me on the news!" she sang. "A William somebody of PBI." Her family was gathered around the kitchen table while Maurice scrambled eggs in long basketball shorts, no shirt, high white socks, and black flip-flops. How could he cook with oil and no shirt on?

"PBI? What even is that?" Janae asked.

"I'll find out when I meet up with them in Greenbelt. He says they have experience outbidding Pemberley. He thinks we could be partners!" Liza finished the last part in a squeal.

"Liza, what do you think they're going to do? They are only going to make it seem like they were in charge of your little protest the whole time," Janae said. She pulled plates out of the dishwasher.

"The cause is won by more than one soldier, Janae. I can share the spotlight with the PBI."

"I don't think there'll be much sharing going on," Janae said. Her phone buzzed for the third time in a row, and she looked down and laughed.

"Are y'all texting now?" Liza asked.

"Who?"

"Heffa—"

"He's cute and funny, okay? That's it. I like to talk to him. Look at this meme he sent."

Liza looked over at her sister's phone. The picture was neither funny nor cute. It was the sort of thing you laugh at only when you like a guy. Liza's face must have shown her opinion because Janae snatched her phone back.

"Janae, he seems . . . nice," Liza offered.

Janae held her phone to her chest. "You just don't think he's genuine."

"She doesn't think anyone is genuine," LeDeya chimed in. "Didn't you break up with a guy because he still kissed his mom on the lips?"

"And I'd do it again," Liza said.

"Don't listen to her, J, she got burned at the party by that big K-pop dude, and now she's salty," Maurice said. He shoveled eggs on everyone's plates.

"Nobody got *burned*, Reece." Liza pushed down the annoyance bubbling up. "I would never dance with a man like that. And K-pop is fun and bursting with energy. That man was more like Special K."

Janae stabbed her eggs. "Yeah, David thinks the world of that guy, but he was pretty standoffish with everyone."

"'Standoffish'? He was a snob," Liza said.

LeDeya pulled out Liza's laptop. "Okay, while you two are on Mars pretending that that man isn't a snack, the internet says differently. And she's got stories." LeDeya easily reguessed her sister's password and got to stalking. Liza leaned in to see what LeDeya found.

"The big guy is originally from the Philippines. His mother started like fifteen charitable orphanages all over Africa and Asia for AIDS and war orphans. WCO, I think." Deya scrolled through pictures of a thin blond woman with her arms wrapped around three children. They looked like Colors of the World skin-tone crayons.

"WCO?" Years ago, Liza had written her senior thesis on

Patricia Fitzgerald. She had even applied to serve in one of their orphanages for two years, but unrest broke out in Ghana. "Wow, his mother is Patricia Fitzgerald?" Liza couldn't hold back her astonishment. WCO *actually* did great things. They had pioneered nonexploitative international adoptions and had incredible women-centered initiatives all over the world. The apple fell pretty far from the tree.

"His parents were like the nineties version of the Jolie-Pitts. He has a little sister from Kenya and another brother from like, Russia someplace, but the brother died along with the parents in this big accident."

They all paused for a moment of genuine sadness—to lose one's mother, father, and brother in one accident sounded terrible. They all avoided Janae's eyes.

"Anyway, he's loaded, dude. Like, he spells his millions with a *B*," LeDeya said. "And, Janae, your David is big shit in society with old, *old* money. He and his sister live in New York but they're all from Maine. Like his granny came over on the *Mayflower*. But they're trying to get their money to stack like Dorsey's—which is why they're partnering with Pemberley."

"So, the Bradleys aren't developers?" Liza asked.

Janae shook her head. "They're financiers. They manage and count the money."

"Wow, so David understands your inner math nerd," Liza said to Janae. "How sweet."

"I'm an outer math nerd. People just refuse to see it because of this." Janae flitted her hands around her face.

"'Oh, I'm so beautiful. If only I could be plain so people could let me do math in peace,'" Liza teased.

Janae punched her sister. "I know how it sounds, okay?" In fact, finance whiz was only the tip of the iceberg for Janae. In

another life, before tragedy struck, Janae had been part of a committee sent to investigate a major bank opening accounts for
clients and moving money illegally. She knew all the ways to
detect fraud on a financial account. Janae was appalled at how
easy it all was. From that point on, she demanded to handle all
of Bev's and Granny's finances. They had seen their savings
grow and Granny even had a tiny bit to retire with. It was scary
that the sweetest one of them all had the mind of a heist flick
hacker.

The plates clinked noisily in the sink as Liza lazily ran dish
detergent over them and returned to the table. "Imagine if you
used your snooping skills for good, Deya."

"She'd be unstoppable," Maurice added.

"Wait, I'm not even done!" LeDeya protested. "They're hir-
ing financial managers in New York and Singapore. You get a
discounted apartment, top salary, great benefits, and other
perks," she read. "For questions, call Pamela, assistant to David
Bradley."

"Oh no, Janae." Liza saw the fire ignite in Janae's eyes and
immediately tried to stamp it out.

"Liza . . ." Janae's eyebrows rose. "Don't let this be like the
time you forced us all to go vegetarian."

"The worst three months of my life," LeDeya howled.

Maurice held his stomach. "You watched *one* documentary
and put us all through hell!"

"Maurice, you got over that chubby phase because of me!
How dare you." Liza crossed her arms. "Janae, how would it look
if you were working for Babylon?"

"Liza, I just want a proper job, not embarrassing guest appearances for two hundred dollars here and there."

Maurice leaned on the table. "Why does my sister have to be

held hostage by your moral code? You want her to starve for your beliefs?"

"No, Maurice, I agree with Liza," Janae said. "We're all still in Granny's house because we couldn't afford rent, and the Bradleys of the world aren't making it any better. I've just had this long gap in employment since"—she exhaled—"since the baby, and I want to flex my calculator again." Everyone was silent. Janae *never* mentioned the baby. They all exchanged looks over the top of Janae's head. So David had sparked some joy in her sister? Had he done what the family had been failing to do for three years?

"I say since you have ol' boy on the hook . . ." Maurice pretended to throw out a fishing line.

LeDeya flopped around like Maurice had hooked her. "Reel him in."

Liza shook her head. Yes, they were all Bev's children. But the motivation had changed. So Liza swallowed her spectacular grandstanding speech and stepped up for Janae.

"I guess it's time for you to earn your keep around here," Liza teased. "I'm frankly tired of supporting you." On cue, everyone erupted, knowing Janae had used her pageant money to help with what she could for all her siblings. Speaking ill of Janae was a great way to unify the family and get herself out of an argument.

KENDRICK LAMAR BLASTED ON THE SPEAKER SYSTEM, and Liza absently bounced to the beat. The afternoon was chilly, and the forecast called for heavy snow and a drastic dip in temperatures. PBI was a new, promising opportunity, and she wanted to see what social change could look like with likeminded folks. Liza took a chance and wore her cute ballet flats.

She would be indoors before any crazy weather began anyway. She had to admit she looked good with her snap-front fitted flannel shirt and her high-waisted slim jeans. Dorsey's dark eyes flashed in her memory, how he had appraised her in a quick flick of his lashes. It was the smallest of gestures, but it was the detail her mind kept returning to, that tiny sweep of her body. Her stomach flipped traitorously, and Liza shook her head. *Not him. Not ever.* Liza had lost enough credibility with the "I'll pass" meme.

"Are you registered to vote?" a big-eyed middle-aged volunteer in a headscarf asked Liza.

"Oh yes. I'm here as an organizer." Liza tapped her badge.

The woman nodded. "Two doors down and to the left."

Another volunteer looked Liza up and down. She clearly disapproved of Liza's tiny jacket and shoes. "Is it snowing yet?"

"No, not for a long while yet."

The lady huffed when she saw a couple file in with white flakes of snow in their matching locks.

"Okay, so it started early." Liza shrugged. She followed the signs down the community center hall and turned into a low-ceilinged multipurpose room with deep stains in the flat blue carpet. A sign saying ORGANIZERS' BREAKFAST sat on an easel. Liza floated into the room and found her way into the center circle.

"I say we occupy those buildings." A beefy Black man stood in the center of the circle. "They can't *rejuvenate* what they can't take down."

"Please, brother, we'd be wasting our potency."

There were shouts and clamoring agreements.

Liza cleared her throat. "We should hit them where it hurts," she said. The crowd quieted, waiting for her response. "Their wallets."

"Aren't you that lipstick revolutionary girl?" the man asked.

Liza's chest caved in a bit. He didn't say it like a compliment, and he'd called her "girl."

"That's lipstick revolutionary woman to you," Liza shot back.

Mr. Muscles chuckled. "I saw a TikTok of you trying to bump and grind with that big wallet in the room." He smiled, and women and men turned to look at her with half-scornful, half-incredulous laughter. They all looked dressed for a prom she didn't know she was invited to. The room was made up entirely of elaborate clothes, hostile glares, and headdresses; even the men wore elaborate turbans. Liza was about to dip on this Afrika Bambaataa look-alike contest. This was a bust.

"Yeah, the 'I'll pass' meme! That was you?" More laughter.

Liza breathed deeply. She was just about to open her mouth and give these self-righteous goblins all of her vocabulary when a rich voice boomed behind her.

"She was also the mastermind behind the Netherfield Must Go hashtag, and she was invited," the man said.

Mr. Muscles clapped his mouth shut. His stupid smirk was nearly gone.

"I'm glad you could be here," the rich voice continued.

Liza looked up, and her mouth popped open. He was smooth, uniformly brown, with a graphic tee that had a picture of Oprah with ALL MY LIFE I HAD TO FIGHT printed across it. No headdress, no robes, no calling her "girl."

Tall.

Dark.

Handsome.

The Color Purple reference.

Liza was already halfway in love.

"I'm honored to be a part of this," she said. *Just as soon as I find out what* this *is.* She smiled broadly—too broadly—and was suddenly embarrassed to still be looking into his eyes. "I, um, hope I can be of use."

"William Isaiah Curry, but my friends call me WIC." When she reached her hand out for a handshake, he pulled her into a hug. His cologne was sweet and cool, and just when Liza was getting cozy, he released her. He looked down and pointed to her bosom, and Liza saw with embarrassment that the top snap from her blouse had come loose in the hug, showing a bit of neck. But the women gasped like she had just ripped open her shirt.

"Cheap snaps," she mumbled, snapping the shirt back together and zipping up her jacket. She tried to play it cool, but her face was hot with indignation. *What is this Hester Prynne bullshit?* WIC clapped above his head to get the attention of the other organizers.

"Okay, let's all introduce ourselves and get to work. Remember, there is no such thing as a stupid idea. We're leaving this room with a solution, and I, for one, really like the idea of hitting them in their wallets." He put a hand on Liza's shoulder and smiled reassuringly.

Liza was bolstered and fluttery at the same time. She took a deep breath and explained her plan.

THE DRY HUMPING

From: WQUR
To: DFitz@PemDevCo.com

Dear Mr. Fitzgerald,

Thank you so much for your gold sponsorship of the *Liza Bennett Hour*! Your contributions entitle you to three separate scripts and one appearance per quarter. We can also provide you with analytics about the effectiveness of your ads.

Good luck,
Martin R.

Dorsey's eyes narrowed. How long was this farce of an interview going to last? He saw Liza's timid sister through the glass doors in the office. She looked perfectly poised, but young David looked like a nervous wreck. He fidgeted, twisted, and crossed and uncrossed his legs in the chair. He was on fire for this woman, and she took notes and nodded coolly like a court stenographer. David would surely put in a good word for her with his friends in New York. She would get what she wanted. What else needed to be discussed?

Finally, she stood up and smoothed down her skirt. What was her name again? For the life of him, "Liza's sister," was the only name that came to him. She shook his hand, but David's hand lingered. He gestured around the office, looking as if he might give her a tour, and Dorsey rolled his eyes. The snowstorm rolling into DC was going to be huge, and they needed to go. What on earth was David thinking? Dorsey got up and passed through the double doors to talk some sense into his friend.

"David, we were supposed to leave at two, and it's already three. We *really* need to get out of here before it comes down any more."

"Oh, Dorsey, stop fussing. Are you afraid of a little snow? We'll be fine. I just want to show Janae my office. I think she's going to like it." He had a look in his eye, calculating and a little lusty. Dorsey was pretty sure of what David wanted to show this woman in his office. God help him if a woman ever reduced Dorsey to a rutting teenager like this.

"Hey, can you open your bar?" David wiggled his brows. "We could really use some drinks."

"No. The facilities manager is making his final rounds, so we need to go." Dorsey patted his pockets for cigarettes. This was stressing him out.

"Are we renting these floors, or do they belong to the facilities manager? So what if he's making his last rounds? Let's have a drink, and then we'll go. It'll warm us up before the car service gets here."

"David, you're killing me. What about your sister?"

"Jennifer is a hard worker, and she doesn't even know we're alive. Do you see her head in paperwork? She's in her happy place. She'll be fine."

"I know I'm going to regret this."

———

THE WIND WHIPPED AROUND LIZA'S FACE, FLIPPING HER pressed-out hair all around and sticking it to her glossed lips. The afternoon clouds had grown dark, and the wind was swirling, thick with heavy, wet snow.

"This wasn't supposed to be here until this evening," Liza mumbled to herself.

"This is going to get bad," WIC said. "Where are you going?" His eyes were kind.

"Just down the Green Line," Liza said.

He put an arm around her shoulders. "Where is your coat?"

"At home, Dad," she teased.

"You headed to Anacostia?"

"Near there. Merrytown."

"Do you want a ride? I think the trains are shutting down." He pulled her hair away from her sticky lip gloss.

Liza thought her heart would stop from the tenderness of the gesture. "Not for a couple of hours, I think. I'll be fine." Liza smiled. She *did* want a ride. She just wanted him to insist.

But he didn't.

"Sure. Well, keep warm and dry."

"I will." Liza tried to keep her eyes from stinging. *Who do I have to be to get a man to extend just a little extra effort? Janae?*

She parted from him and made her way to the platform. She didn't know how long she stood in the train station as she tried to make a memory of the nicest man she'd met in a while. *Was this the moment everyone talked about, when you know?* She pulled her phone out and tapped her sister's picture. The phone rang twice, and Janae answered laughing.

"Hello?"

"I take it the job interview is going well," Liza said.

"David was just telling me about the time he stole fifty *golf balls* from the store," she replied, still chuckling. "I mean, for what?"

"Because he would never *actually* be held accountable for his actions?" Her sister was silent on the other end of the line. "Sorry, Janae, I don't care about golf balls. You should get home, though. It's already snowing."

"Oh, stop fussing. It's not supposed to get bad until the evening. I'm fine." Her words slurred. *Is this girl drinking at a job interview? Oh no.* Janae and alcohol always ended up in a pool of tears and a relapse of depression.

Janae had had the perfect life at one time. She had a bouncing baby boy, a promising career in finance, and a town house in Bethesda. Everything was perfect. She even had the obligatory drugged-out, womanizing, football-player fiancé, Trevor Nolan. It all ended one night when Trevor ran a red light into a busy intersection with Little Trevor and another woman in the car with him. Janae's son was dead before he'd made it to the hospital. On a busy street in broad daylight, there were no eyewitnesses. Trevor would never play football again, and the other woman walked away without a scratch. Janae was so devastated that she couldn't work and was let go. She moved in with Bev and Granny to get back on her feet, but it had been slow going. Janae was kinder, gentler, and more fragile than anyone she'd ever met. For a long while after, Liza wondered how God could have allowed this to happen to someone so unambiguously good.

But now Janae was drinking again, and the pain was going to wash over her, and it would be at least three weeks of locked doors and bleak silence. Three years later, Janae had never seen a therapist, despite Liza's nudging. She just drank and disappeared into herself. She was one year sober—until today. Liza had to get there.

"Janae, I'm coming for you, okay?" Liza couldn't hide the fear in her voice.

"Liza, you are so dramatic. But come. I'll wait for you here." Janae rattled off the address for Pemberley Development before hanging up, and Liza took a seat on the metro. She had gotten only five stops when a watery voice sounded over the intercom.

"I'm afraid this is our last stop. The train ahead of us is stuck in the snow. We cannot move forward and have no timeline for when the train ahead will be moved. Please try to make other travel arrangements."

Liza did not know how much the weather had changed in her hour underground. As she climbed the stairs, she was greeted with a near whiteout. Her thin ballet slippers seemed like a cruel joke now. Pemberley was still about a mile and a half west, according to her phone's navigation app. She squared her shoulders and braced herself for the cold.

THE GLASS REVOLVING DOOR SWOOSHED HER INTO THE deserted office building, and a heavenly warmth blasted down from above. She glanced at the directory. The offices of Pemberley were on the top five floors. She stepped into the elevator and pressed all five. When the doors opened at the first stop, Liza saw Jennifer, David's icy sister. She was just as sleek as ever, and her eyes narrowed in recognition at Liza.

"Do you need a job too?" Jennifer said, stepping inside the elevator. She sounded perfectly polite and genuinely uninterested at the same time.

"I do." Liza's voice was deceptively cheerful. "But I try to stick to light clerical stuff, you know? Nothing that might damn me to hell for all eternity."

"Ha. Being rich was my original sin." Her tone was slightly less bored.

"Okay, Eve. Do you know where my sister is?"

"One floor up. Probably sitting on top of my brother by now."

"Excuse me?" Liza asked, shocked.

"Oh, come on, let's not pretend. She's a beauty queen. She knows her effect on men. Dorsey's the only man not swayed by her . . . face."

Liza did not miss the touch of pride in her voice, the hint of ownership. "Your brother seems like quite the willing participant."

Jennifer sighed with a bit of a laugh at the end. "You are right in that." The elevator doors slid open, and Liza stepped out.

"Down the hall and to the left. You can't miss the dry humping."

The doors closed behind Liza. The office was uniformly gray, with random pictures of smiling children or pithy coffee mugs on top of desks.

She turned the corner and saw her sister, a clear cup of white wine in her hand. She sat in a glass-walled office the size of the entire apartment at Longbourne.

"Liza, you came!" Janae—rosy-cheeked and glowing—glided across the empty cubicle maze. Janae gave Liza a heavy hug, and Liza held her sister's wrists together, checking for signs that it was all about to break loose.

"Let's go, sissy. Let's get out of here before the weather gets too terrible."

"Too late." Dorsey stepped out of a frosted-glass conference room. Lord, but this man could hang a suit. He looked dashing in his slick Italian clothes, and Liza had to look away for a moment as an uncharacteristic blush rose to her cheeks. Surely she was brown enough that no one noticed. She was vaguely embarrassed to see him after the meme fiasco. Though he must have been equally surprised to see her, he didn't break his composure.

"Over a foot of snow has fallen," Dorsey said. His gaze met Liza's. She saw nothing but cool professionalism in his eyes. Whatever discomfort being the subject of a viral meme had caused him did not show on his face now. He looked up when the elevator dinged and a blank-faced Jennifer blew out of the double doors.

"The car is stuck. The trains are stuck. Everything is stuck. *We* are stuck."

"No." Liza groaned. "Can't you guys just helicopter out of here?" What was the point of being rich, after all?

"What kind of irresponsible pilot would helicopter here in whiteout conditions?" Jennifer asked.

"This will be over soon, Liza," Janae cooed.

"No, it won't. DC won't get to shoveling this snow until at least tomorrow. Traffic and trains are at a standstill. And we all should hope the power stays on."

"Sleepover!" David shouted cheerily. Then he and Janae chanted, "Slum-ber party, slum-ber party." David stood up and looked around. "We have all of this leftover champagne from Jean's retirement. We could play charades, raid the downstairs cafeteria, roast marshmallows in the toaster . . ."

"Leave it to you, Davey, to turn lemons into lemonade." Jennifer's tone was annoyed, but her eyes were loving as she chided her brother. She then eyed Liza's wet feet. "Dear god, did you walk here? In those?"

"I needed to come and get my sister," Liza said defensively.

"Your sister is fine, fine, fine," David sang.

Janae echoed, "Fine, fine, fine," and laughed.

Liza fidgeted. How much champagne had her sister already drunk? Was she already too late to ward off Janae's downward spiral? Her face must have shown her worry because she looked up to find Dorsey eyeing her with a raised eyebrow.

"We won't starve," Dorsey said.

Did he think she was worried about her next meal?

"You could come downstairs with me to grab some salads and wraps from the cafeteria," he offered.

Like Liza needed proof that there was food? How destitute did he think she was, or did everyone seem dead broke to a billionaire?

Jennifer held her finger up like a church usher. "Oh, I have a much better lay of the land and know where the baskets are. I'll come with you." She smiled tightly and followed Dorsey toward the elevator.

Liza looked at the two of them departing, his broad shoulders and her slim, elegant frame. They would have made an excellent stock photo under a "wealthy couple" search. If they were dating, they didn't exactly seem hot for each other. But Liza imagined it wasn't in Dorsey's nature to be hot for anything.

BAD WEREWOLF PORN

From: DFitz@PemDevCo.com
To: Facilities@PemDevCo.com

I would like a briefing of our protocol for our Philadelphia
building in case of weather emergencies. Blankets, food
storage, generator policy, and cots. Especially cots. I
shudder to think about our employees being forced to
huddle together with no provisions.

Today just got interesting, Dorsey thought as the elevator
doors swiftly opened on the bottom floor.

"Can you believe she walked in this snow with those little flats
on? Poor thing. By the look of them, they'll be torn apart in a
week. Cheap shoes can't take a lot of wear and tear," Jennifer said.

"I'm sure . . ." Dorsey said absently. He could see Jennifer
gearing up to try again.

"David told me about the Netherfield conversation." She
laughed. "When she overheard you say something about her hair."

Dorsey did not answer. Something about seeing Liza again
jarred him. He had fully expected that her Instagram would be

the only means of ever engaging with her. Yes, he was *very* well acquainted with certain pictures on her Instagram feed. But just like that, she popped up at his DC office, red-nosed, shivering, a halo of snow on the crown of her head—and gorgeous. Jennifer— *Dear god, is she still here?*—continued.

"I bet it was the first time anyone's ever rejected her," Jennifer said lightly. The cafeteria was gray and austere, and Dorsey remembered why he rarely came down here. It was downright depressing.

"I'm sorry . . ." Dorsey was having so much trouble following the strand of Jennifer's conversation. "What are we talking about?"

"Liza," she muttered, but when Dorsey broke eye contact again, she huffed. "Oh, never mind."

"Liza, yes, she looks different today. Maybe it's the hair, or I think the cold brought out a little sparkle in her eyes. She obviously cares for her sister. It's actually quite—"

"Oh," Jennifer interrupted. Her voice had taken on a high-pitched tenor that made Dorsey wince. "Here's the food." She jerked open the glass door holding various refrigerated items. Jennifer scooped up a few Caesar chicken wraps in cellophane while Dorsey grabbed cookies and bottled water. "And the baskets are here! See, I told you I knew where they were."

"Her birthday," he mumbled, flicking through the icebreaker texts his baby sister sent him from time to time. "That's lame." He shook his head. There had to be something he could say to get her bright eyes on him again.

They made their way back to the elevator. Jennifer punched the up arrow impatiently.

———

LIZA BOUNCED ON A BALANCE BALL OFFICE CHAIR IN A man named Kenyon's cubicle. Was this what her sister wanted—

to be seated across from Ken in accounts receivable in a gray box all her life? What made people run toward these awful choices?

As the hours passed, Liza had taken to secretly watering down her sister's drinks. In fact, she was pouring water in a half-filled champagne glass in the office break room when Dorsey, materializing from what must have been thin air, opened the refrigerator next to her.

Besides the fact that he wore ridiculous suspenders, his style was impeccable. She knew a well-tailored trouser when she saw one. Even his shoes looked hand-stitched by some arthritic cobbler in Italy. He seemed to have a bit of an outsider energy to counter his straitlaced clothing choices. His hair was the ultimate puzzle—for a man keen on structure and order, why would he keep his hair long? He was all rigidity and cultivation, but in that hair Liza could see flashes of lupine opulence that spoke of a man not fully domesticated. He had taken off his jacket, and his hands in his pockets exposed the curve of his buttocks and thighs. How had she not noticed the snug fit of his trousers before? Now it was all she could look at.

Without a word, he placed a bottle of Ariel Brut Cuvée non-alcoholic champagne on the counter.

How did he know what I was looking for?

Unless he had been watching her sneaky little substitutions. Unless he had been watching *her*. The thought of it excited her more than it should have. She grabbed for the neck of the bottle, but Dorsey's hand had not yet left it. They touched for a split second, and his eyes rocketed to hers. She was positively pinned in place. His touch was icy. The pads of his fingers grazed her knuckles and stayed a beat too long. Still, without a word, Dorsey tore his eyes away. She wished she had read something there, but he was inscrutable. He walked away toward the cubicles, and she watched his form retreat. Why had she been holding her breath?

She took the Brut and, with hands shaking, filled her sister's glass. *Deep breath*, and with a plastered-on smile, she called out, "We're not done partying yet." She walked back into the office space, holding the cups in her hands.

Janae smiled and whispered in her sister's ear, "I feel so happy for the first time in a long time!"

Liza squeezed her sister's arm. "You deserve it. Enjoy." She handed her sister the cup, and they made silly party faces for a rapid succession of selfies. A few minutes later, her sister sat with David in an uncomfortable-looking office chair. It looked more like conceptual art than an actual functional chair. Liza left them to their privacy and turned down through a darkened hallway. *Is this place just cubicles as far as the eye can see?* She pushed open a door and gasped at the view. With the lights out, the world outside sparkled. The capital was lit up around her, and the weather coupled with the full moon had turned her bustling political town into a quaint village covered in a blanket of glittering snow. It looked like she was being shaken around in a snow globe as the flakes and wind whirled against the window.

A deep voice from across the room jolted Liza. "You found my office."

She turned to find Dorsey staring at her with those unnerving dark eyes. "Oh god, I'm sorry. I didn't mean to snoop." She was surprised. This was not the largest office on the floor, or the flashiest. There was a smooth dark-wood demilune desk with a pony-skin upholstered armchair that begged you to sit. He had a vintage apothecary cabinet installed on the wall with tiny undecipherable words written on the drawers. On an adjacent desk, there was a bronze statue of galloping ponies.

This probably wasn't even his primary office, but Liza imagined it must have taken thousands to outfit it to his specifications. On the other side of the small office was a floor-to-ceiling window. It seemed to Liza that Dorsey's taste leaned toward the supple and sumptuous—another surprise. What did this austere man know of sensual pleasures—the feel of leather and lace and feathers, the smell of freshly ground coffee, the taste of deep red wine? What could he know about feeling first, then thinking?

What his office lacked in space, it made up for in location. It was the best spot positioned to see the entire cubicle space. It also had the best view of the city. She turned her back to him and admired the impressive vista again.

"I didn't take you for the corporate espionage type," Dorsey said, crossing the small room. He looked at the light but did not turn it on, gazing instead at the view as well. He stepped closer to the window—closer to her, until his spicy, woody cologne snaked around her.

Is that a joke?

"Thank you for finding the . . . that bottle," Liza said, still facing the window. She didn't dare turn. Why did she bring that up? Now she was thinking of the icy pads of his fingers on her warm skin. Thankfully, he didn't respond. But his silence was neither rude nor oppressive. She saw his arm rise over her shoulder as he placed his palm on the window. Suddenly, she could feel the heat of his body directly behind her. She didn't even want to take a full breath for fear that her back and his chest would touch. Her breath tightened. She would hyperventilate if he got one inch closer.

Dorsey pointed to a spot in the distance. "Do you see that church over there?" His voice was slightly above a whisper.

Liza nodded.

"My father was born there. My grandparents were on a trip

to talk to President Eisenhower. They got into an accident and had to stop at the church."

"Wow, on a casual trip to see the president, huh?" Liza teased. She wondered if those same church steps had held many less fortunate 1950s babies.

"Babies are so helpless." Dorsey sighed. "You know they're all just one poor decision away from being left on those same church steps."

Liza spun to look up at him, ready to tell him she had thought the same thing. Or maybe ask him about his own adoption. *Had he been left at his mother's door?* But she had underestimated how close he stood behind her. The wide collar of her shirt had gotten caught on the jagged metal clip of his suspenders, and her cheap snaps gave up the fight. Her fitted flannel shirt unsnapped nearly down to the navel, exposing the tops of her breasts as they fought with the old, too-tight bra. The cheapness of the bra and the holes in the lace and her view of his Ferragamo shoes irrationally made Liza want to cry. *From this day forward, no skimping on underthings.* She took a deep breath and heard a sharp exhale in response as her breasts brushed against his chest. Dorsey tried to turn around, but her shirt was still stuck to his suspenders and Liza lurched after him. He reached for the fraying collar but thought better of it and held his hands high.

"Don't breathe." He growled. Liza held her breath without question and attempted to pull her shirt out of the metal clip of his suspenders. Why would a man this rich wear suspenders this raggedy? Something about her jarring movements angered Dorsey, because he steadied her shoulders and gritted his teeth like he was defusing a bomb.

"May I?" he clipped out. Liza nodded, and his enormous hands slid carefully around the collar. Liza was hyperaware of the millimeters between his knuckles and her semi-exposed breast, and she watched every micromovement. She willed her nipples to stay flat. But she could already feel gooseflesh spreading over the tops of her breasts. When she took an involuntary breath, Dorsey's thumb trembled, and his Adam's apple bobbed like a boiling egg.

"What on earth is going on here?" Jennifer, who had, of course, followed Dorsey down the hall, had her fists balled at her sides.

Liza heard Dorsey groan. This had all the trappings of bad werewolf porn.

- Heaving bosom of the damsel in distress
- Man inexplicably sweating in a cool office
- Ripped-open shirt
- Ripped bra

Liza took one hard yank on her shirt and pulled it loose—not without an adequate tear in the fabric, however.

"That's what I was trying to avoid," Dorsey said. To Liza's surprise, Jennifer rounded on *her*.

"What on earth do you think you're doing?" Jennifer demanded.

Liza snapped her shirt closed, as mortification mixed with anger and something else, something hard to name, washed over her. She didn't know what to feel first.

DORSEY WANTED TO ROLL THE SHIRT OFF LIZA'S SHOULDERS and bury his face there. He should have said that, if only to knock the presumptuousness out of Jennifer's tone. Even if the woman had walked in with Liza bent over the desk and him balls deep inside her, Jennifer did not have the right to outrage. "My suspenders got caught on her shirt just as you were walking in. It's no big deal." His voice was strained.

"Why were the lights off?" The steam had come out of her voice.

"Better view," Dorsey and Liza said in unison, and he turned around again. He was abuzz with energy. Mercifully, she'd snapped that damned shirt closed. He had been nearly paralyzed at the sight of her skin. The sugary-brown tops of her breasts nearly bursting out of a lacy black . . . oh, this was no good. The blood rushed away from his head and pooled in his midsection. The beginnings of an erection. *Think of skeletons, think of soccer. Think of skeletons playing soccer.* He was no thirteen-year-old humping pillows, but he had never been so overwhelmed with raw sexual feeling. He was *in* his body—and finally, for once, not in his own head. Had he been alone, he would have roared, beat his chest, howled at the moon, or whatever primal beasts did to display potency, but he wasn't alone, and he had to get this bad boy down. He risked a glance at Liza. Mistake number 307. He saw the gooseflesh rise on her neck and thought about how it might feel to kiss her there.

Did I do that to you, Liza? Did I give you goose bumps?

He was roaring back to life, and skeletons playing soccer wouldn't save him for long.

He left with no valediction to either woman.

LIZA WAS LEFT WITH JENNIFER IN A WEIGHTY SILENCE. Her stomach was still upside down from the surprising physical reaction she was having to Dorsey's nearness.

"I'm sorry I misunderstood what was happening," Jennifer

said, contrite all of a sudden. "I should have known. One time I got my hair stuck in those same dumb suspenders. He wears them with almost everything. I think his biological family gave him all sorts of trinkets and knickknacks when he went to Manila."

Liza wanted to shake this woman. *You don't have to do this, honey.*

"I feel like we got off on the wrong foot, you and I. Do you want to take a walk around and chat?" Jennifer asked.

Liza looked up, surprised. *Maybe she's apologizing?* "Sure," she said warily.

Jennifer looped her arm around Liza's arm. It was a forced intimacy. Liza noted how often Jennifer craned her neck looking for Dorsey.

"How rude of him to scuttle out of here without a word. Like we're taking up his time," Jennifer said.

"Is he always so . . . ?" Liza searched for the right word.

"Stern, glacial, disaffected?" Jennifer guessed.

"Unknowable," Liza finally settled on.

Jennifer stopped short. She looked like she was about to agree, then shook her head vigorously.

"Oh, I don't know . . . Once you get to know him, he's just a great big old teddy bear," Jennifer said. The lie must have tasted foul coming out of her mouth, because she made the slightest frown when she said it.

Liza walked with Jennifer around the dark side of the building. Jennifer's face suddenly lit up. *Uh-oh, she's scheming.* Liza didn't know what she was about to be a party to. They walked outside the hallway and back into the cubicle space.

When they saw Dorsey again, looking less troubled and a bit refreshed, Jennifer asked him, "Do you want to use the office workout space downstairs, maybe do some yoga?"

"Why would I do that?" he grumbled, apparently still annoyed.

"To stretch your limbs, exercise. Relax," she said pointedly.

"There are two reasons you would ask me that, and not one of them is to relax," Dorsey said smugly. He was responding to Jennifer but looking in Liza's direction—trying to get a rise out of her, she knew. She wouldn't take the bait.

Jennifer smiled coyly and elbowed Liza. "What is he talking about? What is he trying to say?"

Liza shrugged. "Please don't pretend to be curious," she said, rolling her eyes. "He's bursting at the seams with some cockeyed theory."

Dorsey's full attention was rattling Liza. "Are you the only one allowed cockeyed theories, Liza?"

Jennifer pushed her way back into the conversation. "What did you mean, Dorsey?"

"Two reasons you would ask that. You want to see *me* do yoga, and if so, you can look at me all you like right here. Or you want to do yoga in front of me—"

"Dorsey!" Jennifer hit his shoulder. The false outrage made Liza want to hurl. This man needed no extra boost to his sense of self-importance.

"And if you want to show me *your* downward dog now, I won't object. Either way, I'm better served sitting right here."

"You are terrible." Jennifer turned crimson. "I've never heard you talk this way. How often are you watching me do yoga, you Peeping Tom?" She pretended to be scandalized. "Liza, don't you have that feminist blog? Are you going to write about his chauvinism?"

Liza blinked. She walked around the table, conscious of his dark eyes following her. "Hmm, nothing so obvious as that. I'd write about his ego, and his assumptions that everything is about him."

Jennifer scoffed, but Dorsey's eyes fixed on Liza and did not move. Liza could only meet his gaze in quick glances. The atmosphere of the room was thick. They were doing this, somehow changing the very chemistry in the air.

"You accuse me of ego because I use discernment in whom I choose to downward dog with?" He paused. "Or dance with?"

Jennifer's shoulders slumped in defeat. "Oh, is this personal? Are you talking about each other?" When no one acknowledged her, she cleared her throat. "Dorsey has a very particular taste, you know. It's not just in friendships, but also relationships and business deals. His standards are so high because he holds himself to a perfect standard as well."

"And what happens when one of those friendships or relationships falls below his standards?" Liza asked.

"I drop it," Dorsey said without blinking. "Never look back."

"Well, thank goodness I'll never meet your particular standards for friendships," Liza said. "It seems like maintaining your high regard is a full-time job."

Dorsey's voice had dropped a register, and he leaned in, giving off a kind of energy that Liza had never felt before. "I can assure you that the benefits are excellent."

Liza swallowed. "With such a tiny applicant pool, it's a wonder you have any friends at all. As for the ones you do make, god forbid they make a mistake . . ." She drew a line across her neck.

Jennifer thrust herself between them, blocking their intense eye contact. "Oh, Dorsey has many friends. And if he chooses to not slum it for friendships," Jennifer said pointedly, "then that's his prerogative."

"I didn't know friendship was something one could slum for,"

Liza said. Why did Jennifer need to come to this grown man's defense? Couldn't she see he held her in the same contempt he held everyone else?

"When you're a billionaire, everything is slumming," Dorsey said, wearily eyeing Jennifer for a split second.

Liza whistled in her head. *Yass, drama.*

Jennifer's eyebrows creased at that. "My family has produced five senators, one president, and three business tycoons in three hundred years in America. They built this country," she said coolly. "And they did it without owning one slave, without shipping one job overseas, and without an ounce of corruption."

Her blood was bluer than his, and her privilege went deeper. He was an adopted child of a wealthy family. He did nothing but luck out of some godforsaken Asian peninsula. *Yes, you're obscenely rich, but I'll always belong here, I'll always be white,* she was telling him. He deserved to be taken down a notch, but Liza wondered how many microaggressions Dorsey had to field from families like this.

Jennifer squeezed Liza's wrist and smiled. "You really bring out the beast in Dorsey, don't you, Liza?" It was as if she was realizing just this moment that Dorsey was an asshole. "I guess I don't need any help getting my blood flowing anymore."

"You guys are so boring." David emerged from a dark corner, drunk, with swollen lips and pants in a semi-tent. Liza looked away—that was none of her business.

"I say we play a little game." Janae, wonder of wonders, was up and not yet pulled into the darkness. Maybe she really was happier. Or the fake champagne had done its job. Her lipstick was completely kissed away, and her bra strap sat high on her shoulder, a sign of overcorrection.

"How about Never Have I Ever?" Jennifer suggested.

"No," Liza and Dorsey said at the same time again, then looked at each other.

"We don't know these people, Janae. We maybe shouldn't tell all of the family secrets just yet," Liza said with a look to her sister.

"And I have zero tolerance for games," Dorsey added.

"Gosh. What are we up to now? How many things are we going to add to this list of things Dorsey doesn't tolerate?" Liza asked.

"DJs," Dorsey said. His delivery was so dry that she once again did not know if he was joking or serious.

"Okay, let's play a game," Liza said, never taking her eyes off Dorsey. "I think hide-and-seek is just the thing to—how did you put it, Jennifer?—get the blood flowing."

ACTION OVER DELIBERATION

HOPE YOU ALL ARE STAYING SAFE IN THIS WEATHER. Thank you for joining me tonight. It's so weird to call into my own show, but I am stuck, y'all! We're gonna play a prerecorded quiet storm session for y'all. I hate that I can't be live. But you can! Show me your winter cozy poses and make sure you use the hashtag #Bennettblizzard so I can see all of your pics," Liza said.

AN HOUR LATER, LIZA WAS HUDDLED UNDERNEATH A desk, enjoying herself despite the circumstances. Dorsey sat out the game in favor of reading what was no doubt a terribly pretentious book. But Liza thought everyone was having more fun because of it. Even Jennifer had an impish grin on her face as she ran to hide, instantly looking more like her more carefree brother in that moment. Liza struggled to keep her eyes open, because every time they closed, she saw Dorsey's trembling thumbs over her collarbone. What if Jennifer had not come in when she did? Would she have moved his big shaking hands over her breast? Would he have taken her cues and pushed her against that damn floor-to-ceiling window? She wasn't against a rough, quick tumble. *Liza, he's not the hot waiter. He's the rich asshole who is destroying your neighborhood. Focus.* She found it strange that she had scarcely thought of WIC this whole time. Normally, when she liked a guy, she would be halfway through their imaginary wedding ceremony by now and constantly thinking of him. But her fear for her sister was foremost in her mind. She was glad she had come to at least intercept the liquor.

Liza saw the red EXIT sign aglow and smiled. No one had thought to go to the *other* floors. Before David finished counting, she was out and down the stairs to the eighth floor. They would be forever looking for her. The eighth floor was some kind of tech start-up. The atmosphere was fun and inviting. Cool little cylindrical pods that looked like giant aspirin pills lay at the ready for any hardworking developer who wanted to catch a nap. Liza thought once again that she was in the wrong business. There were no naps in international studies or DJing. And there certainly wasn't a fully stocked fridge. She found a desk and crawled underneath it and laid her head on the interior file cabinet. The next thing she heard was the door click open. Liza covered her mouth to keep from laughing. *Has someone finally found me?*

"Everyone's drunk or sleeping. I thought I'd tell you before you hid here forever."

Liza jumped at the sound of Dorsey's voice. She saw those hand-stitched leather shoes stroll toward the desk, and she wanted to save herself the indignity of crawling out from under it. But he squatted down and tilted his head.

"You coming out?" Dorsey said.

"Yes," she grumbled and crawled out from under the desk.

Dorsey took Liza's hand to help her up, and she slipped out of his grasp as soon as she steadied herself. He stood with a rigid and formal posture next to her.

"Why didn't you play?" Liza searched for one of her soggy shoes.

"I told you I have no tolerance for games. It's silly."

"You sound one hundred and seven."

Dorsey kicked the missing ballet flat to her from underneath the chair. "I'm an adult. At least thirty."

"At least?" What kind of a loon didn't know his age?

"My birth year is a little fuzzy."

Liza slipped on the shoe. Thankfully they didn't still squelch when she walked. "I had a friend who was adopted, and she got to choose her own birthday."

"I did too." Dorsey pointed to a nearby fancy bagel toaster in the kitchenette.

She waited for him to go on and gave up. "And what did you choose?"

"Uh, Thanksgiving. It was the holiday with the most food. Little did I know Thanksgiving changes every year." He pointed to her ballet flats.

Liza laughed ungraciously. "So now your birthday is just on a dry-ass November twenty-fourth or something?" She slipped off the flats. It wasn't a *terrible* idea to dry her flats over a bagel toaster. She was just surprised that it was his idea. What did he know of making do?

"Laugh all you want. I'll hit Thanksgiving again someday." He turned the toaster to its highest setting. Now he was actively avoiding looking at her rainbow-painted toes. "How old are you anyway? Nineteen, twenty?"

Liza curled her toes inward. "Twenty-six *with* a master's degree. And, dude, thirtysomething's not that old."

"I'm old enough to have never uttered the word 'dude' in serious conversation."

"All that tells me is that you're missing out on America's most zeitgeisty phrases." Dorsey pulled open the stairwell door, and Liza stepped out of the office—bare feet cold against the polished cement floor.

"How did you know I was down here?" Liza asked. She was sure she had slipped out undetected. Again, she wondered, *had he been watching me?*

"The chair wasn't pushed in," Dorsey said blankly, ushering her toward the stairs.

"See, you would have been great at this game!" Liza bounced good-naturedly up the steps. The game and the quick nap had worked wonders for her mood and had gotten her mind off that embarrassing shirt business. "Do you think you can beat me to the next floor, old-timer?" Liza challenged.

"Of course I can. But I don't *want* to—"

Liza jetted up the flight of stairs before he could finish. A throaty laugh escaped her when she saw him quickly step, then break into an all-out sprint up the flight of stairs. He caught up with her effortlessly, his long legs doubling and tripling the steps. Dorsey never lost his momentum once he reached the top and stumbled up the stairs behind Liza, nearly tripping to avoid her bare feet. He looked as if he would totter for a minute and pulled Liza close to him, using her to steady himself.

"You're going down with me!" he said. His laugh was small and rusty—unused, Liza guessed. The way his arms wrapped around her, the way his lopsided smile lit up his features, *beautiful.*

She bit her lip. Squirming in his grasp, she was prepared to tease him for losing but found a look in his eyes that stopped her cold. The grip on her waist changed from slight to firm. Things seemed to go in slow motion from here. Something had flared up in him—the gleam in his dark eyes, the rapid rise and fall of his chest, spelled trouble. How could he not see her pulse jumping out of her throat? Up close, he seemed impossibly tall, with a shadowy beard already growing in. She wanted to reach up and stroke the dark whiskers, anticipating that bristled feel. It was the second time in as many hours that she found herself pressed against his body, and the effect was drugging. She leaned in, waiting for something, waiting for him. Dorsey looked down at her, and the surrounding air seemed to bubble up like they were two trinkets at the bottom of a glass of champagne.

Then gently, so tentatively, he brushed his lips to hers. Was it a kiss? Or did their mouths just accidentally pass each other? Every touch was a featherlight question. Had he grazed her breast? Did he brush her hips? Was that his breath on the slope of her shoulder? It was perhaps better that his touch was so light as to be indiscernible. Liza feared Dorsey might brand her if he touched her with any deliberate pressure.

His expression changed, and he released her suddenly. Liza felt like she'd suddenly burst out into oozing sores the way Dorsey acted. David's slurred voice sounded through the door.

"I found them in the stairwell!"

Liza saw Jennifer stride toward them with eyes full of questions, then halt and pretend to check her phone messages.

She'd give a million dollars to get into that woman's head. What made smart, capable women like her chase men who were only interested in themselves?

Dorsey straightened his trousers and smoothed imagined

wrinkles from his shirt. "Like I said, this is silly. I am an adult. You would do well to remember that." The chill in his voice was definitive. His tone was an ice pick popping the fizzy bubble of warmth that had formed around them.

I guess he suddenly remembered I'm not Ms. Venezuela.

How dare he make her feel childish and stupid and unattractive in one dismissive sentence. Liza cocked her head. He had tricked her somehow, and now she was angry at herself.

"You know what your problem is?"

Dorsey pulled the door open wider, nudging her to exit the stairwell.

"You mean besides being a friendless, vain sociopath?" he offered wearily.

"Oh wait, I actually think that covers it," Liza snapped. *Where is that smoldering man from just two minutes ago? Liza, Hot Waiter does not exist.*

"I went downstairs to get her," Dorsey said, his voice cracking slightly. "She would have been hiding on the eighth floor for days."

What made his pronouncement more peculiar was that there was no audience for his big fake show of joviality. Janae and Jennifer were scrolling on their phones, and David had already passed out again on the chair.

"Do you know what *your* problem is?" Dorsey whispered to her.

He had been thinking of a comeback. Ha! Slow on the draw. He turned on his heels so swiftly that Liza stepped back to anticipate him falling.

"You let your first impression be your only one. It's incredibly shallow and intellectually lazy," he told her.

"Oh, so now I'm lazy." Liza rolled her eyes. "Where have I heard this before? Oh yeah, that's right—the cotton field." *There, that'll sting him.*

Dorsey's eyes tightened around the edges, and he scowled. "You are willfully misunderstanding me." He carefully pronounced every syllable. Liza was glad he looked pissed. How dare he turn off like a faucet. Why would he pull her along to the edge like that and drop her like a sack of potatoes? Her hands were *still* shaking. She knew there was no mistaking that look from the stairwell. It was the look of a man who absolutely knew what he wanted to do to her.

"Add that to your list."

Then the room went black. In the windows, Liza saw the city go dark block by block.

"Ah hell," David slurred.

"Surely this place has a generator," Jennifer said.

"Only certain federal buildings get emergency generators. Besides, they evacuated this building at two p.m. for that very reason. Do you both remember when I suggested four times that we should leave if they decided to close the building?" Dorsey sounded like a bureaucrat nearing retirement.

"Thank you, Dorsey. We remember it and won't be allowed to forget it," David said.

"We should have listened to you," Jennifer simpered.

Liza wanted to barf. Did anyone ever tell him anything he didn't want to hear?

Liza turned to face everyone. *Someone* needed to herd these cats. "Congratulations on being right. Is that gonna keep us from freezing our butts off?" Jennifer's head snapped in Liza's direction. "It's twenty-eight degrees outside. With no generator, it's going to be twenty-eight degrees in this office soon. What are our choices?"

Dorsey's turn to look at her; he nodded. "We need to scout the building for blankets." He disappeared into the darkness with his cell phone light.

Liza paced the room like a drill sergeant. "The floor is going to be cold."

"The floor is not happening," Jennifer agreed.

Dorsey returned to the common space with a few decorative throws. "We should really spring for basic office furniture. All of this furniture disguised as modern art was a mistake."

Liza took the folded throws from Dorsey. "Okay, the floor is not an option to sleep, and neither is the modern art, so maybe we can use tables?"

"Too unstable," he said.

"Hey, when I went to the eighth floor, their offices had—"

Liza and Dorsey spoke in unison. "Nap pods."

Liza turned back to the center of the room and addressed the others. "There are nap pods downstairs. We don't have a ton of blankets, but we should generate enough heat if we keep the lids closed."

"No, I don't think heat will be a problem."

Liza's eyebrow rose. Was he flirting or agreeing? He delivered everything in that flat, arrogant-ass tone. It was impossible to know the difference. The five of them gathered their belongings and made the quick trip downstairs. Liza rushed past the spot of the *almost* kiss, then made the sign of the cross over her body to protect herself. That spot had bad juju.

When they got to the common area of the tech start-up, Jennifer stated the obvious. "There are five of us and only three pods. This won't work."

"The pods are roomy but not huge. If we sleep on our side, two people could comfortably fit in there," Dorsey said.

Liza inched toward the middle pod. "I think since it was my idea, *I* should get first dibs on the solo one." It made sense. The couples would share, and she'd have her own.

A huge hand clamped down on her shoulder. "That's ridiculous. It should be two siblings to a pod and I get the solo one." Dorsey said this as if *that* made perfect sense.

David and Janae shouted their disapproval. Janae sounded like she was being interrogated by a tough cop. "Liza's a night snuggler—and open-mouth breathes right on top of you. She's going to make me sweat my hair out. I won't do it," Janae said.

"Janae!" Liza exclaimed. She would betray her sister to protect her dang roller set?

"And Jennifer sleep-toots," David blurted out. Jennifer elbowed her brother in the ribs as her face exploded in shades of deep pink and a strangled cry of anger escaped her throat. David clung to Janae, using her as a shield against his sister's wrath. "The worst little farts you'll ever smell. Silent too, so they take you by surprise. So we'll make this easy for you all. Janae and I claim this pod." He held Janae's hand as she climbed into the pod, then climbed in himself. "Good night." He slid the hatch over his head, and they all rolled their eyes at the sounds of giggles and squeaks. As if they gave a damn about sleeping.

"Jennifer and Liza, I think it only makes sense for you two to—" Dorsey started.

Oh, hell no. Dorsey will not stick me with the silent-but-deadly night tooter.

"It looks like the gods favor action over deliberation." Liza made a fast break for the third pod. But Dorsey was faster and reached the pod seconds before Liza crashed into it. Before he wiped his expression clean, she caught him smiling.

Jennifer smiled so tightly it looked like her face might break. "Well, it looks like you two have chosen." She took off her shoes and stepped into the second pod. "Good night." She slammed the pod door so hard it bounced back open. It took her three angry slams to satisfyingly close the hatch.

Liza's shoulders shook. All she could do was laugh. This fucking day would not stop. "I guess it's you and me."

Dorsey's face was stone. He didn't even acknowledge the ridiculousness of their tight quarters. Instead, he got up and stormed off into the darkness.

Would he rather freeze than lie next to me?

DORSEY STEPPED INTO HIS OFFICE, CLOSED HIS DOOR with a soft click, and let out a silent scream. He had spent a lot of money on peace and comfort. Retreats, vacations, yoga, meditation. So much of his life was spent pretending, acting like a man who deserved his father's last name. His only release was that he got to take off the mask at the end of the day and find his own peace.

Dorsey had spent the entire day acting as if he would not burst into flames at the sight of Liza's exposed skin and the feel of her soft hip against his dick. *Get ahold of yourself.* He couldn't maintain this kind of physical and mental anxiety. Did she know she could knock him over with a feather right now? If she gave him *any* indication that she wanted to, he would absolutely fucking rock her to sleep, her head tapping against the top of the pod and his mouth on her breast.

He grabbed his headphones and searched for a meditation app on his phone. He needed one hour of Liza-free peace. Being flustered in front of a crowd was one thing, but to be so agitated in his peaceful bubble was unheard-of. He had once gone to a meditation retreat and hadn't uttered a word for a week and a half. The organizers had reached out to him to teach the retreat the next year. External things he couldn't control gave him anxiety, sure, but the one person he *always* fought to be at peace with was himself. Now he was a live wire and would burst out of his own skin if he didn't keep himself at a safe distance from her. No distance was safe enough, though. Liza Bennett had committed the unpardonable sin of making him uncomfortable in his own head.

When he got back down to the eighth floor, he was prepared. Dorsey had held out as long as he could, but the cold had crept up. His soundproof headphones and the mountain of pillows—to build impenetrable borders between his body and hers—teetered as he made his way back to the pod. He looked like a hockey goalie. But when he pulled open the pod, Liza was already asleep. She had some silk scarf wrapped around her head. Lying there with her brush of black eyelashes resting on her cheeks, she looked like she had been lifted out of a charcoal sketch. He exhaled a shaky breath and placed the pillows inside the gleaming white pod. When he closed the hatch above his head, he was enveloped in blessed warmth and the smell of coconuts and some other nutty bouquet. Before he carefully fashioned his pillow wall so that he could avoid accidental contact, he allowed himself to study her body outlined in shadow. She looked like she'd been drawn by a master. She was alternately lush and lean, full and hollow. The shimmering brown of her skin reminded him of the warm, tropical riverbanks he fished from as a child. Would she be that warm and wet? Could he submerge himself and let her wash over him? He lifted her head and wedged a pillow underneath her to make her more comfortable. The warmth and coconut smell weaved around him, and his eyes got heavy. Then, immediately, his eyes popped open wide.

An ass.

The soft rise of a perfect peach ass on his hip. Was it? It was. It was grinding now.

Nope.

No.

He shook her shoulder.

"Liza!" he whispered. The panic rose in his voice. "Liza!" Her eyes fluttered open.

"What?" Liza looked confused, but how could she be? She had to feel her entire ass on his leg.

Dorsey knifed an imaginary line down the middle of the pod. "You're over the line."

"What line?" Liza asked groggily.

He hacked the air with the flat of his hand. "This line."

"You're just making gestures," Liza said and settled back into her position.

"You. Your butt is over the line."

"Should I apologize for being a Black woman, then?"

"It's not about that. It's just bad sleep technique. You're like the letter *S*. You should be straight like a lowercase *l*."

Liza turned over to face him again. Dorsey bit his bottom lip. Had her eyes been that intense shade of brown yesterday? Had her lashes been this long? The snaps on that cheap shirt could easily come undone in the night.

He shifted a pillow over his cock. It pulsed in response to an unasked question. *No, you are not fucking invited.*

"A lowercase *l* like you?" she asked.

"Yes, like me. This is good bed-sharing etiquette." Dorsey demonstrated his perfect form.

"You look like you're doing a side plank." She poked at his shoulders and biceps. Didn't she know not to bother a cornered animal? "You are fully flexing. You can't even relax in your sleep." Liza shook her head.

How could he sleep with that ass resting on his leg, those breasts threatening to burst out of that shirt? That pursed mouth dying to be shut up with a kiss?

"Your sister was right. You're a night snuggler."

"Oh, don't flatter yourself, sir. That was not a snuggle."

"Just keep your body parts to yourself," Dorsey said. When she didn't move, he patted her bottom with the back of his hand. She nearly hit her head on the hatch door in surprise. He stuffed a pillow in the space she made, re-creating his impenetrable border. "Now, stay over there."

Minutes passed. Had it been an hour? *Okay. This wasn't terrible.* He was warm. He was comfort—

No.

Liza's thigh frog-legged over his middle. His cock rocketed to life, and he instinctively palmed the inside of her thigh to lift it off and away from his now-straining midsection.

"Liza," Dorsey whispered. It sounded like a plea. Liza turned to the other side with a heavy sigh. Dorsey turned also so they would be back to back. He was trapped with his penis boring a hole through his slacks. He cracked the hatch door for a burst of frigid air. It cooled the beads of sweat accumulating on his brow. But the cold was so harsh and uninviting that he immediately slammed the hatch door shut. The sound jolted Liza awake.

"Oh my goodness, what now?" Liza's voice was thick with sleep.

"Liza, keep your body"—he paused—"over there."

"Dorsey." He could practically hear her roll her eyes. "It's just a body. Don't worry, you can't catch poverty by contact."

"I'm not afraid of catching poverty. I'm trying to get some

sleep." Dorsey turned to face her. *Let her see what her reckless snuggling has done to me.* But the pod was too dark.

"Don't blame your guilt-ridden insomnia on me nudging you once in a while in your sleep."

"Nudging? That was not a nudge." This woman was insane.

"I'm being fair to you by even admitting that I touched you. I've been adhering to my side of the pod pretty well actually."

"You're delusional. Your body was way over the line."

"Show me. Show me what I did that was so out of line," she said. Always a challenge with Liza.

"I don't have to show you. Take my word for it," Dorsey said. Sounding all of seven years old.

"Then you're exaggerating." Liza rose up on her elbow. Lord, but this woman could actually have all of him wrapped up with a bow right now.

"Then I'll show you," he said.

Dorsey pulled at her thigh again, palming the inner part near the knee, then stretching it over his middle. In the dark, there was no seeing, only feeling. She must have felt his erection. God, he was metastatic with desire for her. It had started in his fingertips hours ago. Now, it was everywhere. She exhaled hotly on his cheek. There was no top clearance, so her breasts pressed flat against his chest.

Had a body ever arranged itself so well onto his? It was perhaps not the *best* idea to pull her nearly on top of him, thighs sprawled, just to prove a point. It wasn't lost on Dorsey now that in their current position, if he pushed her down *just* a little, the head of his penis would be at her hot center, with nothing but blue jeans and Italian wool between them.

Liza, if you move, I'll move.

"It's more than a nudge." Dorsey's voice sounded foreign and harsh.

Liza pulled herself off him devastatingly slowly.

Safe choice.

"I didn't know you had it in you." Liza's voice had also taken on a husky quality. *Can she feel it too? The danger we're in?*

"A dick?" Dorsey massaged himself.

"Exactly. It's just external stimuli, Dorsey. Or are you surprised to have a biological reaction to someone other than Ms. Venezuela?"

Aha, there it is. So she *had* thought about his stupid little comment as much as he had. She'd had her little ego bruised and wanted to get a trophy hard-on out of him. The joke was on her; lately, well-buttered buns could get a hard-on out of him.

"We can test your theory, Liza. We can test my biological reaction." His voice was a low promise. "Or you can stay on the other side of the line."

He heard her kiss her teeth as she turned her back to him. After hearing Liza's deep and rhythmic breathing, Dorsey toyed with the idea of heading to the bathroom and rubbing one out just to get the tension out of his neck. But freezing in the men's bathroom with his balls out did not appeal to him. He ran his hand over his chest where she had lain. Once. Twice. Finger lightly running over his nipple. He turned to her again, her figure silhouetted like a cello in the dark. What would it feel like if she reached for him? Allowed him to play her chords? No one would have to know but them. This pod was their universe. Dorsey felt himself relax.

———

DAYLIGHT STABBED LIZA IN THE EYES. BUT SHE REFUSED to wake up. She was an old pro at burrowing under the covers when her mother rolled the curtains open. She buried her head into a cushion.

"We found a plow." Liza's eyes flew open. A blast of freezing air cracked through the warm cocoon she and Dorsey had made. Jennifer's cool face was mere inches above her. The night's events came rushing back to her. Her cushion was also shaking himself awake. *Shit.* Liza scrambled to untangle her arms and legs. What in the spooning hell was going on here? Had she slept on his chest? Like a bland after-sex scene in a sitcom? *Ugh, girl.* And where had his hands landed? She found them cupping the rise of her hips.

The hatch door only opened so far. No one could see his hands, and she was so cold. *Surely there was no rush to move them.*

Jennifer's eyes cut like a scalpel. "You've missed half the day." She looked immaculate with her deep red lipstick, perfectly powdered face, not a strand of hair out of place, clothing meticulous. This was how a woman went into battle. Liza wanted to tell her she had wasted her war paint. She didn't feel sorry for Jennifer exactly. She had not known Dorsey long, but she knew he had the power to make people feel like that, like they weren't worthy of him. Jennifer was just his latest victim.

Liza patted her own silk scarf and wiped the crust from her eyes.

Dorsey raised himself up. "What time is it?"

Lord. Have. Mercy. How dare he wake up this sexy? His hair was tousled. His voice was low and tired, and the sound rumbled pleasantly in her chest. Warmth unfolded in the seat of her belly. *Really, vagina—turning on me too? You're as bad as Janae.* There had been a moment last night with her legs spread over him that Liza thought she might have . . . She didn't want to think of what she might have done. What did it matter now, here in the blinding light of day? She tucked her hands into her lap. It was not lost on her that their legs were still touching. Neither one of them had snatched their legs apart the way one does in the light of day.

"It's eleven thirty-six," Jennifer said with a flash of impatience.

Dorsey's eyes rounded. "I haven't slept past ten since college." He rubbed his chin, and Liza looked away, afraid to be caught staring. There was something strange about seeing him in the morning before he'd put himself together. She should get up before she embarrassed herself, stealing swoony glances like a tween girl.

Liza pulled herself out of the pod and made her way to the bathroom. The normally weak winter sun had gotten a reflective boost from the snow and now shone brightly through the window blinds, streaking in alabaster light on the eighth floor. She checked her phone and saw that her mother had called no less than thirteen times.

Shit. Janae. Liza washed her face and finger-brushed her teeth in the bathroom and went searching for her sister.

Another call. "Yes, Ma?"

"Where is Janae?"

"I'm looking for her."

"Don't go barging in on her and her man. Give them some privacy. You should have taken your butt home. You get yourself stuck overnight in a whiteout, then don't pick up your phone until damn near noon."

"Sorry, Momma. I thought . . . She was drinking so I . . ." Bev quieted at this. Liza moved toward the steps and faltered when she saw Dorsey waiting for her at the exit, looking like an awkward sentinel. He was actively not looking her in the eye. *So we're doing this, huh? The I-was-never-here, it-was-all-a-dream shit? Fine.*

Bev's voice howled through the phone. "Oh, my poor baby. Why would you let her drink?"

"Ma, I watered down her champagne and traded it for non-alcoholic. I did what I could, but she's a grown woman," Liza tried to whisper. She didn't want Dorsey overhearing all this, but Bev hung up without saying goodbye.

She and Dorsey took the stairs up to the ninth floor in absolute silence so tense that Liza raced up the remaining stairs.
They found everyone else in the common area neatly assembled
and ready to go. It was at this point that Dorsey handed her the
dry ballet flats. She had forgotten all about them. She took the
shoes and slipped them on.

Everyone eyed them like they were glass slippers and Dorsey
had been searching the damned kingdom or something.

"Nice of you and Dorsey to finally join us," David finally said.
Liza smiled tightly and looked over to her sister, reading her face
for worry or strain. Janae had a blank expression and tears brimming in her eyes. She didn't talk to David and only nodded to
Liza. It was time to get her out of here. She should have insisted
yesterday. It was nobody's business to see her like this, and certainly not these snobs.

Liza picked up her mother's phone call on the third ring.

"Liza, just get my baby home," Bev wailed.

"Okay, Ma." When she looked up, Dorsey was gone.

Jennifer walked into the common area. "I found a private
contractor who can clear the garage and streets. Janae and Liza,
you can ride with David. He'll take you home."

"Thank you," Liza said, genuinely grateful. She couldn't stay
here another minute. Dorsey had taken to completely ignoring
everyone here, with his head in his laptop. David was obviously
hurt at Janae's sudden change in temperament, and Jennifer was
moving mountains to get them gone.

Liza gathered her things and walked over to Janae, who sat
looking at nothing. "Up, sissy. It's time to go."

"Just leave me," Janae mumbled.

"Up," Liza said more insistently, and Janae plopped her arm
around Liza and stood up.

"Hangover," Liza mouthed to David, who sat in openmouthed concern. She didn't have time to think about how to tell them about Janae's pain. Her loss seemed like something they could never understand. It struck Liza with a sad finality that the gap between their worlds was unbreachable.

They took the ride in unpleasant silence. David tried to engage Janae and made those types of jokes that Janae loved—dad humor, just shy of corny. Liza insisted he drop them off a block away, so the truck driver didn't have to do any tricky maneuvering out of the neighborhood. The air was chilly and wet in a way that clung to the inside of Liza's lungs, and the sky was still a tepid gray. David hopped out of the car and walked with them to the building awning. A wet brown leaf tousled his hair, and he didn't correct it. They crunched through knee-high snow, hardened at the top with sleet. David was sweet and incredibly compassionate. An ungracious pang of jealousy shot through Liza at the type of attention her sister inspired. Perhaps if she were prettier, less prickly even, she could elicit that type of unquestioning devotion.

"Here we are. Thank you, David," Liza said.

"Thanks," Janae said. She sounded like a phone operator, distant and staticky and dispassionate. David nodded curtly, as if he were suddenly understanding something, and patted Janae's back.

"You two are fine from here?" David asked, his eyes searching hers earnestly.

"Yes!" Liza almost pushed him down the street.

Janae gave him a weak and watery smile. "Keep warm," she mumbled.

Liza hustled them inside and leaned against the door to the foyer. She exhaled and pulled Janae close to her.

It was the last the Bennetts would see of them for sure.

BUTTERMILK PIE

WE HAVE A SPECIAL GUEST WITH US TODAY! LONG-bourne's own golden boy, Colin Gruthers." Liza leaned on the applause button. "You may remember he was interviewed by Channel 4 when he won no less than four scholarships to top universities. I don't remember which ones, but he certainly does and will let you know repeatedly exactly who he turned down to strive for the gold.

"He graduated middle of his class at Drexel. He is the author of *Up from Nothing: The Harrowing Tale of Escape from Southeast DC*, for sale exclusively out of his trunk. He just recently won a bid for local office in Virginia. You can call him City Council-man Gruthers, but to me, he's the same ol' pain in the ass." Liza leaned on the laughter button.

"Well, thanks, Liza. I appreciate the brief introduction. There are quite a few things that you left out of that intro, including the fact that I was geography bee champion in middle school and that I'm working on a second book entitled *Can't Hold Me Down: Getting to the Top with No Sacrifice*."

"Tell me, Colin, what brings you down here?" Liza used her best curious voice. In truth, she was in over her head writing the proposal for WIC, and Colin's city council background had actually proved helpful. Now she owed him, and he planned to milk it dry.

"Oh, you know I like to come back occasionally to the place that raised me. Your own mother used to pack my lunch every morning. It's good to see where you never want to go back. It makes you strive to do so much better."

"So glad we could be a negative example for you, Colin," Liza quipped. "I consulted Colin because I was drafting a plan to get more affordable housing in our city. I thank you for that, Colin."

"Liza, anytime, anywhere, whatever you need, I'm there for you. You know, folks out there in radioland, I recently bailed her younger brother out of jail. If it was anyone else, I would have hung up the phone and said don't call me back. But when Bev and her daughters need something, I come running."

"And we can't thank you enough. Literally. All right, folks, this is your chance to ask Longbourne Gardens' own golden boy questions about success and failures. Hit us up!"

"Thank you, Liza. And congratulations on the station expanding your show to two hours."

"Yeah, I have to find out who this mysterious donor is when I get next week's commercial list." Liza pressed the kissing-sound button. "There's a big juicy kiss for you, Mystery Moneybags."

"Okay, Liza, I will be around y'all's way for that homemade buttermilk pie your mom loves to make for me." He winked.

"MOM, YOU NEED TO BUY A BUTTERMILK PIE," LIZA SAID as she jimmied the key out of the lock.

"You look like hell," Bev commented.

"I haven't been sleeping well." Honestly, the nap pod was the best sleep she had gotten in weeks, but that knowledge did not help her sleep better. Would she ever be that warm again?

"Mom. Buttermilk pie. You have, like, two days to buy it," Liza said.

"Oh, Colin's coming by?" Bev perked up.

Everyone in earshot groaned. Granny shook her head.

"Yes, he's coming for his annual poverty tour," Liza said. "It's my fault. I had *one* question."

"You all need to hush. That boy made something of himself because of me. He listened to me when none of you did and now look at him." Bev straightened her shoulders.

"Mom, have you told him why you were always across the hallway making sandwiches for him when his mother wasn't there?" Liza asked.

"Mr. Gruthers was a friend. He was a shoulder to cry on when Deya's father up and left us." LeDeya's father didn't "up and leave." He simply reunited with his wife.

"Yeah, but Mrs. Gruthers never spoke to you again," Janae said.

"I was young. I've made my mistakes. But that doesn't mean their boy doesn't deserve love," Bev said.

"Mom, we try," LeDeya said. "He moans when he hugs us."

"Remember he visited last year with cameras to get us on a show about broken homes?" Janae said.

"And so what? There was ten thousand in cash in that show. Janae, all you had to do was that bikini shot and—"

"What about when he made you a cosigner of his first car without even asking you? You found out five years later."

"Yes, after he *paid* it off. Have any of you ever paid a car off?" Bev asked. "Look, the boy's not going to win any popularity contest, but he's as good as family and I expect you"—she eyed Liza—"to treat him as such."

"Why are you looking at me?" Liza huffed.

"Cuz you got a mean streak a half a mile wide," Maurice said.

"I'm not mean, I'm pissed. Colin's got all of this money, and he's still trying to squeeze what he can out of us."

Liza didn't say what she wanted to say because it was the nuclear option. Bev was a serial side chick. She had a string of relationships with unavailable men, but jaded was the only thing she got from it, not to mention children who never knew their fathers. It made her hyperaware and focused on the relationship status of her children, but blind to her own secondary status in the lives of men.

The Gruthers had lived next door, and while Mrs. Gruthers struggled through chemotherapy, Bev fell in love with her husband and all but established herself as a housewife in the Gruthers' apartment. But it was all for nothing. When Mrs. Gruthers died, Mr. Gruthers did not marry Bev like she had hoped. He went to his grave soon after, claiming that Mrs. Gruthers was the only woman he'd ever loved. Colin became a permanent fixture in their home, sullen and obnoxious. But when his ticket out of Longbourne Gardens came, he didn't do so much as write a note to say goodbye. He had nothing but disdain for the place and a strange sense of entitlement to what he called the Bennett Beauties. It was a weird mix of guilt about his mother's death and devotion to his father—a man who never acknowledged her—that kept Bev bound to Colin's whims. Liza would never be so bound up in someone that she would be willing to accept him in small pieces.

"You don't know what it's like to lose someone that close to you. The bond between a mother and son—" Bev stopped herself.

"Mom, you can say it."

"Janae, we weren't trying to upset you."

"I want everyone to stop tiptoeing around me. I know I've struggled . . . am struggling with . . . things, but I am starting to see myself differently, and I want you all to try as well."

"I think we can do that," Liza said.

"I'm going to try a grief counselor like you suggested," Janae told them.

Liza and Bev looked at each other in a moment of shared surprise.

"David called me. I was sure I'd never hear from him again. He called to make sure I was okay. At first, I just held the phone. And then he spoke. He told me his father is ill, and he's seeing a grief counselor. He told me it helped him feel less out of control."

Liza held her tongue. She had been telling Janae for three years to talk to someone, but David mentioned it in passing and Janae already had an appointment. Could falling in love really be this transformative? Liza doubted it. She had never met anyone who made her rethink her whole self and probably never would. And despite living with her mother and not having a job that was her true calling, Liza was pretty sure nothing else about her life needed to change. But for Janae, maybe that was what it took.

Liza had thought that Janae and the man-boy's little spark had faded, but instead, it was glowing. Would Janae tell him about her son? Would she open up and risk her heart to grasp at happiness? Liza hoped she would, even if it came in a chinless, goofy package.

"No one is rushing your grief, Janae," Liza said.

"I know. The loss will never not crush my heart every single second I'm alive. I just want help with the weight of it," Janae said. "I . . . I can't do it on my own."

"You'll never have to," Bev said, then grabbed her for a hug.

Liza's eyes shot to the nearby wall at the sound of a hard thud, followed by rapid yelling in Spanish. Liza looked at Janae, who sighed.

"Go and get her, Liza, before that man knocks a hole through the wall," Bev said.

Chicho's family was at it again. Her mother was a nice enough woman, if a bit mousy, and her father was a brute. Liza and Janae were out the door before they uttered the next Spanish curse word. The hallway was poorly lit, and a few bags of trash sat outside dented doors. She knocked on the Ochoas' door with authority. That always put the fear of God into Chicho's father. The door flew open, and Javier leaned on the doorjamb.

"Don't knock on my door like the law, little girl! I told you about that." The liquor and marijuana smells wafted outside into the hallway.

Liza threw on an old smile like a worn housecoat. Janae tilted her head up in a smile as well. "Mr. O., is Lucia here? I need her. It's an emergency."

"Chicho! Las Gatas!" he yelled behind him.

"Oh, and Granny is trying to rest and would love it if you kept it down over here?" Liza added.

"Yeah, how is your grandma?"

"Doing well." Janae nodded.

"Ask if she can get me some of those peppers from that garden."

Liza doubted he would remember. "I will." Liza grabbed Chicho by the sleeve and pulled her out. "See you!" Liza and

Janae shuffled their friend down the hall and through their front door.

"Oh girl, I am so over that house," Chicho said. Liza saw her hand tremble.

"How did your second interview go?" Liza asked.

"They went with someone else again. I don't have the look for fancy retail." She waved at Janae and Bev as they made their way to Liza's room.

"Chicho—" Liza started.

"Girl, please, I'm a realist. I'm not the girl they want in front. That's reserved for you and your sisters."

"I wish everyone would stop lumping me in with my sisters all the time."

"Liza, you can never take the simple way. That's always been your problem."

Liza rolled her eyes. This was an old fight. "Not everything is about a cheat code, Chicho."

"Why can't it be? If I had your face and body, I'd leverage it to get the hell out of my mom's house, but you want to fight a revolution that's only gonna get you more broke."

"Came swinging today, Chicho, geez."

"I'm sorry, I'm not mad. I'm just tired of working so hard when so many people don't have to," she said, her voice tightening.

"I have some gossip, anyway," Liza sang.

Liza filled Chicho in on the events of the previous week, delicately skipping any mention of her and Dorsey sharing a nap pod and avoiding talk of them pressed against each other in the stairwell. And certainly omitting that ghost of a moment when he had burned her alive with a searing look down her open flannel blouse. No, Liza would take that look—and whatever it conjured in the pit of her belly—to the grave. Chicho clapped with appreciation after Liza vividly told the tale.

Janae, who had been listening, popped in. "Liza, you are skipping your new love!"

Liza panicked. *What could she mean?* Had Janae seen them during the snowstorm? *No way.* She had been passed out. "No, there's no new love, Janae!" Liza crossed her arms in front of her.

"Oh, there definitely is," Chicho said. "I can tell by the way she's denying it."

"The guy you met, Liza! He's with the Black Israelites or something? He's fundraising to outbid Pemberley on the Netherfield Court development?"

"Oh, oh, oh!" Liza exhaled with something uncomfortably close to relief. Of course she didn't mean Dorsey. "He's from Philly. His name is WIC, and he. Is. Fine."

Liza met her sister's eyes. There was a touch of disbelief there. Janae's squinty-eyed scrutiny made Liza shift her eyes away.

"Yeah, right. A guy that *Liza* likes!" LeDeya popped back into the room, waiting for gossip. "Give this one a week. He's gonna pronounce 'coup d'état' the wrong way, and she'll be done with him." Janae and Chicho laughed behind their hands.

"Deya, I have a particular taste."

"Look at your outfit and say that again," LeDeya said. Liza wore slim jeans and a hoodie with a paint-splatter design. Liza wanted a man to meet her at her mind—a man who could be wise and learn new things. She wanted to be a student with someone for the rest of her life. Everyone she met was so in love with their own thinking. It wasn't too much to ask for a thoughtful, measured, kind man who could also lay pipe.

Deya tapped her shoulder. "Now tell me his complete name

so we can google the hell out of him." LeDeya pulled out her phone. Her cracked screen, fluffy dangling charm, and ornate jeweled case were almost painful to look at for too long.

"Deya, this is none of your business—"

"I'm better at this than you, and I know you've already tried. You search the overall social media scene, but *I* be researching their DMs and subtweets. I'm on another level."

Liza looked up sheepishly, letting her curiosity cushion the blow to her pride. "William Isaiah Curry."

All four women stood over a small screen with their opposite ears touching.

"Okay, so you know he's from Philly. You know he's with the Black Israelite movement. *Ew*, does he scream at people on the side of the road?" LeDeya scrolled. "Gross. Not much info about it, though."

"Keep scrolling," Janae said. It surprised Liza to see her sister so interested.

"You too?" Liza rolled her eyes.

"Oh, look. He atted DFitz about a year ago." Janae, Chicho, and Liza all looked confused. "Mr. Congeniality himself, Dorsey Fitzgerald," LeDeya clarified.

Liza's eyes widened. She would never think that those two could ever be atting each other. "What does it say?"

"'This is the new CEO of Pemberley Development? #unfit #trainingwheels.'" It was a grainy photo of Dorsey, surrounded by women, smoking what looked like a blunt. His eyes were low. Liza smirked. Mr. Cool and Collected was a womanizing troll. She was actually relieved to see these photos. Her stomach could stop dropping when she thought of his hand gripping her thigh.

"See if Dorsey responded," Liza said almost frantically.

"Nope, no response."

"Can't defend himself," Liza said.

"Nah, I think it's like Jedi deep." LeDeya stretched her arms out.

"It's not Jedi deep, it's just arrogant. It is exactly the reason he can put luxury midrise condos up in the poorest part of Southeast. People like us don't matter to him."

Maurice, now also crammed into Liza's bedroom, shrugged. "Your pretty boy WIC started it, if you ask me," he said. "If you come for the king, you best not miss." He quoted *The Wire*, but Liza wasn't sure if the boy had ever really seen the show. That was so like Maurice, using a thing in the right context yet with so little understanding.

"Look at you, already standing up for your WIC." LeDeya pushed Liza with her shoulder, but Liza did not allow herself to smile.

Her WIC.

To: DFitz@PemDevCo.com
From: CoolPodz

Thank you for your interest in CoolPodz for your office!
We're so pleased that you had an amazing experience in
one of our pods! Could you recall which model it was? We
could have 3 shipped to your Philadelphia offices by the
end of the week.

Best,
CoolPodz Sales

Four weeks later, on a crisp November morning, Dorsey was
counting himself lucky. He had scarcely thought about Liza's
sugary-brown skin all day and hadn't stalked her Instagram in
thirteen hours. And moreover, for three days, he hadn't lingered
on that one picture where her shorts hugged her ass. An ass he
had pushed out of the way. He sat in a DC municipal building
with Virginia State Corporation Commission's chair, Christopher De Berg. Representatives from Maryland also crowded the

table, but the way they genuflected to the senator, it was like the president had walked in. When he spoke to Dorsey, the clamor hushed.

"People are looking into your developments in DC. This whole gentrification chatter is getting louder." He had a forty-inch computer monitor in front of him. Dorsey didn't know if it was tech-savviness or Luddite tendencies that would make a man purchase a monitor this obscene, then lug it around for meetings so he could fact-check in real time. There was no privacy. Dorsey could see an email from Lighthouse Marriage Counseling: "36 Questions to Bring You Closer." The senator also bet on fantasy football quite a bit. When someone at the table asked him about the gigantic screen obstructing their view, he replied, "I like my own data, and I don't know what the hell a cloud is." Everyone chuckled, except for Dorsey. It must have been that absence of a chuckle that drew the senator's attention. De Berg's white hair, probably once blond and thick, was slicked back and clung to his collar. He inexplicably wore golf shirts year-round and had prominent front teeth that made him look like a member of the British royal family.

"What are you going to do about the chatter, Fitzgerald?"

"I'm not sure there is much I *can* do. People have a right to protest. I have a right to build. One thing shouldn't prevent the other."

"I think you could play up the social media component of this." The senator clicked through a few images on his screen and turned the monitor. It showed the two viral memes of him and Liza. Dorsey unbuttoned his jacket in an excuse to look away.

"How do you mean 'play up,' sir?" Dorsey was an expert at making his tone unaffected.

"The little girl that started this whole thing. Maybe a photo of you two being friendly. It would make it seem like you're hearing their concerns." The senator pulled the monitor back. "Make it seem like you're being responsive." Murmurs of agreement washed over the room.

"So a photo op?"

"Not a photo op, a *viral* photo op. Use social media to either discredit her or prove that you're a bleeding heart."

"That's gross," Dorsey said coldly. The room went still.

"That's politics. If you don't have the stomach for the ugly underside of progress, you're in the wrong profession."

Dorsey stopped short at that. Perhaps he *was* in the wrong profession. He didn't enjoy smiling and glad-handing with people he had no chance of ever liking. His mother would have thought of a better way. She would have tried to understand.

"The developments are a net positive for the community *and* the district," Dorsey insisted. "The facts should speak for themselves."

"Ha." The senator slapped the oak table. "You need to come down off your high horse, son. People don't deal in facts and figures. They know how a thing makes them *feel*. And pushing a boulder through the projects while little Black and Brown kids watch and cry is bad for business. Like a damned SPCA commercial."

"I'm sorry, everyone is just going to have to grow up. I will not associate myself with Liza Bennett"—he took a thoughtful pause—"*just* for the sake of building more buildings in DC," Dorsey said. He wouldn't mind being huddled up in the cold with her half straddling him again. But the senator thought people's lives were chess pieces. Not to mention he'd just compared Black children to those sad anti–animal abuse commercials. He had the strength of his mother's convictions about this. He would not use Liza.

"That's a lot of money to throw away for the sake of your pride."

The senator's marriage-counseling email gave him an idea. "Self-respect is a perfectly good cause to spend your money on." He rose and closed the buttons on his black tartan sport coat, which had stayed remarkably wrinkle-free.

The senator looked him over. "And when it's all gone, can your self-respect keep you dry in the rain? Can you eat your pride?"

With his hand still on the doorknob, Dorsey asserted calmly, "It would take me seven lifetimes to run into that problem."

THE HOTEL
WASHINGTON TREATY

YOU'RE LIVE WITH LIZA B., THE ONLY DJ WHO GIVES A jam." Liza put her feet up on the desk. The DJ booth was less cluttered now, and Liza could finally see the walls behind the posters, the only upside of massive layoffs.

"It's Friday night, Liza. Could you give us some energy?"

"Hey, I have to play what's on the list."

"Well, I can listen to dad rock on my own. I like your mixes."

"Say no more. I'll have some Louisiana bounce after a few words from our sponsor. P-Pem—oh no." Liza rubbed at her temples. She saw a nervous woman tap on the Booth G window across from hers. She saw the DJ's shoulders slump, and the woman led him down the hallway. Another pink slip. This man was the king of assholes.

"Pemberley Development, s-saving DC one c-community at a time. Call the care line if you have c-concerns about Netherfield. That's 1-800-Care4Yu." Liza choked out the words. This man was appalling. Liza looked at her script schedule. Dorsey was a gold sponsor! Did he know the station was in trouble? Would he risk expanding her show just to humiliate her with commercials? Liza wanted to be furious, but the blockhead didn't know that he had likely saved her show.

Liza laughed for a full three minutes before it was time to go back on air.

LIZA LOOKED AT HER CALENDAR. IT WAS DEFINITELY Wednesday. She paced at the busy intersection, dodging waves of cold slush as cars rushed past her. She would be an army of one today. The municipal building was supposed to be the site of a rally. But Liza had been here for an hour already. She was cold, her fingers red and swollen. Today *was* Wednesday, right? It was just another example of people not showing up for a cause.

Lately, her charm seemed to be wearing thin. Dorsey had laughed at the thought of dancing with her, and WIC hadn't really been returning her texts. It was confusing because she and WIC had such a vibe. He was just the type of man she thought she *should* like. But in activism and in love, it seemed like her enthusiasm was never returned, and she was alone at a rally (again), texting a guy who rarely texted back (again).

In the meantime, she couldn't go long without thinking of the tiniest interactions with Dorsey. He was permanently part of the things that took up space (rent-free) in her head:

- Who was the first person to realize we could drink cow's milk and, like, what were they actually up to?
- In Mean Girls why did everyone believe Cady wrote the Burn Book? She was new!
- When Dorsey spread my legs over him in the nap pod, had I been seconds from throwing this man my whole ass?!

They were all rattling around in her brain, popping in her head uninvited when she showered or lotioned or curled her hair. Should she have pushed her nipple in his mouth? And grabbed his length underneath her? Told him to shut up? That didn't sound very consensual. But she liked the idea of getting a little bit of power back—make him scream her name and beg for her. He deserved it. It was uncomfortable and confusing when her body and mind were running in opposite directions. Shouldn't she dislike him completely if she disagreed with everything about him? How could his touch still make her heart jump out of her chest? Why would the sound of his morning voice make her grab at her abdomen like she needed to protect her eggs? He was so entitled to female attention that he had scarcely given her another thought. But now that Janae was wrapped up so tightly with David, Liza couldn't help but feel lonely, and it was hard for her to share her feelings with her family. Chicho also seemed to see her mostly as a whiner.

"Okay," Liza said to herself, "time to split. Cut your losses."

She had resigned herself to sitting in the café next door and applying for positions she would never hear back from, when she saw Dorsey through the windows of the municipal building.

Keep your head, child. It was Granny's voice that popped into her head now.

Granny, I'm trying.

Her head knew all the reasons he was just wrong, but Liza's body only remembered his cock under her thigh, so thick and throbbing.

For me?

For her.

He seemed to pop up when she was in want of an audience. His shoulders were high, and his brows were creased. He looked angry. *Good, I hope some official finally told him no. I should go before he sees me.* It made sense in her head, but her body moved itself into Dorsey's line of sight.

DORSEY STOPPED WALKING MID-STRIDE. HE NEARLY dropped the phone at the sight of Liza outside the government building. She stepped right out of his Instagram feed like he had conjured her out of purely lustful thoughts. He saw her in the thick glass, and she tilted her chin up defiantly.

She sees me.

Dorsey knew she did. He was stuck there momentarily, gazing at her. She walked up to the building and pressed her fist onto the glass. Then she pretended to crank her middle finger until it was straight. Ah, she must have heard about her new sponsor. He stepped out of the revolving door. Once again, he found himself anticipating her reaction.

"What are you doing here?" he asked. His heart was hammering like a son of a bitch.

"This is *my* city government. I have a right to be here." Liza held up her sign. One side read TRANS RIGHTS ARE HUMAN RIGHTS; the other read VOTE NO ON PROP B.

"Where are your comrades?" Dorsey asked.

"Don't you mean *our* comrades, Gold Sponsor? Thank you for joining the fight." Liza said this like she had won something.

Wait, *had* she won? Dorsey wanted to get a better look at the activism he was funding.

"Let me see that sign." This had all seemed brilliant a few weeks ago.

"Oh no, you don't. I know what you do with signs." She held her sign behind her back. Dorsey thought if he reached for it, he could feel her pressed against him again. He balled his fist instead.

"No combustibles." Dorsey held his hands up, then unbuttoned his blazer. "Search me," he offered. Liza touched the inside of his jacket. For a half second, he thought she would touch his stomach.

"Silk lining . . . Shit." She was more impressed with his clothing than with him. "Just checking for vape pens."

Dorsey laughed, then held out his phone. "'Vote no on Prop B' is next Wednesday. The trans rally was last Wednesday. You have the right *place*, at least." He buttoned his jacket.

"Right place wrong time is kind of my brand," Liza said. It was a criminal offense how easily charmed by her he was. She wore a snug cream turtleneck sweater. Snug made him think of that warm night in the nap pod.

He wanted a redo.

He would be much more efficient with his time. He scanned her black leggings and black fur boots. He needed to find something safe to focus on. Her hair was in long twists down her back, and she wore a black beanie and the biggest pink glasses he'd ever seen. Her lips were two-toned like his—a soft pale brown at the top and a lush full pink at the bottom. Something she was wearing made them look like she'd just licked them. He didn't want to stop looking at her.

"My friend thinks he knows the best place for drinks in DC. Do you want to prove him wrong?" Dorsey asked. He didn't know *how* he knew that this way of asking her out would yield better results, but the proof was in her offended pose.

"Is your friend even from here?" Liza asked. Dorsey opened his mouth to speak but was cut off. "You know what? I know he isn't. But I can't say no to trash talking overpriced drinks," she said.

"You're on." He smiled back. A breath rushed out of him. *Relief?*

"Is this your car?" Liza pointed to a moderate sedan. "My brother went to real jail for unpaid parking tickets. How on earth did they let you park right in front of this building?" Liza asked.

"Really, the first bland midsize sedan you see is mine?" He couldn't keep the slightest offense out of his voice.

"No, the first car illegally parked with no sign of tickets is what I thought was yours."

Dorsey pulled out his phone again and pressed the screen. Liza turned around in every direction, and Dorsey pointed to his Tesla as it unparallel-parked itself and drove toward them. *"That's* my car."

"Holy shit, tell me there's a person in there."

"No, it's the Summon feature. It's slow but reliable and pretty handy on a cold day." When the car arrived, Dorsey pressed another button, and both doors opened up like bat wings. Liza actually clapped like the machine had stood up on its hind legs.

Do cool cars work for women like you? Dorsey kept his face firmly inscrutable. As he slid into the buttery leather seat, he sobered.

She doesn't think you're cool, idiot, just your car.

"Navigate to Hotel Washington." When he saw Liza pulling out her phone, he smiled. "Not you, the car," he said through laughter.

"I'm not used to the spoils of capitalism. You'll have to explain your ways."

"So glad you said that. I think I *can* explain my ways so we can understand each other," Dorsey said. "I read this article from the *New York Times.* They paired people off and asked them a set of thirty-six questions ranging in intimacy, and the people came out . . ." Dorsey suddenly started stammering.

"In love." Liza said. "I read that article."

"Not *all* of them. I mean . . ." Her directness made him sputter. "That's not what *I'm* trying to do. No. The people understood each other better. I think we could try to—I just don't think I'm your enemy." His sentences crashed into each other like bumper cars. But he meant it. The only things he consistently felt for her were curiosity, annoyance, and a hearty dose of lust.

"We want the exact opposite things. The only thing we *can* be is enemies. You said yourself that no one can ever screw up around you. And all I *do* is screw up." Liza picked at her leggings.

"Even if that's true, won't we negotiate better knowing exactly what those things are? Sometimes the stars align, Liza." He enjoyed saying her name.

"Aligned stars don't mean aligned goals."

"What about tonight? Right now, you and I both want a drink. Could we just start there?" Dorsey hated the crack in his voice. It sounded like he needed her. The pleading tone in his voice made it sound like he was lonely.

"Okay. Start your interrogation." Dorsey hoped she could not hear his sigh of relief. He was glad she had spared him the wattage of her smile.

He pulled up the questions on his phone. "First question: How do you feel about your relationship with your mother?"

"No way is that the first question."

"It's the first in my app."

"There's an app! The precision of your weirdness is . . ." Liza laughed, a high, sweet sound, and kissed the tips of her fingers. His eyes watched her soft mouth.

"Your job is not to critique the question-delivery method," he said.

"Okay, wow. My relationship with my mother is . . . fraught. There are so many land mines. I could effectively avoid them when I had my own place, but since I got evicted, all I seem to do is set her off." Liza said the last part facing the window. Something seemed to latch into place for Dorsey. She had been evicted. Liza could not pay rent with the job she had, with a degree—with two degrees. She was personally affected by the lack of affordable housing in her neighborhood.

"Mothers fully understand you when you're six, then they sometimes forget that they have to keep understanding you," Dorsey said.

"What about your mom?"

"See, with me, you get a twofer. My relationship with my biological mom is . . . well . . . I think I remind her of a time in her life that she can barely stand to remember. She was treated pretty poorly by my biological father. Now she has a new family and wants nothing to do with me." Dorsey wanted to sound funny and lighthearted. But his delivery tanked. The truth just wasn't lighthearted.

After his family's horrific accident, he'd traveled back to Manila on an ill-fated soul-searching trip to find his mother. It had been so simple that he wondered why he hadn't done it before. He'd found her by some miraculous happenstance. Some part of him wondered if his mother hadn't been coerced into the adoption. As much as he loved Patricia, he'd heard so many stories of less-than-legal international adoptions. He'd thought maybe when his mother saw him she'd open her arms and exclaim, *My son!*

His mother had recognized him instantly. Something about

the configuration of his face brought on the painful memories of his biological father. He found out from her that she had been abused repeatedly by two brothers in the household she was working in. Her life had been a nightmare. She told him with frankness that it was only her fear of hell that made her not suffocate her baby in his sleep. She had a new family now and didn't want to be reminded of her secret shame. His biological mother was not beautiful by Asian standards; she had the burnished brown skin of the working class, the diminutive height and round face that he never saw in Filipino TV and film, unless the person was a thief or the comic relief. But in the hours of his visit, she had made him a pot of *arroz caldo* and spoke with her head down. He saw a gracefulness in her movements, a kind of moving beauty he rarely witnessed. Afterward, she had shooed him out of her kitchen before her new husband came through the front door.

He never reached back out.

"Dorsey . . ." He hated that low tone in her voice. Why had he even told her that? He had told no one about that miserable and desperate trip. It was the beginnings of the cold cynicism that pervaded his thinking these days. He had seen too many people crushed under the heel of money to be idealistic about mere ideas.

"My adoptive mom was a mother in all of those perfect ways, though. She was warm and supportive, and I've molded my life after her."

"Why are you building unaffordable homes in poor neighborhoods, then?" The sharpness was gone from her voice. It was simply a question.

"For both of them, actually," he said. "Any sufficient humanitarian effort requires financial support. Sometimes we can't be precious about where that support comes from." If Netherfield Court didn't go through, his mother's foundation was finished. All his plans for learning centers and schools for girls all over the world would never receive the funding to get off the ground.

Liza huffed and crossed her arms. "How does one ethically amass this much money?"

Dorsey shrugged. He touched the big screen on the dashboard, changing the playlist from his conspicuous "Planet Money" podcast to some nice and safe pop music. "How does one ethically consume in a capitalist society?"

She didn't look convinced. "Is that your answer—we're all trapped in an inescapable web?" Dorsey smirked and shook his head. Liza lived in a world of fair-trade coffee and museum gift shop scarves sewn by women's collectives in Sudan. He had been where she was. Ten years ago, he'd thought like Liza; he'd built awareness campaigns and read Karl Marx. But going around the world and witnessing such miserable conditions confirmed one thing: that money, and *only* money, was power. It was a Swiss Army knife. To change the world, ideas alone wouldn't do a thing. As the CEO of Pemberley, he'd allowed a hard, protective crust to form over him. Liza would do a lot better if she didn't always walk around with her heart and politics on her sleeve. But that wasn't an argument he expected to win tonight.

He had managed to get her to agree to drinks. Now all he had to do was *not* fuck it up.

BULL VS. COW

DORSEY WAS SURPRISED THAT THE HOTEL WASHING-ton was only two blocks from the White House and that the building was more than two hundred years old. He marveled at the architecture, a blend of 1930s federal and old British Empire styles. The ornate lobby had dramatic marble columns wrapped with holly and lights in preparation for Christmas. He turned to look at Liza, whose eyes were up on the detailed tray ceilings with intricate paintings representing each state in the country. She reached out and touched the lush greenery, and her boots swooshed lightly on the detailed tiled mosaics on the floor.

"This is next level," was all she said. Liza didn't put on airs. If she thought something was cool, she let herself like it. While he was constantly gauging what others thought to determine his level of enthusiasm. The way she had clapped in delight unselfconsciously about his car—he would give anything to feel so comfortable in his skin. She moved toward the enormous tree in the middle of the lobby and took a big dramatic breath. "Do you smell that natural pine smell? Isn't it gorgeous?"

"It smells like Christmas."

"Is that what Christmas smells like? We've never had an actual tree. Granny would just take the plastic tree out of storage and we'd put it up together. There were still awesome memories, but what I wouldn't give for a real tree one day."

Dorsey found them a table. The sun was setting and the light at such a slant made little rainbows dance out of Liza's earrings and onto her face. Miles Davis's "My Funny Valentine" played, and this whole evening felt like a woozy dream. He ordered something bland; she ordered something on fire. They drank, and no matter where he looked, he crashed into her eyes. He stuttered out a comment on the architecture, on the weather.

His heart beat unnaturally fast in his chest. It was the same feeling he had when he bombed that board meeting. He was bombing this social interaction. Gigi couldn't bail him out now. He exhaled. What if he tried not pretending?

"I didn't want what I just ordered," he blurted out.

Liza nodded as if that was what she expected. "Why did you order it?"

"I thought that's what I *should* order. My dad always ordered whiskey neat. It just seems like a drink I should like." Dorsey did not know why he was suddenly telling her this.

Liza tapped his forefinger. "What do you *actually* want?"

You, he thought, but dared not say. At least not tonight. So close to the holidays, the loss of his family was most acute. His loft in the city was too cold and empty. He dreaded going home. But some kinds of honesty were not useful.

"I wanted that drink that was on fire too," Dorsey said instead.

Liza smiled and slid her mug across the table. The setting sun hit the reddish highlights in her hair, and Dorsey wondered how long she had to sit to get her hair so intricately twisted. He remembered his sister getting braids, and it seemed like an all-day affair. Liza's eyes found his. "Taste it, then, and order again." The teddy-bear-brown pools were so soft, the heaviness seemed to lift a little from his chest.

He took the mug of Mexican Sunset *a fuego* from her and encircled her entire hand with his in the exchange. She didn't move away. What the hell kind of parallel world had he walked into? She didn't pull her hand away and slap him or laugh. Reluctantly pulling his own hands away, he lifted and turned the glass until he saw the rosy half-moons of her lip gloss stained against the rim. He took a sip and squinted.

"A lot of mezcal," he said. Dorsey unrolled the napkin and placed it on his lap. He only stopped when Liza looked at him laughing.

"You're so precise with that napkin," Liza teased. *Here we go.*

"Do you mean correct?"

She tucked her napkin into her collar. "I mean persnickety."

"If you keep that around your neck, I'm going to have to report you."

"Oh no, not the napkin Five-O." Liza pulled the cloth down. "I definitely can't make bail." She still placed it on the table like some kind of napkin heathen.

Liza squinted. "Speaking of bail, why did you sponsor my program?" Her question was direct. Her eye contact was direct. He wouldn't bullshit this question.

"David came up with the idea of a care hotline for the community to voice its concerns, and we needed to publicize it. I thought I could discredit you and help us by forcing you to tell the community about it." Dorsey didn't flinch under her stare.

"But you miscalculated." She smiled. "People like you throw money at a problem and expect it to right itself. But at the heart of that method is a lack of vision. Money can't go anywhere without vision." She took a liberal gulp of his whiskey. "So instead of muting me, you've amplified my message." She looked pleased with herself, and pointed to the whiskey, "I like this better."

"Believe it or not, I'm not *against* your message. I'm against your method. It's *all* vision, all luck, all movement. It's a bull with no cock."

"Help me navigate your masculinist analogy. By *no cock*, you mean without . . ." Liza raised her brow.

Dorsey met her eyes. "Power." He played with the mug in his hand. "Force. Weight." He finished her smoky cocktail and ordered her another whiskey and himself another Mexican Sunset *a fuego*. "Let me give you an example. *I* was given this job with no real qualifications or desire to lead the company." He settled into his chair. Liza took long looks at him, and the color rose high on his cheeks. He could get used to her attention.

"Sounds like falling up."

"I know to you that makes me sound like even more of an asshole, but I've never seen myself as CEO of anything. After I joined the Peace Corps, I saw firsthand that clumsy development organizations did very little. Idealism does not work." The waitstaff returned with their drinks but placed the Mexican Sunset in front of Liza and the whiskey neat in front of Dorsey. Honest mistake. When Dorsey moved to switch them, Liza took a small sip of hers, then slid the drink over. He followed suit and took a sip of the whiskey and placed it in front of her. It felt like a kind of truth ritual. The warmth in his chest was definitely just the whiskey.

"You know what works?" he continued. "Money. Cold hard cash changes circumstances—nothing else. My mother's foundation is tied to the strength of Pemberley. I would hate to see that work ruined. It helped me, my brother, and my sister. It can help a thousand more like us if I keep my eye on the prize. Without money, vision is impossible. Thus, my vision has *power* behind it."

"Wow, I got a 'thus' out of you. Well, my vision isn't a bull. It's . . . just a nice cow, but it still has power. It's got a womb and udders." Dorsey nearly spit out his drink. "Don't you dare laugh! I mean it. I want to build a coalition and *create* something together with the community—to *nurture* ideas, create a self-sustaining model. Think about how sustainable *your* model is. How long will the board pay for the WCO's *entire* operation? A cow can provide milk to *all the* calves she births. At some point you will have to build and create."

Dorsey nodded. She was half-right, he allowed. He had been thinking of how to make WCO independent from Pemberley Development. "I take your point."

"Thusly, you will pack your spaceship back to Philly," Liza added.

Dorsey could not keep the corners of his mouth down all night. A surge of boldness coursed through him. "I want to send you something," he said, holding up his phone.

"Send it." Liza shrugged.

"Um . . . on your phone." Dorsey's face burned.

Smooth, Datu. Real smooth.

"Oh." Liza fumbled with her phone. It slipped out of her hand like a slippery bar of soap and landed neatly near his drink. Sounding somehow winded, she recited her number in small, halting syllables.

He sent her the meme of them at Netherfield Court. They had both probably seen it a thousand times, but the scene morphed into the fight scene with Aaliyah and Jet Li, and when Liza unfurled her napkin, the print read ROMEO MUST DIE. Dorsey was curious about how she had taken the viral moment and wanted to ease into conversation with her about it.

"Oh my god, people have so much time on their hands! This is good." Liza laughed, a big, gorgeous sound that bubbled up inside him as well.

"It's a deep fake, but the best one I've seen," Dorsey said. They relaxed into a comfortable conversation about being the center of a meme. He told her how it changed people's perception of him at the company. He wasn't overthinking their conversation. Was she making this easy, or was he trying harder? He didn't feel himself searching for the exits or checking the time. He had even made her laugh.

The server came to settle their check, and Liza rubbed her palms together.

"I propose to you, Dorsey, a Hotel Washington Treaty. I was wrong about this place." Liza smiled through her admission. "It is, in fact, a cool place to have drinks. This was a good idea. Seeing each other as people. So I decree on this day . . . Shit." Her eyes shot to him.

"What?"

"Today's your birthday," she said, half-astonished.

"Oh!" He pretended to check his phone. "I guess it is." His face must be on fire right now. *How did she remember?*

"Happy thirty-one?" she ventured.

"-Ish," he said. "Do you have to get home?"

Stop torturing the girl and let her go.

"I don't have a curfew, if that's what you're asking."

"I wanted to grab a bite if you want to come," Dorsey said. The invitation was out before he could think better of it.

"I had a big argument planned with my mom, but I guess I could reschedule it. Do you know any Filipino restaurants?"

He didn't, and hot spikes of shame prickled at his chest. He would always feel this way. Like he should know more, speak better. He didn't know *any* restaurants and it was a damned shame.

"I don't see why I have to know—" Dorsey stopped short. The terror in her eyes made him whip around to assess the danger.

But there was no danger, only Isaiah, slick and wolf-fanged.

The man Liza knew as WIC.

ONE OF THOSE "NO" WOMEN

LIZA'S CHEST DEFLATED. *SHIT. HOW DOES THIS LOOK?* She suddenly felt the eyes on her now and all the cameras the eyes must have had.

"Wow, what a lucky coincidence. I didn't know you two knew each other like that." WIC turned to look at Liza. She smiled and pushed her chair out. Stepping back and away from the table with too much fumbling to go unnoticed. It was half cowardice, half discretion. How must they have looked together at this tiny table—cozy, even familiar?

"You guys come here often?" WIC was all levity and charm, and Liza wouldn't have known there was any bad blood between him and Dorsey at all. Except when she looked at Dorsey, his stormy expression had turned imperious and disdainful. The shy, soulful man who liked sweet drinks and precise napkin placement was gone. Liza took another small step away from the table. He must have registered the movement because now he settled his disdainful gaze on her.

Shit. The room chilled twenty degrees.

WIC nudged her arm. "You two are bold. Anyone with a

camera could accuse you of anything." He held out his phone. When neither of them spoke, WIC continued affably, "Nah, I'm kidding. I dig it. A little diplomacy."

Liza saw a camera flash and shook her head. Not this again. "No!" It came out louder than she meant it to. She saw Dorsey and WIC wince a little.

"We don't come here often. Never, actually. We don't go anywhere. Together."

Nervous laughter bubbled up in her as she continued creeping away from Dorsey, so she'd no longer be drugged by his warmth and his cologne. Yes, best to get doused with this humiliating bucket of ice water now. Why was Dorsey so silent? Did he want another meme situation?

Dorsey pulled out his phone and looked at what Liza could only make out as a blank screen. "Liza, I forgot, I have a meeting kind of early tomorrow morning. I can't do the thing tonight." He offered a cool look in Liza's direction. Sixty to zero again in one minute.

What had made her say yes to Dorsey's invitation to drinks? Curiosity? No, loneliness was more likely. WIC was closer to "the struggle" than Dorsey would ever be. He understood her. They were a natural fit.

"No problem. I have shit to do too." The spell really was broken. Their night ended here.

"I can drop you off," he offered.

"No!" Liza rushed. "We, like, accidentally met here so . . . no need to drop me . . . it's not like this was planned, so, no."

"Thank you for such a thorough explanation of the circumstances of our meeting. I was glad to hear them again." That he could hurl veiled accusations at her without even looking up from his phone was a fucking skill set.

"All right, maybe next time we can all go out together. Maybe get some *Philippine* cuisine?"

Dorsey shot WIC a look that was as clear as a statement. *Not on your life, pal.* WIC's brand of charm seemed to slide right off Dorsey, because he took his coat and slipped it on with an angry jerk. He flashed an impatient glance at Liza. Oh, he wasn't cool; he was pissed.

"Liza, allow me to take you home," he said. He seemed suddenly intent on getting home, even though he'd just bailed on dinner. It seemed like he suddenly realized he was in *inferior* company. WIC went out of his way to be kind to him, and Dorsey did everything but spit at his feet.

"I'll take the train," she said, and waited a beat for WIC to offer, but he must've been stunned into silence. She lifted her chin and shouldered past both of them.

"Liza!" She heard Dorsey call out to her, but she let the wind swallow his cries.

IT WAS WELL BEFORE HAPPY HOUR AS DORSEY SAT TWO days later swirling a cocktail.

"What in the hell are you making, Dorsey?" David Bradley sat on the other side of the empty bar room on the ninth floor of their offices.

"I'm trying to get the ingredients just right on this terrible drink I had the other night. It was a smoky mezcal and honey-pineapple syrup cocktail set on fire for the drama."

"If it's so terrible, why are you making it?"

Dorsey stuck a match dramatically and touched it to the rim of the cup. A sparkling blue flame leapt to life. "Because it's a wonderful memory," he said.

"Does this memory involve a person?"

"Most do." Dorsey blew out the fire and sipped his drink and winced. Not enough mezcal. Though there was nothing he could add to reproduce the inebriated feeling he'd had that night. What a boozy watercolor dream Liza had been. It was the perfect night—until it wasn't.

"So, I've been talking to Janae," David said.

"Why? Didn't she ghost you?" Dorsey huffed. These games were tiresome. Why waste time on people who couldn't return your feelings? Not that he had this deep well of feelings, but there had been something warm and welcoming blossoming between them under the twinkle of the Christmas decorations— until Liza crushed it under her UGGs. He hated to think it, but *is Liza ashamed of me because I'm not Black?* Did she think he couldn't understand her because of his wealth? This was all too complex. Dorsey hated complexity.

"I think Janae was embarrassed after the snowstorm. She got a little too tipsy. We went a little fast," David said. "We're taking it slow. I'm getting a sense that she needs that right now."

Dorsey poured the drink out into the sink and started again. "There are rooms full of women who would've called you back in minutes, you know."

"I don't want those women, and if you're honest with yourself, neither do you."

Dorsey tipped more tequila into the mug. "Against my better judgment, I followed up with one of those 'no' women. I thought we were having a great time, and then she runs into someone she knows, and it's like she didn't want to be seen with me in front of anyone. And do you know what I did?" Dorsey asked. "I suggested she ride home with the asshole."

David shook his head. "It just sounds like she was being discreet, Dorsey."

"What do you mean?"

"I mean, since this meme stuff, you're a pretty public figure. It just sounds like discretion to me."

Dorsey blinked. It was like someone splashed a warm bucket of water over his head.

Discretion, not rejection.

Liza had a hell of a reason to play it cool with him in public. Hell, if *he* was in his right mind, he would have been walking five steps behind her himself—especially in front of an absolute wolf like Isaiah. They were recognizable people on opposite sides of a struggle.

What if the board had seen images of him looking like a besotted fool? He would be out on his ear. And how could he have put her in that position of choosing between a fun night out and her entire reputation? He remembered her burning look. He had misunderstood, and worse, he had been unchivalrous. The phone burned in his hand. He took a deep breath and texted Liza.

> Question number 18: What is your most treasured memory?

Nothing.

Okay, he deserved that.

"Dorsey, I'm starting to think your phone is the only person in this room." David stood up to go.

"I'm sorry." Dorsey snuck another glance at his phone. "But I see your point in giving Janae another chance. Is there some gift you can give her to make up—I mean, *you* have nothing to make up. I'm just thinking aloud here. Maybe we could get them a Christmas tree?" Dorsey's mind raced, and his heart did a little flip. David's eternal optimism was actually useful.

"A Christmas tree? Are you insane? Why?" David laughed.

"I think it would mean a lot."

"I can't lug a Douglas fir up five flights of stairs!"

"I'll help you deliver it." If he had misinterpreted Liza and left her to take the train, there weren't enough trees in the world that would bring him back into her good graces.

MODERN WOMAN

YOU'RE ON THE LINE WITH LIZA B., THE ONLY DJ WHO gives a jam. Welcome back to our hip-hop world tour! We're taking you around the world. Come visit the station for prizes—shirts, tickets, and albums. Last week we took you to Paris with free drinks at Le Diplomate restaurant with a cool collection of French MCs. Next week we're giving you some South African flavor! I'm taking suggestions for our next country. Caller One, do you have any suggestions for our hip-hop world tour?"

"First of all, it is so great to finally talk with you," a woman said.

"Thank you." Liza beamed.

"But yes, have you put any thought into the Pinoy rap scene, like Filipino hip-hop artists? The Philippines were really the start of hip-hop in Asia with N.E.R.D. and the Black-Eyed Peas. There is some early Francis M. that would blow your mind."

"Oh, I like that! We didn't catch your name, caller."

"Just G."

"Well, Just G., I think you just filled our last slot. The Philippines will be our big finish."

___

THE MORE LIZA THOUGHT OF HER AND DORSEY'S NIGHT out, the more she knew that she and Dorsey had both lost their damn minds. She didn't *actually* have to maintain a cordial relationship with Dorsey. After his project failed, he would be off to ravage another city. But WIC was a freedom fighter in the trenches with her. Dorsey had to know that. His single text burned in her brain for two days. Until finally she relented and texted him back.

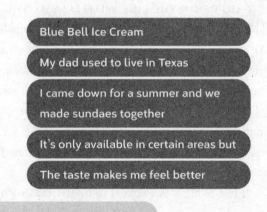

> Blue Bell Ice Cream
>
> My dad used to live in Texas
>
> I came down for a summer and we made sundaes together
>
> It's only available in certain areas but
>
> The taste makes me feel better

Noted

Typical one-word nonanswer. While Liza saw the intellectual reason she should distance herself from Dorsey, her body acted of its own accord. At night, she burned with the memory of his touch. She wondered if she would die with the knowledge of the feel of Dorsey's hard dick against her thigh.

WIC had called her every day since he'd seen her that night.

Her right mind said that she was glad to be back on WIC's radar. It took seeing her out that night to jog his memory. Good. She was starting to think she had imagined their banter. Her phone rang, and she picked it up. WIC again.

"Hey, Liza."

"This is she." She tried to sound breathy and cool.

"Oh, hey girl, I wanted to check on you again."

"Aw, WIC, you're such a sweet man."

"Gotta make our queens feel like *queens*, don't we?"

Liza couldn't stop the flash of Dorsey's dark gaze at the hotel. He had started off the evening quietly, but it wasn't noncommunicative silence. His eyes washing over her, his sweet blushes, his flustered speech, made her feel . . . lovely.

You. Get out, she told an imaginary Dorsey. *This is WIC's time.*

"Did I lose you?" WIC asked.

"Oh no, sorry, right here," Liza said as she scrolled through job boards. WCO was looking for a project manager. She would give an eye to work there. Should she ask Dorsey to put in a good word? No, she would rather die.

He laughed. "No, seriously, you are intimidating. I had to step my game up before I approached you."

Liza was lightheaded. Her single biggest flaw was how much she loved to be gassed up by men. A Leo through and through.

"Flattery will get you everywhere with me, WIC. Keep it coming."

There was a bubbly silence. At any moment, either of them would break out into giggles.

"So what do I have to do to get you down to a place like the Hotel Washington?" WIC said.

"Ask," Liza replied.

"You mean I don't have to be financially set up like a Fitzgerald to get you to pay attention to me?" Wait . . . she had given him her number *ages* ago.

"Quite the opposite, actually."

"Do you know Dorsey like that? You both looked cozy."

"Not really." Liza's skin tingled. *It isn't a lie, is it? You never really knew anybody.*

"Has he ever talked about me?"

"What? No."

"Yeah, I used to know that guy." WIC chewed the words out.

"Wow." It was all she had. She didn't want to share that she had creeped on him online.

"Yeah. I was in this young entrepreneur program and had a bright idea. You know, it was a great opportunity. His dad, who I had mad love for, promised to invest."

"Like a venture capitalist?"

"Yeah, but when Mr. F. died, Dorsey just let me and my business twist in the wind. He threatened me with the cops. It was a bad situation."

"Wow," was all Liza could say again. This sounded just like him.

"He ended up doing me pretty dirty in the end."

Liza kept quiet, but none of it surprised her. This type of thing happened all the time. She was glad that WIC already seemed so comfortable opening up to her.

"So you guys parted ways and you haven't spoken since?" Liza asked.

"Sorry, I didn't mean to bore you with my personal drama. It was just so . . ."

"No, it would have been weird to not talk about it, considering all the commotion."

"So, when can *I* get you to the hotel?" WIC said, changing the subject.

"We weren't at the hotel." Liza's voice was louder than it needed to be. "It was a bar, and I bumped into him."

"Chill, Mama, I would never question your honor. I just want to take you out too—wanna know if my money's gotta be this tall to ride."

Liza smiled. He was jealous? "It doesn't have to be the Hotel Washington, but I should warn you, my dance card stays full."

"Oh, I saw that. If you had Dorsey smiling from ear to ear, you must be able to charm a snake," WIC said.

Thinking of Dorsey's smile stopped her short for a moment to check her phone for more texts.

"Are you still there?" WIC asked. *Lord, what has this man been saying?*

"Oh, WIC, I'm sorry. My reception went out. Could you repeat that?"

"I actually wanted to talk to you about your draft proposal. Everyone was really wowed by your idea, and I'd love to see it expanded. If we raise enough money, we can buy Netherfield ourselves!" Liza smiled; his enthusiasm was catching. The proposal was pretty meaty work too. It would normally cost thousands of dollars to hire someone to write one of these up. And he trusted her to do it.

"Oh, I wanted to tell you. We're going to this event in Philly soon. My granny won this garden competition, and I want you to hang out."

"Cool. I'm there," WIC said without hesitation.

"Wait . . . But it's Dorsey Fitzgerald's company party."

Long, cold pause.

WIC cleared his throat. "I don't think I'd be a welcomed guest there."

"We don't have to stay the whole time," Liza said.

"You told Dorsey I was coming?"

"Not . . ."

"Did you tell him?" His voice had an edge of impatience.

"I'll get to it. Do you want to go?"

He let out a muffled yes, and Liza smiled.

"What will you be wearing?" she said over the background noise. "I want to match—

"I'm sorry, the train is coming," WIC said tersely.

The phone hung up abruptly, and Liza shrugged. *Must be underground.* Now this party wouldn't feel like so much of a drag.

WIC sounded confident, and Liza wanted to feel hopeful with him. He was wary of being seen with Dorsey, she could tell, because he was a revolutionary down to his bones. This is what it looked like to want the same things. It wasn't a drink for a moment; it was justice for all.

HOW YOU DOING, DC? WE'RE HEADING INTO THE Christmas season. Who's alone out there? Are you thinking about someone tonight?" Liza played the Jazzy Jingle Bells snippet.

"Call me on the loveline, and I'll send a special song their way. I'm getting a request from a Datu Ramos online. He wants to hear some soulful Sam Smith, 'Lay Me Down.' Goodness, I wish somebody wanted me the way Sam Smith wants whoever they're singing to." Liza pressed the dials. "Coming right up for you, Datu. I hope she's listening tonight."

***

"YOU ARE SPRUNG, GIRL," CHICHO TEASED TWO DAYS later. It was the week after Thanksgiving, and the women were seated around the large faux-leather sectional in the Bennetts' apartment. It was a nice-enough evening that Granny wanted everyone's help putting up the Christmas tree. Janae had sheepishly admitted that David had bought a tree for them and wanted to bring it over. David had pursued her, even when she lost heart, so Liza supposed she could grow to like him for her sister. But she was unsure if Janae had shared every part of her life with David yet. Liza hoped that David's heart was big enough to see all of Janae, not just her beauty.

Beverly kept asking if David had "hit it" yet, and Janae deflected with the skill of a used-car salesperson. Beverly kept suggesting she and David be alone and "let whatever happens happen."

Liza continued to alternatively string popcorn with a needle onto her Granny's red embroidery floss and eat it out of the bowl.

"Liza, that popcorn is for the garland, not your stomach," Granny said as she smacked at Liza's hands.

"Then why pop the movie theatre butter flavor?" Liza shot back.

Janae tapped her phone and announced, "He's downstairs."

Liza and Janae began to frantically clean the living space. Bev opened her mouth to protest but begrudgingly fluffed the couch pillows and threw away LeDeya's colony of Doritos bags. Liza finally stopped cleaning when she smelled the Glade PlugIn kick in. Country Lemon could cover a multitude of sins. The knock at the door came quickly, and the entire family including Chicho jumped into some sort of stage setting of Bennett family life.

Beverly went to the door and let out a dissatisfied grunt when she saw who was on the other side. Liza nearly choked on the popcorn kernel in her mouth. Taking up the whole doorway, dark and lean, fully bearded now and still bunned, was Dorsey Fitzgerald. He was holding the top branches of a bushy evergreen tree and returned her mother's look of slight disappointment.

Liza smoothed her hair and turned to fake a cough and put ChapStick on. Nothing she could do about being dressed like a hobo, though. He, however, looked like a full-course meal. Liza snatched her eyes away from his strong thighs in the slim jeans, but then made the mistake of looking up into the full force of his gaze. How was no one else pinned to the floor like a butterfly specimen? A low-voltage current buzzed from her center out to the tips of her fingers and toes. *Okay, avoid eyes.* But then she would be forced to focus on the outline of his abs in the thin black sweater, or that damned messy man bun that she wanted to braid then mess up again. There was no place on that body safe for Liza to look. But she had to admit that—scratch that, she didn't *have* to admit anything.

She scanned for faults. She supposed this was his attempt at casual. But the worn leather jacket was so soft and buttery-looking that she knew it had to be Italian. His shoes looked like simple high-tops, but she had dated a sneakerhead once and knew those were Rick Owens Geobasket shoes in some type of animal skin. Liza was pleased to find something she could scorn. Those shoes cost about the same as a used Honda Civic, and he was walking around Merrytown in them?

"Do you have it?" David, ever cheery, was holding up the tree's trunk as he pushed Dorsey through the door. The crisp smell of evergreen flooded the apartment. They obviously should have called *someone* to get a sense of the apartment dimensions before they purchased this Rockefeller Center tree.

Granny grinned. "I always wanted a real tree," she said. "You can put it here." She motioned toward a worn-out tree skirt and a tree stand. David made a funny show of grunting, gaining laughs from the women in the room, while Dorsey's face was flat and impassive. David let the top of the tree drop to hug everyone. Dorsey grunted as the weight of the tree tipped him forward. Wide-eyed, David touched ceramic Precious Moments figurines and examined Liza's moving boxes and the plastic-covered carpet like he was touring the Vatican.

"You guys want to stay to help us decorate it?" Granny pointed toward her boxes of ribbon ornaments and tinsel. Granny's voice must have knocked David out of his poverty tour because he dropped a faded doily into the hanging ferns.

Dorsey blustered, "No," at the same time David said, "Yes."

"Yes," David repeated firmly. "We would love to. Let's water this bad boy and get started." David completely abandoned his friend and the tree and moved into the kitchen, leaving Dorsey to lift the whole thing inside the apartment. His shoulders flexed, and the soft material of his sweater lifted to expose a smooth abdomen with deep V cuts. *Lord have mercy, this man comes with penis arrows?* Liza looked around, but everyone was huddled around David as he rummaged in a messenger bag.

Granny offered David and Dorsey some leftover oxtails. David nodded and Granny shoved two plates on the table. "For you and your friend."

But Dorsey was busy pulling the gigantic tree into the small living room. Everyone hovered over David eating oxtails, but the fools were missing the show of the century: Dorsey single-handedly dominating that immense tree and flashing those Olympic swimmer's abs. Nothing was more interesting than this.

When the tree teetered, Liza rushed to steady it as Dorsey closed the clamps on the tree stand. The top branches of the tree bent under the low, yellowing ceiling and the fat branches obscured the television. But it was glorious. A bit grander than the surroundings, but so the fuck was she.

David cleared his plate of oxtails. "And before I forget, here are your formal tickets to the Pemberley anniversary ball, your plane tickets, and your hotel accommodations." David handed everyone a ticket. "Yours was truly an excellent garden, Granny."

"Thank you." Granny beamed under his attention. He had finished her grandmother's oxtails and complimented her garden. David was batting a thousand.

Liza rolled her eyes. "Yes, thank you for making our homes unaffordable. I'm sure this *party* should make up for it."

If looks could kill, the one Bev shot Liza would have her cold in the morgue.

"We host our Garden Sweepstakes in *all* of our developments in nearly every neighborhood across the country. Your grandmother's creative use of space and variety and health of her greenery beat out *everyone*, fair and square," David said. It was the most serious tone Liza had ever heard him use.

"I'm not saying Granny didn't deserve an award," Liza said.

"Then what *are* you saying, Liza?" Bev asked tartly.

"And all of you are allowed a plus-one, so . . ." David continued awkwardly. "Except you." He winked at Janae, who laughed that truly terrible laugh of hers. Everyone else in the room winced. God bless David if he could live with that laugh for the rest of his life.

"I know exactly who's coming with me." Bev spoke before Liza could say another thing. "The reverend is finally coming around, and I'm bringing him to Philly." Bev thought for a minute. "But if we all get a plus-one . . . My word, that's gotta be, what, ten thousand dollars for all of those people and the hotel and the food?"

"Momma," Liza said under her breath, mortified.

"What? It's a lot of money. No point in pretending like it ain't. Liza, you can use your plus-one for Colin."

"No. Nope. I have a plus-one, Ma. Let Deya use hers."

"No! I'm bringing Derek!" LeDeya protested.

"I have a date too," Liza said.

"Since when?" Bev smirked. "Chicho, have you seen this date Liza has?"

"Not exactly yet. But I know he's—" Chicho started, but Bev had already turned away from her.

"Your own best friend hasn't seen this very real perfect man of yours?" Bev asked.

"No! Dorsey knows him," Liza shot out. "William Isaiah Curry. WIC." Okay, they didn't like each other, but he could at least vouch that WIC was a real person.

Dorsey's back straightened. "I know of him." His tone was clipped.

"He's into, uh, public service and Black empowerment." Liza muffled the last bit and put a handful of popcorn in her mouth.

"Of course he is." Dorsey pulled the popcorn string from her other hand and threw it absently around the tree. He inhaled. "Smells like Christmas, doesn't it?"

Liza flushed. She must have looked like such a bumpkin to him that night. Surely *he* didn't have anything to do with David getting the tree? Was the tree for her?

"Liza, go and get some more tinsel from the closet." Granny directed her granddaughter like a general. Liza padded toward the closet; she threw Dorsey a look over her shoulder, and he wordlessly followed her down the hallway. Part of her wanted to ask about that night at the hotel bar, and why they kept reset-ting every time they saw each other. Because after the drinks wore off and the sun came back up, they both came tumbling back to their senses. During the day they inhabited the real world—which made this daytime family visit all the more surreal.

"How long have you been seeing WIC?" he said without any preamble.

"Oh, hi, Dorsey, how have you been?"

"Uncomfortable. How long have you been seeing him?"

"Well, we're not *seeing* each other . . ." Liza put up air quotes. It was exactly the impression she had meant to give her mother, but it sounded wrong coming from him.

"Can you say in one sentence what you know about WIC?" Dorsey looked more concerned than interested.

"He's a community organizer . . ." Liza started.

"Who does he work for?"

"For his organization, the Black Israelites."

"An organization which you—with a *women's studies* degree—find no fault with?"

"Not true. An organization is made up of people. You can't paint everything with a broad brush. For example, I find hella fault with Pemberley Development, and yet here you are."

"Point taken. A few more questions. What is his organization trying to do?"

"Outbid you on Netherfield."

Dorsey rolled his eyes. "Netherfield is already mine." Something about the way he bared his teeth at the word "mine" made Liza avert her gaze.

"Well . . . request that they reopen the bid." Liza was now piecing together holes in the story for herself. She didn't know the whole schema yet, but how dare he try to make her unsure of her cause?

"Do you understand *precisely* why he needs the money?"

Dorsey said slowly, like he was talking to a toddler. Liza couldn't put a fine point on it, but why did she need to for Dorsey's sake?

"How do you know he's raising money?" *He must have spies everywhere.*

"It's all he's ever doing," Dorsey said flatly.

"I don't have to tell you anything I'm doing. It's a violation of the Hotel Washington Treaty," Liza reminded him.

"You're right. But you should know WIC and I aren't cordial."

"So he's not invited to the gala?" Liza threw him a dusty box of decorations. "Honestly, Dorsey, if we only invited people that you're cordial with, then that would leave you in a room with Jennifer and David."

"It's *your* plus-one. I'm not your father." He looked at her, unblinking. *Why does everything seem so intense with him?* "I can't stop you from making terrible choices." Dorsey shrugged stiffly.

Liza sucked her teeth. He couldn't even *shrug* casually. "I wasn't *asking* permission."

"It sounds like you want permission or a reaction," Dorsey sniped. "I don't care to give you either."

Liza snapped her neck back as if she'd been slapped. The nerve of this man assuming she would need his approval!

"It's *your* party. I was trying to be respectful."

"It's my company's party."

"You know what, whatever. I'll come with whomever I want," she whispered.

"If we're doing whatever we want, there's a thing I wanted to do." Dorsey shifted the box to his hip.

"If you ask to touch my hair—" Liza warned. But instead, Dorsey leaned in close. Liza instinctively pressed her palms to his shoulders. Her loud, nosy-ass family was right down the hall. He wasn't going to try to kiss her right now? Her belly plummeted. He dropped his head even lower. She was so afraid that he might try it, and even more afraid that she would let him. She parted her lips. God help her if he was going for it. She closed her eyes in anticipation. The scruff of his chin rubbed past her cheek, but his lips moved past her mouth and whispered in her ear.

Not a kiss.

"Can I ask for a little guidance about gentrification?" Dorsey asked. This close, his spiky lashes shot out like stars and his sandstone skin looked soft and pliant. Liza tried to will her heartbeat to slow down. "I want to understand more," he said.

"Um, sure, I can send you some readings." She should be *relieved* that he wasn't leaning in for a kiss. "But I'm not going to be your tour guide through racism."

"I have a degree in civil engineering from Princeton. I don't think I need a tour guide. I realized that I *do* need some perspective, though."

"Ever humble," Liza said. Her hands were still on him. His broad shoulders rose and fell under her palms, the smooth, soft material of his sweater shifting slightly. She was trying not to notice his rapid pulse and instead tried to name this luxuriously soft material at her fingertips. And damn if it wasn't the wool of some poor baby vicuña. She wanted to wrap her arms around his shoulders and flip the tag over. Placing the fabric was a small victory, but it wasn't distracting her from the oceanic depth of his eyes. While her nether regions pulsed and her belly quivered, on the outside, she tried to radiate cool indifference.

"I have a hunch that the literature they gave me at Princeton and what they gave you at Howard was probably pretty different," Dorsey said.

"I never told you I went to Howard."

"You're right. You only mention it every half hour on your radio show."

"You listen to my show?" Liza touched her warm cheeks.

"I may have scanned past your station. I forget." He was teasing her . . . and she liked it. *What is this?* "So it's a date, then?" he asked. His voice cracked in the middle of his question.

The word seemed to snap Liza out of a haze. *Remember how he treated WIC. That's who he really is.* Liza crossed her arms. "It's a class."

They emerged from the hallway with everyone watching Janae and David's chemistry, and no one had even noticed they were gone—except for Chicho, who looked between them with a raised brow.

"The decorations," Liza announced.

"Oh." Granny clapped whimsically. Dorsey's face had such a disapproving look on it that Granny eyed him nervously. "You didn't eat your oxtail, D," she said.

"Oh no, I wasn't really hungry, and just Dorsey is fine."

Liza grimaced. In her family, nicknames were a thing bestowed on you by impressed, mean, or nostalgic adults. It was not a negotiation of identity. You were "Hambone" or "Jughead" whether you liked it or not. And passing up *any* grandmother's food was just signing a death certificate. *Just eat the damn oxtail.*

"How about Mr. Fitzgerald, then?" Granny said. "I wouldn't want to get too familiar."

"If that makes you more comfortable," he replied. All Liza heard were the church bells tolling for the immediate death of Granny's regard for him. Why did Liza want to throw the cooling plate of oxtails at his head?

Liza pulled homemade decorations out of the box, and Granny slowly shifted her attention. All of Liza's, Maurice's, Janae's, and LeDeya's childhood ornaments and Christmas notes came pouring out of the box. Dorsey stood apart from everyone, sometimes pacing, sometimes looking at the door.

Liza took great pains to ignore him. One long look would have her family on high alert. She picked up the delicate ornaments and threw them haphazardly on the tree. Dorsey seemed to curl into himself, overfocusing on tiny tasks like tinsel placement and ornament distribution instead of talking to people. She went behind him and repositioned every perfectly placed ornament he had put on.

"That's not evenly distributed," Dorsey complained.

"Neither is wealth," Liza quipped. "I'm putting the ornaments on the side of the tree that people actually see."

"Yes, the Instagrammable shot," Dorsey shot back.

Another knock on the door had all the women in the house rolling their eyes.

"Are you guys expecting someone else?" David asked.

Liza sucked her teeth. "Yes . . . yes, we are."

"Colin!" Bev's high-pitched false enthusiasm nearly shattered the glasses.

Dorsey's face was a mask of confusion, so much so that Liza rushed to explain.

"He's my play cousin," Liza said.

His eyes widened. "What the hell is a play cousin?"

"A family friend you grew up with that's not related but feels related," LeDeya said and stepped between Dorsey and Liza toward the foyer to give Colin a decidedly fake hug.

"So, why not just say friend of the family?" Dorsey asked, genuinely curious.

"Because this fool is no friend of mine," Liza stage-whispered and walked to the door as well. She attempted to give him a passing church hug, but Colin pulled her in and gave her a squeeze so aggressive that Liza was short of breath. He had beefed up since his skinny days in Longbourne Gardens. He had a face cut right above generic, but his green eyes turned a bland face into a striking one, as they were set in deep contrast to the brown of his skin. He handed them all signed copies of his book.

"I wrote a personal note in there for all of you," Colin said. "Oh, Liza, you ladies are somehow more lovely than those Instagram pics." He let Liza go and let his round eyes settle on Janae.

Bev walked hastily to David and introduced him to Colin. "This is David, Janae's man."

Colin's face fell visibly as he gave David a limp handshake. He then turned to Dorsey, and his face lit up again.

"Wait, are you . . . is this who I think it is?" He stopped to do a quick Google search. "Dorsey Fitzgerald, as I live and breathe. Net worth seven billion, sitting on a peeling leather couch in the hood?" He blinked and laughed. Liza cringed with secondhand embarrassment. The tone and tenor of Colin's voice immediately changed. Liza recognized it as the same voice her granny used when she interacted with white people. He pronounced his *R*s and kept his vowels flat. He stepped across the room, nearly knocking Bev over to shake Dorsey's hand. He pumped furiously, but Dorsey couldn't even be bothered to turn his body in the poor man's direction.

"What an amazing coincidence! Do you know who I just recently sat down with?"

Dorsey said nothing.

"None other than Christopher De Berg, senator for Virginia!" Colin continued on with no encouragement. "He is giving me so much insight into the political world in DC, important movers and shakers . . . donors." Colin let the last word hang. The air chilled a few degrees, and Colin laughed to fill in the silence. "Hey, but let's not talk shop."

"I think David and I were just leaving, actually." Dorsey's tone indicated that this was not a suggestion.

David looked surprised. "Yes. Yes, we have another appointment, I'm afraid."

"Oh, stay for dinner." Colin invited them as if it were his house. He pulled a sliver of meat from the plate of cold oxtail. Liza stopped herself from calling it *Dorsey's* oxtail. "I'm sure Bev has baked her famous buttermilk pie."

Bev unwrapped the package of store-bought buttermilk pie and stealthily threw it into the oven.

"We couldn't possibly," Dorsey said. He glanced at Liza and held her gaze for *just* a beat too long to go unnoticed. He broke his gaze and gathered his jacket to leave. He was out of the house before Bev could say goodbye.

Bev huffed. "That man. I'm sorry he's so damn rude. It pisses me off that a man as nice as David comes with a sack of sad baggage like that!" Bev looked over to Liza. "And what was *that* look for?"

"What look?" Liza asked. She wasn't used to her mother paying close attention to her.

"He gave you some kind of look before he left, like you were gum on the bottom of his shoe. I'm going to have to ask David to stop bringing that man by. All of that hair . . . He don't look professional. Looks like he's in a rock band or something."

"Ma," Janae said. "That's too far. Dorsey is—"

"What? What is he? Standing over there pacing a hole in my carpet, doesn't speak to anyone, tells Granny to call him Mr. Fitzgerald, doesn't even stop to greet Colin, and snarls at Liza on his way out."

"Thank you, Ma, but I'm fine," Liza assured her.

"Now, Ms. Bev, you should be so lucky that a man like that would even come here. It shows his good-naturedness right there. I mean, look around. He must have been horrified—no offense."

"None taken," Liza said sarcastically.

"How many of us can say we know a billionaire? Senator De Berg says half of politics is knowing who to ask for money."

Liza mimed wrapping a rope around her neck, and Bev elbowed her sharply.

"So will you be staying over?" Granny asked too sweetly.

"Oh no, of course not. I can't be seen in these conditions for long."

Liza sucked her teeth and moved toward her room. She could never handle Colin for too long.

"Liza, girl . . ." He let his voice trail, and it sounded practiced. "You have really grown into yourself, haven't you? Can I talk to you a bit?"

Liza stopped in her tracks and plopped on the couch. He *was* a council member in Alexandria and could probably help her more with the proposal for Netherfield since WIC suggested she expand what she wrote.

"Sure," Liza said. Chicho sat down next to her without Liza having to beg.

Colin sat beside her and placed his hand on her knee. "Christopher is giving me all kinds of tips for political life. He really is a beacon in the Democratic Party," Colin said excitedly.

Chicho nodded. "Voted number two in the Power Broker Index."

"Yes!" Colin answered in surprise. "Yes. So, he says the first thing you have to do is find yourself a wife and then immediately pop out a few kids. He says that people absolutely don't vote for single men. There's a creep factor."

"I can imagine," was all Liza said, nudging Chicho. But Chicho's face was serious, and she nodded slowly. She was going too far with her politeness. Colin continued for exactly thirty-seven minutes, imparting to Liza and Chicho the proper next steps for any political hopeful. At the thirty-eighth minute, Liza spoke up. "Well, Colin, we must pick this lovely conversation up later. I have some blogs to write."

"Yes, I've seen some of them. Can I watch your process?" Colin's eyes roved over her.

"I'm sorry, I don't really like to have people around while I'm creating."

"Colin, are you coming to church with me tomorrow?" Bev asked. Colin was Bev's fake trophy child, and she would spend the weekend taking him around all her church-lady events and fawning over his accomplishments. Her actual kids all allowed it because it gave them the weekend off from Bev's inspecting eye. Job searches, boyfriend questions, grade inquiries—all gone. Colin's green eyes and fancy education were here, and his shining corona kept the heat off Bev's kids and all the ways they were failing her. It seemed like a fair trade to the Bennett siblings.

DESPITE APPEARANCES

From: DFitz@PemDevCo.com
To: MK@PemDevCo.com

A while ago, I mentioned not filling my schedule with any office events and holiday parties. You've been a great personal assistant and have kept my schedule relatively free of fluff. I realize in celebration of the season, I should be more receptive to "fun." As such, I will attend the annual Christmas ball and the 50th anniversary gala. I still, however, request as few pictures and extended conversations as can be helped. I will give you a signal when I need to be rescued from excessive engagement.

Thank you.
D.

Dorsey held the phone and exhaled. The loft in Georgetown he rented seemed cramped and small with Jennifer still here milling about. She said she would drop a few papers off that he needed to sign. But it had been an hour. His head was filled with crop tops and glossed lips from Liza's past summer on Insta-gram, and the last thing he wanted right now was company. It was nearing eleven p.m., and she showed no signs of packing up. The moon had long ago disappeared, leaving a quiet and dark night. The only sounds were the sluggish swoosh of the Foundry Branch and Jennifer's anxious heels clacking on the polished wood floors. He winced with every step.

He was going to text Liza tonight. But he wanted Jennifer gone first. It thrilled him to think that he could affect Liza the way she did him. The fluttering in his stomach when she touched his shoulders in the hallway—had her stomach twisted too?

He should've kissed her when she glanced at his lips in the hallway. *Why didn't you do it? You coward*, Dorsey chided himself. He wasn't sure if he'd get a slap across the face or a warmer welcome. A near-constant *What would Alexi do?* rang in his head, but in this case he knew. Alexi would have acted. Dorsey should have coaxed her into the bathroom and taken her on the vanity, rattling medicine cabinets as cotton ball containers and tooth-brushes toppled onto the floor. He would cover her mouth with his to keep her from moaning too loudly. *Is she a moaner or a screamer?* He imagined them walking back into the family living room, flushed and smelling like each other, everyone too polite to mention it. Dorsey groaned and and rolled his eyes. Jennifer approached, looking annoyed.

"Who was that on the phone?" she asked. *Why does she feel so entitled to my private moments?*

"What else is there to look over? I'm getting kind of tired." He glossed over her question.

"Sure. Um, I'll head out, then, unless . . ." Jennifer let the word hang. Dorsey noticed the slightest trembling on her lip, and he groaned. He would have to take the Alexi route.

"Look, Jennifer, I have to be honest with you. We had a few dinners, it didn't work . . ." Dorsey started.

"Who said it didn't work?"

"I just kind of think we don't work—"

"Kind of?" Jennifer looked nonplussed.

"Have you asked yourself why *you* want to hang out with me, Jennifer? Really?" Dorsey said.

Jennifer was nodding before he finished. "This line of questioning wouldn't have anything to do with whoever you were texting with your cock on your mind, would it? I swear, you are off the *charts*, Dorsey." Her fury did a poor job of masking the hurt in her voice. "Do you even want Netherfield to succeed? I thought we had shared goals. That's your answer. I thought we were alike. You said you wanted this. And now I can't get you to sit still for ten minutes to go over the financials. You're all over the place, Dorsey, and it's going to cost us Netherfield Court *and* the Alexandria project. Senator De Berg told me he asked you to make a gesture of unity for Alexandria, and you refused."

"It was beneath me," Dorsey said. He patted his pocket for cigarettes. Nothing. His head was pounding.

"Beneath you?" Jennifer smirked. "I catch you ripping the shirt off a woman in your office, and you are talking about what is *beneath* you? I don't want you to become like one of these men in power that get . . . lusty and end up abusing people. You need to cut a clear line. I mean, despite appearances, you *are* a man in power. The MeToo movement would eat you for lunch," she said. "Now you're late-night texting God knows who, looking like the cat who swallowed the canary. Just promise me it's none of your employees—no paralegals, no secretaries."

"I'm not a predator, Jennifer. I am aware of my position and have never preyed on anyone weaker than me." Something about the way she said "despite appearances" infuriated Dorsey. He just wanted her out of his home and out of his ear. His heart wasn't in this work. He knew it. She knew it. But he would try to be the man his father had been. He *was* trying. But it wasn't enough. He was starting to fear it never would be. "I *should* pay more attention to this work. I concede that. But that's all you get to comment on. Are we clear?"

"I wish that was all I could comment on. Look, I know for you this is a shortcut to increasing the philanthropic budget, but this is my actual life, you know." Jennifer crossed her arms.

"I think I just need some sleep," he offered. He stood up and walked over to the door. "Good night, Jennifer."

She yanked her briefcase up and choked out an angry good-bye as she rushed out. Dorsey closed the door behind her and leaned his head against the cool metal. The phone burned in his hands. Finally. Liza.

———

THE EVENING HAD COME QUICKLY, AND THE BENNETT women were settling in. Maurice had spent the night out as he was prone to do. They had made their polite conversation with Colin, and Liza retired to her room. Colin was still at the apartment and had made no move to leave. Liza's guess was that he would hang around until Bev invited him to stay the night. He probably didn't even have a hotel. She tucked in the last corner of the bedsheet to military snugness. She wanted to hear any movement on this side of the room. Liza was bent over, tucking the other side of the sheet in, when she felt eyes on her. She turned and saw Colin's tiny green eyes squinting in appreciation. She was suddenly conscious of her thin T-shirt and swaying breasts. The ratty material of her sleep shorts seemed transparent and indecent.

"So when are you headed to the hotel?" Liza asked.

"I'm not even sure Ubers come to this part of town. It's gotten so late." Colin leaned against the doorjamb.

"Oh, they do. I can get you one," Liza offered, almost pleadingly.

"I could never. Your mom tells me you're not making ends meet," Colin said. Liza could kill that woman. Colin followed the peaks of Liza's nipples with his eyes.

She folded her arms over her chest. "I'm just gonna pop off to the bathroom."

Liza came back in the room with at least two pairs of everything on. A sports bra, tights with fuzzy pants over them, and a big button-down shirt over her thin T-shirt.

Her phone buzzed on top of her cluttered dresser, and she picked it up, hoping WIC had sent her something funny or thought-provoking. But it was a number she'd only seen once before.

> How's Play Cousin?

Three stupid words, and she was smiling like a goofball.

> New phone. Who dis?

There was a long pause. She was about to put the phone down when it buzzed again.

As a response, a GIF of her Netherfield Must Go photobomb popped up. She did everything she could to hold in her smile, but Colin sidled up next to her.

"Are you cold?" he said, noting her copious layers of clothing.

"Yeah, came down with a big chill."

"Who's got you smirking at this time of night?" Colin asked. He had the nerve to look semi-jealous.

"It's no one," she said and went back to the bathroom. She closed and locked the door and put the lid down on the toilet to sit. Thumbs poised delicately on the screen, she responded:

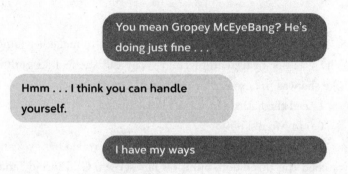

> You mean Gropey McEyeBang? He's doing just fine . . .

> Hmm . . . I think you can handle yourself.

> I have my ways

She snapped a picture of her ankle with both her colorful tights and fuzzy pajama pants rolled into long men's socks.

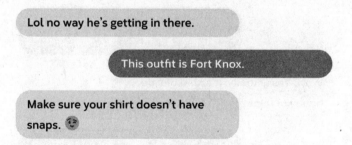

> Lol no way he's getting in there.

> This outfit is Fort Knox.

> Make sure your shirt doesn't have snaps. 😉

Oh, why did he have to mention that night! She was flooded with images—his shaking thumbs attempting to free her shirt, his knuckles and her breast one deep breath away from touching, and those eyes when he'd looked down at her. She had never met a man with such a blistering gaze. After some time, she finally replied and tried to find some chill that she did not feel.

I've been #buttonsonly since that night.

Glad to see you've taken the proper precautions.

A knock on the door scared Liza enough to make her jump. Why was her heart hammering? Why did she feel so guilty? Like she was in here eating the last of Granny's pie.

"I need the bathroom, Liza," Janae huffed.

"Go to Mom's!"

"I need this one, it's got my rollers." Liza rolled her eyes and watched the three dots blink on her screen. God forbid Janae was kept away from her roller set.

"One minute!" she stammered.

Oh, almost forgot. Do you know anything about the Pinoy rap scene?

Wow. Yes actually. It's kind of a deep hobby of mine.

Cool, cool. Let's hook up later. I need help curating a playlist.

She smiled at that and unlocked the door. Janae looked at her quizzically when she blew past her.

LOVEMAKING PRACTICE

From: EliteEvents
To: DFitz@PemDevCo.com

Ok, we went ahead and added the dance floor setup to the room. It was a last-minute request, so the price is more than quoted in the itemized list. Can we expect a dance floor for future events as well?

Awaiting your reply,
Tom, Elite Events

Dorsey spent the entire week blowing through his Treasurer cigarettes. When those were done, he chewed gum. Now, tonight, mere hours before the event, he was a bundle of nerves. He would ask Liza to dance, that he knew. But her reaction was hers. He hoped to publicly make up for the meme, for the embarrassment he had caused her. And to spend a few glorious minutes holding her without the crippling guilt or the threat of memes.

He wanted to rent documentaries and catalog his thoughts and cross-reference them with hers. He knew that was an incredibly nerdy fantasy, but he really was dying to know how *she* would speak about issues he didn't even know about. No doubt Liza had an opinion on them all and a riotous way of conveying it. He had told no less than ten people about her Electric Slide theory, and the surrounding discussions had been telling and hilarious. She was so opposite her diffident sister. Janae reminded him of a masterpiece behind layers of plexiglass, her beauty distant and inaccessible. David swore the woman was interesting, but Dorsey had only ever seen her light up during a conversation about regressive tax. But David had turned his entire life upside down for Liza's sister, not even leaving DC and Janae when the news came down that his father's condition was worsening. Dorsey picked up the phone and dialed David's number.

"David, you need to tell your dad to stop working." Dorsey's voice was firm and deliberate.

"You know I can't do that. This Paris deal means so much to him."

"You take over that deal. It will give him peace of mind. He just wants to feel like everything will be taken care of when he . . ." Dorsey's voice trailed off.

The phone fell silent, but Dorsey could still hear David breathing.

"I can take care of everything in DC," Dorsey continued. "You can't wait for Janae to feel something for you."

"Dorsey, you're so cynical. Just give me tonight. I'll make my decision tomorrow."

Dorsey hung up and held the phone. He had so many things he wished he had said to his father before he died. He would give anything for one more hour with him. One more minute. David was making a mistake staying in DC while his father spent his dying days trying to close a deal in France.

Anxious, he sent off a text to Liza, his thumbs dancing over the phone keyboard.

> Question number 14: Is there something that you've dreamed of doing for a long time? Why haven't you done it?

He waited for a full five minutes and had almost put the phone down when it buzzed in his hand.

> Building schools in Ghana

> I haven't done it because large efforts require coalition building, and I've stumbled getting people behind me for a cause

> You?

Dorsey thought for a moment.

> I have always wanted to slow dance with a beautiful woman.

> You've never slow danced!!!?

> This fact would kill in #NeverHaveIEver

She made him sound like a mutant. He supposed it was a strange thing to never have done.

> Once in public. It was a disaster.

> And dancing in public is kind of an exhibition, isn't it?

> Everyone can see just how much you don't belong there

Dorsey finished, then waited.

> You feel like you don't belong a lot?

> More often than I would like.

> ProTip. next time eat the oxtails.

He eyed the phone in confusion.

> What oxtails?

> NVM 😑

The soft knock at the door was purely performative as his sister, Gigi, draped in pink crystals, pushed through the door.

"Come in." He rolled his eyes at her.

"Aw, you look so handsome." Her hands popped to her slim hips.

Dorsey tugged at his lapel. "My stylist thanks you."

Gigi waited with her arms out like a glitter scarecrow.

Dorsey looked her up and down. She was expecting something. "That dress is very short," he offered.

Her shoulders fell. "*My* stylist points a middle finger." Gigi flopped on the bed, her long legs cascading upward. "Would it kill you to pay your little sister a compliment?"

"I thought we were just talking about what we noticed first." Dorsey shrugged and patted his pockets.

"You're nervous as hell, Datu. Did a communist library explode in your room? What is all of this?"

Dorsey fidgeted with his tie, which was now skewed to the left. "I'm auditing a class at UPenn. In fact, take *Evicted*. Do you have a gift box around here?"

"Why?" she asked warily. "Are you about to gift someone a book?" She flipped the book around. "*Poverty and Profit in the American City*? This is the least sexy gift I've ever seen."

"Good thing it's not for you. Find a box."

"There are no boxes, Dorsey."

"You didn't even look! I keep a ton under my bed."

She pulled up the dust ruffle and pulled out a few boxes. When she found one that fit the book, she scoffed. "I'm not putting this book in a dusty Tiffany box."

"Why not? That's perfect."

"Dorsey." She put her hands on her hips and looked down as if to collect herself. "You can't give a woman a Tiffany box with a used marked-up book inside of it. She will murder you."

"Um, maybe put a bow on it?" His hands shook and he gave up on his tie in frustration.

"Breathe, Datu. I know your meme queen will be there tonight. Do you have some lighthearted conversation ready? I can shoot you some texts."

He did breathe. "No, thank you, Cyrano. *We* don't need that."

If she noticed the possessiveness in his emphasis of "we," she didn't say anything.

"Since when? You *always* beg me to send you tidbits on your dates." She sounded a little hurt, like Dorsey wasn't letting her in on his little adventure with the big kids. "You're afraid I'm too dumb." She flipped the book again. "I can talk about eviction and—"

"No, nothing like that. We just don't need it." Dorsey was honest-to-God trying not to sound smug, but his sister's eyebrows still rose, and she shimmied her shoulders. "We text like every day." Again, it came off like a brag.

"You sound very pleased with yourself," Gigi said.

He couldn't help but feel a tiny flick of pride. A woman had a continual interest in him that *didn't* start and stop at his bank account. Liza asked him about his bent pinky, confessed that she didn't really like mambo sauce but pretended to, and sent him articles about the eviction crisis. Whatever they were doing— these text diaries—it was the longest *thing* he'd ever had. He didn't want to do anything to upset this tender equilibrium.

Dorsey tried to sound casual. "I'm going to ask her to dance." He let the words hang.

His sister froze and caught his eye in the mirror.

"You're joking."

"No, I'm not joking. I'm going to ask someone to dance in public in front of everyone."

"Datu, you're going to try to dance *and* make conversation?" Her incredulous look was way over the top.

"Gigi, don't turn this into a big deal, I'm nervous enough."

"*You're* turning it into a big deal, not me. Does she know about the dancing thing?"

"Of course not. Why would I tell her about Camp Sunshine?"

"You said you two talk every day."

"Not about that," he said, closing the Tiffany box over the book.

Camp Sunshine was a sleepaway camp they'd gone to every summer during their early adolescence. In the cooling last days of summer, the camp held a dance. Thirteen-year-old Dorsey had finally set his mind on asking a girl to dance. Everything went well until he was pressed a little too tightly against Katani Sanders. After they separated, he had a tent in his pants for the whole camp to see. To add insult to injury, her heavy diamond hooped earring slipped out of her ear and connected with his pants, giving his hard-on a disco-ball effect in the strobing lights. To a subset of children in Philadelphia's Chestnut Hill enclave, he would always be *Disco Dick*.

That night also started a long and complex relationship with his right hand that Liza had recently reignited.

Gigi slapped his hands away and rearranged his tie. "I hope you can pull this off. I need her to like me. I've been trying to manifest powerful sisterhood."

Dorsey straightened his back. Gigi had never looked up to anyone he was interested in. His little sister was his whole family now, but he was still surprised by how good it felt for Gigi to like Liza this much. "Just *don't* be yourself," he smiled at her eye roll. "She'll love you."

***

"I'M HEADED TO THE CITY OF BROTHERLY LOVE THIS weekend to get some love from a brother! What are y'all doing this weekend? Hit me up."

Booth G was skeletal. A few of Liza's photos hung on the wall. Her *generous sponsor* was the only thing keeping her show going.

"While I'm in Philly, check out my live feeds on Instagram! You'll be hearing reruns here, but if you follow me to Philly, you can get the scoop as it happens."

"Liza, I wish I had an invitation and half the dresses in your closet. Why are you being so close-lipped about what's happening?" the caller asked.

"Not close-lipped, just discreet."

"Liza, you're not fooling anybody. I have a cousin who works security at that hotel in Philly, and Janae Bennett is on the VIP list for Pemberley Development! Are you going to work out some kind of deal where *we* get screwed and you and your family get a new apartment?"

"I'm not making any deals or taking part in any foolishness. Someone gave my granny a prize for her roses, and I'm going to clap when they call her name and leave."

"Why do I have a feeling you're going to come out of this smelling like roses while we all get evicted?"

"Faith, sister, as tiny as a mustard seed. That's all I need from y'all. Let's take a break and hear from our sponsors, Pemberley Development, who care about our neighborhood's value."

***

TWO HOURS AFTER THEIR FLIGHT TOUCHED DOWN IN Philadelphia, the Bennetts and Chicho were bustling through two adjoining suites at the Four Seasons Hotel Philadelphia. Maurice had donated his plus-one to Chicho after Liza begged him to let Chicho come live it up with them in Philly. When Maurice finally relented, Liza noticed the blush on his neck when Chicho kissed his cheek.

The bathroom was a riot of curlers, bobby pins, lip glosses, and eyelashes, and the beds were covered in Janae's dresses and alternate dresses. Shea butter and all manner of clashing bath and body fragrances wafted in the air. Through the floor-to-ceiling windows was a vibrant city of mostly Ben Franklin statues. This twinkling city view reminded Liza of that moment in Dorsey's office—her shallow breathing, his voice in her ear and his chest against her back, that spicy scent that curled around her, and the tender way he had spoken about his mother. Flashing memories of that whole night kept coming back to her at strange times.

She took a selfie next to the window, hoping she could capture the view. Maurice snatched the phone camera out of Liza's hands.

"Dang, what is that, selfie number two hundred and four? I will admit that Deya turned you from a frog to a human but, my sister, pride goeth before a fall."

Liza let him take the phone. The truth was that she looked damned good tonight, like some Afrofuturist version of herself. Her hair was braided in a complex, elegant updo that left coils at her nape. LeDeya's makeup job was dramatic: a cobalt cat eye with shimmery silver liner. Her earrings were the best part, an excellent knock-off of Beyoncé's ear cuff, where the "diamonds" went from her earlobe up the curve of her ear. She kept trying to get them at just the right angle for the camera.

"Are you wearing that?" Liza asked her brother. She looked up and down at his outfit—a drab sweat suit with large headphones bulging out of the front pocket. "Ma is going to skin you alive."

"Come on, this is for Granny. And I don't want them to think they can just steal our Janae and that we'll be good little minorities. This is a protest!"

"This is not a protest. This"—Liza pointed to his outfit—"is lazy."

"Oh, no one can plan a protest but you? You're the only one who can be political in the family?"

"Of course not! I would love it if you were political. Right now, I just think you're being provocative for its own sake, and at Granny's expense."

"So I'm supposed to go there dressed like a damned chandelier?"

"Just come with a little respect for what Granny has done to beautify the neighborhood."

Maurice huffed and pulled off his sweatshirt, revealing an **I CAN'T BREATHE** T-shirt. He groomed his beard in the mirror while Janae swished around nervously. She popped into Liza's room and delicately put on her drop earrings. Liza noted her hand shaking slightly.

"Janae, what's wrong?"

"Nothing, I'm just . . ."

"Nervous?" Liza finished.

"I think his mom and dad will be there."

"So what?"

"So have you seen what Maurice has on? Have you heard Mama bragging to every person who will listen that I'm never working again? It's terrible."

"I know. But our family is our family. David knows that, and remarkably, he still loves you."

"Loves?"

"Loves," Liza assured her.

"I haven't told him yet," Janae whispered.

Liza only nodded. "Why not?"

"I'm afraid of the sadness finding its way into our relationship. Everything has been so fun and nice. I know if I tell him about my past, he'll . . ." Janae trailed off.

"I think he can handle it, J. Trust him."

"I will, just not now." Janae shook her head, then expertly

shifted the subject. "So are you excited to finally hang out with WIC? I say the texting isn't enough. You guys have to see each other."

"This is how excited I am to see him!" Liza pulled a condom out of her tiny clutch, and Janae burst into fits of laughter.

Maurice groaned.

"Girl, are you falling for this man?" Janae asked.

"I think we'll see! I mean, what if we don't have any physical chemistry?"

"But the two go hand in hand," Janae said. "Have you ever had physical chemistry with someone you didn't particularly like?"

Hell yes. That night in the office with Dorsey looking out over DC. The feel of his broad shoulders under her palms. Even now, her insides tightened, and her pulse lit up thinking about it. But she shook her head rigidly instead. "No, I guess not," Liza lied.

"See, don't worry about that. You two will be fine."

Liza smiled. She was happy to be seeing WIC again after so long. But something trembled in her belly, something a lot like fear, maybe nervousness. Janae flitted out of the room to finish the last of her makeup.

Liza's phone buzzed and flickered in her brother's hand.

No.

She lunged like an NFL receiver toward her phone and successfully snatched it out of Maurice's hand.

Deya shook her head. "You are so pressed for this man!"

It was Maurice who held her gaze the longest. If he wanted to say something about her near-crazed dive to get her phone, he kept it to himself. She looked down at the text. She was still breathing heavily.

> **Question number 8: Name 3 things you and I appear to have in common.**

Her thumbs tapped rapidly.

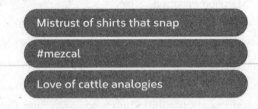

> Mistrust of shirts that snap

> #mezcal

> Love of cattle analogies

She saw the dots undulate.

> **You forgot sisters.**

That was all she would get from the man. Would his sister be there? Of course she would. Would it be presumptuous to introduce herself? Liza was normally so sure of her next move. What if Dorsey had never mentioned her? Liza's thoughts were interrupted by Maurice consulting her on how to seduce WIC.

"You should let him make the first move. Sisters are quick to emasculate a brother with their forwardness. You all remember Nora Dash, all ladylike and feminine? Men love that shit."

Janae sprayed a cloud of sweet-smelling perfume and walked into it. "So we should all record ourselves having sex like Nora did?" Janae rolled her eyes. "We all know you watch that video she made daily, Maurice."

"Is everyone gonna define her by that tape? Does that take away from the fact that she's a real lady? Shit don't sound sex-positive, Janae." Maurice sucked his teeth. "Yes, she made that masterpiece and *I* checked it out, we *all* did. But she was always sweet and knew how to treat a man."

"Damn shame about her." Bev shook her head. "Just goes to show, you can't buy breeding.

Liza was about to launch into a tirade about slut shaming when she heard a soft knock on the door.

Chicho opened the door, and Liza gasped. She looked wonderful in an elegant yellow gown that accentuated her curves.

"Chicho, you look so good, girl!"

"Whatever," Chicho said darkly.

"What do you mean, 'whatever'? Girl, this dress is so classy."

"And then I see your outfit. This looks too plain."

"Trust me, simple is always in style," Liza said.

Chicho smiled at her feet. "You look . . . like, so freakin' beautiful."

Liza pressed the sides of her cream backless jumpsuit. The deep V in the front reached nearly to her navel and was generous to her average bosom.

"Girl, you ain't seen nothing. Wait until you see Janae. She will make you sick."

"Why do you always do that?" Chicho asked abruptly.

"What?"

"When someone calls you pretty, you deflect to your sister."

"It's 'cause she knows she ain't," Maurice shouted.

"Shut up, Reece!" She turned to Chicho. "I didn't know I did that."

"You do. Wait." Chicho's eyes had shifted to Maurice. "You wearing that trash bag to the gala?"

"It's a sweat suit."

"Ignore him, Chicho," Liza said. "Light a candle for Janae. She's waiting to hear if she got the interview for a big position in New York."

Liza didn't know what had gotten into Chicho lately. She was constantly talking about getting out of Merrytown. She played the lottery every day and actually read Colin's book, *Up from Nothing.* It was like she was suddenly so dissatisfied with her life, and with Liza's too. Chicho nodded lately whenever Bev chastised Liza about lipstick, bras, and men. Their friendship seemed to be cooling for reasons Liza couldn't understand, and she didn't know how to reverse course.

"Oh, I hope she gets it. She's too sane to be cooped up with y'all for too much longer," Chicho said, nodding at Maurice.

"And WIC is coming!" Liza squealed. "So light two candles."

"I'm not praying to the saints so you can get a booty call." Chicho crossed herself.

"Why not? I plan to be calling on the Lord all night." Liza shimmied her shoulders.

Chicho pretended to be scandalized. "It's so weird, though. He should have seen more of you by now. It's not like Philly is so far. Why couldn't he just pop over on the weekend?"

"Because he's organizing. The weekends are the perfect time for that, and far be it from me to impede the movement."

Bev slapped the door in impatience. "I want to look at this limo David sent for us!" Liza's mom wore a skintight fuchsia dress with strategic cutouts in risky places. Even at fifty-five, she looked good. But just because she *could* do something didn't mean she *should*. The reverend sidled up next to her. He wore what could only be called a zoot suit. With his broad padded shoulders and slim legs, he looked like a walking isosceles triangle.

Liza couldn't wait for Bev to see WIC—all dressed up, handsome smile. She would have to admit that Liza had gotten it right. Liza was finally going to see Bev eat crow. Nothing could spoil this night.

ENTANGLED

THE LIMO WAS LAVISHLY APPOINTED. THE BENNETTS sipped on champagne and nibbled chocolate-covered strawberries. Deya shouted over Maurice as they fought over the limo snacks, and Janae kept making requests to the driver to turn the music to max volume. The whole time, Beverly was counting up the expenses.

"I looked up our hotel. It's over one thousand dollars a night for suites. And this champagne ain't cheap either."

Janae chided her mother softly. "We get it, Ma. They're being very generous to us."

"Oh, it's not about us, honey. They are giving us the royal treatment because of you and that moneymaker right there." She pointed to Janae's face. "And we'll meet Ms. Liza's mystery man too. This perfect man that is so much better than a future politician."

Liza sat with her arms folded and did not take the bait. It was one of the most adult moments of her life. She should diversify her 401(k) next.

Granny was swinging the limo door open before the car was at a complete stop.

"This girdle is suffocating me." Granny yanked at her hunter green tracksuit. Bev had begged, pleaded, and bartered to get her mother into "something reasonable." The plush velvet tracksuit was as far as she got with the woman.

The Bennetts spilled out of the limo to a surprising number of photographers and curious onlookers. Bev smoothed her dress as she scooted out of the limo and grinned as if she were made for the spotlight. Liza knew that as soon as she stepped out, she would stick out like a sore thumb. She wore a jumpsuit, for one. When she saw it online, she'd fallen in love with the detail, the plunge neck, the shawl lapels, and the side pockets. It was the open back and wide legs that made her feel both exposed and conservative at the same time. She fretted with the chain that went from the nape to the small of her back. It had seemed like a good idea at the time. Now it had the same creeping sensation of a fly walking up her back. Janae swatted Liza's hand away.

"Leave it alone. You look amazing, Liza," Janae assured her. Her sister always knew what she was thinking.

"I'm the only woman in pants here."

"So your WIC can easily make you out, right?" Janae said.

Liza nodded and walked down the carpeted aisle into the building.

The elegant ballroom was laid out on two levels. A formal stage accommodated a large band playing a milquetoast version of an Earth, Wind & Fire song. The walls were dark and draped in crushed velvet with gold inlay. Everything else was fresh and white. Tall ivory calla lilies rose from the table centerpieces. The tables themselves were overfilled with white and gold saucers, plates, and bowls, with matching embroidered napkins shaped like elephants. There was a modest dance floor and a light show that cast the room in various geometric overlays. They were handed heavy bags filled with expensive items, lotions, mascaras, shaving creams, Caterina jewelry, a three-day trip to wherever the hell Sag Harbor was, and a key to a mint green electric scooter.

She wanted to comment on how much of a waste this all was, but she stopped herself when she saw Granny's face looking through all the items, oohing and aahing with Janae. They sat Granny at the winner's table, where she was being waited on and fussed over.

She deserved this. Those slow arthritic fingers had known nothing but work all their life. Let her take center stage and be pampered.

Liza set her eyes around the room to see if WIC had arrived yet and could see no one with that particular build and hair. *No biggie, he'll probably be late.* He was a revolutionary—he couldn't show up on time for these bourgeois events. But he was coming to see her, she reasoned, not to really participate in all this. As if on cue, her mother pulled at her elbow.

"Where's your Mr. Perfect? I thought he'd be standing outside to greet us with a truckload of roses or something."

"Ma." Liza wanted to scream. "He's not a contestant on *The Bachelorette*, he's just a guy I'm seeing, okay?"

"A guy who didn't meet you when you came to his city," Bev shot back.

Liza waved at David in the distance, using any excuse to leave her mother. His blond hair was slicked down, and his face more somber than Liza had seen before. She realized she was getting closer to a throng of reporters and cameras and was attempting to back up when the man in the center of the throng spotted her. Dorsey's gaze was sharp and perfunctory; he looked over the Bennett clan with cool disinterest until he met Liza's eyes. When his eyes met hers, Liza's head buzzed pleasantly. Dorsey was in a soft wool Continental tuxedo with peak lapels. His beard was neatly trimmed, which was the exact opposite of his devil-may-care raven's wing hair, coiffed perfectly to look as if he'd just tumbled out of a French model's arms. It was probably a thousand-dollar haircut—and, jeez, she sounded just like her mother. He took the remaining steps toward her, and the cameras and reporters seem to flow behind him like a cape in the wind. Wordlessly, Dorsey held out his hand rather dramatically to her, and the crowd parted to see her. She took his hand with a tremor because she didn't know what else to do. It seemed like the entire room had quieted to a hush. Cameras popped all over them, and Dorsey squeezed her hand, bringing her attention back to him—back to those inky eyes. *Is he talking?* Everything was suddenly underwater.

"Save me a dance, Liza?" Dorsey asked. His dark eyes twinkled and reflected the lights in the room. Even with all his chivalrous grace, his hand still shook when it held hers.

Is he nervous?

"I got you something. It's at your table. I'd love to talk about it."

Liza nodded dumbly. He nodded in return and went back to his speech regarding upcoming changes for the company.

Did I just agree to that dance or acknowledge a gift? She had meant to return his earlier pettiness with a slight of her own. But damn if he didn't trick her with the cameras and the crowd. She would have agreed to anything under those conditions.

Liza elbowed her way out of the mass of people. He would forget he ever asked; there was too much commotion for him to remember. He was the host, after all. Liza looked around for

WIC, not wanting him to see her being dazzled by his greatest foe.

Chicho's warm hands clamped on her shoulders. "Did I just see Dorsey ask you for a dance in front of all of those people?"

"Yes, because he knew I couldn't say no, which is exactly what he wanted."

"Couldn't or wouldn't?" Chicho bit into a flower, then realizing it wasn't fancy, tiny food, put it back on the plate.

"What's the difference?" Liza changed the subject awkwardly. "I'm so excited for you to meet WIC!"

"Yeah, if I ever meet him. The night's going to be over before he comes. He better be worth all of this waiting."

"Chicho, you sound like my mom. I don't know what's gotten into you lately."

"You know Hot Boy's not coming," LeDeya said as she neared the girls.

"What are you talking about, Deya?"

"I saw the message come through on your phone."

Liza opened up her tiny clutch to find only her lipstick and a Ziploc bag, just in case the buffet was legit. She must have left her phone with Janae. She sighed. "Okay, fine, let's just enjoy the night."

Disappointed, Liza tried to settle into the evening and enjoy herself. She saw David take Janae all around the room to meet his friends. *Good for Janae.* He was just the type of man she needed. She saw the robin's-egg blue box sitting prettily at her assigned seat. She already knew she couldn't accept whatever this was. A Tiffany necklace? Liza felt a little let down. Ostentatious gifts like this really weren't her style. It felt like it was out of some rich-guy playbook.

Liza's belly jumped when she heard his soft baritone behind her. "Liza. I'd like to introduce you to Gigi, my sister. Gigi's getting her MBA at Wharton." Dorsey took a half step back.

"In a sprint to build a better mousetrap, eh?" Liza smiled.

Liza, what the hell are you saying?

"Something like that." The young woman seemed embarrassed. She fanned her eyes and Liza realized she looked like she might cry. Was the joke that bad?

"Gigi, Liza is—" Dorsey started but was interrupted by Gigi wrapping her arms around Liza—cutting off her breath.

"I am just so . . . Wow! You look like you have a filter on. You are really . . ." Gigi said.

The girl couldn't seem to string together a full sentence. Liza didn't know how to respond to any of these half thoughts. Not that she could, as Gigi's embrace threatened to produce a real-life faint. Liza took in a short breath, and Dorsey pulled his little sister to a respectable distance.

"It is truly an honor to meet you, Liza. Dorsey just goes on and—" She stopped abruptly, as if she'd been jabbed. She held her hand to her heart. "It is a pleasure."

"Same. This dress is gorgeously put together and you look lovely in it," Liza said. His sister *was* a lovely thing. Long and graceful, with prominent front teeth, skin as brown as wet bark, with the kohl-rimmed eyes of a Bedouin—she was runway striking. They shared no blood, but the woman had something of Dorsey in her bearing. The straight shoulders and imperious nose. Gigi twirled around.

"Same to you. Who are you wearing? I *have* to get the name of your stylist," Gigi gushed.

"Oh, it's uh, Chez Moi." Liza rubbed the back of her neck. "My sister and I made it."

Gigi froze. "Like with needles and thread?"

"Exactly that." Liza nodded.

"That's dope. That's like pioneer-woman dope." Gigi still looked at her with half-moist eyes. Who did this poor girl think Liza was? What had Dorsey told her? Liza looked up at Dorsey, and he had the strangest look in his eyes. She had something sharp and prickly to say—right at the tip of her tongue. But that look chased the words right back down her throat.

"So, about that dance . . ." he finally said.

"How about an Electric Slide?" Liza blinked prettily.

"How about a slow song?" Dorsey countered.

"A slow jam! Dorsey, I never expected to see you bumping and grinding in such a fancy place," Liza said, a smug grin widening across her face.

"In polite company, we can get away with a bump at most. Were you expecting a grind as well?" He smiled with satisfaction as Liza snatched her eyes away. "Soon," was all he said.

Wait, did he mean soon for the dance, or soon for the grind? Oh god, why am I even entertaining the grind comment?

"I feel like I should tell you both that I'm still here." Gigi waved her hand. It was as if she had reappeared in front of them.

"Sorry, Gigi. It was a pleasure." His sister said her goodbyes, and when Liza looked up, Dorsey was gone.

She sat at the wide circle table alone while her family wreaked havoc on the party. Maurice tried to go onstage twice to say his spoken-word piece about police brutality. The second time he got out at least a stanza before security ushered him offstage. LeDeya was on the dance floor, twerking to songs from *Porgy and Bess*. Janae came to sit next to Liza with a desperate look in her eyes.

"What?" Liza said.

"It's Ma. You've got to stop her."

"You know I can't—"

"Liza, she is going around telling everyone that will listen that me and David are practically engaged, and that she's going to have mixed grandbabies," Janae whispered frantically.

"Okay, she is on another level of crazy," Liza said. She saw her mother and made a beeline for her, just in time to overhear her conversation.

"Right! I say she pokes a hole in that condom, and she is set for life!" Everyone around her groaned in response, but Bev didn't seem to notice.

"Momma!" Liza said. She saw Dorsey eyeing them but kept pulling her mother away.

"Let me go, girl, what is your problem?"

"Watch your mouth, Ma!"

"I'm a grown-ass woman. You watch your mouth." A few people turned to watch.

"Momma! You cannot—" Liza was interrupted by Maurice bum-rushing the stage again.

"I am the white man's burden!" he screamed with all the patterns and gesticulations of a slam poet.

Liza and Beverly both looked at each other in mutual agreement for the first time in a while: they needed to get that fool down. They both rushed over, but security was quicker and escorted Maurice firmly off the stage. Bev wound up her hand and smacked the back of his head loudly. Now everyone really did turn. Liza wanted to melt into a puddle. The Bennetts were really showing their asses tonight. Liza pulled at her brother's arm.

"If you get back on that stage, I will murder you. Do you hear me? You will be dead. Do not do it again, Maurice. This is for Janae and Granny. Look at the time they are having. Stop trying to turn it into the damn Maurice show."

"Oh, you salty because Prince Charming stood you up?"

"Grow up, Maurice."

"You shouldn't feel bad. I see Money Bags has been whispering in your ear."

"What?"

"Oh, you think little brother don't see, but I do, and ol' boy has had his eye on you all night."

"Maurice, you think you know something, but you don't. Could you sit down somewhere?"

"You fight Ma all the time, but you're just like her. You're destined for side-chick status, big sis. A man looks at you like that for one reason, and it ain't to plan the wedding."

"Seriously, Maurice, you are the *worst*. Please sit and don't get up again, or I *will* plan your funeral." Maurice's mouth popped shut.

Liza shuffled across the floor. The night was ruined. She was completely deflated. Guilt already ate at her for shouting at her brother. Was she so pissed because his words had a pang of truth to them? She was not naïve enough to ascribe anything innocent to the way that man looked at her. Was she setting herself up to be hidden away? As his secret shameful desire?

She yelped when Chicho tapped her shoulder.

"Uh, chill." Chicho laughed. "What's up with your sister?"

"Oh god, which one now?"

"Janae." Chicho shoved the canapés on her plate into a Ziploc bag.

"Janae is fine. She looks great."

"She doesn't seem that interested in David," Chicho said.

"Well, she is," Liza said, annoyed. Liza made her way over to the food table as well, intent on filling her own Ziploc bag with hors d'oeuvres. Chicho always thought the only way around something was straight through it. She was mostly right, but her ruthless practicality could make her very black and white in a gray world.

When Liza returned to the table, she continued. "You know how shy Janae is, and she's not a public-display-of-affection type of person."

"She needs to display something, because she's looking real sometimey right now."

"Chicho, you know—"

"I know, and you know, but does *David* know?"

"She'll open up and tell him on her own time." But Liza examined her sister's coolness. Janae looked like David's *friend* up there. Liza wondered if her sister could ever truly open up to anyone ever again. If sweet, kind David couldn't get her to do it, perhaps no one could.

"Liza." The partygoers moved around them and feigned disinterest, but at some point, every eye in the place had turned to her. That voice behind her made her stomach twist. She turned and saw that the dance floor had cleared behind Dorsey. A middle-aged Black man checked the mike, and the smooth opening bass guitar of Smokey Robinson's "Cruisin'" started.

"I love this song," was all Liza could say. She hated how breathless her voice sounded in her ears. Dorsey held Liza's hand as if she were made of glass. He drew her to the middle of the floor, never taking his eyes off hers. He smelled like lemongrass and deep red wine. She was sure if she kissed him now he would taste of some vineyard in Argentina.

Don't you dare look at his lips, you basic heffa. Remember the oxtails.

He wrapped his left arm around her waist, and she looped her arms around his neck. Still, Dorsey said nothing. He only looked at her. Liza could somehow read his gaze as a charged mixture of *How are you? You look lovely. I want you.* Liza's throat was dry, and she swallowed. It was almost the chorus, and Dorsey had still not said a word. She had to escape those eyes, bottom-of-the-ocean-black and teeming with life. Oh great, Billie Eilish's "Ocean Eyes" was looping in her head.

No fair.

Liza cleared her throat—anything to break the intensity of his gaze. "Um, normally at these things, people have something to say."

Dorsey pulled her closer. Her body was flush with his. It was indecent. Everyone could see it. "What do you want to hear?"

"In these types of instances, people have remarked on the weather outside or the song they're dancing to, like 'Dang, girl, this is my jam,' or something like that," Liza offered.

"I'm not as gifted as you are in small talk," he said dryly. They fell silent again before he made an attempt. "So . . . how often do you walk through blizzards to take care of your sister?"

"Can you believe it was my first time?" She smiled tightly. "I was already on the train because I went to a rally in Greenbelt."

"A rally . . . where you met Isaiah?" Dorsey said, taking her by the wrist and twirling her slowly. The chain at her back caught on his tuxedo button. And the jerking sensation made them both gasp. They were always finding themselves entangled. Dorsey quickly unlooped the chain from his button.

"WIC, yes." Liza turned to face him.

"Isaiah is excellent at making new friends, but terrible at keeping them," Dorsey said. His hands were at her back again, and his thumbs stroked the gold chain. Tight bolts of electricity shot out from where his fingertips touched her skin. "Time is Isaiah's only enemy."

Her breath kept hitching at the touch of his warm hands and

the cool metal at the small of her bare back. She remembered the heat of his body when she'd been pressed on top of him in the nap pod. He kept snatching looks at her mouth. He'd be insane to kiss her here with his board and her family looking on. But she wet her lips anyway.

Liza, remember WIC. She closed her eyes and focused on the image of her eviction notice. "And if WIC did anything to offend *you*, God help him. What was it you said? You'd drop them and never look back?"

Dorsey opened his mouth to comment but was tapped on the shoulder. His hands whipped back to his sides. The reverend, her mother's date, stood with a grin you could play piano on.

"Everybody here is talking about you two! You are lighting up this dance floor!" The reverend clapped enthusiastically.

Liza saw Dorsey's face twitch with the slightest bit of embarrassment.

"Our Liza is a fine girl, you know, and she's gonna need some company if her sister runs off with that white boy." The reverend laughed, stretching the thin mustache atop his lip wide. "You both look made for each other when you dance!"

"Okay, Rev. We'll be seeing you!" Liza enthusiastically nodded. She was looking for the exits. She had to get out of here. The band started up a smoky rendition of "You're My Latest, My Greatest Inspiration." She knew she couldn't survive Teddy Pendergrass. It had all the ingredients for a mistake:

- Feeling rejected by man of your choice
- Drinking more than you should
- Man not of your choice pressing you near and wearing some kind of human pheromone cologne
- Teddy Pendergrass

She moved to bow out of the dance. But Dorsey's hands curled around her back, then slightly stiffened. The singer crooned on—a soft encouragement.

Dorsey's breath puffed in her ear. "So, I drop people and never look back. Is that all you know about me?" he asked.

Heat crept up her neck, and she needed about forty gallons of water to get this lump out of her throat. "I . . . keep trying to get a sense of you. But everyone I talk to has a different opinion of you," Liza said, surprising herself with her honesty.

"Have you been persuaded one way or another?" he said while swaying her. Liza tried not to sigh into him. "Or are you just pleased to hear the gossip?"

Liza smiled. "Column B, I think."

"Well, far be it from me to deny you *any* pleasure."

Okay, I need to get out of here, or Dorsey is going to get all my cookies tonight. The part of her—with the tiniest sliver of self-respect—scrambled for safer conversation.

"Who would you most like to invite to dinner, living or dead?" Liza asked.

Dorsey tilted his head down in surprise. "You downloaded the app?"

"Just answer the question." Liza rolled her eyes. She'd downloaded the app ages ago.

Dorsey looked thoughtful. "I think I would invite my biological father."

Her eyebrows rose. "From what you told me, he probably wasn't a good dude."

"I know. He was probably a rich, abusive asshole who thought he could take advantage of a poor foreigner in his home." The pads of his fingers traced up and down the small of her back. She let go a soft breath. Degree by fractional degree, Liza was unspooling.

"So, what would you even do at dinner?" Liza asked.

"I would be a rich, abusive asshole."

Liza thought she should close this line of questioning, but he asked her—

"And you?"

"Uh, honestly?" Liza asked.

His gaze was dark and intentional on her. There was no bottom to those smoldering eyes. "Always."

Liza felt for the first time how far out of her depth she'd waded once again. Every turn in the road led to Dorsey. "I would invite Patricia Fitzgerald," she said.

His Adam's apple bobbed as he swallowed. "Why my mom?"

"She was just this middle-class lady from the Rust Belt, and she built an entire ecosystem of goodness all over the world. WCO's work is unimpeachable, and she did it all by making rich people pay for it. I did a paper on her for my international studies thesis."

"Um, that's . . ." He trailed off and squinted like he was trying to make something out. "I think that may be the mayor that LeDeya just asked to hold her shoes?" Dorsey stopped swaying.

Liza turned to see her sister with her sky-high heels off, twerking and popping her booty up and down.

"How do you twerk to Teddy Pendergrass?" Liza wondered aloud. "Lord, all she needs is a pole." This was the Bennetts' worst showing. Dorsey took a step back from her, and Liza's body chilled. Had they been dancing *that* close?

"Where are David's parents?" Liza asked, putting her hands to her sides.

"They sent their apologies," Dorsey said. Liza sighed in relief. "And I think your mom has had enough champagne." Dorsey's arms loosened around her, and Liza sensed the chill creeping into his demeanor. Mr. Freeze was back. Liza turned just in time to hear Bev laugh loudly, sloshing her drink all over her wrist.

"And she better poke a hole in that condom if she knows what's up!" She laughed while onlookers exchanged pained looks.

"Oh God, that joke again. She is too much." Liza freed herself from Dorsey's arms and walked toward her mother. Dorsey walked in the opposite direction, toward the bar.

The night only dared to get worse, as her brother was eventually kicked out of the party for rushing the stage yet again. Granny went thirty-five minutes over her seven-minute presentation slot and spoke for ten minutes alone on her fertilizer mixture ("for sale at the Bennett table; just ask the girl in white without a date"). Bev got so drunk that she was cursing everybody out at the end. She had seen a man walking with his wife and checking out another woman, and screamed, "Men gon' be men!"

Liza left the party, dragging Janae, Bev, Granny, and LeDeya into the limo. Somehow, she'd lost her brother.

———

DORSEY PRETENDED TO BE OCCUPIED WITH HIS FINGER-nails when Jennifer's skirt swirled around his feet.

"You look pleased with yourself, Dorsey," she said. He hadn't spoken to her since her dressing down at his loft. But she was right. He was pleased with himself. His nerve endings were still on fire from the sensation. Every eye on him was a sharp pinprick, but he had done it. Dancing in public felt like the ultimate test of belonging somewhere. The type of dances you knew and the way you did them marked your class, your personality, even your age. He just didn't want to be marked like that by the people around him. He was already different enough. But his sheer

force of desire to be close to Liza had chipped away at that pho-
bia. His chest expanded, and a smile kept creeping up his face no
matter how hard he tried to keep a neutral expression.

"I just might stay the whole time," Dorsey said.

"What was that? Some kind of good-PR dance? Finally
following Senator De Berg's advice? It'll make the policymak-
ers in DC a little less nervous." Jennifer looped her arm around
his.

"No." He scratched his nose as an excuse to unlock their
arms. "I just *really* wanted to dance with her."

"After everything I've seen tonight, there's no way I'm letting
anyone in that family near anyone in my family. I think you owe
it to David to tell him what you heard Janae's mother say."

"I've already told him. He needs to move on. But he's his own
man, and she's really got her hooks in him."

Liza isn't her family. Dorsey kept repeating that mantra in
his head. But there was no way they could seriously date with
those albatrosses around her neck. She came with too many li-
abilities. He couldn't be dragged under by scandal.

He saw Liza's little brother sauntering toward him. Jennifer
excused herself, probably to avoid any and all Bennetts. Dorsey
braced himself. He knew little about Maurice, but he recognized
that purposeful walk.

"Salutations, D-baby." Maurice slapped hands, then began a
complex handshake, which Dorsey allowed himself to simply be
a passenger for.

"Just Dorsey is fine."

Maurice nodded and shifted his feet. "So." Maurice exhaled.
"My sisters. Look, each one has their own type of beauty. Janae
in the boring way, Liza in the annoying way, and Deya in the
dumb way, right?"

Dorsey froze. This was definitely a trap. "I honestly don't know how to answer that."

"Like, Liza, for example, is pretty in the way that you hate, because she gets on your nerves. You just wish she had boils and warts and shit to match her soul."

Lord, someone help him wade out of this conversation. How was he supposed to respond? "Maurice, please help me get there with you," Dorsey pleaded.

"Liza talks a lot of shit, but she is actually scared a lot."

Dorsey could sense the beginnings of a don't-fuck-over-my-sister speech.

"I'll make this simple. My sisters think I don't pay attention, but I saw Liza's hand shake when you took her hand to dance. And I've only seen her tremble like that when Marcus Davison asked her to the prom in the school cafeteria."

Dorsey nodded. He was getting it.

"Don't fuck around is what I'm saying." Maurice's face was serious.

Dorsey returned his gravitas with a solemn nod. He would do the same for Gigi.

"You have my word, sir," Dorsey said with formality. Maurice's lips turned up at the word "sir." He nodded and slipped back into the crowd.

Jennifer, who had been loitering in useless circles nearby, found Dorsey again.

"I hope he wasn't shaking you down for money," Jennifer said with a brittle laugh. Dorsey remembered a time when he would have laughed at that joke. But now it made him turn to Jennifer with contempt. He saw a woman trying to hold on to what felt right to her, desperately clinging to what she thought she deserved.

"Jennifer, great joke. Remind me, was that funny because they're poor or because they're Black?"

"Oh God, it's her, isn't it? Who you've been texting and neglecting your work for?" Jennifer's smile tightened when Dorsey offered no answer.

"Wow. This is an epically bad idea, Dorsey." She looked genuinely concerned. "What have these women done to you and my brother?"

"Do I need to remind you that I'm not your little brother? I know exactly what I'm doing." Dorsey shoved his hands in his pockets. He had no idea what he was doing.

"I'm just concerned that you're only setting Liza up to fail. Look, I think she's fun and positively lovely. But she doesn't belong here, and a rich boyfriend won't make her belong. You've seen so many couples like this at the club—some man has a midlife crisis, dumps his sensible wife, and marries a waitress. They're divorced in two years, and she has half of his money."

"Am I having the midlife crisis? Are *you* the sensible wife in this scenario?" Dorsey didn't mean for it to come out as hard as it sounded. But before he could apologize, she stomped away in anger. Dorsey tilted his head. He had been trying so hard to color within the lines since his parents died. Dorsey knew if he didn't play the shareholders' game, he would not hold on to the legacy his mother and father built. And now he'd just pissed off the daughter of a major shareholder.

CAT GIFS

LIZA HELD UP HER PHONE WITH A SELFIE STICK IN HER hotel room in front of the Philadelphia skyline. "While I'm away from Booth G, this is where you can catch up with Liza B. Thanks for all of the love you showed the Bennett clan getting ready for the gala. Now that it's done, I get to show you around Philly. Follow me tomorrow morning for day three in the City of Brotherly Love . . . Okay, you all have a lot of opinions."

@TinyTot73, that's right. Hang on and you just might see exactly the brother I'm tryna love. Liza smiled at the heart emojis.

@SexxiKitti, I love your energy. Thanks for the support!

She caught images of her and Dorsey dancing in the comments. *Oh no, not this again.*

@Tomkat09, I've seen those pictures already, and that's not the man I'm talking about.

Then new pictures and comments started to flow in.

Slut.

Whore.

Sellout.

Wannabe.

"Okay, okay, this is not okay."

I thought I had a thick skin but this . . . is a lot.

"Okay, you've all had your fun. You can stop now." When more invectives poured in, Liza disabled comments.

───

LIZA PLOPPED HERSELF ON THE PLUSH BED. SHE HAD SPENT the entire night managing her family, then batting away internet trolls, and she collapsed like an overworked event coordinator.

Her phone buzzed. WIC. She picked up.

"You finally got time for me?" WIC cooed.

She didn't reply.

"Look, I wanted to come. My tux was all picked out. But your boy has a real mean streak, you know?"

"What do you mean?" Liza asked, curious.

"Dorsey tracked me down, threatened me, calling me racial slurs, the whole gambit."

"Racial slurs?" Liza's stomach twisted. "What did he say exactly?"

"'I don't want people like you at my party.'"

"And then he called you the N-word?"

"He didn't exactly say it, but you know how they code it. 'Your type,' 'your kind.'"

"When did he call you?"

"Like three days ago. It was hell. Somebody like that—"

"So you've known for three days you weren't coming?"

"Liza, you're getting the wrong information out of this."

"WIC, it's been a long night. I'm tired."

"Did you dance?"

"Not really." The beginnings of a pounding headache pushed against her temples.

"That's not what the internet says."

"Oh?"

"Oh. You let him use you. Now you look like you're chummy with these developers. I mean, I have pictures of you looking absolutely dazzled by this guy. They're saying you left with a Tiffany box. Now that's the new narrative: 'Residents make nice with developers, nothing to see here, folks.'"

"I'm sorry, there was too much on my mind to be playing chess."

"Right," WIC continued, "and I didn't go because you know I can't be used by them. I won't be their little dancing monkey."

Liza opened her mouth to speak but stopped short. Had she been a tool the entire time? Had she missed something entirely? If she was honest with herself, it didn't feel that way. At some point during the dance, everything they had ever said to each other had just fallen away. What was left was just a man and a woman slow dancing.

"Tell you what, I'll stop by the hotel tomorrow and take you out."

"Thank you. I'd like that." How had she gone from stood up to angling for forgiveness? This night had to end. Had to. She closed her eyes, and her throat clenched at the thoughts that rushed over her. Dorsey's smoky eyes and his warm hand on her bare back as he pulled her flush with his body. He had been ex-cruciatingly intentional. And she had registered every stray thumb press, every flick of his eyes to her mouth and then down her bodice, every intake of breath shorter than the one before it. He had given so little, and somehow it was like a flood.

"Weren't you stood up? Why do you look all gooey?" LeDeya

said. She surprised Liza with her perceptiveness sometimes. LeDeya walked out of the bathroom, all legs and swaying breasts. God help her, she looked ten years older than her tender sixteen years, even with all the makeup off.

LeDeya laid her head on Liza's belly, and the two girls formed a crooked T on the overly soft hotel bed. She grunted and moved over something uncomfortable. "Ew. I opened this Tiffany box and it was just a used book. I would be so pissed. Does Dorsey hate you that much?"

Liza's head shot up from the bed. "Don't open my gifts, Deya. Gimme the box."

She must have looked feral, because Deya squinted her eyes. "Damn, here. You look real pressed right now."

Liza took the box, trying not to snatch it out of her sister's hands. Whatever this was with Dorsey belonged to her alone.

It didn't mean she wasn't excited about WIC coming tomorrow. She wanted so fiercely to protect her choice to her mother that she told no one of the creeping doubt that came over her about WIC sometimes. The way a surprise frost ruined the first buds of spring, Liza fought the coldness that threatened to creep in. But she always did this, found *one* fault with a person and turned them into the villain in her story. If she was honest with herself, it had kept her single for longer than she liked. WIC was handsome, charming, woke, and a brother. He already had three traits up on Dorsey. Liza stopped herself right there. Images flickered in her head like a faulty projector. *No. Get thee behind me.*

"Have you guys, like, done anything?" LeDeya asked.

"Who?" Panic constricted her throat.

"Who else?" Deya laughed. "WIC."

Liza bristled. Why had the thought of sex with WIC seemed so great that morning? Now it turned her stomach, which was not something she'd admit to anyone. Her mother and LeDeya would tease her mercilessly. *Liza found a flaw again! One hair's out of place, so Liza dumped him!*

"No, and I won't until I'm married," Liza said. LeDeya huffed and reached out to pinch her older sister's thigh.

"I'm not a child, you know," LeDeya said, without real conviction.

"That is exactly what you are," Liza said. LeDeya fell asleep then, her head still resting on her sister's belly. Liza slowly uncurled herself from her sleeping sister and padded to the balcony. Slowly, she opened the box. A book from a Harvard sociologist on eviction. Of course it wasn't a necklace.

He knew that this was what she would love from him.

She flipped through the book. It was marked up around the margins with his brusque handwriting. She ran her thumb along the grooves of the earnest markings and a tear fell and spread the dark ink across her fingers. She finally saw the note.

Liza—God, the way he wrote her name!

Let's discuss! This was illuminating. It really is all coming together.

He was self-educating. He had a blind spot and he was doing the work. Shit. All she ever wanted was a little effort. She held the book to her heart. It was such a tiny gesture. But it was worth more than what would have been in a real Tiffany box. She rocked in her chair. Two fifteen a.m. was no time to grip her phone so tightly. Ugh, she had to text him.

> Was I a prop?

She had to ask now. She wouldn't be brave in the light of day. He would get this text in the morning and be faced with how to answer, but she had gotten her part out. Liza was surprised to see three pulsing dots on her phone.

> No.

Typical Dorsey response—concise, to the point. No fat on that bone for Liza to chew through. Now he had placed a response back on her, and she fumbled for once in her life for a witty reply.

> Why did you dance with me?

Liza bit her lips. The reply came quickly.

> I wanted to.

> Well, it's kind of a 😮 🍿 now. Wanting to do something is no reason to actually do it.

> If I didn't do it, how would I know?

> Know what?

> That I want to do it again.

So many questions swirled in her head. She couldn't explain why, but it *felt* like the truth. More than WIC's sly explanations for not showing up. Dorsey felt more solid, more human to her than WIC did, and Liza felt a twinge of shame for not believing WIC.

Am I a sellout?

> We're memes again

It was all she could come up with.

> We're establishing a bit of a pattern.

> I got your book.

> Had you already read it?

> No, I'm going to dive in tomorrow.

> Why don't you stop by my home and
> I can show you all the books from the
> class I'm auditing.

> We could have a study group.

Liza wasn't thinking about studying even as she typed that. If she went to his house she would want his hands on her, his mouth on her. She would show him effort. And from the way he held her at the gala, Liza knew she wouldn't be alone in that wish.

Shit.

Damn.

She'd already planned her day away with WIC.

> Um scratch that I overbooked myself
> tomorrow

Liza waited while the three dots wavered, then stopped. Finally, a GIF popped up of a dad telling his son, "I'm not mad, I'm disappointed."

> Just remembered

God she wished she could take back her agreement with WIC. *This* was what she wanted. Whatever this feeling was.

> No Worries. I slow-danced in public
> with a beautiful woman.

> Bucket list conquered.

Liza's cheeks burned, and she quickly found a GIF of *The Beverly Hillbillies,* a black-and-white comedy her granny used to watch about newly minted country millionaires arriving dusty and uncouth in LA.

> Travel with Family

> Fuck it List Conquered.

> #neveragain

Three ROFL emojis.

Three ticking dots.

The next time Liza looked up, the morning sun was streaking pink across the sky. Somehow, she'd texted Dorsey all night—GIFs and haikus and four a.m. selfies. They had their own language and jokes and lexicon now.

Last night, she and Dorsey were an entire universe. Now she had the whole day with WIC to get through.

———

THE NEXT MORNING WAS GRAY, WET, AND LIMP. LIZA DID not want to move, much less curl her hair and put makeup on. Her phone vibrated, and she moved with a little too much speed to find it in the folds of the bed. LeDeya sat eating a heaping plate of eggs and hot sauce—expensive room service, Liza was sure.

"You finally up?" Deya asked. "You look like hell."

"Is that Mr. Thang?" Beverly pushed open the door from the adjoining suite. She, like everyone else, was already de-scarved and dressed. Liza finally found her phone twisted in the sheets. Why was her heart pounding?

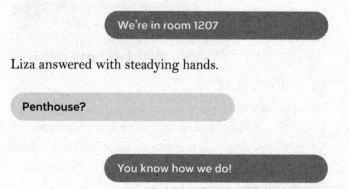

> I'm downstairs

Her heart hammered, and then she remembered. WIC, of course. *Who else could it be?*

> We're in room 1207

Liza answered with steadying hands.

> Penthouse?

> You know how we do!

She responded, then rushed to the bathroom to wash her face

and brush her teeth. She was throwing her headscarf onto the messy pile of sheets when she heard his soft knock. Liza looked around. Why was her family draped over the furniture like a *Vogue* front page?

Liza opened the door and beamed. WIC did the rest. He came with gift boxes and flowers and all the things to bowl everyone over with his magnanimity. Liza could not have played it out better. WIC floated in, all warmth and smiles, with fragrant pink roses for everyone and a cheesesteak for Maurice. He even *mistakenly* called Bev by her oldest daughter's name, "thinking" she was Janae, and coaxed Granny's turban off and wore it around the suite for ten minutes pretending to be Madea. He had turned a gray day into a bright one. Liza leaned into his magnetism, late-night texts forgotten. Her sisters were all laughs and lashes.

"You're famous again!" WIC said.

"Oh, the memes, I know." The family gathered around WIC's phone as he searched Liza's hashtag #Bennett2winit on Instagram. As he scrolled through all the social media around the event, the banter and laughter faded at the latest memes that popped up with Dorsey and Liza dancing.

That feeling when your mom made you make up with your brother.

Black lives matter sees green.

When you get fried chicken at Asian carryout.

Hater to Dater.

Gentrify me, Mr. Fitzgerald.

Some Tiffany for Liza

There were also a lot of jokes about the "dark side," and even more jokes with some combination of Asian and Black racism.

"This one was all over Reddit. Did he get you a Tiffany necklace?" WIC smiled. It was a great one. Everyone in the room relaxed a little. Liza only noticed how large his canines were.

Liza rolled her eyes. "No, he did not."

"He got her an old book," Bev said.

Liza's hands popped to her hips. *Is there anyone who hasn't already looked in my gift box?*

"What was it? A rare first edition of *Rich Dad, Poor Dad?*" WIC's look was a notch past curiosity. "He's using expensive gifts to try to get Liza off his neck. But it won't work!" He clapped again. "But what was it?"

Liza had no idea why she was absolutely unwilling to tell him what was in that box, but she would rather rip it up than have him flip through it and see her doodles and notes on top of his notes. Hear him mock it.

Maurice stood between them. "WIC, my brother! Mr. Dorsey is nowhere to be found. Why does every conversation have to be about him? I'm very interested in your plan to save Netherfield Court."

Liza squinted at her little brother. He had these flashes of intuition about people that sometimes surprised her.

Bev tsked. "I see Mr. High and Mighty ain't out there contradicting this mess. He's just gonna let you take the heat for how this looks."

WIC pulled up his slacks and sat at the foot of the bed. "I hate to say this, Ms. Bev, but this is typical Dorsey. Letting the Brown people endure the blowback of his decisions. He's enjoying this."

Janae winced. "There are just as many disparaging Asian remarks as there are Black. He can't be too happy about that."

"The power differential is too high, Janae. He should be out in front because he has the power to do so. But he's gonna let the laborers do the work for him," WIC said.

"He doesn't seem like the out-in-front type," Janae said thoughtfully. "When David and I hang out with him, he almost disappears into the wallpaper. I was shocked Liza got him to play along with us at the office."

WIC's eyebrows rose. "He played along to what?"

Janae laughed prettily at the hazy and mostly wrong memory. "We were snowed in and bored to death and played hide-and-seek. I forget most of it, but I do remember Dorsey chasing Liza or something. Or maybe he had caught you? Y'all slept in those pods . . ."

"It's all fuzzy!" Liza interrupted. "The point is, he's a stick-in-the-mud who's not out in front."

"You spend a *lot* of time defending him when you should denounce him. Post something on the 'Gram to tell people how you feel about being used," WIC demanded.

She could feel herself bristling. "I think it was simpler than that," Liza said defensively.

"What? That he just happened to ask the person leading the opposition to his development work to dance in front of a thousand eyes and cameras?" WIC shook his head. "Look at how bad it's getting."

He brought his phone to her face. It was a picture of two people, Liza's and Dorsey's faces pasted on them. The man was vigorously fucking the woman from behind and whipping her with some sort of medieval contraption—while the woman shouted out, "Master!" Liza looked away, practically vibrating with shame.

"We have a cousin in the permit office," she told WIC, her voice softened. "I'm sure I can get her to slow things down."

"That should buy us some time to do more fundraising. How's my proposal coming along?" WIC's smile lit up the room. It was like she'd been kicked out of some enchanted garden. Everyone was having fun but her.

"It's coming." That was all Liza was willing to say. Her shame was transforming into a slow simmer. *What did he mean to do by showing me that disgusting video?*

WIC touched her shoulder. "Fine, be mysterious. You're beautiful when you're mysterious." Liza saw Bev elbow Janae out of the corner of her eye. Liza was about to let them know she saw them, but she was stopped short when LeDeya walked out of the spacious hotel closet with a scarf around her head and thigh-high boots.

"Deya, what are you wearing?" Janae asked.

"It was in the boxes WIC brought up."

"My gifts are better and you can wear them home," WIC said, winking at Liza.

"You brought us head wraps?" Liza asked. She hoped to heaven this man was not thinking of converting her into any of this head-wrapping nonsense. She worked too hard laying her edges to see them go to waste.

"Modesty is the true source of beauty," WIC said and winked at Bev.

"That's why I always keep a modesty cloth over my knees for church," Bev said. Liza bit the inside of her cheek. Bev was perhaps the most immodest person she knew.

"I also think that you all would be perfect faces for the movement. Janae, I know you can work your pageant magic to bring awareness to this fundraising campaign. Liza, your social media following is enormous, and Deya is even attracting a large following with her makeup tutorials."

"You know about my tutorials?" LeDeya's eyes were saucers.

WIC nodded. "You're quite the businesswoman."

LeDeya beamed, but Liza frowned. She was already spending a lot of her extra time writing a proposal. She also didn't like that he had researched her sisters to rope them into the effort. Janae especially hated doing pageant work, trading her face to add value to a friend's tire shop or a new grocery store chain. If he had researched them, why wouldn't he have asked Janae, with her finance degree, to do this damn proposal? Not that she would have been fool enough to do any of this for free. Liza took a deep breath.

No. She was doing that thing again. Finding faults and messing up a thing before it even started.

"These scarves are dope. And they would really take a well-made-up face to the next level," LeDeya said. WIC smiled that damned smile, and Liza saw every woman in the room's heart skip a beat.

Except hers.

Bev glanced approvingly at Liza. Bev liked him. Liza had actually done something right in Bev's eyes, and she'd be damned if it didn't feel good. But she knew this was going to be her high school boyfriend all over again. Once Bev liked someone, she asked about them endlessly, even when Liza had someone new. This would be the beginning of years of "How's WIC?" It made her dread messing anything up for fear of hearing "Whatever happened to that nice WIC fella?" every month for the rest of her life. Everyone loved him. WIC seemed to even like her family, and there were no cultural or class translations needed. He would know to eat the damned oxtail. He would have known to do it. Liza would just have to squash her own asshole tendencies and settle into a good thing.

"While I applaud your attempt at modesty, you sound only interested in scarves to highlight the expert application of immodest makeup," Maurice said.

"While I applaud your attempts at being a thesaurus, you still sound stupid," LeDeya shot back. Maurice took a scarf and attempted to whirl it around and snap LeDeya with it.

"Leave the girl alone. She knows what she likes," WIC said.

"She doesn't know anything," Liza said.

"I know I look better than you in these scarves," LeDeya said.

Liza threw a pillow at her sister's head and missed.

***

WIC TOOK THE FAMILY TO FIFTY-SECOND STREET IN WEST Philly, where Granny bargained for cheap knockoff purses and bought shea butter and bags of incense. Then they went to a café where they bused their own tables and washed dishes in a collective afterward.

He was the perfect freedom fighter. Fist bumping old men and rubbing the heads of young boys with fresh cuts—in her world, WIC made sense. But a slow shadow still slid over the day for Liza. Not just because she was exhausted, but because she was trying so hard to *want* to like it.

Time is Isaiah's enemy.

By four p.m. she'd just hit a wall. Janae had fidgeted with her phone all day, and she seemed pretty out of it too.

Liza caught up to her in front of everyone. "Janae, are you ready to leave?"

"Yeah, I guess I didn't get a lot of sleep last night, and it's catching up to me."

"Yeah, me too, you ready to go?"

"Almost." She looked down at her phone. "Actually, yes."

"Janae?" Liza held her sister's shoulders.

"I just thought we'd talk more, David and I, I thought he would invite me over after the gala. And now I haven't really gotten a text since last night . . ."

Liza laughed. "He's probably still asleep."

"Probably." Janae didn't look convinced.

———

THE BENNETTS DROVE HOME TO DC IN A SLIGHTLY LESS luxurious manner than before. Granny didn't trust her new plants to survive the frigid airplane cargo section, so they sat in a cramped van. Bev and the pastor chatted about the gala the entire time and speculated on the price of every morsel of food.

Liza, Janae, and LeDeya were glued to their phones. Liza was alternating between mean comments and uplifting cat GIFs.

The phone vibrated in her hand, and she nearly threw it down at her feet. Gosh, she was on edge.

> Leaving my city?

Dorsey's number popped up. She had refused to save his contact info. It was like an admission of some sort.

> Yep, if only you'd do me the same favor

> Ouch.

Liza's smile broadened, and LeDeya smirked. "You look so goofy right now. WIC is *that* funny?"

"Mind your business, Deya."

> Am I bad for your street cred?

>> Yes

> Does this feel too complicated?

>> Yes

> Do you regret our dance?

>> No

Three wavering dots.

> Good.

>> I wanted to come by before we left. It just got a little . . .

> I know.

> I underestimated how interested in us people still are.

> Had you come it would have been a

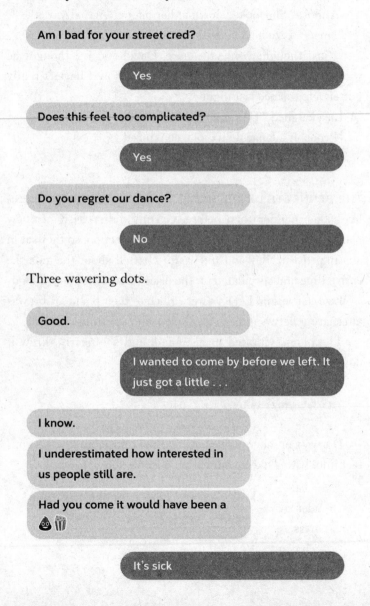

>> It's sick

Yes. I'm seeing some terrible stuff

It will go away

Still, you OK?

Steady streams of cat gifs are helping.

You?

You're helping.

Warmth crept up Liza's cheeks. She looked around and pulled the phone closer to her. Maybe they should make a statement?

Long term strategy tho, we should publicly denounce it at some point right?

Let them know we're not #crazyinlove

Three wavering dots.

Would that be the truth Liza?

The question felt electric, and her fingertips buzzed as she flipped the phone screen facedown on her lap. When her heart wouldn't stop pounding, she pushed the phone down to the bottom of her purse. The question still didn't feel far enough away.

She shoved her purse under her other bags despite herself. Dorsey's directness steadied Liza's whirling thoughts. He was a lot of things, but not a liar. She didn't feel up to the challenge of answering his text.

What does he want me to admit?

What is he admitting?

They pulled up to their apartment in record time.

Colin was waiting outside the building. No doubt Bev had told him when to show up. Liza pulled at her suitcases. Colin did not offer to help her but buzzed around her anxiously.

"Can we take a walk, Liza?" he asked.

"I'm a little tired," Liza started.

"Liza, you been staring at that phone for two hours. Stretch your body out. It will do you some good," Bev said. "Y'all take a walk." Liza rolled her eyes. Bev was always trying to orchestrate something with Colin, and Liza was over it. She got out of the van and slammed the door behind her, leaving Colin to talk with Bev. If she loved him so much, let *her* get wrapped in one of his endlessly self-referential conversations. When Liza got to their door, she saw a small brown paper package with her name scrawled in calligraphy.

LeDeya's eyes rounded. "WIC is so sweet. What is it?"

"It's for me." Liza snatched the box. It was cold. Inside, when she finally neatly cut away all the packaging, she saw the gold rim of Blue Bell Homemade Vanilla ice cream. It was one of her answers to the thirty-six questions. She'd told Dorsey about the time she had spent with her father in Texas and the taste of Blue Bell ice cream. Liza blinked back hot tears.

Deya was unimpressed. "Why would WIC get you off-brand ice cream?"

Liza's voice was thick. "It's not from WIC and it's not off-brand."

Colin cleared his throat. Lest anyone forget for a second that he was here. "Liza, I'm sorry if this dessert is making you so emotional, but"—he let out a shaky breath, then nodded at Bev— "I'm not leaving until you talk to me."

BROWN, BUT NOT TOO DARK

'M BACK IN THE SADDLE, DC! THANK YOU ALL FOR CHECK-ing me out on my live feed. I want to apologize for losing it a few days ago, but Philly was tougher than I thought. Let's talk about the way we treat each other online. The messages I got and the pictures I received were just relentless." She pressed the answer button.

"Can I offer you a word of advice, Liza B.?" an older voice asked.

"The whole country is giving me advice, so go ahead," Liza said with a sigh.

"You'll never find me defending the rich, but that boy, the one with you in the photos, doesn't deserve all of that garbage people are spewing about him either. We don't want to win that way. You two should work together! Yeah, and build something better for Merrytown! He's actually the person with the resources to fix it." The caller's excitement was palpable. Working with Dorsey was impossible. Right? He simply wanted to take his profit and go. He didn't want collaboration. Besides, the way her body acted around him—all of that breathing and eye contact. She wouldn't last an hour without passing out.

"The community can help itself too. We don't have to wait for manna from heaven. There are a lot of good people behind the scenes who are working on this problem."

"Take the hard way then," the caller said. Liza laughed. It was the type of thing Chicho would say.

The phone lines buzzed, but Liza didn't have the heart to take any more calls. Nearly everyone was gone from the adjoining booths. Most of the offices were stark-white boxes. Booth G was one of the last booths standing. Liza knew her high-profile sponsor and international artist showcases were keeping her solid for now. But one false move and Liza knew she was out of a job.

LIZA WOKE UP TO THE SOOTHING SOUND OF HER GRAN-ny's steady rocking. She smiled and stretched herself out on her tummy. The carton of ice cream tipped over empty in her bed. Her eyes were puffy and gritty. She'd cried all night, and she wasn't sure it was entirely because of the internet taunting. Dorsey wasn't turning out to be the petty tyrant she needed him to be. He was no man of the people by any means. But he was soft and careful with her, and no matter how hard she tried to deny it, his cerebral attention, his intellectual earnestness—turned out it was her brand.

She wanted desperately to feel this way about WIC. But Dorsey charged through all her thoughts like a—well, like a bull. She remembered him fastidiously setting his napkin on his lap at the Hotel Washington bar and insisting it would save his clothes. He was a man not so in love with his own opinion. He would do the work and learn when he had a blind spot. That was worth its weight in gold.

Why couldn't you just eat Granny's oxtails? You had an in! Then maybe she could start to explain to her family what was happening inside her heart.

When her eyes popped open, she saw Colin cross-legged on her granny's rocking chair at the foot of her bed. Liza had been dodging him for two days, feigning cramps and a migraine to stay in her room. When she saw him suddenly rising out of the chair, she let out a clipped scream.

"Holy!" she said.

Colin closed his eyes. "I didn't mean to surprise you."

"Yes, you did."

"I just wanted to see you relaxed. You always have this mad scowl on your face. It is really remarkable to see you sleeping so peacefully."

Liza tried to keep her face flat. "Colin, did you need something?"

He drew in a deep breath. "Liza, you are all I ever think about. You're bold and funny and though your breasts are below average compared to your mother and sisters, all I need is a handful"—he held out his palms—"and you still excite me physically a great deal."

Liza pulled the blanket over her head. What could she do to make him go away?

"I need a Michelle Obama–type counterpart. Down, but not too militant. Brown, but not too dark. You polled excellently in Senator De Berg's focus group. And I want you to be my wife." His words tumbled over one another. "I know what you're thinking: *How can a woman like me ever measure up to the pressures of political life?* You'll meet a lot of public officials."

"Colin," Liza said warningly.

"I know you're excited, but let me finish. I even thought of a way you can use that degree in international studies. We pulled some strings and got you a position on the evangelical station, focusing on women's issues all around the world. Your segment is called *The Prayer Corner*. It's a six-figure job, but you have to be done with all of that LGBTQ stuff. Keep some of those crazy opinions to yourself." He made a fussy face. "Senator De Berg has even added a podcasting booth in our town house. I mean, the man is beyond generous. One theme he's interested in is women taking on all of this MeToo nonsense. He thinks Christian women should stand up to this."

"Colin!"

"Wait, I just made a few notes."

"I'm sorry, but—"

"Wait."

"No."

"Liza, be reasonable."

Liza picked up her bell hooks reader and hurled it at him. Next came Zora Neale Hurston. It was the Nabokov that got him square between the eyes. Colin rushed out of the room, holding his head and his midsection. The thundering hooves of her entire family shook the hallway.

Bev rushed into the room not two minutes later. "Are you soft in the head or something?" she shrieked.

"What are you talking about?"

"A man just offered you a home, a six-figure job, some social standing, and you throw bell hooks at him?" Bev read the spine of another book. "He poured out his heart to you, and you threw Zora Neale Hurston at his penis? This man can fix every. Single. Thing. Wrong with you in a snap of his fingers. Just who do you think you are? Drop-dead gorgeous like Janae? Funny and lively like my Deya? Or, hell, a man like Maurice?"

"I don't think I'm any of those, Ma."

"You're damn right you're not, so act like it. If you don't know a meal ticket when you see one, I've never taught you anything."

"I don't want to spend my life using someone."

"Why not?" Bev said. "Men will use you up. They will take your youth, your joy, your beauty, and leave you with babies. Uneven trade, if you ask me."

"Dang, Mom." LeDeya's eyes peered over at Liza from behind Bev. They were secret sister eyes. *I understand you, but I can't stand with you.*

"Whoever you're waiting for, Liza, the perfect man with no problems, who's rich and will take all of your troubles away, he doesn't exist." Bev's face was suddenly cold and serious. "You need to get your head out of books and into the real world. Colin is what a good man looks like. Your granny's gonna have a fit when she hears this."

Bev stormed to the back of the apartment with Liza trailing after her and pulled a still sleepy Granny out of the bed. She had deep brown skin and a wide, bulbous nose that sat on her face like a wise Buddha. Her full cheeks and deep dimples gave her an ageless mischievousness that everyone loved. Liza couldn't bear her granny being disappointed in her.

"Colin asked Liza to marry him. Live in his new town house in Alexandria and meet with senators. He had a job lined up for her, making good money, and this fool told him no. I have half a mind to kick her ass all the way down the street," Bev threatened.

Granny yawned. "Well, you got your answer right there, child."

Liza's eyebrows wavered. *Granny too?*

"Your mom is going to kick your ass if you don't go with Colin, and *I'll* kick your ass if you do."

———

LEDEYA BURST THROUGH THE DOOR INTO LIZA'S BEDroom. "Look at David's Insta. Is this real?"

Liza stared at the shot of David with a playful smile biting into a croissant, the Arc de Triomphe artfully framed behind him. #Parisinthespringtime #6weekfoodbaby

"He's in Paris?"

"When?"

"Why didn't Janae tell us?" Liza asked, then squinted at LeDeya's Instagram. "How did you get this many followers? Momma just let you get an account three months ago!"

LeDeya snatched the phone back. "People are looking for marketable content."

"*Marketable content?* Who have you been speaking to?" Liza asked. She didn't have time to be agog at her sister's fifty thousand followers because Janae walked in.

"Who kicked your dog?" she asked. She had been packing for interviews in New York and had nearly cleaned out all the closets in the apartment. The woman needed an outfit for every mood.

Janae had secured an interview not only for the position she applied for, but from four other large companies in the same week. She had made arrangements with her father's family to stay for the week. This was interesting to Liza for a few reasons:

- *Janae had talked to her father, a man she avoided in her adulthood as much as he had avoided her in her youth.*

- She could easily plan and manage multiple job interview prep documents and schedules without getting overwhelmed anymore.
- Only Janae could fill out one application and get four interviews.

For all those reasons Liza had misgivings about showing Janae David's social media post. Her sister had been improving, and maybe it was because of the joy David had brought to her life. But LeDeya pressed forward.

"Janae, do you know?" LeDeya haltingly showed Janae the photo of David enjoying himself in France.

"This doesn't make sense," Janae said softly. "I just spoke to him three days ago. He never mentioned."

"What does 'six week food baby' mean?" Liza said.

"It's a project. He told me he was going to get his sister to run it. A project in Versailles." Janae's voice softened. "I guess he decided . . . I . . . I don't understand."

"He just went to a whole other continent without telling you?" Liza huffed. "Why would he do that?"

"I'm sure it was urgent."

"What do you mean it was urgent? This boy *internationally* ghosted you." LeDeya crossed her arms.

"You're too good for them, Janae." Liza and LeDeya were unified for once.

Janae pulled out her phone, searching for missing texts or calls. Her hands shook almost imperceptibly. Janae straightened her back and exhaled. Liza touched her shoulder. Her big sister was so used to disappointment, and so used to not getting what she needed from people.

"I think you should tell him. Tell him everything," LeDeya advised.

"Deya, he's gonna—"

"No, Janae, maybe you should trust that he'll understand," Liza said.

"No one has before."

"Maybe not, but this is the happiest I've seen you. You owe it to yourself to give it a better try than this."

"What do I do? He's in Paris!"

"Phones no longer work?" LeDeya asked.

"I guess I'll text his sister and get his schedule in New York," Janae said.

Liza rolled her eyes. "Ugh, Jennifer is the worst. Just call him before you head to New York, Janae. You know you're going to get every job you're interviewing for."

"His sister likes me. I'll text her."

"I don't think Jennifer likes any of us that well," Liza said.

"Yeah, her and Dorsey are so different from David. I wouldn't be surprised if the rumors are true about them."

"Wh-what rumors?" Liza stammered.

"That they're together. You see them everywhere together." Janae sounded exasperated.

"I don't."

"You had to notice during the snowstorm how she would flutter after Dorsey every time he swiveled his head."

Liza remembered that night differently—burning looks, ripped shirts, waking up wrapped up in him. *Was Jennifer even there?* "I'm starting to think you weren't as tipsy as you pretended to be that night. The memories you conjure up!" Liza laughed nervously and left the room.

LIZA WOKE TO A SOFT NUDGING OF HER FOOT AND
jumped to grab her baseball bat from under the bed.

"Liza! Liza, chill. It's me, Chicho."

"Oh my gosh, girl." Liza held her hand to her chest. "What's
up? It's early, right?" Liza grabbed her phone, but Chicho lunged
for it.

"Don't look at that."

Liza tapped her Instagram notifications. Chicho had posted
a story?

"I wanted to tell you before you saw it online. I wanted you
to know first." Chicho's tone was so pleading it raised alarm
bells.

A video played of Chicho's wheat-colored hand wearing a
lovely princess-cut diamond ring.

"What, you're pretending to be engaged?" Liza laughed but
noticed Chicho's left hand was conspicuously behind her back the
entire time.

"Not pretending."

"What do you mean?"

"Colin asked me to consider a proposition, and I said yes."

"You're marrying *Colin*?"

"Yes. He said with the demographic change in DC and Virginia, a Latina wife was polling better than he realized." Chicho
said this with no recognition of how ridiculous it sounded. Liza
winced at her friend's language.

"Don't. Don't look at me like that," Chicho said.

"Oh, Chicho. No. He's . . ."

"He thought you were beautiful and got a little beside himself. Colin admitted that to me. But he said you turned him down."

"I'd do it again."

"Liza, marriage can be full of love, but it can also be a cheat code. I rarely agree with Ms. Bev, but if you find someone who can take you out of a dangerous cycle, you gotta go for it."

"Do you think he's the best you can get? You're better than this."

Chicho's face snapped back as if she'd been slapped. "Liza, you're perfectly okay with me being the sidekick, the plain girlfriend who you never have to worry about taking your man. They're going to give me a six-figure job and my own house. I can take my little brother and enroll him in a better school district. I'm so sorry if Colin isn't as hot as WIC, but I think I've done pretty well for myself here."

"Chicho, that's not what I meant."

"You know who you remind me of? That arrogant *come mierda* Dorsey. You two are more alike than you think. You think you're so much better than everyone."

Now it was Liza's turn to recoil. "Fine. Have a nice life. Don't call me when you have to stand by your man at a press conference when he inevitably gropes an intern."

"That was a shitty thing to say."

"This is a shitty thing to *do*. There are better ways to secure your future."

"Excuse me if I don't take self-help advice from you. This time next week, I'll be in the damn PTA and making three times your salary." Chicho stormed out of the room, and Liza's face fell. It wasn't until she heard the front door slam that she allowed herself to cry. She pulled out her phone and shot off a text to Dorsey. She didn't know why she thought of him first. Why did her thumbs hover over his number in her phone all the time now? She just needed a different kind of interaction.

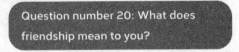

Question number 20: What does friendship mean to you?

Liza wiped her eyes to see the phone clearly. Three wavering dots appeared.

Having someone you can show your scars to without their judgment.

Someone who shows up for you when you're emotionally, physically exhausted.

Someone you can laugh with so hard you fart and pee a little.

💩

She laughed an ugly-crying laugh and drifted off to sleep.

CHEAT CODE

BACK, SOMEHOW, BY POPULAR DEMAND, IS LONG-
bourne's own Colin Gruthers, self-published author of *Up from Nothing*. Colin, I believe congratulations are in order? You found the best girl in the neighborhood and put a ring on it?" Liza turned her face away from the mic. She didn't want him misreading her anger.

"Yes, asking Lucia Ochoa to marry me is the best thing I've ever done. I've tried these other neighborhood women. They all seemed to be dazzled by my persona, not seeing the real me. I daresay even *you* got the jitters when I sat down to chat with you." His oily giggle made her stomach turn.

"By jitters, do you mean reservations?" Liza pressed the applause button and put her hand over the mic. "Do not press your luck, Colin."

His green eyes flashed, and his smile flattened. "All jokes, folks, all jokes," he said. "But I have a question for the host, if I can turn the tables a bit. Where are these perfect men that our high-minded sisters are holding out for? I see sisters eating alone and passing up a free meal. For what? I just don't get the psychology of it. What would make a person say no when they have absolutely *nothing* else going for them?" He had the decency to avoid eye contact with her. Was this man's help on the proposal worth two appearances on her show? Liza was rethinking her strategy.

"So women should be grateful for *any* man's attention if they are single?" Liza clipped through her teeth.

"If she's single, and she's not all that." Colin laughed.

"Can you believe this gem's all snatched up, ladies? Mediocre single women! He's taken and we missed our chance to grovel." Liza cut the feed.

⎯⎯⎯

"SO, THIS IS WEIRD," LIZA SAID TO HER FRIEND THREE weeks later under the dingy fluorescent lights of the district courthouse. Colin had had ten dozen roses delivered and also handed the guests expensive cards with his and Chicho's information on them. It was a perfect combination of putting on airs and extreme haste. Chicho's mother cried the entire time, but Liza wasn't sure if it was despair or happiness. The flowers were just about the only thing that was nice about Chicho's ceremony. Colin signed the papers with the flair of a man signing the Declaration of Independence.

"You made it weird by not being happy for me," Chicho said. Her eyes were flat and narrowed. Liza's smile was as brittle as spun sugar. She didn't want to focus on unpleasantness on a day like this.

"I was shocked, Chicho," Liza said.

"You need to admit that you preferred me single so I can attend to you and your love life. All the time."

"Lucia." Liza rarely used Chicho's proper name. "I will admit no such thing. Look, I have been complaining about that boy since we were kids. You can't expect me to fall out of my chair with excitement because he gets to marry my best friend. You're the best of all of us! Why does he deserve you? What has he done?"

"For one, he's going to give me a career and a respectable zip code, give my brother a stable home and an excellent school system, and put my father in rehab. For those of us without your body or your face—"

"Whoa, whoa, why am I suddenly a plastic Barbie when you want to make a point?"

"Or your brains, I was going to say—if you would have let me finish." Chicho took in a slow breath.

"So now I'm astronaut Barbie and can't possibly understand actually wanting a better life? All the ways *my* life is fucked up is my fault because I won't activate the cheat code?" Liza tried to keep her voice down. It was her best friend's quickie wedding, and she should put on a cheerful face.

"Liza, I don't need you to like my choices. But a little understanding would be nice. I'm not trying to find the perfect love. I'm trying to change the circumstances of my life. Do you see the difference? You assumed we agreed on that, and we never did."

"Just know there is no shame in backing out. Call me if you ever feel in over your head."

"Oh, I will. I still need your help with the podcasting stuff."

Liza bit down on her tongue. "Why did you even take the job?" God, she didn't want to do this here.

"Like DJing was your dream job, Liza? Like you wanted a podcast? *Ay bendito*, it's six figures. And I can learn it just like you did." Chicho fussed with Liza's collar. "Okay, here comes the senator and Colin."

"Senator De Berg, I'd like you to meet my lovely *esposa*, Lucia Ochoa-Gruthers," Colin announced loudly, then mumbled, "and her friend Liza." Liza pulled her mouth upward in her best imitation of a smile. "Everyone, your state senator." He wasn't Liza's state senator, but she didn't press the point.

The senator nodded deeply and encircled Chicho's hands with his large ones. "Excellent match! And a Latina too! This is great for the Thirty-Fifth District." The senator kissed Chicho's hand. "A real accessible beauty. Excellent. None of that beauty queen nonsense you were talking earlier."

Liza rolled her eyes. Did Colin really think he could have pulled Janae Bennett?

"And you must be the woman we've all been hearing so much about." The senator raised his eyebrow. His eyes traveled around Liza's face and body as if he were a cat following a laser pointer. He smiled tightly. "Don't see what all of the fuss is about, really."

Liza straightened her shoulders. *Attacks coming in on all sides, I see.*

"Liza, stop by my offices and see some of the work we're doing with affordable housing in Virginia. Some of the progress you're protesting has transformed Alexandria," the senator said.

"Oh, I agree, the city has transformed. Depends on how favorably you see those transformations," Liza said.

"Higher tax revenues, full occupation of formally abandoned buildings? How can you see that transformation as anything other than favorable?"

"Progress for you seems to mean pushing off those who can no longer afford to live in your district to other districts, so they aren't your problem anymore."

"Liza! Excuse me. Everything he has done for our community! He is an Obama Democrat, I would remind you," Colin said with a sneer.

"Congratulations on your allegiances, Senator." Liza turned to Chicho, wished her well, and stalked out of the courthouse. She heard the phrase "dodged a bullet" muttered behind her.

WHEN LIZA GOT HOME, HER MOTHER WAS ON A TEAR. "I tell you what, I better not see her little Puerto Rican ass here again. She's a skeezer, bottom line."

"Momma," Liza warned.

"A skeezer! That girl was waiting like a dog at the table for what you threw away. She's always been like that. I wouldn't be surprised if she got a picture of you up with some pins in it."

"Ma, that's enough."

"I hope you saw the town car they rode in while you came in soggy and tired from the train. I hope you saw that princess cut on her fat hand and compared it to your ashy, chipped-nail-polished hands. I hope it eats you alive that your fat, plain friend got one over on you."

"No one got one over on me, Ma. Chicho . . ." But Liza didn't have the energy to be nice. Her friend had made a huge mistake for money, and it made her feel queasy to defend her right now.

"Well, at least you have WIC. How did you say he made his money?" Bev looked through her purse, a poor attempt at casual.

"I didn't say." Liza had to get around her to get down the hallway. But Bev cocked her hip and blocked her way, primed for an argument. Liza was emotionally near the end of her rope.

"Well, do *you* know?" Bev asked.

"Ma, I told you I'm not like that. I don't ask for a man's bank account before I date him."

"Okay, Ms. High and Mighty. You're *proud* of not even having that man's business card?" Bev put her purse down.

"Don't you like him?"

"I actually do. But I'd like him a lot more with a job description." Bev picked up her purse again and walked toward the door.

"Can that be enough right now, Ma?" Liza asked the back of her head.

"If it's enough for you, Liza, I haven't done my job as a mother." Bev's bracelets jingled as she clicked the front door closed.

CHICHO'S INSTAGRAM WAS INSUFFERABLE FOR A WHILE. Every hashtag was "the Lord this" and "blessings that." Liza had never heard her friend speak this way. Chicho had also swapped her wild thick curls and heavy mascara for a straightened bouffant and shimmery eyeshadow. Her very Catholic friend was lifting her hands at a nondenominational megachurch and mouthing songs Liza knew she didn't know. Chicho sat at children's bedsides and went to food pantries and fundraisers. Liza had to admit that her friend looked made for this job. She was compassionate and approachable and was the perfect complement to Colin's egregious self-promotion and outright buffoonery.

Liza shifted her phone to the other ear. "Chicho's posts are unrecognizable lately."

"Liza, do not comment. You can't help but sound petty and she is going to think you're jealous," Janae warned.

"Trust me, I am not. We just aren't talking, and this is the only way I can catch up with her."

Liza could hear her sister's annoyance over the phone. "Why don't you just call her?"

"I don't want to burden her with how much my life sucks right now. Our cousin in the permit office is running out of reasons to deny the permit. Our time is running out. I just feel like getting people here to care about what's really happening is hard. I'm going to every council meeting. Plus, WIC and I keep missing each other, trying to connect. And nothing's really official." This was a small white lie. She knew how much the family liked him, but she had been sending some of his calls to voicemail recently. Every call was half flattery, half asking her to do something new. She didn't like to feel used. But Bev had been terrible after Chicho married Colin, and the imaginary deep relationship with WIC was the only thing that kept Bev from flying off the handle with her. Family acceptance was a powerful drug.

"And you think talking to her about what's really wrong is going to make her think you regret turning down Colin?"

"Yep." Liza nodded.

"So you haven't spoken to your best friend in four weeks? You got it all figured out, right, Liza?"

"No, I never said that I did. What about you? You got two offers in New York, and you still haven't responded."

"I know what you're trying to do."

"David is bound to come back to New York soon. You have your pick of jobs there. Talk to him instead of stalking his Instagram and looking around puzzled. You two are the worst."

"Well, don't *you* have all the answers for somebody else's life?" Janae's voice crackled over the phone. "Even if we hung out here, he'd have to go back to France for another four weeks, and he did this without even telling me. Nothing changes the fact that he up and left the country without so much as a text."

"Isn't that something you can talk to him about to his face in New York?"

"It's not always that easy, Liza."

"Janae, I'm not saying that it's easy. I'm saying that at some point you have got to let yourself love again. You've got to let yourself open up. You can't just let love pass through your fingertips. Do *I* like David? Meh. I think he has a weak chin and a goofy laugh. But I think he works for *you*, and he makes *you* happy. You should *fight* for what makes you happy, not run away from it."

"You are so great at mapping out what everyone else should do. But can I share something with you? You're lukewarm on WIC. I can tell. You're only pressing it to shut Ma up. If he stops by, Deya said you're barely even in the room. You leave Ma and Deya to swoon over him while you text with an unsaved number. Like all day, every day."

Liza was glad Janae was on the phone and couldn't see her face. Her ears burned at the mention of her frenzied texting. She thought she was being discreet. But in the past month, she'd waited for Dorsey's thoughtful questions or awkward interpersonal struggles with a little too much breathless anticipation. After all the hateful memes, she helped him deal with the darker, intrusive side of internet fame, and he . . . well, he *listened* to her. He made her feel like she didn't have to shout from 1600 Pennsylvania Avenue to be heard—that she could whisper and he would come running. But it was a spell that was broken too easily by reality.

"So do you want to talk about everyone else's secrets, or do you want to talk about your mystery man?"

"Mystery *man*? Your heteronormativity disappoints me, Janae." She fumbled for something else to focus on. "Deya needs to stay out of my business."

"Is she lying?" Janae challenged.

"Janae, look, I—"

Liza's phone vibrated in her hand. It was a FaceTime request from Chicho, who never FaceTimed since she thought the camera was "too truthful."

"Um, it's Chicho." Liza was as confused as she sounded. She'd probably realized the enormity of her mistake. Liza would not go into "I told you so"s She was bigger than that.

"Chicho? Her ears must be burning."

"Yeah, really. I gotta hop off." Liza pressed the button and answered. "Chicho, is everything okay?"

"No, everything is not okay. The podcast for the inaugural episode is next week, and I have nothing. This is supposed to go on for a year. I don't have one thing written. This is hard, and I want to quit. I need your help. Can you come?" Chicho's face showed guileless panic. A small part of Liza had hoped her friend had finally seen through the fraud that Colin was and wanted to come back home, but she just needed help with her six-figure job.

"I can come."

"Oh, thank god. I can pick you up in a town car. We have a bomb-ass guest room. I want you to stay for the week and hear the first episode."

"I can't hang out at your house for a week."

"Why? Because Mama Bennett is such a charmer?"

"Ugh, she's been terrible for months."

"I know. My mom can hear her telling you and me off through the walls."

"Oh, I saw your dad. He's looking pretty cleaned up."

"Rehab can do that for you. He says he liked the rehab so much that he applied for a job there."

"That's right, I haven't been seeing him during the day, and it's been silent next door." Liza let the silence ring between them. Quiet next door meant Chicho's father hadn't hurt her mother since he'd been back. Liza could hear Chicho's relieved exhalation of breath.

"Come on, Liza, let me call the car for you. I can ask my mother to make mofongo for you. You can eat it all week without me judging you or calling you gordita."

"Oh snap, your mother's mofongo is the best in DC. Okay, call your boy. I'll be packed and ready." All she had to do was play nice with Colin—easy.

BOILED POTATOES

From: JPARK@AjummaTruck.com
To: dorsey@yourmail.com

I'd love to pop over to DC with you. I can't wait to meet this "friend" you keep talking about. Been scrolling through the feeds, and OMG she looks like that French woman I was obsessed with for like three years, Cindy Bruna . . . with an American ass tho and funny captions too. Punching above your weight, bro! You need all the help you can get. Be there @6pm.

Park

"I'm going to tell it to you straight. You need to shit or get off the pot with this Netherfield deal." Senator De Berg squinted at the copy of *Making Marriage Work* he had been flipping through, then turned to Dorsey.

Dorsey was once again in a DC municipal building, getting a lecture about how he should handle this situation.

"We're hungry for new development. You can't allow these

permit tricks to stall you. The Alexandria council welcomes you with open arms, and you don't seem to want to make a move," the senator said.

"Do we know anything about the communities that we're bulldozing?" Dorsey asked.

"What communities? These are mostly abandoned homes. If people cared about them, they wouldn't be abandoned. It really is simple. Don't let those people get under your skin."

"No one's *under my skin*. I just don't understand why this isn't going the way these things usually go."

"You can get away with a lot of stuff in Philly that won't fly in DC. Everything is linked here. If you screw up in DC, you can kiss the federal government, Maryland, and Virginia good-bye."

"I am aware of the stakes, Senator." Dorsey pulled up the knees to his pants and sat.

"If you are aware of the stakes, what were you doing making goo-goo eyes at that Bennett girl at your company's event?"

"Her grandmother won a contest fair and square." It seemed like every step was a misstep where Liza was concerned.

"You can sell that horseshit someplace else. I've been young and rich before. She's a pretty girl who's got the balls to tell you no and doesn't give a damn about your money." The senator turned his attention back to the workbook. "It makes your dick hard and your head soft."

"Senator, I don't appreciate being told how to interact with someone like I'm a child. This is a complex situation that calls for a complex solution, not a whitewashing. I need the room to do that."

"Can I give you a piece of advice, kid? You got a stick up your ass about something. Everybody sees it. I'm rooting for you, but your board, you should know, is *not*. But I'd rather work with you than some new asshole."

"I appreciate the sentiment, but I can handle my board myself."

"Sure, sure." The senator held up his hands. "Look, I have a little friend in that district making a lot of things happen, Colin Gruthers. Why don't you have dinner with us a couple of nights next week? They also want to bring over that Bennett woman from the memes. Apparently, they're friends or related, but not really?"

"Play cousins," Dorsey mumbled.

"What?"

"Nothing."

"I want you two to hash things out so we can get moving. It will also help you see that she's a pain in the ass."

Liza *was* a pain in the ass, mostly because she wouldn't get out of his head. Whenever he got out of the shower. Any time he touched his zipper, he thought of the cool metal chain from Liza's back, and how he wanted to push her against the hard length of him and pound and suck and squeeze until his heart gave out. He thought of how neatly she had fit the hard planes of his body. This woman had been driving him insane. He had never been inclined to have dinner with this politician before, but suddenly his invitations were welcomed.

"What do you like to eat? Maybe my wife, Anne, can make a dish for you?"

"Oh, there's no need for that." Dorsey did not want to over-commit himself. Say yes one time, and he'd be on the calendar for a month.

"How about some Russian food, in honor of your departed brother?"

"My brother was from Slovenia. We've never been to Russia. Don't know much about the cuisine."

"It's settled, then. A night in Moscow with the De Bergs."

Dorsey shuffled his feet.

"A different country each night, and on the last night, the Philippines."

"There's really no need."

"Oh, Anne'll love it."

"I can't come over every night," Dorsey protested.

"Should I just let you know when the girl will be there?" The senator raised his eyebrows. Dorsey nodded and left the room without a goodbye.

WHEN BEVERLY SAW THE TOWN CAR DRIVER BUZZ THE apartment for Liza, she crossed her arms roughly. "Your limousine is here. Enjoy this week with your friend. You're going to need it to realize everything you gave up."

"See you, Ma." Liza's relationship with her mother had never been great. But these six weeks since Chicho had left with Colin tested her more than ever. She would never understand why she and her mother were so at odds about what was important and fundamental. It seemed like an unbreachable gulf. After all the arguments, after all the boiled-over anger, the only thing left was hollow sadness. She wanted a mother-confidante, a mother-cheerleader, a mother's unconditional love. But those things always seemed to evade her.

The ride was quick. She could have taken the train, but Liza knew Chicho wanted to make a point.

Look what I can do now.

I made the right choice.

The cobblestone streets in old Alexandria rumbled pleasantly underneath the town car. It was amazing how a thirty-minute ride could change the landscape so dramatically. From harsh brutalism to quaint eighteenth-century brick homes. A horse-drawn carriage pulled up alongside them at a red light, and Liza tapped on the window to get the sleek black horse's attention.

When the car stopped, Liza pulled a tight smile across her lips. No matter what was said, she would keep her face in a neat, friendly smile. These ankle boots seemed like a great idea until the low tread met the cobblestone.

The ground was slick with chilly rain that had iced over, and Liza's foot slipped on a shallow pool of ice. She braced herself for the fall by flinging her hands out, and she hit the pavement before the driver could catch her. It was softer than she expected, and she was relieved that she hadn't broken anything until she realized the softness was warm and stinky, and her hands and shoulders were covered in horseshit.

"Oh my god, girl, what are you doing down there?"

Colin reached for her, then quickly withdrew his hand.

"Liza! Are you okay?" Chicho rushed to Liza's side, but then also pulled herself back. "Sorry. This is a Rosetta Getty blouse. Can someone help her, please?"

Chicho's little brother, Alfredo, scuttled out of the house and smiled. "Ew, you stink." But he graciously took her arm anyway.

Colin covered his face and shooed Liza and the boy around the building. Once they were out of earshot, she nuzzled Alfredo.

"Ew, gross!" He laughed.

"Do you like it here, Fredo?" Liza asked.

"My school is awesome, and the people are nice."

"That's good," Liza said. "Go get my bags and put them in

my room. Tell your sister to take out my good jeans and the gross shirt. She'll know what I mean."

Half an hour later, Liza was showered and sitting awkwardly in the living room in her snug jeans and a **GRAB 'EM BY THE PUSSY** shirt, listening to Colin describe every politician he had ever met. She tapped her phone to call up Dorsey's texts. They were becoming a comfort to her, something she had come to expect every day. She texted:

> At Play Cousin & BFFs house.

His reply was quick, as if his phone had been in his hand.

> How is that going?

> I fell in horse manure so . . .

> Genius plan! Make them want to make you leave immediately.

> I think I still have shit somewhere. It's coming off in waves

> It's the hair clip.

> You're right I should take it off

Three dots.

> No, wait. It's the bra.

> Good idea! That's off too

> I'm on my way.

Liza laughed out loud in the quiet room and jolted everyone out of their polite and quiet agreement on the grandeur of the home. Colin touched her arm. "Did you know I brushed past the First Lady at a book signing? She's not *that* nice," he stage-whispered.

"Honey, why don't we show Liza around the place?"

Colin walked Liza around their historic home, giving her infinite details about the original windows and the procedures associated with changing the baseboards in a historic home. "Senator De Berg has been kind enough to supplement the cost of some upgrades like central heating. Do you know how expensive installing central heating in a historic home is?"

"I bet it's a lot," Liza mumbled.

"Tons," Colin corrected. For the third time, he looked down at her shirt.

"If we dine out with Senator De Berg, you won't be wearing that shirt, will you?"

Liza looked down innocently. "I was thinking about it."

"Once again, he is an ally," Colin warned.

"Then he'll laugh it off."

"It's crude."

"It's true."

"Liza," Chicho interrupted. "What about that cute little military-style blazer you have? Did you bring that? It would go great with your jeans and can class up your shirt."

Liza loved that jacket. Chicho knew this. They looked at each other for a minute.

"C'mon. It gives you Janet Jackson 'Rhythm Nation' vibes," Chicho wheedled.

"I know." Liza rolled her eyes and slumped her shoulders. "I'll wear the jacket." Chicho mouthed, "Thank you," and Liza checked off a box inside her head.

- Smooth sailing with my BFF

Honestly, she and Chicho hadn't talked much these past several weeks, and when they did, the conversation had taken on a new strained quality. Liza was frantically asking after everything with fake cheerfulness, and Chicho tried to tamp down her enthusiasm for her new life.

"The senator's friends with Only Ms. Venezuela." She used their nickname for Dorsey. "You're just now getting over all of the memes, but I couldn't tell him no."

"No, it's fine." Liza pressed her lips firmly together and tried not to make any sudden moves. She knew Chicho would read her like a book. She would sniff out Liza's wobbling facade of dislike before Liza even had a chance to truly understand it. Whatever this companionable texting thing that had sprung up between her and Dorsey was, Liza knew what it *wasn't*. It wasn't sex, and it wasn't cheap. The depth of vulnerability they had shared with each other over text was just the tenderest thing in her fucking life right now. And she wasn't ready to spoil that feeling just yet with flashlights and cross-examinations.

"Y'all, I thought we were going out tonight. But this one is better. We've been invited in!" Colin squealed. Chicho and Alfredo cheered.

"Invited *in* is about six times as personal as being invited out," Alfredo said sagely before Colin could say it himself. Liza saw a tinge of pride in Colin's eyes. It was clear he had come to love Fredo, and for that, Liza gave him a break and held up one hand in a limp "raise the roof" pantomime.

"The senator said he's especially excited to see you again, Liza!"

DORSEY SAT IN THE BACK OF THE TOWN CAR PEELING away calluses on his hands. He had a nervous habit when he was a child of biting the rough skin, which had suddenly surfaced again out of nowhere. He planned to close the loop on his strange preoccupation with Liza Bennett and had called in his closest friend for reinforcement. Park was one of the most affable people he'd ever met, with a rare combination of charm and substance that made him irresistible to ladies even when he'd had empty pockets. They had met when Dorsey was on an ill-fated date at a Korean dumpling class in New York, and Park was the instructor making ends meet. The girl didn't last, but the friendship had.

"You look like you're about to get hit by a bus, dude."

"Maybe I am." Dorsey shifted in the back of the car.

"Oh, I have got to meet this woman. Instagram is not enough. All the lovely ladies I try to set you up with come back and tell me you're an impossible *kkadonam*."

"I don't know Korean, but I have a feeling that's some kind of asshole. Why? Because you keep trying to hook me up with your chatty Korean cousins?" Dorsey rolled his eyes.

"They're women, aren't they? And you mean to tell me that *this* woman tolerates you? A sister? From Wokeville, USA?"

Joseph Park was from a diverse and culturally fluid space that gave him the ability to relate to just about anyone. He had grown up in Flushing, Queens, and had one foot in old Korea and another foot in the hot food truck scene. His Ajumma House Korean food trucks were parked in nearly every major metropolitan area.

"Well, I think she more than tolerates me? I think we're kind of serious."

"Serious? Have you been on *one* date?"

"It's complicated. We can't be out in public. It's a whole thing."

Dorsey handed Joseph the phone and scrolled through the text messages quickly so he couldn't read too deeply.

"Is this just today?" Park whistled.

Dorsey nodded.

"Damn. This is more than I've ever texted anyone. Like in my whole life. Wait, what is IFF?"

"Don't read my texts."

"You handed me your texts!" Park was incredulous.

"To see the amount. Not to read, you nosy mofo. IFF is International Food Friday. Liza and I choose a country—it started off as a joke about the senators little parties—and we FoodDash—"

Park swiped at the air. "Never mind. I thought it was some freaky shit. But that sounds boring."

Dorsey ran his fingers through his hair. "Park, I want to take a big step, and I want her to feel safe and—"

"Which is why you're bringing your Korean lucky charm?"

"You *are* charming and Korean."

"I'm honored to be your wingman, Dorsey, but my job is to be the voice of reason for you. You've never been this close to the L word. I'm gonna have to play bad cop with her. If a woman who looks like that Instagram photo gets anywhere near your dick, you're going to buy her an island. So, you need to be sure."

Dorsey blew out his breath and opened the car door. It was not Park's charm or discernment Dorsey was relying on tonight; it was his ability to make Dorsey feel safe and normal, even funny. Park's presence was more courage-inducing than tequila, without the headache in the morning. His heart hammered in his chest, and before he could knock, the door swung open. The housekeeper's face met his with a deflated sigh. Joseph snorted and pushed Dorsey's shoulder.

The housekeeper led them down the hallway, brimming with glossy prints of the senator's wife, Anne. Anne on a horse. Anne blowing out candles. Always the same angle, always the same sullen face. The hallway was a shrine to Anne's discontent with her life. When they rounded the corner, the smell of German pretzel bread, sauerkraut, and sausage made his stomach churn. What on earth had he signed up for? Wasn't this Russia night?

"Happy Fasching!" Liza popped up like she was bursting out of a birthday cake. *Is she happy to see me?* Dorsey's eyes zeroed in on her chest. Did she have her bra on? He vowed to check personally. Liza laughed out loud, probably because she knew the direction of his thoughts. *Yes, she is happy to see me.* That small realization made his throat feel thick and his face hot.

Dorsey cleared his throat, too afraid his voice would crack with emotion if he spoke. Liza was radiant. Bright teeth, reddish brown curls swept up in a high puff, and curly bangs across her forehead. She wore a dark military-cut jacket with a shirt on which, as hard as he tried, he could only make out the word "pussy" across her low belly.

That's it. She was taunting him. He knew it.

"It's German Lent! Can I interest you in some boiled potatoes?" Liza asked, the teasing still in her eyes. Dorsey turned to see Park beaming. So much for bad cop.

Colin stood up. "The best boiled potatoes you'll ever have, I'm sure!"

"I think if you've tasted one boiled potato—" Park started.

Liza shook her head. "No, *these* will be the best boiled potatoes you've ever had." Park laughed a funny little laugh, and Dorsey was suddenly struck with the fear that Joseph would see Liza's magnetism and sparkle too. Why would he then want to be his wingman when he could have her himself? He was everything a woman like Liza would like.

No, I'm being paranoid.

Liza walked around the table, and when Dorsey saw those jeans, his eyes shot heavenward in a prayer for mercy.

Where would you even buy pants that snug? The children's section? The jeans hugged her curved thighs and slender hips. A fine figure, his father would say, a fine-figured gal. *Her ass is a damned masterpiece of biological engineering.*

Dorsey greeted the senator with a tight nod, still not completely over the kick in the chest those jeans were. "I want to introduce Joseph Park, one of my closest friends." He could see Colin scrolling on his phone.

"Celebrity chef, the king of Queens, Asian fusion guru, affordable-chic food magnate Joseph Park?" Colin asked.

Park pulled at the collar of his shirt. "Yep, all of that!" Everyone at the table laughed. Park made the rounds, shaking everyone's hands and charming them effortlessly. Dorsey made an undignified sprint, just beating out Chicho for the seat next to Liza, while Park sat across from him. A woman came to pour the wine, and Liza and Dorsey reached for the same wineglass.

"Wineglasses go just above the knife, which will be on *your* right." Dorsey managed a smile. *I'm doing it. Relating without sounding like a robot.*

"I really should brush up on my Emily Post," Liza quipped. She looked slightly embarrassed.

Oh god, did I call too much attention to her mistake? I'm terrible at this. Every time he looked up, his eyes met Liza's. She would flit her eyes away, or he would pretend to look down into his drink. Drinks that were flowing a bit too freely for Dorsey's liking. He was suddenly glad he hadn't driven, because his head was swimming. He wasn't sure if it was his prolonged proximity to Liza or the wine. Her sparkle made everyone seem like such dull company. It wasn't just him who seemed to think so—everyone asked her questions and picked her brain for outrageous tidbits.

"Ron absolutely didn't deserve Hermione," Liza finished. "He negged her the entire series!"

Park scoffed. "Get out of here with your Hufflepuff sensibilities. It's a Gryffindor or Slytherin world out there."

"Hermione chose exactly who she wanted!" Anne said. It was the first topic Dorsey had seen her passionate about. Had everyone seen this film? Anne was a generation ahead of him and followed this conversation. Why hadn't he just sat down and watched the damn movies? All he knew was Harry was good and the green dudes were bad, but he had never understood why.

Liza crossed her arms. "I ship Hermione and Harry all. Day." She clapped her hands for punctuation.

"Why would Harry do that to his friend?" Park asked.

"Now who has Hufflepuff sensibilities? The heart wants what the heart wants." Liza shrugged.

"Forget Hufflepuff, that is so Slytherin of you." Park laughed. "Dorsey's got a Slytherin streak too."

"I will not even pretend to understand what exactly you all

are talking about," Dorsey said quietly. When Joseph rolled his eyes, Dorsey added hastily, "But I vaguely remember the green guys—"

"Slytherins," Liza said.

"I think Slytherins get a bad rap." The table groaned around him. *Oh boy, am I bad at this.* Only Liza slapped the table decisively.

"Oh my god, thank you for your bravery," she said. "What is wrong with ambition? That is J. K. Rowling's Britishness erupting all over the page." Liza smiled at Dorsey, and he smiled weakly back. How could he steer this conversation to a comfortable place?

"I enjoy the animated series *Avatar*," Dorsey said haltingly. Why couldn't he be the man he was in texts? Why was it so hard to push out these words?

Liza's brows rose in surprise. "I . . . I think Katara was underutilized."

Dorsey nodded. "I mean, she could blood-bend."

"Right, just do what you have to do to win the war," Park said.

Dorsey, buoyed by the positive reactions, continued. "And Aang and Katara were a terrible match."

"Zuko and Katara . . ." Dorsey and Liza blurted out at the same time. He nodded, and Liza finished.

"Zuko and Katara were a better couple," she said.

Park scoffed. "He was a jerk to her. Just like Ron."

"The heart wants what it wants," Dorsey said. When Liza looked up at him, the bottom dropped out of his belly.

"What do you think, Lucia?" Park asked.

"Liza and I have been down this road before. We have a binding agreement. I won't talk about *Unsolved Mysteries* and *The*

First 48, and she won't talk about her cartoons," Chicho said, and Liza laughed.

"Yes, we called that the Treaty of Paris, I think," Liza said.

"Do you all name your friend truces?" Park asked. "Dorsey, we have to do that."

"What is your Magna Carta?" Dorsey asked.

"Don't like the same boys," they both said in unison.

Dorsey looked over to Colin. "Solid pact," was all he said. Liza put her hand to her mouth like her wine might spill out.

A tiny droplet fell onto the fabric of her white shirt, spreading and staining just above the peak of her nipple. He couldn't believe she actually hadn't worn that bra. He could make out the sway of her breast easily in the snug shirt. Maybe he could get that wine stain out with his mouth? His balls tightened. He must have veins bulging out of the side of his neck.

Shit.

How long have I been staring at her nipples?

Liza's speech was slowing down. Could she be as nervous as he?

He looked over at his glass and realized she had been drinking from both his and her own glasses. Perhaps the unflappable woman needed a little liquid courage tonight. Dorsey looked down at his hands, then surprised himself by grazing Liza's thigh with his knuckles. He couldn't keep his hands off her. She looked up at him, grabbed his wineglass, and finished the contents in one swallow, her eyes never leaving his.

The game is afoot.

WHAT ARE THE TOP THINGS TO DO IN ALEXANDRIA?"
After a moment, Liza continued, "Wrong answers only."
Liza posed with her selfie stick in the senator's bathroom. It
was so luxe with its red cloth wallpaper, gold finishes, and
Tuscan tile that Liza didn't think she'd find a better spot to
stream. Let her followers think she was joining them from a Ro-
man bath.

"'Oh lord . . . the men . . . Stay away, Liza girl,'" she read from
the comments.

"Don't worry about me and men tonight," she replied to the
comment. "You ever had the feeling that the room is full of gaso-
line and you have a match in your pocket?"

Oh, you gon' burn it up tonight, Liza?

She laughed. "I want to do damage, DC family. Okay, I have
one more post tonight, and you'll never know where I'll be. This
WQUR live cast is, as always, brought to you by our friends
at Pemberley Development. They put the *trust* in 'trust fund
kids.'"

WHEN THE FAMOUS POTATOES WERE FINALLY SERVED,
Dorsey found them lifeless, saltless, and hard to boot. The sauerkraut was bitter and the bratwurst greasy. It was one of the worst
meals he'd ever eaten. Liza had artfully spaced all the food on
her plate to give the illusion of an eaten meal. His thigh pressed
against hers. It was everything he could do to hold his hands at
his sides. Seeing her, being near her again, was just too intense
for him. They had kept a loose correspondence in these three
months, with quick teasing texts or memes. Their communication seemed almost easy. And communication had *never* come
easy to Dorsey. Liza didn't know how he agonized for hours
before he sent her a message. She would shoot back something
pithy, and he would be reeling all over again. It was what made
him get over his second thoughts about her family and come to
see her.

"Liza," Senator De Berg boomed across the table, "I hear
you're here to help Lucia with her podcast. Are you a good inter-
viewer?"

"Not really. My show isn't really that format."

"Have you heard that podcast *Serial*? Can you make the podcast a little like that?"

"A true-crime mystery women's Christian podcast?" Liza
smirked.

The senator nodded wistfully. "I could've been a reporter. I
have an instinct, you know? And I don't give up. With a little
training, I could have been at the *Washington Post*."

"Oh, most definitely, sir, and excelling at that as much as you
do your public service work," Colin simpered.

"It's a similar skill," Chicho said.

"That's right. I could see this wall full of Pulitzers had I just pushed in the opposite direction." The senator pulled up his high school newspaper pictures, kept at the ready on his Facebook profile. He passed the phone around. Everyone nodded politely. Except for Colin, who sighed in awe.

"We're all so glad you chose public service, Senator."

"Public service," the senator said, pausing wistfully, "chose me."

Dorsey saw Liza and Park roll their eyes together.

"So, Liza, how's your crusade against progress going?" the senator asked.

"Progressing, actually." Liza smiled tightly.

"I got a look at that amateurish proposal you drafted."

Dorsey saw Liza look over to Colin, then to him. "There are still some wrinkles to iron out," she said.

Dorsey kept his eyes on her sleek hands and the tiny little gold rings on each finger. A cracked-screen Apple Watch looked incongruous on her slender wrist.

"People aren't taking you seriously after those photos, huh?" Senator De Berg's response was tinged with a touch of glee. Dorsey couldn't read Liza. She just blinked and held her composure at the senator's remarks. Maybe she had a lot of practice dodging mean comments. "If you're still having trouble getting into the room where it happens, call me." The senator was smug. Dorsey wanted to punch the smile right off his face.

"I have had trouble being taken seriously since the gala. I've lost followers and credibility." Liza was clear-eyed and focused. The vulnerability she could express while still looking like a badass was a thing of wonder to him. "But if I got into this work just for the likes, I would have quit a long time ago." She gave the senator a hard stare. "My work doesn't have to be public and loud to be good. In fact, you'll find that my 'amateurish' proposal has been vetted by several council members and may quietly land on their desk for approval. And then my quietly drafted legislation will make it just a little harder for companies to come in and overturn apple carts."

"Dorsey, you hear this? Liza's got plans for all of your work." The senator was out for blood.

"I wish Liza luck in *all* of her endeavors. I hope in the future we can work together toward the *same* goal."

The senator's face did some facsimile of a smile. But his eyes burned in anger. "Okay, cut the horseshit," he said through forced laughter. "You don't want her to succeed. How could you? She's your enemy."

"A wise man said I should choose my friends for their good looks, and my enemies for their intellects." Park looked from Dorsey to Liza, then to the senator. "Who said that, Dorsey?"

"Oscar Wilde, I believe." Dorsey dabbed at the corners of his mouth.

Liza looked up. "You know, it's funny, when it rains, it pours. They got money for wars but can't feed the poor." Liza smiled and took on the same confident air as Park. "Who said that, Chicho?" Liza looked at her friend.

Colin shot daggers at Chicho, and Chicho put her head down.

Before Liza's face could fall, Dorsey answered, "I believe it was Tupac."

Park winked at him, and Dorsey had to stop himself from kicking him under the table.

Dorsey was egged on nonetheless and continued. "It's interesting how government deprioritization of the poor gets trans-

lated into corporate responsibility." Dorsey was rewarded with
a surprised look from Liza.

Liza moved her food around her plate. "Dorsey, you know
Tupac, but not *Harry Potter*?"

"Oh, I can explain this." Park put down his fork. "Dorsey is a
die-hard West Coast rap aficionado."

Dorsey shook his head. "Not this again." It was Park's favorite piece of knowledge about Dorsey.

"Even when faced with the superior lyrics of Biggie, Jay Z,
Nas, and Meek Mill. Despite growing up in Philly, he still stans
Dr. Dre, Tupac, and Kendrick Lamar—as if they compare." Park
laughed.

"I have no coastal allegiance for hip-hop," Colin said.

Liza's improperly placed napkin fell from the table, and
Dorsey caught it before it hit the ground. "Liza, my brother,
Alexi, is—*was*—into West Coast rap. Those lyrics take up a
ridiculous portion of my brain."

Liza took the napkin from his hand and put it back on the
table. *Why does she never put napkins on her lap?* She had made fun
of his persnickety napkining at the hotel bar. But he didn't care;
there was a wrong and right way to do things. Dorsey took the
napkin again and folded it over her lap. Not missing the opportunity to run his thumbs across her thighs. He realized that the
table had gone quiet when Colin cleared his throat.

"Chicho and I are really moving away from the violence of
hip-hop into safer, calmer music. Right, Chicho?" Chicho nodded, and Liza put her fork down noisily. Dorsey wondered how
she and Chicho were doing. It must not be easy to see her friend
attached to someone like Colin, who seemed to always be cam-
paigning for elected office, even at dinner. Silence once again
rolled over the table.

"And that, folks, is how you entertain," the senator boomed, cracking the silence, and Colin immediately began hooting with laughter, followed by Chicho and Fredo. Liza looked impatient for this night to be over. It was time to get down to the business of his visit.

Be bold, Dorsey. Say what you want.

"Liza," he began, his voice coming out too loud. *Keep your cool.* "Park is an avid Korean rap fan. I know you were looking for worldwide collections."

Liza's eyes widened. "Oh yes. I'm doing these hip-hop show-cases on my radio program."

"Can we show you his collection and mine? He's out with me in Georgetown," Dorsey said hopefully.

"I could come hang out, sure. I'd"—she risked a glance at Chicho—"I'd have to get back here, though. We have work to do tomorrow."

"Of course, of course," Park said through smiles, lifting up from the table so forcefully he tipped his plate. "Which jacket is yours?"

"Oh, you mean right now?" Liza looked like she was holding in an eruption of laughter. "Chicho, wanna come?"

"Um . . ."

Colin popped up and called out, "Lu-Chee-yuh."

Liza handed her friend a jacket and wiggled her eyebrows. Daring her to ignore her husband.

"Lucia and I still have a bit to do this evening, and we have quite an early morning. So we can't afford to be so impulsive," Colin said.

Chicho put her light jacket back on the hook and, after a beat, smiled brightly. "It's crazy over here tonight. You all go, and I'll see you back tonight, Liza."

Park put his arm around Liza and pulled her into the night.

———

WITHIN FIVE MINUTES, DORSEY SETTLED IN THE BACK OF the town car next to Liza. Dorsey reached over her to finesse a missing seat belt strap out of a crevice. Liza didn't bring her jacket. She was either a notorious underdresser or she meant to torture him all night. If he looked down at this moment, he would be achingly close to her mouth. He couldn't feel any puffs of air on his neck, so he knew she was holding her breath. Just two inches and a mile of courage separated his face from the graceful hollow of her neck. He wanted to kiss her there. *Would she taste like cinnamon and sugar?* Finally, he pulled the strap across her, and he saw her exhale shakily when his knuckles grazed her nipples, pressing out prominently through the fabric of the shirt.

"First things first: I'm sensitive to smells. Did you find out what was still smelling like horseshit?" Dorsey whispered, even though they were the only people in the car.

"I took my bra off just to be safe." Liza kept her eyes on him. Dorsey looked down again at her hardened nipples—that red wine stain spread out over her taut peaks.

His throat went dry.

Park was saying his elaborate goodbyes, and, God help him, Dorsey wanted to ditch his friend. He'd begged this man to make the four-hour trip from New York to DC. Now Park has designated himself "bad cop," and his only plan is cock-blocking Dorsey.

His voice was thick with desire. "I'm glad you took the proper precautions."

Park opened the door to the town car and smiled. "Y'all ready for some proper food?"

Dorsey and Liza both nodded vigorously.

"My tongue was in jail," Liza said.

"My spirit left my body," Dorsey complained.

"I know a cry for help when I hear one," Park said. "What stores are still open?"

Dorsey sighed. He wanted food, especially Park's food, but not more than he wanted Liza alone in his bed.

Fifteen minutes later, they stopped at a grocery store and raided the aisles. Liza rolled her basket down the aisles and raced with Park to find the ingredients he listed. Dorsey laughed along with them. He wished he could make her laugh like that.

Liza counted all the items in the basket, carefully switching out Park's ingredients for items on sale. "What are we making, Park?"

Park slapped her hands when she reached for his expensive rice. "Woman, don't mess with a chef's rice. We're making *arroz caldo.*"

Liza gave up her item swapping with an eye roll. "What is it? Rice something?" Liza asked.

"It's a rice porridge with chicken," Dorsey said.

"Are you gonna show us how to make it?" Liza rubbed her palms together.

"*We* know how to make it. I'm gonna teach you," Park said.

"Taught by a famous chef!" Liza said. Dorsey's heart hammered with a mix of fear and anticipation. *She likes Joseph Park. Who wouldn't?* Why would he introduce two of the most charming people he'd ever met and think they wouldn't hit it off?

"And D here is gonna be the taste tester," Park said.

"If he doesn't like it?" Liza asked.

"Back to the drawing board," Park said. Still teasing, slightly flirting. Dorsey was already reading their wedding announcement in the *Washington Post*.

When it was time to check out, Liza and Dorsey pulled the cart toward the attendant while Joseph pulled it toward the self-checkout.

Liza and Dorsey spoke up in unison, "Oh no."

Park's shoulders slumped. "Liza, don't tell me you're like him."

Liza lifted her haughty chin. "Self-checkout is a scam."

"Truer words were never spoken," Dorsey said.

"You two are ridiculous. There is no line, and there is an eighty-year-old cashier in aisle four! This is a no-brainer," Park said.

"It will always take longer," Liza said. Her tone was imperious, and her little button nose tilted even higher in the air. "There is always something that doesn't scan or that doesn't work. It is a time suck. Not to mention they fire tons of employees to build those things."

"And you have to bag your own groceries!" Dorsey said.

"So the part you hate is bagging your own groceries?" Liza teased.

"Among other things."

"How about this? I'll take half the groceries, and you take care of the others. The first person bagged and at the exit wins," Park said.

Liza looked positively gleeful. "What do we win?"

"Let's focus on if you lose. If you lose, you two will have to do this same thing again tomorrow night but with my favorite food, Korean dumplings."

"And if we win?" Dorsey asked, liking the sound of "we" on his tongue.

"You get to be right. It sounds like winning is enough for you two," Park said.

Liza shook her head—unhappy with the terms. "I want you to cook my favorite meal. Butter chicken with garlic naan."

Dorsey knew that the little fact of Liza's favorite food would rattle around in his head forever—the way her ice cream memory had. He thought of this little place in London Liza would love—best butter chicken he'd ever tasted.

Park, secure in his own victory, only shrugged. "Bet."

Liza turned and raced toward lane four, holding Dorsey's hand to pull him along. Dorsey filed this date away. *The first time we held hands was . . .*

He let himself be pulled until they got to the checkout. She still hadn't let his hand go. Even still, he hoped no one in the store recognized them. He never wanted her to go through that intense bullying again. She didn't deserve it. Her touch was suddenly everything he wanted to feel. God, he had to stop before his erection burst out of his jeans. The aisle was tight enough to hide his arousal, thank God, but one wrong step and Liza would feel just how excited he was to have her so close to him. He reached for a gossip magazine and pretended to examine it. He would need something to cover his embarrassment when they were out of the checkout aisle. Liza's jeans were positively painted on. And her ass was incredible. Damnit, he was only making it worse! *Look up and count the fluorescent rectangles.*

The cashier greeted them warmly and Liza stepped back absently, pushing her plump bottom onto Dorsey's rock-hard length. The gasp she let out set him aflame. But instead of shouting out in disgust, she leaned into him, pressing her shoulders to his chest. Dorsey's throat was suddenly parched.

He wanted to spread her open right now on the conveyor belt. Let the eggs tumble to the sticky floor as she held on to the periodicals for support and he pounded into her. Before his fantasy became too X-rated, the cashier pulled Dorsey out of his

lull by shouting the total for all the items. After Dorsey paid,
Liza looked down and handed him a bag of groceries. She smiled.

"Button your coat or we'll have to explain yet another meme."

He awkwardly walked around with the throbbing in his midsection. He had worked his entire life to cultivate a polished restraint. He didn't want to be the adopted child who did not live
up to his father's name. He had worked hard to be thoughtful,
slow to react, and dispassionate for fear of what they would say
about him if he was anything less. But this woman had him in a
constant meme loop on Twitter and Instagram. She had him in
the company of people he would have otherwise avoided. She
also had his pants tented in the grocery checkout. How had he
gotten here? He heard her laugh as she saw Joseph Park trying
to wave down an attendant for a finger of ginger without a sticker.

"Lane four is open," Liza called. "Betty's a real wiz!"

Joseph Park punched in numbers on one hand and held up his
middle finger with the other.

"Any of you have a damned Savers card?"

THEY REACHED DORSEY'S LOFT, LOADED DOWN WITH
groceries. Park seemed to remember every embarrassing story
he had about Dorsey and relayed them all to Liza on the way
over. Liza laughed that full-belly way he was coming to know as
her genuine laugh. She threw her head back, giving Dorsey a
view of her slender neck. He would bury his face in the crook of
that neck by the end of the night, he vowed.

LIZA DANCED TO KOREAN HIP-HOP AS SHE STIRRED THE
onion. Joseph threw finely diced ginger and garlic into the sauté

pan. She was aware of Dorsey watching her dance. She was aware of Dorsey, period.

"How do I know when it's done?"

"You'll smell it," Joseph said. "Dorsey, how is the rice coming along?"

"You put me in charge of the most boring activity."

Liza had never seen Dorsey so relaxed and natural. She shook her head. She had been half on fire all night because of him. He stripped her of all her finely held ideas, all her notions, grinding everything down to one crystallizing fact: she wanted him. Maybe not forever. Maybe not even for a week. But right now, for tonight. It bothered her how primitive it all was. A rich, out-of-reach man, a tight butt, and an erection—it was some kind of basic recipe. And she hated to be lured by it. It would mean that she wasn't who she said she was. Was she principled, or would she bend the rules when they suited her? Could happiness really be found in the arms of a man? Her body screamed, *Yes.* God, she was just like her mother but with a master's degree.

In her pensiveness, she had stopped stirring, and Joseph furrowed his eyebrows at her in question. Liza snapped back and swirled the onions, garlic, and ginger vigorously—too vigorously, it seemed.

"Whoa. Your head's in the clouds," Dorsey said.

As if you didn't put it there.

He was suddenly behind her. His hand covered hers, and he slowed her furious mix down to a steady swirl. "Easy," his voice rumbled in her ear.

His other hand rested loosely on her hip. The heat of it warmed her insides and made her pulse. If she didn't release this pressure, she would burst.

Liza blushed to her toes. *Dear lord, how would she last the night?*

When her eyes flicked down to Dorsey's hands, he flitted them away and returned to the sticky rice sitting in cool bowls. He looked chastened. How could he still be unsure of where he stood with her? Liza wondered if she was aware of what she wanted herself. When the food was finished, Joseph seasoned the flavorful bowl with salt and pepper, then garnished it with green onion and lemon slices. She took pictures for her Instagram feed, carefully disabling the location as she bragged online about her bowl of rice.

When Joseph Park popped up to take credit for the dish, her feed exploded.

He took a video of her dancing to Korean hip-hop and posted: **The face behind the voice. The moves behind the jams. #givesajam #goodgirl #wherewereU #askingforafriend**

Liza looked at her profile. She had over a thousand new followers in twenty minutes.

"Dorsey? Are you ready to taste?" Joseph asked.

"I've been ready for a long time," Dorsey said. His eyes were not on the steaming bowl, but on Liza.

Liza crept toward him, careful not to spill the contents of the wooden spoon. She nestled between his thighs and lifted the long-handled spoon to Dorsey's lips. He parted his mouth and tasted the first bite. His eyes closed. "Mmmm, damn." Dorsey swallowed. "That's missing something, though." Liza's shoulders sagged. Dorsey reached behind her and pulled the bottle of fish sauce off the counter. He then poured nearly half the contents of the bottle into the bowl, splashing it everywhere, then mixed it in with the wooden spoon. "Try me again."

Liza held the spoon up again, and he took a generous portion and rolled his eyes. "Good lord, that's delicious." Dorsey took the spoon from Liza's hand and held it up to her lips. "Taste," he said.

She parted her mouth tentatively, and Dorsey wiggled the spoon. "Open for me." He coaxed and when she made a soft slurping sound, the spoon trembled in her mouth and the softest whimper escaped his lips. The soup *was* delicious. So warm and perfect for the still chilly March weather.

"It's amazing."

"Thank me later!" Joseph headed to the stairs. "I'll be back down in five."

"Thank you, Joseph," Liza said. Dorsey's friend was a breath of fresh air. She was surprised by her immediate fondness for him.

"Call me Park."

"I've always tried to make this myself, but it never comes out this good," Dorsey told Liza.

"I have a golden-brown thumb. It's like a green thumb but for cooking," Park called as he disappeared up the stairs.

"Don't take credit for my masterpiece," Liza teased.

It was insane how quickly their spoons clattered against the bowl. Liza met Dorsey's gaze. He still looked hungry.

"Done eating?" she asked.

"Not even started," Dorsey pulled an old iPod and speaker out of a messenger bag, placed them on the kitchen counter, and hit play. "Shall we?" he asked. He poured enormous glasses of dark red wine that clinked as he padded barefoot to the living room. He placed the glasses down carefully on a wooden slate and pressed a button on a gray remote. Instantly, a fire sprang to life in the chilly room. "Dim the lights," he said aloud.

Liza smirked as the lights immediately turned down.

He sat wide-legged on the carpet and patted the soft spot near him.

The red wine was warm and buttery, and Liza let her back rest on his chest. So this was what it was like to feel completely at ease with someone. His big hands moved across her belly.

He looked up at the loft. "Liza," his voice rumbled in her ear. "I want to— Can I?" Liza was prepared to say yes to just about anything:

- Butt stuff
- Another chick
- Strap-ons

He asked for none of that.

"Kiss you?" he finished. He pulled her up to straddle him faster than she could say, "Hell yes." Liza gasped as his mouth opened over hers, and his tongue swept inside. The tight bowstrings of her body were suddenly cut all at once. *Why had he taken so long?* He held her tightly and coaxed and teased with his tongue. His hand slid up her rib cage and caressed her back before it found her aching breast.

"No bra. This drove me crazy all night." He rolled the firm bud between his thumb and forefinger. He used his other hand to push her hip harder into him. Liza placed her hands on his chest; the rapid pace of his heartbeat was like a drum under her hand. He stretched and hardened underneath her.

"Is this what you came for, Liza?" Dorsey said, rocking her again on his hardness. She fluttered open like a dark-petaled peony. When she arched her back, he took her breast in his mouth, sucking greedily over the thin T-shirt. A loud moan escaped her, and Dorsey clamped his hand over her mouth and continued his intense sucking and grinding. She moaned into his hand and bit the rough skin.

Shit, this got intense fast. If he found the right spot, she would come with her clothes on like in high school. He was too damned in control of himself. Liza knew Park was just upstairs. She understood Dorsey's restraint, but feverish need pulsed through her, and she wished he'd lay her down on this fancy-ass rug and fuck the way his eyes had told her he wanted to. Park could watch, for all she cared.

Liza didn't expect this. Or rather, she didn't expect for his kiss to be so jarring. His hands found the flimsy snap of her jeans, then the lace of her panties.

Gentle strokes, lord help her, such tiny tender strokes separated her folds.

"Liza, this pussy is as hot and wet as I thought it would be." His mouth closed over hers again. He had thought about how hot and wet she would be. Well, she had the benefit of knowing exactly how his hard dick felt against her.

Something frayed inside her. Because suddenly she could see why people threw themselves into the arms of lovers, despite the wreckage it would cause. She understood how so many things could fall away in someone's arms. He rubbed her clit and she ground into his hand.

"Shit, he's coming." He pulled away from her, and his eyes were just as surprised as hers. As if he didn't know he would kiss her until his lips met hers.

"What, you're coming?" Confused, Liza's head swirled with sensory input.

Park came back from wherever he had scurried off to and made conspicuous noises announcing his presence.

"Damn! Mood change," Park said. Liza hopped off Dorsey like he was made of hot coals and folded her hands over the wet spot on her shirt. It was translucent now, and one could make out the brown edges of the nipple underneath. Shit, she would need to go to the bathroom to finish herself off. From the looks of him, Dorsey would beat her to it. He didn't even try to hide his glossed lips and dazed expression.

He licked his fingers. Actually licked. Like she was the last bit of sticky, sweet dessert. He got up and made for the bathroom, and it was a herculean feat to not follow him there and help him out. Minutes passed in deeply awkward silence. Park's eyes bounced away from her as she looked toward the bathroom. That she knew what he was doing in there continued to light her on fire. The thought of him stroking himself, wanting her so badly, maybe calling her name out, had her rocking in her seat.

After a few minutes, Dorsey opened the bathroom door and found her eyes again. The intensity of his gaze and the set of his jaw would have terrified a lesser woman. Even if she had never seen an I'm-going-to-fuck-the-shit-out-of-you face, it was the type of look she knew when she saw it. She wouldn't get out of this untouched tonight.

They spent the night writing, listening, choosing songs, and guzzling wine. Liza absorbed a ton of information about the history of music in the Philippines and Korea, and she built playlists that would tell a story of the people. Dorsey played "Respeto" in the background and got into a real shouting match with Park over Filipino rapper Gloc-9 vs South Korean Keith Ape. Liza held her hands up when they looked at her to confirm a point. She wasn't interested in telling someone else's story and co-opting it. She lined up culturally appropriate guest DJs and librarians who would come onto her show. Park even gave her a few restaurants where she could go on location and promote. The result was a full sensory experience completely mapped out. When it was time for this radio installation, it would be her best. Liza checked her phone. *Shit, it's three thirty in the morning.* She needed to keep her promise to Chicho.

Dorsey caught her looking. "I know you have to go."

"I'm having a great time. I just promised Chicho . . ." Her tone was tinged with a little regret. She wanted this night to end differently.

"I understand. I'll take you in the town car." Dorsey was clutching his wallet.

Liza's eyebrow shot up. "Is Raymond still up?"

"Who is Raymond?" Dorsey asked.

"Your driver. He has two kids. I may have told him you would tip him an insane amount."

"When did you have time to get the driver's life story? And exactly how much did you promise him?" Dorsey asked. When she shrugged, he continued. "Yes, I informed him I would be returning you safely to Alexandria."

"Shall we?" Liza asked.

Dorsey smiled a wolfish smile. "We shall."

Park lowered his chin and made no move to join them, and Liza felt a flutter low in her belly. With Park gone, they had nothing but themselves and the attraction between them, which still flowed and crackled like an electrical current. Dorsey closed his loft door and showed her to the car idling out front. And just like that, they were alone.

WHY WAS THE ATMOSPHERE SUDDENLY DIFFERENT? THE molecules and atoms had re-formed themselves as soon as Dorsey closed the doors. They always did this—boil the air around them. Walls closed in. Lights dimmed. Dorsey's scent filled the car. He seemed to take up the whole other side of the vehicle.

She could finally look at him as long as she wanted. Liza had only ever allowed herself short, sidelong glances—so afraid that someone would pop up out of nowhere, screaming, "I knew it!" But lord, Dorsey looked like the king of this town car. But what would that make her? A serf, a concubine, a jester, a queen?

Liza touched his lapel. Maybe if she focused on tiny details like this and not this whole gorgeous man in front of her, she wouldn't make a fool of herself tonight.

"Gosh, the stitch detail on that shirt is amazing," she said absently.

Dorsey looked down at his shirt. "Is . . . is this shirt turning you on?" He smiled a wicked smile.

"A little." Liza laughed. "My grandmother is a seamstress. You get to notice fine detail work and high stitch density." She ran her index finger up his collar. Then she unbuttoned the third button of his cream shirt, which exposed the muscular divot of his collarbone. *What would it feel like to kiss him there?*

"Want a trick to know if your shirt is outstanding quality or not?" she asked. Her eyes danced playfully. The way he had looked at her tonight. The way he touched her. It told her everything she needed to know. She was drunk off more than the drink tonight. It was a heady thing to be the center of a man like Dorsey's desire.

"I'm not sure how I would happen upon a low-quality shirt." His breath had taken on a measured slowness as Liza fiddled with the button.

"Thick mother-of-pearl buttons. Do you feel this?" She ran her hand down the length of buttons until she touched his belt buckle. Liza was pleased to feel his stomach tighten. "Four millimeters thick, I would estimate," Liza murmured.

Dorsey began rapidly unbuttoning his shirt.

"What are you doing?" Liza saw smooth pecs with taut brown nipples. Rigid abs flexed and corded muscles moved under smooth skin as he dispensed with his shirt. Liza's tongue clicked. She wanted to put her face on his chest. She took a moment to absorb the sheer tangible certainty of him being here tonight and not in her daydreams and night dreams. There were so many false narratives flying around about them. Right now, though, his heat, his smell, that same cologne that had her spraying sample fragrances at every men's perfume counter in DC, was the truest thing in the world to her.

"I'm going to just give you the damned thing. I should be obsessed with your shirt tonight," Dorsey said. He crawled over her in the back seat. His biceps rippled on either side of her head and the hard length of him rested heavy and pulsing on her thigh.

"Let's switch." She pulled her own shirt over her head, freeing her breasts, but trapping her arms in the material. He kissed the space between her breasts. Once the shirt passed her eyes, she opened them to find Dorsey's lips just above her own. She saw his mouth coming like a freight train. His huge hand cradled her neck; the other arm pulled her so close the air rushed out of her lungs. The kiss burned right through her.

Liza's belly flipped as he deepened the kiss. She tasted the rich wine on his lips and kneaded the soft skin of his shoulders. His mouth covered hers, and she struggled to pull him closer so she could feel the weight of him. Damn this car. Not enough space. Liza ground her middle into his hardness.

"Partition," Dorsey growled out, and a black mirrored separator pushed itself up from the driver's and passenger's seat. His voice was gravelly in her ear, and his breath was hot against her collarbone. Then she moved her mouth, letting his prickly chin drag gently across her face until she found his mouth again. He kissed her like he had all the time in the world. But Liza knew they didn't.

She broke the kiss. "We're not that far from Alexandria." His mouth wandered down her face, and he nuzzled at her nipples, which had gone hard as pebbles underneath his attention.

"Plenty of time." His hands kneaded her breasts, and his mouth flicked her nipples mercilessly.

"I'm not gonna come in five seconds," Liza warned. He kissed her again. She wasn't sure if it was to shut her up or not, but this time it was more urgent. Good, she needed him to know that it was now or never. But he seemed to mistake the warning tone in her voice for a challenge.

"You want to go all the way? Liza, who told you I was that type of man?" Dorsey bit her collarbone.

"I won't fake it. And you have fourteen minutes now."

"Fourteen minutes is an eternity. You're gonna come in seven." He peeled her tight jeans from under her hips. They had never come off in such a fluid motion. Her own pants wanted to obey this man. For a minute, he just looked at her. The pads of his fingers touched the scalloped lace of her panties. His knuckles grazed the wet heat at her center. Liza sucked in a breath and clenched her teeth. If he started now, she just might finish. No foreplay, no sweet words, just carnal grinding, squeezing, thrusting, grunting.

"You're still wet." He said this almost like an accusation. Like he didn't think she would cop to being turned on by him more than once.

"Damned sexy shirt," she joked, raising her hips in impatient insistence.

"Where did you get this scar on your knee?" He pointed his chin toward her knee, then kissed her there.

"Roller skates are deadly instruments and should never be given to kids."

He kissed her thighs—left thigh, then her right. Those kisses burned right down into the core of her body. "Pull your panties down."

Liza pulled quickly at the waist of her panties. She wanted him inside her—that was undeniable, but maybe if she didn't come, it *wasn't* sex? If he was lousy, she could just forget about him. Either way, she needed some hard physical data on Dorsey Fitzgerald. Maybe her body could give her clarity, because her heart was all over the place. Her hands shook, but his hand stayed hers at her waist.

"Slowly," he said.

But Liza didn't want to go slowly. Urgency burned a hole in her chest. Didn't he know that in the light of day, too many things separated them? Didn't he know they'd only work in the dark, and the dark never lasted? "You're wasting your eleven minutes." Liza pushed the panties down her legs with her feet.

"I told you, I only need seven." He kissed her inner thigh. Liza looked down at the bulge in his pants, and her mouth watered. She could take him in her mouth right now and show him exactly why they'd be fools to waste their time. That would shut him right up. Dorsey kissed the crease at the juncture of her thigh. Liza's belly jerked when the pad of his thumb grazed her sensitive folds, then found her clit.

"Nine minutes." Liza moaned the last bit as Dorsey's thumb increased the pressure. He moved up to kiss her again, rubbing her clit until wetness seeped into the soft seats of the town car. He kissed her collarbone, then dragged his tongue to the rigid peaks of her plum nipples again. Liza's entire body arched to meet him when he kissed her rising rib cage, then the hollow of her belly. She realized too late that he meant to go all the way down. When his rough tongue slipped over her clit, Liza shuddered. He palmed her full ass with both of his hands and pulled her closer, his face meeting her wet warmth. His tongue lapped at her greedily and his palms kneaded her ass. The intensity of his tongue had Liza inching herself away.

"Don't run away now, Liza. I still have four minutes." His voice was husky. She wouldn't last four whole minutes with his rough, hot tongue licking her clit like she was the last thing he would ever taste. She was sinking. He was pulling her deeper into his warmth, and she could no longer see the surface of the water. The opening churchy chords of Aretha Franklin's "Spirit in the Dark" trilled in her head.

"Dorsey . . . I . . ." Liza warred with herself. She would never live it down. But shiiit, her body was running the show now.

"Say it."

"I'm . . ." Liza began, then he slid his two fingers inside her and Liza clenched around him like a vice. She bucked against his hands and mouth. His fingers slipped in and out, and she heard loud, wet, sucking sounds as his mouth covered her clit. The sound of enthusiastic sexual enjoyment had to be reaching through the partition. Liza covered her mouth with one hand and tapped his massive shoulders for mercy with the other.

"Say it," he demanded. Liza's thighs clenched around him. She was going to come so hard right on his mouth. She had no shame. The orgasm powered through her and mushroomed out like an atom bomb.

"Fucking say it, Liza."

"You made me come! You made me come! Oh my god!" Liza's words came rushing out, her hips still rocking on his fingers.

"Yes, I did. And next time, it'll be on my cock." It was then that the town car came to a slow stop. Dorsey looked up at her. His eyes were heavy as he scrambled to dress. He took her shirt out of her hands before she could protest and instead wrapped his own shirt around her shoulders. Liza's skin buzzed with the contact, and her hands shook, buttoning the mother-of-pearl buttons.

"Even trade," he said.

She shuffled out of the town car, knees weak, eyes glossy and dazed. Liza turned around just in time to see him fight and stretch her GRAB 'EM BY THE PUSSY T-shirt over his head. He had certainly earned it.

BETTER JUDGMENT

From: DFitz@PemDevCo.com
To: VL magazine

I know you all are normally the ones keeping me abreast
of new music and events, but I'm turning the tables today.
There's a radio program I want you to listen to in a couple
of weeks. This local DJ gathered a ton of resources and a
playlist for Pinoy rap, and I think it's going to be a
worthwhile event to cover.

More details to follow.

Dorsey lay on the back seat of the town car as it rocked gently en route to his loft. The same stupid smile crept across his face every five minutes. *You did it. You and Liza are a thing.* As soon as he thought it, a new kind of panic crept in. What if he was being presumptuous? What if she didn't want anything more?

He would just have to make it plain the next time he saw her. That's right. He was going over there and just saying it. What was he going to say? *Liza, I want to be with you because your eyes are like shimmering dark amber?* Those kinds of interactions left a foul taste in his mouth. And Liza was unlike any other woman he'd ever known. She didn't need tasteless flattery to be convinced that they were making an excellent decision. No, they had gotten this far on candid truths. Liza would expect and *respect* him telling her the flat-out truth. She wouldn't want to be flattered to death. Maybe he could write up a quick cost-benefit analysis, maybe a SWOT analysis of their relationship, and go over it with her. They could problem solve together. He had three things to convey:

- That he was fully in love with her
- That their relationship was a very smart decision
- That he could overcome the obstacles: her family and her inflexible economic views

He would manage it for her because everything *else* about them was *so* right. So right. God she tasted so sweet. Tonight was a slick, wet, hot fever dream. The smell of her—like the forest after it rained—lingered over him. Tomorrow his only goal would be feeling her clench and come all over his dick.

Would people be surprised that a man like him would date so far outside his social circle? Sure. But the people that thought they were in his social circle never were.

What would he *really* be giving up? Invites to country clubs? Golf tournaments? Charity balls? Could Liza suffer such terrible company when he, who was expected to join in at these events, could barely be bothered? Dorsey was feeling more and more confident about his plan. Go straight for logic. Go straight for the benefits. Smooth over the doubts.

He imagined Liza would probably need some convincing. He knew she didn't enjoy living with her mother, so maybe he could talk about a new apartment—anything that would make her get over any misgivings.

She probably never dreamed she would be the center of a Cinderella story. She would also probably prefer to keep their relationship quiet until this whole Netherfield deal was done. Whatever Isaiah had said to convince Liza that their fight was winnable was the worst kind of lie. But the *worst* kind of lies were Isaiah's specialty. What made women fall for such bullshit artists? Netherfield was a fait accompli. Liza *had* effectively slowed it down to a crawl, but she could never really stop it. Maybe he could build a community center next door? She might take this defeat hard, mostly because Isaiah had deluded her into thinking she could win. But he thought of a million ways to ease her out of her anger. When the car came to its gentle stop, he was still semi-erect with Liza's too-tight shirt stretched across his broad chest. When the driver opened the door and frowned, Dorsey beamed back and shrugged. He had learned from Liza that the driver's name was Raymond.

"Have a good night, Raymond."

CHICHO WAS PISSED, AND LIZA COULD SEE IT.

"Girl, I am so sorry."

"Liza, it's four in the morning." Chicho leaned against the sofa.

"I know." Liza fidgeted with her shirt.

"And you smell like liquor and cologne."

Liza grabbed a bottle of water from the kitchen. Her knees were shaking. She was still seeing stars. If she came like that with an appetizer the entree would kill her.

"Whose shirt is that? Park's?"

"Chicho, I'm so sorry. I know tomorrow is really important for you." Liza leaned against the wall.

"I know," Chicho mumbled. "I'm not mad. Well, I am, but not for a reason you think. I wanted to hang out with Joseph Park too. The food at the senator's was so terrible. I just knew Park was gonna prepare some fancy food for you." Chicho raised a curious eyebrow. "You smell like you had fun."

"No, no, that's fish sauce." Liza was mortified.

"Of course it's fish sauce. What kind of fun did you think I was talking about?" Chicho and Liza shared their first genuine laugh in three months. "What did Joseph make?"

"We made *arroz caldo*, a Filipino dish. It was amazing and gone in five minutes."

"What did y'all do for the other ten hours?"

"Um, just some research for my DJ spot."

Chicho looked doubtful at this, then her expression cleared. "Liza, if you lie to me, I will never forgive you. Did you fuck Joseph Park? How did you ditch Dorsey?" Chicho leaned in, positively begging to be scandalized. "I know your face. You look peaceful AF right now. That happens when you're listening to the *Lemonade* album, and when you get a piece."

"Chicho . . ." Liza begged.

"You got a piece! Joseph was paying a ton of attention to you tonight," Chicho accused.

"Let's stop talking about this and focus on your podcast. I'm gonna get a few hours of sleep, then we can plan."

Chicho threw her hands up. "You smell like expensive cologne, you're not wearing a bra, you're in a man's shirt, *and* your panties are crammed in your back pocket, but we'll stop talking about this," Chicho said. Her voice had a sharp bite to it.

Liza padded off to her room. She didn't know where to put her emotions. Liza wanted to stay in that car and sit on Dorsey's hard-on until it went away; she wanted to punish herself for how much she wanted that man; she wanted to get back to right with Chicho. This was a moment she knew she wouldn't get back with her friend. But there was just too much to explain.

A few hours later, Liza awoke to a phone call from Janae. She picked up on the first ring.

"Janae—"

"Oh my God, Liza, I am having a terrible time," Janae said, cutting Liza off.

"Well, I'm having the opposite time, girl—" Liza pushed on. Janae would flip when she heard what Liza had let Dorsey do.

"You were right, by the way," Janae said.

"About what?" Liza asked. Liza was a sucker for that phrase, and Janae knew it.

"About Jennifer not liking me."

"Not exactly happy about that," Liza said.

"I'm in New York, right? Settling in."

"Right." Liza was proud of her. Her sister had taken the first step to living a new life.

"And Jennifer knows I'm in New York. She didn't text me once. Then *I* called her and told her I was in the city, and right after that she tagged me in her Instagram with her and Dorsey's little sister." Liza went into Instagram and found Jennifer's post. Liza read the hashtags: #Friendsarethefamilyyouchoose #sisnlaw #birdsofafeather.

"That *bitch*," Liza said. That is how you treat someone you like. You introduce them to your family; they are involved in your life. Jennifer had made it to the "front page" of Dorsey's life.

"She sent me a DM."

"Send it to me!"

Liza waited for the screenshot.

I guess you saw the post! Can't keep people who are
meant to be apart! Sorry you got mixed up in all of this.
David is such a man-child.

"Yeah, so her and Dorsey are together, and I guess she wants
to hook David up with his sister," Janae said miserably.

Liza gulped. "Her and Dorsey are together?" Someone
breathed in her ear, or in her head, she wasn't sure. *Side chick.*

"I don't know. I hate to gossip. It's just you were right about
them. The whole family's trash."

Liza only nodded. "Mm-hmm."

LIZA WAS EXHAUSTED, AND THE DAY HAD ONLY JUST BE-
gun. "The trick is to find something interesting, even in the
least interesting places," she told Chicho.

"Find something interesting in uninteresting places, check."

A whole seven hours later, Liza had a topic schedule laid out
for fifty half-hour spots and also started calling and lining up
speakers. In the next few days, they would record a few of the
episodes to bank.

"Okay, Liza, I think my head is about to explode. Can we be
done for today? I want you to tell me all about Joseph Park. I
know I'm a newly married woman, but he is a man of mystery,
and I have to know what happened yesterday."

"Joseph Park is a great guy, but really, nothing happened between us." The only way to lie was to tell the truth a little.

"I don't get you. Why don't you want to tell me things all of a sudden? This is something that we would both be squealing over, and now you're keeping this to yourself."

"Chicho, I'm telling you there's nothing."

"Joseph Park just texted Colin to say he wanted to come by and make you butter chicken for lunch tomorrow. Can you explain why a world-famous chef is coming over here to make *you* food?"

Liza shrugged. "Maybe he lost a bet."

"You are full of it, Liza, and I'm going to find out why."

THE NEXT MORNING, COLIN TOOK LIZA AND FREDO ON A tour of Alexandria like it was a Tuscan village in Italy. He went on and on and on about the architecture, about the culture, and by noon, Liza knew an extraordinary amount about old houses in Alexandria. And absolutely nothing new about Colin and Chicho.

Part of her wanted to make sure that her friend was truly happy. She hated to say this, but she was looking for clues or signs of regret, for Chicho to run to her and say, "I was wrong about everything."

But it didn't look like that moment was ever coming, and Liza had to come to the slow realization that her friend was happy with her choice. Perhaps the least she could do would be to be happy that her friend was happy.

Joseph Park came over at lunchtime with bags of groceries. He went over everything in his bags with Liza and Chicho and shared his butter chicken recipe as he made it. The entire time he cooked, he also chatted and flirted with every woman in the house, making Chicho blush and threaten him with her flip-flop. Liza watched the door, thinking that Dorsey would stop by, text, or call.

Park caught her eye and casually mentioned that Dorsey had

meetings all day until the evening and would probably catch up with them separately. That was the last time Liza looked at the door. She settled into Park's friendliness.

When Chicho left to take a conference call, Park sidled up next to Liza. "So explain something to me." Park put fresh coriander and garam masala back into his bags.

"Sure."

"Last night, my friend was pacing and smoking like a maniac in his loft with *your* tiny little shirt on. He'll need surgery to get that shirt off!" Liza laughed.

"Seems like things got wild on your ride home, so I feel like I don't even need to tell you that Dorsey is really one of the nicest guys that I know," Park said.

"Wow, I'm getting the 'don't eff with my friend' speech," Liza said. Should she ask Park about Jennifer? About whether he had given her the same speech? Did men like this even see her in the same way as they saw a person like Jennifer?

"Well, yes, he's serious about everything. And if you're not . . ." Park let himself trail off. "I'm just telling you he's a fantastic guy. He just recently stopped a friend from making the worst mistake of his life."

"Oh really?" Gossip? Liza was all in. She didn't care if she knew the parties or not.

"Yes, really. His friend was dating a complete ice queen. He says that the girl's family was really embarrassing. And the girl was this beauty queen, but she didn't really seem that into him except for his money. But this guy was head over heels for this girl, like about to go down on one knee. No prenup, no discussion, just like that." If Park noticed Liza's face fall, he said nothing. "My boy Dorsey was like, 'Oh hell no.'"

"Was he?" Liza's grip tightened on the plate. She knew it was

Janae like she knew her own last name. Dorsey had plotted to separate her sister and David while dating Jennifer. It was exactly what men like him thought of women like Liza and Janae—fuck, don't marry.

"Liza, you okay? Did you eat too much butter chicken? Anyway, he told his friend to get a grip and recognize when he's being played. I cannot stress to you how trash this woman's family was. The stories I heard, Liza." Park took the cup Liza was holding and placed it in Chicho's sink. "He probably saved that young man's life. That's the kind of dude Dorsey is."

"That is exactly the kind of man he is." Liza's tone had a sharpness to it.

Park checked his phone. "Dorsey and I keep missing each other. I gotta head out, but he's headed here." Park squeezed her shoulders and smiled.

Liza got up to put her plate away. She dropped it in the sink with apparently too much force and the delicate plate smashed to pieces all over the sink and countertop.

———

"COLIN AND I ARE GOING TO A BENEFIT DINNER. DO YOU want to come?"

"After all of this butter chicken? I'm going to burst," Liza quipped. "I'm just gonna sit here and nurse my food baby instead." What she was really nursing was a simmering anger at Dorsey's nerve that only expanded for the rest of the day.

It was nearly two hours later when she heard a tentative knock at the door. She opened it to find Dorsey filling up the doorway with a confused look and a lopsided grin. He had dark circles under his eyes and his hand shook with a tiny cup of espresso. *Did he even sleep last night?*

"Oh my god, Liza." Dorsey tumbled past the threshold. "Every waking thought of mine has been from last night. I see you in everything that I do. I feel you."

"Dorsey . . ."

"I know. It's completely insane, right? Everything in me says to leave you alone. Your family is well . . . They would always draw negative attention." Dorsey laughed out loud, manic with his own confession.

All he needed was a corkboard with red yarn and thumbtacks. Was he trying to explain a conspiracy theory or tell her he loved her?

"Everything about you and me does not work on paper. You know what it's like? It's like one of those bad reality TV shows you swear you will not watch and then you're so hooked and you actually love it. I . . . I actually love you." Dorsey seemed to marvel at the words coming out of his mouth. He looked like he hadn't slept in days. She smelled strong coffee and cigarette smoke on his breath.

"Dorsey, I—" Liza started.

"You brought me to my knees last night, Liza. And I want to wake up with you in my arms." His voice rumbled over her, and she hated herself for the effect it had.

"Dorsey. What we have is great for a night at Hotel Washington, but what about the light? What about at big corporate events when I drink the wrong wine, or family reunions where you don't Electric Slide? Those little things build. I'm not from your world—"

"I know, but I can make you a part of it. I could get you an apartment, some place hidden away, but tasteful. Maybe something in Georgetown."

"And would you still live in Philly, while I'm in Georgetown?" Liza folded her arms.

"Of course, Philadelphia is my home. But I want to give you some peace, Liza." Dorsey paced. "Like you mentioned your relationship was fraught with your mother. Maybe we could minimize our interactions? I can see how it can be too much," he stated.

Too much? Liza wondered if she should let him continue to plan out his secret fantasy, but it was all she could do to not grab a paperweight from the table and throw it at his head.

"Dorsey." Liza's voice was calm in contrast to the absolute riot inside her. "I am so sorry that I gave you the indication that I wanted any part in your *Pretty Woman* fantasy. The other night was fun, but it needs to stop right there. You're probably the last man I would ever have a serious relationship with, *if* that's even what you're proposing. It sounds like you're trying to set me up as your permanent side chick before you even have a main chick?"

"Side chick? Liza—"

"As in your woman on the side. The one you give head to in a town car while your sister visits with Jennifer."

"No. No, Liza, Jennifer and I are nothing—"

"You have me all wrong if you think I would hop at the chance for a half-life with you. You can take your cocaine intensity and see yourself out," Liza said coolly.

Dorsey's face twisted, then darkened. "Is that it, then? I texted you last night to tell you I had a great time, and you sent me three eggplant emojis and a peach! What the fuck happened since then? Are you telling me I was alone in what I felt? Give me some reason why suddenly today you don't want anything to do with me."

"Excuse *me*, but it sounds like you want nothing to do with *me*. Saying we should minimize my interaction with my mother because she's too much!"

"No. *You* said she was too much at the fiftieth anniversary gala, after she told everyone that her grandkids would have 'good hair.'"

Liza winced at that last bit. "So what? *I* can shit on my mom, *not* you. If that were it," she continued, "then that would be enough to *never* see you again. But you're also a really shitty friend. WIC told me that before your dad died, he promised his business an investment. He told me you did everything in your power to keep that money from him."

"Why is WIC suddenly coming out of your mouth?" Dorsey seethed. "I haven't heard you say his name in months. Now you're so concerned with what he's feeling while throwing *my* logical and truthful confession back in my face? This is all petty bullshit. I know if I hadn't bruised your little ego when we first met, you would be all over me."

Liza's jaw tightened. "How *dare* you accuse me of having an ego when you compare loving me to loving trashy reality TV."

"Okay, I—"

"And I will *always* be concerned for my family and friends when people treat them like shit," Liza said. "I could never be with a man who is the reason my sister is depressed right now. You told David my sister—who is the sweetest person in the world, would never hurt a fly, is the definition of all goodness— you told David to leave her." Liza's voice wavered.

"Your sister's lovely, but you have to admit she didn't seem interested in him at all. And it also seemed like she may have a drinking problem. I saw you that night of the snowstorm watering down all of her drinks, and that next morning you were afraid. I saw it in your eyes. David's father is dying, and he's not in a good place right now, so I told him to focus on his family. Because, yes, Janae seemed a little cool toward him."

"Do you know anything about my sister? Do you know that

her child died, and she had a nervous breakdown and is slowly building herself back up from the ground?" Liza's voice wobbled. "She leaned on alcohol in the early stages of her grief, and I *was* afraid. But she's just shy and cautious. Nothing wrong with that. It's not up to you to decide how much she loves him. She's desperately in love with David, and she was seeing a light at the end of the tunnel and turning into herself again. And then you tell your friend, 'She's just not that into you'? How dare you? Who do you think you are?" Liza was yelling at this point.

"I can tell you that David didn't know any of that. And if your sister is so in love, maybe she would have shared that huge part of her life," Dorsey said.

"I mean, whatever, but it wasn't your business. You made yourself the arbiter of someone else's love, and you were wrong."

Dorsey was quiet for a moment. "Well, it sounds like you have quite a few reasons not to ever see me again." He took his coat. "I'm sorry I misunderstood our relationship. It will *never* happen again." Dorsey opened the door and nearly knocked Chicho down to get himself out of the town house.

"Was that Dorsey?" Chicho's eyes widened. "What on earth did you say to him?"

—

"YOU TOLD HER *WHAT*?" HIS SISTER'S VOICE RICOCHETED around the room, even over FaceTime. "Dorsey, what type of woman would ever say yes to that?"

"I thought of it as more of a logical presentation of the benefits of a relationship. Show the other party why they're getting a good deal." Dorsey heard how it sounded as he said it. His no-sleep logic had made sense in his head the other night, but he groaned inwardly at his reality TV comparison.

"But she had just given you some major sign of liking you, and you really threw it in her face. No woman wants to be made to feel so cheap. I mean, she's dead wrong about Isaiah, but you're not doing yourself any favors."

"She mentioned you and Jennifer . . ." Dorsey said, letting his sister in on the most perplexing part of the conversation, the "side chick" accusation.

"My visit to her father's bedside? Why?" Gigi asked.

"I have no idea," Dorsey said.

There was a long pause on the phone. "Oh no . . . Jennifer's post the other day." Gigi sounded alarmed. "She posted an old photo of us with these crazy hashtags about us being sisters."

"If Liza saw that . . ."

"Oh, she definitely saw that. She thought you were—"

"Making her the other woman," Dorsey finished. She should have just asked, *What about you and Jennifer?*, and he would have set her straight. She had all the wrong ideas about him. "Well, it's too late now," Dorsey said. Why did he keep getting it wrong with her?

"What do you mean?"

"I told her I wouldn't be back again and to have a nice life."

"Wow, I can't believe I used to date men. Why don't *I* just tell her the truth about Isaiah?" Gigi said this with a nonchalance Dorsey did not believe.

"Gigi, I'm not sacrificing you on the altar of my broken relationship."

"No, I want to tell her." Gigi's voice hardened. Dorsey knew that stubborn tone. She was settling in.

"I don't want you to."

Gigi looked genuinely disappointed in him. Damn, that face stung.

"Are you still trying to protect your family's pristine reputation to Liza? Look, she has the facts wrong, that's simple enough to fix, but you—your whole mind-set is still about self-protection. You came to the table trying to be superior. The reason she doesn't know that Isaiah is bad news was because you were looking out for your image. You've had so many opportunities to tell her about him. Liza needs to know Isaiah lied about everything. That will fix the facts problem, and then *you* can apologize for the rest."

Dorsey groaned. "Do you know the last time I apologized? It was 2006."

"And it will be 2046 before you find anyone as remotely interesting as Liza."

THREE DAYS LATER, LIZA RECEIVED A TEXT—MORE LIKE A thread. Another one of the thirty-six questions:

> Number 27: If you were going to become a close friend with someone, please share what would be important for him or her to know.

> Don't worry. I won't be falling all over myself for you again. This text is just so we can move on with a clear conscience.

> 1. I told David to move on. I didn't know your sister's history. For that, I am sorry.

2. Jennifer and I are not and have never been an item. I would think you'd know how it is when someone feels entitled to you with no encouragement. #playcousin

3. I won't apologize for holding myself and my potential partner to a standard of decorum, but I struggled to find an apt comparison for the complete surprise loving you was to me. That was not the best way to communicate it. I am sorry.

4. Isaiah is not a good man. This also isn't my story to tell. My sister wants to share a story with you if she can call you at 8:15 p.m. Thursday.

Liza wanted to delete the text, but curiosity snaked around her and instead she read it three times more. What could his sister possibly say to change her mind?

8:15

YOU ALL ASKED FOR MY PLAYLIST. YOU'RE GONNA GET
it. Listen or don't."

Liza jabbed the call button.

The caller's voice was tentative. "Sis, is everything okay?
These past few days the music has kind of been all over the place.
I normally like to jam on my way home from work, but every-
thing is so angry and sad."

"Don't worry; the station also wants me to change up my
catalog to a nice, happy Top 40. There will be music to shake
your ass to in four minutes." Liza hung up the call.

There was a tiny knock on the door. Her executive producer
appeared with a clipboard in her hand.

"Hi, Liza, there are at least five new complaints. And Upstairs said you need to play the list they gave you, and only the
list of songs that they gave you. I'm sorry."

"What about my Pinoy showcase next week?"

"Only the list of songs they gave you."

SETTLED BACK AT HOME, LIZA LOCKED HERSELF IN THE bathroom at eight fourteen and waited for a call. When the phone rang, a sweet voice answered when Liza said hello.

"Hi, this is Gigi Fitzgerald. We met at the—"

"I remember you, Gigi. I don't know what you'd have to do with Isaiah, but Dorsey thought we should talk."

"I just want to start off by saying that my brother can be a little shy about interacting, but he's not mean. I don't think he meant to—"

"Oh, that's okay. That's all . . . that's not important." She wasn't in the mood for a rousing defense of Dorsey right now.

"Okay, so I won't hold you up. When I was a young girl, Isaiah's mom used to braid my hair. I'd probably had a crush on him since I was eleven years old. So, imagine my face at my eighteenth birthday when he told me he wanted me to help him start a company."

"Gigi, I'm sorry if Dorsey told you—"

"Liza, just let me get the whole thing out before I lose my courage."

"Okay." Liza's grip tightened on the phone.

"In a year's time, he had fleeced me for over fifty thousand dollars in free labor and a hundred and seventeen thousand dollars out of my trust."

Liza was trying to process all that. "Wow, um, Gigi. Did he steal from you?"

"No, I gave it freely. In fact, I stole over forty thousand dollars from my parents' friends for him. Once everyone found out that it was a scam, I was the one who got busted. I was looking at max fifteen to twenty years and a felony on my record for the rest of my life. My parents had the money to clear this up and get my charges reduced. But I still have a record, and it will follow me for the rest of my life. I found out later that Isaiah had signed an affidavit stating that everything was my idea, then left the country. Whatever you're doing with Isaiah, make sure you don't get caught holding the bag. He wraps himself up in legitimacy and just takes from people."

A slow, creeping shame began to inch its way across her chest. "Thank you for letting me know the type of man he is." The knowledge seemed to crack inside her like ice. She believed Gigi. But surely this work with Netherfield, her proposal, wasn't a scam. They were going through all the proper channels. She'd seen to the necessary financial checks throughout the proposal *herself.*

Surely this was different.

She wasn't a lovesick eighteen-year-old. But something still and quiet in the back of her mind knew it was true.

"Liza?"

"Yes?"

"If we ever meet up again, could you show me that thing you did with your hair at the Netherfield Gala? Dorsey said it was the most beautiful style he's seen you in."

"Oh, that twist-out? I would love—" Liza cut herself off. Damned hair vanity almost got her back in that man's house. "Definitely, Gigi."

After they hung up, Liza drew a ragged breath. WIC had been so quick to enlist her in his campaign. She had given over her movement to him even when Janae had told her not to. This locked so many hanging questions into place. Why had she never been able to find out much about him online? Why had he ditched her at the gala? Why was he so insistent that she take a swing at Dorsey? How could she have been so wrong about someone? Her stomach lurched when she remembered how readily she had lapped up WIC's lies.

When Dorsey had confessed to her, he told her nothing but his own truth, even when it cast him in a negative light.

How could she tell him those things when he had been so frank about his feelings for her? She could never face him again. Her arrogance, her stupidity, her willingness to believe any story about him—any *terrible story*—embarrassed her. She was ashamed of herself, and if she ever saw him again, it would be too soon.

Would she ever live down this egregious mistake in judgment?

This was how Granny found her, crying into her pillow—shoulders shaking, eyes red and puffy.

"Liza, baby, I know this kind of cry."

"I'm just sad, Granny." Liza's voice cracked with the sheer force of trying to sound okay.

"This is the kind of sad only Aretha Franklin can fix." Granny pulled out Liza's phone from underneath her. Aretha was reserved for top-tier emotions only. It was the liquor on the top shelf at the emotional bar. She'd heard Aretha as she orgasmed in the back of that town car. Her heart had been so full. And the Queen of Soul would soothe her heart now that it was empty.

"How do I get to 'Ain't No Way' on this phone?" It was a pitch-perfect song. Aretha pleaded to her lover to just let her in, and Granny patted Liza's head, sliding her hands through the square parts in her twists. It was restorative, and Liza let herself cry into her granny's chest.

"I think *I* broke someone's heart," Liza finally said through sobs. "They didn't deserve it."

"Liza, are you actually having second thoughts about Colin?" Granny sounded incredulous and a little worried.

Liza's head jerked up from her granny's breast. "What?"

"Ever since you came home from Alexandria, you've been beat down, and I thought—"

"No, Granny."

"Look—I know that your friend Lucia has this big ol' fancy life right now. She's in expensive cars and meeting fancy people and she's got a great big old ring, but you wouldn't have been happy like that, Liza, I know you wouldn't."

"Oh, Granny, I know. I *don't* want her life, and"—she rushed out the last bit—"I'm happy for Chicho." It wasn't all the way true, but if she said it enough it would become so.

"Well, what's the matter, baby?" Granny looked all out of options. Why had she kept Dorsey from her?

"There *was* someone," Liza started.

"I hope you don't mean that flashy one . . ." Granny quieted down. "I mean, WIC is a charmer. But I just didn't like that he couldn't show up for you that night." Granny paused to think. "You ended up dancing with that Mr. Shit Don't Stink."

Liza lifted her head from Granny's chest again. Her voice had lost its tremor. "No, his shit *is normal.*" Liza shook her head. "No, I mean, he's not like that. He doesn't think that."

Granny huffed, reminding Liza a little of Bev. "Well, he's not winning any congeniality contests over here."

"He's not like David. He's probably never ordered anything with sprinkles on top. But he's *not* unkind. It's important to me that you know that, Granny." Liza searched her granny's face for agreement.

"Okay." Granny look perplexed. "Okay, I know that now."

If she held on to any suspicion about Liza's pointed defense of Dorsey, she didn't let on.

"Granny, have you ever messed up really bad and didn't know if you could fix it?"

"Oh yeah." Liza could see her wrestling with speaking again. She sighed after a long pause. "I stepped out on your grandfather, you know." She waited for condemnation from Liza that did not come. But surprise did roll over her. Her grandmother had always chastised Bev about her penchant for married men. She'd never dreamed her granny would ever make a huge relationship mistake like that.

Liza stayed quiet. She didn't want to break the soft spell of this truthful moment. Slowly Granny continued.

"Your grandfather was in Vietnam, and I had just gotten so lonely. In the end, I just had to ask his forgiveness. Forgiveness will take you a long way, Leese." The use of the old nickname combined with the soft trilling of Aretha turned Liza's stomach inside out.

"I think this person is a kind of cut-'em-loose-forever type," Liza said.

"Someone's capacity for forgiveness says more about *them* than you." Liza burrowed deeper into her grandmother—loving the enveloping softness, the astringent smell of arthritis ointment and the soft curl of rosewater perfume and Pink oil hair cream. Granny had been the most solid thing in her life for so long, but her sturdy presence made Liza think of another person who always put her at ease. She pulled away from Granny; her mascara made two spidery crescent moons on the older woman's shoulder. Liza reached for the silk-lined turban, and Granny pulled it off, letting the bone-white cloud of hair rise with static electricity.

"Can you oil it for me?"

Liza stood and settled herself behind her seated grandmother. She was happy to occupy her hands, happy to toil with the cottony strands until they parted into neat little rows. Dipping her finger into the Blue Magic, she slid it across her granny's soft scalp.

Should she trade a secret for a secret? Tell Granny everything about Dorsey—about how wrong she had been? But everything had already slipped through her fingers. Did she *want* to see the look of disappointment on her granny's face when she told her how much free work she had done for weeks? How many lies she'd lapped up? How she had faked her smiles and let WIC shit on Dorsey just to seem "down" and worthy of his attention? She didn't want to share that part of herself with her granny— the shallow, weak, silly, gullible side. Instead, she dragged Blue Magic down another row.

THE DAYS ROLLED INTO WEEKS, AND LIZA COULDN'T LIFT herself out of her fog. She hadn't received a "36 Questions" text since the last one. No IFFs, no four a.m. selfies, no GIF parties, all of it sixty to zero. Dorsey really was done with her. She had also lost more than ten thousand followers. There didn't seem to be a bottom on this roller coaster from hell.

When the day came for her Pinoy hip-hop event, Liza threw out the schedule that the radio station gave her and played all the artists that Dorsey and Park had recommended to her. Listeners came to the station to taste Filipino dishes from local chefs and dance on the makeshift dance floor. The Filipino embassy had even come by to take a few pictures, and magazines and newscasters interviewed her about her choice of musicians. She gave all the praise to her advisers, Joseph Park and Dorsey Fitzgerald. When she walked outside the booth to pass out radio station T-shirts and beer cozies and interview community members, she scanned the crowd constantly for Dorsey. He wouldn't be coming, she knew, but hope was the last thing she had, and even that was wearing thin. What had he said that night of the snowstorm? Once he was done with someone, he cut them off completely.

Everything was going so well. Her last international hip-hop session was a raging success. It *should* have made Liza happy.

She laughed and smiled and did and said all the right things. All the media articles were complimentary, saying she was on her way up, not knowing her station was handing out pink slips like a paper factory. She had thrown out their contractually mandated playlist, and however popular she was, her big final insurrection would not go unnoticed.

When it was dark, Liza slept, and when it was day, she compiled playlists, ate, and watched Marvel movies.

Liza, I see you in everything I do. I feel you.

She was never sure how much time passed between her time at the studio and her time at home. Her interactions were generic, and her family, who were always the most annoyed by her sharp tongue, seemed lost with its absence. It occurred to Liza that little by little, the days had become hotter; the birdsongs of spring were replaced by the neighborhood children outside. Her sister was thriving in New York without David and was sending money back to the family. Granny put her window AC unit back into her room. It was summer, but Liza's cinnamon skin had lost its bronze glow and her hair stayed in a silk scarf—hoping but never getting to be unwrapped. Bev would weave in and out of the room commenting on the state of her hair, the smell of her room, and the puffiness of her face.

She was on her third shot of Crown Royal Apple when her mother dropped an envelope on her bed. The envelope was thick and creamy white with gold foil type. Somebody with money wanted her somewhere. Her heart leapt. *Could it be Dorsey?* Liza let the idea linger for a moment. He would not be renewing any friendships, or any "-ships" with her. She would not feel bad for standing up for her sister, but her throat still clenched at the thought of WIC. She had to stop herself before she spiraled down into guilt again.

Liza, I want to wake up with you in my arms.

When she looked back up again, her mother hovered at the door. Granny pretended to dust the floor near her door. LeDeya craned her neck and stepped past Granny to snatch the letter out of Liza's hands.

"Why does it take you forever to do stuff?" LeDeya pulled the thick paper out of the envelope.

"This could be another invite to meet some people with money," Bev said.

"Unlikely, with the way y'all acted in Philly," Granny said.

Bev looked only slightly chastened. "Next time I won't invite that tacky pastor."

"Oh right, the *pastor* was tacky," Liza said.

"Excuse me?" Bev's neck swiveled in Liza's direction. Liza didn't bother staring back and jumped for her letter.

"Deya, don't you open my mail!" Liza jumped again for her letter.

"Too late, you little hobbit." Deya easily held the letter out of Liza's reach and read with a fake British accent.

The Filipino American Heritage organizing committee invites you to join as our honored guest in a three-day celebration of Filipino culture, heritage, and history during several events taking place at the Embassy of the Republic of the Philippines in the United States.

Thank you for using your platform to highlight and celebrate Filipino hip-hop and other cultural means of expression.

Among the scheduled activities are a film screening, lecture, Filipino studies conference, and a Barrio Fiesta! Also featured will be an ongoing exhibit showcasing Filipino Americans' contributions to the Philippines.

"Boring." LeDeya dropped the letter into Liza's hands. The entire family's shoulders seemed to sag. Even Granny had been hoping for something. She shuffled back into her room wordlessly.

"I got a better invitation!" LeDeya said. Bev smiled knowingly. "Tickets to a young entrepreneurs training." Deya danced around Liza. "In New Jersey!"

"How much does it cost?" Liza asked.

"Ugh, do not start, Buzz Killington. Granny gave me her banking information so I can make a small withdrawal. It's an investment in my future."

"Oh, *hell* no," Liza said vehemently.

"I wasn't asking you," LeDeya retorted.

"Momma, you're gonna let this sixteen-year-old girl go to an MLM scheme conference in Jersey?"

"I'm not going to the whole conference, just this one training. And I have an opportunity to do some makeup there and make up Granny's investment. This could bring in actual cash, not to mention followers," Deya said haughtily. "Liza, you're always trying to steal someone's shine. If it is not about you, you don't want anyone to do anything."

"This is the dumbest thing I have ever heard. No one in their right mind is going to let a sixteen-year-old go to a conference like this. Does Granny know what her money's going to?"

"Liza, you're just jealous. I happen to know for a fact that your boy WIC ain't really feeling you that much anymore, and ever since then, you've been real sad. Posting emo songs and sucking the life out of every room you come into."

"Don't talk about what you don't know, Deya," Liza warned.

"You'd be surprised at what I know," LeDeya shot back.

Liza pushed past LeDeya and her mother and knocked briskly on Granny's door.

Granny answered with an annoyed raised eyebrow. Apparently, they had caught her right in the middle of an *SVU* marathon, and she was not happy.

"Granny, Deya is trying to go to a multilevel marketing conference in Jersey. Did you give her your account info? That's insane, right?"

"Granny, I'm just trying to get my makeup business running. I'm actually really good at it. Janae is sweet and good and always going to be pretty. Liza is smart, if extremely boring. Maurice has the entire Nation of Islam to fall back on. What do I have? What do I get to build? Liza just can't stand to see someone be more of an influencer than her," LeDeya whined.

"Granny—" Liza started.

"You gotta let me try at least," LeDeya pleaded.

Granny pursed her lips. "Oh, Liza. What kind of trouble can she get into doing makeup? MLM—that's like Avon, right?"

"Granny—"

"Liza, you gotta let the girl live a little. You should go too."

"No way!" LeDeya shouted. "Liza, let me have those scarves WIC gave you. You're not modest enough to really pull them off."

"You're such a brat, Deya!" Liza retorted. She hated those scarves, but she would rather see them in the trash than on LeDeya.

"You get ready for your lame-ass embassy art show and watch my money stack live on Insta!" LeDeya yelled back.

Liza huffed and slammed her door. As angry as she was at her sister, Liza was too wrapped up in her own self-pity to stand up against both her mother and her grandmother.

TWO TYPES OF PEOPLE

From: RVillanueva@PHEmbassy.gov
To: DFitz@PemDevCo.com

Dear Mr. Fitzgerald,

You may have missed our earlier invitations, but we wanted to remind you about the place of prominence the WCO's work in the Philippines will have at the event at the embassy! We would love for you to accept an award on your mother's behalf and ask you to RSVP as soon as possible so that we may prepare your VIP spot.

Awaiting your reply,
Roberto Villanueva

Dorsey was ill. At least that was what he kept telling everyone who had asked about him in the past six weeks. He had used the excuse so much that he was getting flowers of condolence. The articles about Liza's nephew, Janae's son, raced through his mind. Dead on arrival. It was the same pronouncement for his parents and brother. He could not imagine losing a child. He had speculated about the poor woman's mental health. It was a damned miracle she got herself up in the morning. He'd been simply wrong. He was unaccustomed to feeling such clear guilt.

His misunderstanding of Janae was one thing. But he was ashamed of his absolute diarrhea of the mouth trashing Liza's family and trying to set her up in an apartment and hide her away. Even if he'd meant it to be an oasis for them both, he'd said it like she was a toy he would hide in a hole until he was ready to play. She wasn't a woman to hide away; he was proud of her, and he should have said that. Dorsey had preached to Liza about decorum after he had propositioned her like a mistress. He had buried the story of Gigi and Isaiah because it was a black mark on the Fitzgerald family—on *him*—but now Isaiah was back to scamming people, maybe even the community Liza cared about, because Dorsey held his *own* secrets in such high regard.

I fucked it up.

He'd fucked everything up.

He had driven by Longbourne a few times—he'd even parked and walked around, hoping for a *coincidental* run-in with *any* Bennett. He saw the neighborhood differently now, the unique two-story cottages with Italianate-style architecture and Queen Anne–style homes. He got his ass handed to him in a few pickup basketball games at the Fort Stanton Rec Center. On the court, they only cared about the skill he brought to the team. He was absolutely haunting her neighborhood trying to feel a fraction of the joy she brought into his life.

He'd even bumped into Maurice on some of his longer walks. Liza's little brother never even broke his stride and started walking the neighborhood alongside him—quietly and thought-fully. Maurice took him on a tour of Cedar Hill, the former home of Frederick Douglass, hidden away in her neighborhood like any other house. He, Maurice, and Gigi had even taken a touristy photo next to that enormous chair. He walked her neighborhood without calculation and saw beauty where before he had only seen ashes. He wanted to love what she loved.

She would be fine without him. And he would be fine during the day. But at night, memories of her chased him around his bedroom. Her lips, the way her body rose to meet him when he kissed her, that hollow in her neck that he *now* knew smelled like honey and vanilla, the way she'd moaned when he kissed her most sensitive spot—he remembered everything with encyclopedic accuracy. He had taken to drinking at night to ensure dreamless sleep. But when he woke, his heart and his body still ached for her.

She had been quiet on social media. He had typed and erased so many direct messages and texts to her. In the end, what he'd said and done was too much to overcome.

It wasn't like he would ever see her at any of the events he was turning down. And his sister had done a bang-up job convincing the world that he was lying low in Korea, posting year-old photos of a business trip.

The only event he *wanted* to attend was a Filipino heritage celebration at the embassy in DC. He knew they would be celebrating his continuation of his mother's humanitarian work. He wanted to be there to make his mother proud somehow. His middle-class mother had faced so many snobs who thought his father was *slumming*. His mother would be ashamed of the way he had treated Liza and the Bennett family.

Dorsey skimmed over images of his mother with messy fingers, eating barbecue and dancing traditional dances with villagers. She was equal parts elegant, untouchable, down-to-earth, and motherly. Liza's proclamation about communal dancing popped into his mind. *There are two types of people in the world.* He suddenly understood it so perfectly now. Those that give themselves over to a moment, and those who are too inside their own heads to really experience anything. He had been the latter for far too long.

LIZA WAS STALLING.

"So tell me what else are you planning when the summer comes?"

"Well . . ." The caller searched for more to say. Liza's eyes darted from the door to the phone. "I suppose I could buy some new sandals."

"Oh, I love sandals! Do you like the strappy ones?"

"I guess." The caller had clearly run out of steam. "Am I caller number nine or not?" she asked.

"Oh, we found caller number nine ages ago—" Liza heard the soft silence of dead air. "Guess we lost her; let's try to get her back." But a woman in a pantsuit pushed through the door, and Liza quickly threw it to a cued-up song, dread growing in her stomach.

"Ms. Bennett, you are popular today."

"Every day," Liza corrected. "This is the third-highest-rated show in the region."

"Yes, well, about that. It seems like the radio station is going in a different direction."

"So I've heard." Liza scratched at the table graffiti.

"We plan to start our station rebranding in the next few months, and your brand is just a little outside our tent of offerings," Pantsuit said.

"What exactly are your offerings? Christmas music in October? Top 40 adult contemporary?"

"Now, Liza, I understand your frustration—"

"Frustration! Why am I always the only person who gives a damn, and nobody gives a damn about me?"

"I know this is hard news, but everyone is feeling the crunch. You're internalizing a simple business transaction that's not personal at all."

"I'm curious if these lines really work for you. When you say 'don't take it personally' and 'it's just business,' do people really just dry their eyes and perk up?" Liza was shaking.

"Well—"

"What sense does that make when someone is losing their job?" Liza's mic swiveled and nearly hit Pantsuit in the face. She hopped back and straightened her suit. Liza pressed her nails into her palms.

"I'll just leave you to collect your things," Pantsuit said quietly.

The door closed with a soft click, and Liza threw her headphones into the cluttered corner. Everyone was right about her, and she had been wrong about everything. What had she gained for sticking her neck out? Liza's mind tumbled forward into the inevitable conversation with her mother. She would sigh. It would be impossible for her to pass up the chance to say "I told you so." Her brother and LeDeya would laugh behind their hands. Granny would shake her head.

She had been blinded by WIC's charm, but she had done actual work on that proposal, and she deserved to be paid for it. She'd been avoiding WIC, but if she could get a small fee for her work, it could hold her over until she got an inevitable office temp job. It was time for her to get real about her future. If she wanted to do international human aid, she would start where she was—improving the city block by block.

OFF THE RAILS

From: DFitz@PemDevCo.com
To: DupontS@PemDevCo.com

Sharon, this is my third time reminding you that DFitz and DFatz are two different accounts. I have not had the board meeting yet, but I appreciate the company's speculation about my job security.

I hear we've put an intern on suspension for excessive tardies. After investigation, I found that he lost his apartment and now has to make it here from Jersey every morning. Reverse this suspension immediately. And let's try to supplement his train ticket or flex his hours. In the future, I would like us to be more thoughtful in our punitive approach to changes in work performance.

Respectfully,
D

Ten men and one woman sat with lips pursed and arms folded around a polished oak table. The weather was warm, but

the temperature inside the boardroom was glacial. No one fidgeted, no one coughed into their sleeve, no one reached for the
carafe of coffee on the table. They sat in stony, unified silence as
he reported the lack of movement on the Netherfield properties.
He was launching into reason number seven why permits had
been blocked and agreements were unsigned.

"Dorsey, look, this thing has gone off the rails. My grandkids
are showing me memes of you and that rabble-rouser every time
I turn around. You brought her to our gala?"

"Her grandmother's garden—"

"You brought her and danced with her. You looked like a
damned fool out there."

"Don't you see she is turning the tide of public opinion? Do
you see she is winning?" a dark-haired man said.

"She has you right where she wants you," Hampden warned.
"Which is why we did a little digging." He slid a manila folder
toward Dorsey.

The other board members eyed one another warily. "Hampden, we agreed not to do this," one began.

"Sorry, but it's gone too far," Hampden said. "We were able to
chat with Liza Bennett's sister's ex, who says that the sister is a
mentally unstable alcoholic. Moreover, her mother has quite the
reputation for sleeping with married men. My grandkids know
how to turn some photos of her into memes so that it seems
organic."

"Is this the same ex that killed their baby boy driving drunk?"

Anger shimmered around him. Who did these people think
they were? Who did these people think *he* was? "Is this the same
sister that paid her way and part of her siblings' way through
college?" His voice shook. "This is not who we are. If we get this
deal, it will be by the sweat of our own brow, not on the backs of

people who can't defend themselves." Dorsey pounded the oak table.

"This naiveté is precisely why this project is failing," Mr. Hampden roared.

"What about all the other development deals? I've come in and closed them without exception," Dorsey said.

"You know how important Netherfield is to the strategic plan of the company. We want to bid on federal building contracts, and this was our way in. You bungled it because you wanted to get in someone's pants." The table erupted in censure. Hampden was letting it all fly today.

"We can find another way in," Dorsey said. He would not let them rile him.

"We're tired of waiting, Dorsey. I'm afraid this little experiment isn't working out. We have begun a search in earnest for a new CEO."

"The WCO—" Dorsey started.

"You're fired." The word ricocheted through the room like a gunshot.

They would dismantle WCO. They would close up every school and orphanage, citing financial pressures. He had failed his mother and, as a result, failed women like his biological mother. For the first time in his life, he hadn't gotten what he wanted. Liza had rejected him and dismissed him outright. He was being unceremoniously fired. And his mother's legacy would be washed away with his job.

LIZA HAD EVERY REASON TO DREAD THIS MEETING. WHY had she called him? Oh right, she was desperate.

WIC walked into the coffee shop like a celebrity. Pretty

women's heads turned. He flashed a brilliant smile and sat down next to Liza.

"Hey, lovely."

"Um, hey." Her heart rate was as slow and steady as an athlete's. Amazing what information could do to your libido.

He sat wide-legged with the chair turned around like a cool substitute teacher. "I looked over the proposal doc you sent. Can we talk about it?"

"Sure. I wanted to go over some things with you and—"

"It's a great idea getting these tax breaks, but it won't help with our capital problem," he cut in. He handed Liza the thick portfolio. He smiled, and Liza was happy to see he had spinach or broccoli in his teeth.

Liza flipped through the packet and noted all the red lines through the writing. "You've cut a lot."

"Just the portions that involve a lot of red tape."

"These are the portions that ensure financial oversight," Liza corrected. "How do we know that the money goes where it is supposed to go?"

"Our organization has its own oversights," WIC said smoothly.

"And that's the Black Israelites, right?"

"Liza, of course."

"It's just I've called everywhere, and no one has heard of this fundraising effort."

"Okay, Liza, why are you calling around behind my back? What exactly are you accusing me of?"

"Not accusing you of anything. Just can't seem to map out your connections." Liza saw the anger flash quickly in his eyes. She was glad to be in a public place. She brought this on herself. It was due diligence she should have done months ago. She *wanted* him to be right, and she just filled in the gaps along the way. She'd turned him into a knight by sheer force of will. He'd validated her feelings about Dorsey, and she had lapped it all up like a puppy.

"Oh, I know what this is about." His handsome face twisted in a scowl. "You let Money Bags hit it, didn't you?" He let out a mean laugh.

"WIC—"

"And he fed you some sob story about his thirsty-ass sister. But answer this. Gigi is a big lesbian. How did *I* lure her into some trap?" he said. He was offering up information Gigi hadn't mentioned. It was all the evidence she needed.

"WIC, before this meeting goes off the rails—"

"You're damn right it's off the rails. Give me a proposal with these hoops to jump through. Do you know how many lawyers and accountants you need to even make this profitable? This is useless to me."

"WIC, this was a lot of work. I was recently let go at the radio station, and—"

"Were you hoping to get paid?" WIC let out a guffaw. "For *this*?"

Liza held her face together. "My time and expertise are worth something, WIC." She hated the shaky tone in her voice.

"How much, Liza? Maybe I should give Dorsey a call, because I have a feeling ol' boy knows *exactly* what you're worth." He opened his jacket. "But I'm fresh out of Tiffany necklaces."

Liza's vision blurred and she bit the inside of her jaw so hard she could taste the metallic tang of blood. Without a word, she threw her cup of lukewarm coffee in his face. She gathered up the paperwork and pushed her way out of the coffee shop before the tears fell.

DATU

This will be my last live post for a while here on my personal account, everyone. I've decided to take a little social media break. By now you've all heard the news that I've lost the station. I tried, y'all. I worked myself to the bone, and I really tried. Netherfield was a loss. I was fooled by a scammer. My platform is gone.

I will rise from the ashes. I just don't know how yet.

Aww, thank you, @TuffGrrl56, I will keep my head up. Next time you all see me, I'll have a new perspective. I just can't give you hope right now if I am having trouble feeling it myself. Peace for now, hotties!

LeDeya took off to New Jersey without so much as a word to Liza. That was hurtful. It wasn't like they were as close as her and Janae, but they were still sisters.

". . . And when you're traveling, you should leave things in order," Liza said.

"It's rude. But what do you expect? It's Deya," Janae said. They were video chatting, and Liza let Janae critique her hair and outfit while she spoke.

Liza pulled at her hair, and Janae winced. "Not that ponytail; try something sleek."

"Ouch," Liza complained as she pulled the fluffy Afro ponytail off with the bobby pins still attached.

"I told you to flat iron that stuff," Janae admonished her. Liza slicked back her hair in a sleek ponytail, attaching an EZ long yaki ponytail to her head. Next, she put a hairpiece in the front for a straight full bang. Liza stepped back so her sister could see the whole look on her phone screen.

"You look gorgeous," Janae said. "But try a different ponytail."

"Thank you for letting me borrow this bandage dress." Liza rummaged through a plastic bin of hair and accessories.

"What can I do with it all the way in New York? You can have it, actually. I've put on a few pounds since that dress, and it's downright indecent on me now."

"Are you loving New York?"

"I am! It was such a necessary step just going to the interviews," Janae said.

"I know you've been talking to David," Liza said.

Janae sighed. "I know you've seen his post, Liza." Janae and David were both posting deep quotes and pictures of their hands encircled. They were back on and obviously serious, and Janae seemed hopeful again.

Liza knew Janae probably didn't want her textbook pessimism, so she didn't push too hard. She was so glad she had never blabbed to her sister about her thing with Dorsey. She would have never lived the shame down.

"I'll let you know if there is anything to report," Janae said and then deftly changed the subject. "Have you spoken to WIC?"

"Thankfully, no. I never want to speak to him again."

"He is a manipulative asshole," Janae said. "To think he could have gotten you involved in some criminal activity! So you two never . . . ?"

"No."

"We were all wondering why you were so slow to warm up to him. He seemed perfect." Janae nodded curtly in acceptance of the second weave ponytail Liza offered for her inspection.

WIC never really had a fighting chance to take root within Liza—not after BB. Liza sectioned her life into two segments: Before Blue Bell ice cream and After Blue Bell ice cream. Liza hated hiding something like this from Janae, but if she told her *one* thing, she would have to tell her everything. And after remaining silent for so long, it got harder and harder to tell the entire truth.

"Okay now, punch up that tight little dress with some jewelry. You'll catch some eyes tonight, little sister."

"Yeah, eighty-year-old Filipino dignitaries' eyes!" Liza quipped.

"If I were you, I would take what I can get!" Janae joked.

Liza pressed the end button and finished up her gloss in the mirror. "Dress how you want to feel," she mumbled to herself.

Liza took the train in five-inch heels and remembered the comfort of Dorsey's town car. The way he had searched for the seat belt and grazed the peaks of her aching breasts with his knuckles. He didn't know it, but he'd had her then.

Liza chided herself for acting like a spoiled princess. *You're wistful over a damn town car.*

Janae had been right about her dress. It was getting a lot of eyes. Unfortunately, in the subway, most were the eyes that threatened instead of appreciated. She would Uber home for sure. She checked her Instagram, just to confirm. A picture of Dorsey in Seoul, Korea, popped up. Liza was more than a little relieved. She had seen Pemberley on the donors list and had feared Dorsey might be there. The last thing she wanted was for Dorsey to think she was keeping up with his whereabouts. But he was off living his best Gangnam-style life.

***

DORSEY REGRETTED COMING AS SOON AS HE SAT DOWN. Everyone was uncomfortably reverential to him. A fifty-year-old man gave him *mano po*, a customary respectful greeting usually reserved for elders. He would be out of here in the next half hour, he determined. He would thank everyone, smile for pictures, grab Gigi, and slip out the back.

Exactly twenty-seven minutes later, he found a side door and closed it quickly behind him—moving farther outside to the wrought iron gates. Surely that was enough glad-handing for a lifetime. Hands shaking, he reached for his Treasurer cigarettes and noticed the gold heels as they caught the light of the flame in his lighter.

She was walking from a metro station. She looked like she owned the street, and her knee-length body-con dress fit her like a second skin. The deep V-neck in the front had some criss-cross strappy details that stretched over her breasts and demanded his attention. She still walked like the heels hurt, but it didn't take away a damned thing.

He must have been staring openmouthed because his lit cigarette tumbled out of his mouth, flickering into the wet pavement.

The flitting light caught her attention, and she froze. "Who's there?" she said.

Dorsey stepped out from the shadows. "Hi, Liza."

"Oh my god. Um, hi. I didn't think . . ." Liza stammered. It was the first time Dorsey saw her positively flustered. Good. It was his constant state around her. "Aren't you in Korea?" she said.

"Right now?"

"Yes." Liza doubled down. "At this moment."

He dragged his eyes up to hers. "I'm right here."

"They give you all such nice uniforms," Liza said with a smile and touched the organza and silk of his barong tagalog, a traditional high-necked tunic shirt with intricate swirls elegantly embroidered down the front with gold thread. Dorsey's stomach jerked at her touch—such a tangible visceral desire he had for this woman. It was thick enough to cut with a knife. He'd spend the rest of his life making up for what he said if she would let him. But she wouldn't let him. She would be polite and smile that thousand-watt smile and kindly leave him to his "*Pretty Woman* fantasy."

He heard Gigi clodding behind him and rolled his eyes. "Datu, I swear to God, if you're smoking out here . . ." Gigi burst into the light. She was winded, like she had been looking for Dorsey for a while. Her gaze shifted to Liza. "Whoa."

"Whoa is right," Dorsey mumbled.

"You're such a fox," Gigi burst out.

Liza smiled, big and beaming, and Dorsey's heart sped up in his chest at the sight of it. She nodded in Gigi's direction. "You're not too bad yourself, lady," Liza said. Gigi hugged Liza warmly while Dorsey still stood awkwardly.

"So, Liza," Dorsey started. "What, how—"

"What brings you here?" Gigi finished.

"I was an invited guest. My"—Liza corrected—"*Our* Pinoy hip-hop event was an enormous success."

"I listened. You curated such a perfect list for the Philippines," Dorsey said.

"It was your list, Dorsey."

"And you curated a fire playlist that told a story with tracks I wouldn't have thought to put together."

"Thanks. That means a lot."

"No, thank you."

"And thanks for—"

"Okay, I need to get off this thank-you train before the next stop," Gigi interrupted.

Dorsey had never been more grateful to his sister. He eyed Liza's big brown doe eyes under her dark sooty lashes. There were so many things he wanted to ask her:

- *Do you still hate me?*
- *Can we laugh and feel like we did nearly two months ago?*
- *Can I touch you like I touched you then?*

For the past two months, his mind had been playing a highlight reel of his interactions with Liza. If she just gave him tonight, he wouldn't ruin it with prideful confessions of love. In fact, he had no pride left. He would settle for her in the same room as him for the next three hours.

———

LIZA TOURED THE EMBASSY WITH THE INTENSITY OF A graduate student.

Gigi teased, "You know there's no test afterward, right?"

Liza smiled and ran her fingers against the textured tan wallpaper. She wanted to remember everything about this night. Visiting embassies felt like traveling to her. In the main hall, children weaved in and out of dignitaries, and beautiful dancers with gilded fans performed traditional courting rituals. Liza was even pulled up on stage and promptly embarrassed herself doing a complex rope dance. She noticed how the men followed Dorsey around and how the women preened in his company. Dressed in his traditional finery, he looked like the prince of some faraway kingdom. Solemn and resplendent in his bone-ivory and gold-trimmed tunic, he had what LeDeya would call *drip*.

The gallery tour was starting, and Gigi looped her arm in Liza's. "Let me show you one of my favorite pictures of our mom." Gigi led Liza to a picture of an elegant blonde woman holding a child's hand. "This is the very spot that Mom found Dorsey and the orphanage she established there," she explained.

Liza's eye caught on another blown-up photo. It was Dorsey pulling a child out of the rubble after a terrible natural disaster. He was younger and thinner, but his eyes were unmistakable. The headline was confusing. His name was mislabeled.

Dorsey appeared behind his sister silently and touched the headline. *Same cologne*, Liza noted. She'd thought she would never smell that particular scent again.

"It's my Tagalog name." He answered the question her face was apparently asking. His arm reached up and grazed her shoulder.

"Blank Datu?" Liza tried the name out on her tongue.

"That's Blank Datu-Ramos," he said. "It's a surname. Long story." His tongue rolled over the words so effortlessly. The name sounded like a promise.

"It's nice to meet you, Datu." It *did* feel like she was meeting a new man. One she finally saw completely. But also one she already loved.

"The pleasure's all mine, *Alizé*," Dorsey volleyed back.

Liza covered her face. "Oh my god."

"You failed to mention that you were named after an alcoholic beverage," Dorsey teased.

"I try to forget every day." Liza moaned. "I keep that information under lock and key. Do you have my birth certificate or something?"

"No, but your embassy invitation fell out of your purse." Dorsey held out the thick paper for her.

Liza's hand closed over the paper and grazed the inside of his palm. His eyes sprang up to hers like a gunshot. He hadn't moved away from her. He wasn't giving her space, and her breath shortened at his nearness.

Kiss me like you did that night.

Put your mouth on me so I can die like I died before.

Bring me back to life in your arms.

"I need you to know that I'm well aware that I approached you poorly in Alexandria, Liza," Dorsey said. He took a deep breath. He looked like he was bracing himself for a flogging.

Liza nodded. "I was wrong about nearly everything, Dorsey," she said, meeting his eyes.

"Question number 26. You ready?" His eyes stayed on her.

Liza nodded. He was easing her back into their rhythm. She didn't know how much she missed it until she heard him say it.

"Complete this sentence: 'I wish I had someone to share . . .'"

Why not just tell the truth? She had already lost everything. What else was there? "My bed," Liza said.

Dorsey stepped closer. The muscle in his jaw pulsed and

those impossibly dark eyes were hypnotic and unmoving. He cleared his throat but said nothing.

"Now you complete it," Liza said. "'I wish I had someone to share . . .'"

"My grief," Dorsey said. "I wish I had someone to share my grief with." His eyes traveled up to the photo of him and his mother in a forest chopping wood.

"Remember you caught malaria that trip?" Gigi's question broke the spell. Liza shook her head like she was coming out of a fog. There was a whole damn room full of people here.

"You caught *malaria*?" Liza asked.

"Ugh, yeah," Dorsey said.

"He was sick for weeks," Gigi said. "And this is the school for girls Dorsey started." Gigi pointed to another picture. Her smooth brown shoulders shimmered in the dim light.

"Hold on." Liza held her chest. "*You* built that school for girls in Mozambique?" It was too much. Liza could see the joy on his face, how proud he was of this life. "I remember reading about that. I think half the team went down with malaria, but the school still opened on time." Everything seemed to click into place. He was a philanthropist thrust into a CEO role—not the other way around. His heart was in this humanitarian world, and he was simply playing at the other one.

She looked up and caught his smoky eyes again, then darted away. It was too painful to look at him head-on. The light was so bright now and his true self was so obvious to her, and all it did was make her feel like even more of a fool. Her heart hammered in her chest. She was *not* about to cry real tears in front of these people. *Remember the time I defended a lying asshole when you told me you loved me? How about when I believed an Instagram post instead of just talking to you?* Ugh, the guilt. It churned her stomach.

Liza separated herself after a quick nod and tried to beeline for the exit. It was too uncomfortable to be here.

But Dorsey was faster, and he reached out and caught her wrist at the last moment.

"Don't . . ." he whispered, then shook his head. "Liza, they're starting a Sakuting dance. I would like to show you."

Just keep your hand there.

Just stay holding me, and I'll say yes to anything.

"What do I have to do?" she said.

"According to this program, this dance used to be only for boys, and it portrays a mock fight using sticks."

"Wait, you're reading the program? Why don't you know?"

"Unfortunately, I know just as much as you do, Liza." Dorsey pulled her near the dance floor, where a crowd of people were laughing and shaking bamboo sticks about one and a half feet long and tapered at the end, like a candle. Two people, one representing each side, circled each other and clashed bamboo sticks in a kind of imitation of martial arts sparring. It looked like a European quadrille gone off the rails.

"Is Dorsey Fitzgerald doing a communal dance?" Liza asked in mock horror. "This looks way too complicated. I couldn't even begin . . ."

"The way I see it, there are two types of people in the world," Dorsey teased.

Liza's eyes widened, and Dorsey handed her a stick. "I'm not sure I want to give you a weapon after—"

But Liza did not let him finish and whacked his stick instead, like she had seen the others doing. Dorsey laughed and tapped the floor with his sticks. "Quick study, I see."

Following his lead, she shuffled toward him while circling and interchanging positions with other dancers. She bumped into everyone and clashed the stick when she should have tapped and generally made a complete fool of herself. Eventually they were pushed to the kiddie practice play section.

They were that bad.

Nearing the end of the dance, Dorsey's stick struck hers high in the air. He moved closer to her as their sticks still crossed each other above their heads. One deep breath would have their bodies touching. If he bent down to kiss her, with her arms high like this, she wouldn't be able to stop him in time. Not that he was going to.

Dignity, Liza. You made a mistake. You bet on the wrong horse. Now you have to live with it.

"Liza," Dorsey said. She noticed that his head was bent down at a perfect angle.

Action over deliberation. She didn't let him finish.

She kissed him quickly and deeply, sticks still high in the air.

Fuck dignity.

"Take me somewhere, Dorsey," Liza whispered.

He was breathless. "Anywhere."

"Your place."

Dorsey was calling his car the next moment. Gigi made him take a turn around the room to make his apologies and bid everyone good evening, but Liza saw the rapid-fire handshakes and shoulder pats and laughed. He looked like someone had pressed an invisible fast-forward button.

CLOSED CIRCUIT

LIZA AND DORSEY FELL ONTO EACH OTHER AS SOON AS they crossed the threshold of his loft. Dorsey pushed her toward the kitchen as his mouth met hers in a fury that overwhelmed her and buckled her knees.

He had been so slow, so calculated, before. That measured man was gone. His warm hands explored her body. In the kitchen's gleaming sterility, they were the only two things out of place. Liza was sure he would take her on the dining room floor if she let him. Her hips dug into the countertop as he kissed her neck. Why had she never noticed how strong he was? He picked her up with so little effort, and she wrapped her arms around his neck. Right at the crook of his neck, this close, he smelled like skin, soap, and sweat—like he was finally meeting her the way nature intended.

"I want you, Liza. I've wanted you for a long time," Dorsey told her between kisses. "I know I fucked it up with you before."

"Don't speak." Liza did not want her head clouded with all the ways this could end in tears. *Sorry I misunderstood our relationship. It won't happen again.* His final sentence flickered constantly inside her head. He walked up the stairs with her hooked around his neck and waist.

"No . . . No, Liza, I fucked it up. But I'm gonna make it right. I'm gonna make it up to you." He ground the thick ridge of his cock into her. "And I'm gonna start here." He kissed her again.

Wet friction.

His mouth on the shell of her ear.

Filthy promises whispered against his neck. Liza was shattering. He wasn't proposing or anything, just acknowledging that he had been wrong. But why had his words vibrated inside her?

It was Liza's turn to take a measured approach to tonight. *Just be breezy.* All the judgment she had heaped on Bev, and here she was again, in the arms of a man who could only give her a piece of himself, not all of him, and she would take it, at least for tonight. She was tired of feeling empty. Tonight they had recognized her for an event she and Dorsey and Park had put together. She had a win tonight, and she needed it after a series of losses. Why not try to run up the score while she could?

Once in his bedroom, Liza stood and tried to separate, but Dorsey would not let her go. He bent to kiss her again, but she pulled back and wagged her fingers. "We have plenty of time. More than fifteen minutes this time," Liza teased. He brushed the soft skin of her jaw with his thumb as if he couldn't believe she was actually here.

Liza pulled at his belt buckle. "I was so stupid before," she said. "I kept ignoring my heart. I had all of this evidence, and I ignored it. But I won't ignore this." Dorsey sucked in a breath when Liza pulled his pants down. Liza slid her hands into the warm cotton of his boxer briefs. With her free hand, she pushed his underwear past his hips. His thick cock bounced forward and pulsed for her. A small bead of wetness pearled at the engorged tip. Liza licked her lips—she would swallow it whole if she could, and bent down to kiss the head. It jerked up in anticipation, trying to put itself into Liza's hot mouth.

"Now that we've greeted each other . . ." Liza went to her knees. She was damn good at this and too rarely got to showcase her skills.

"Liza, I have no shame in telling you if you start there, this is going to be a short night. I've wanted you for so long. I cannot—" He stopped short when Liza's mouth closed over him. She kneaded his butt as he thrusted deep into her mouth.

"Liza!" He held the crown of her head. Every vein in his cock pulsed and throbbed on Liza's tongue. He was close, she knew.

"Oh my god, Liza. Fuck it all, I'm coming." His voice was tight, and he seized and spilled himself into her mouth. He fell backward on the bed and did not speak. Liza hurried to the bathroom and spit in the sink. She found some mouthwash and gargled.

By the time she stepped back into the room, he was up and hard again.

"See? You just had to believe in yourself." She smiled.

"You are so beautiful." He covered his heart with his palm.

"More beautiful than . . . Ms. Venezuela?" She took another step toward him.

"This"—he looked down at his cock—"has been yours since I made that stupid comment."

"That's a long time to be hard." She was just in his reach now.

"Oh, you are about to find out how long I can be hard. Clear your schedule."

"My carriage won't turn into a pumpkin this time, Datu." She used his given last name just to see what it would do. His dark eyes softened, and he pulled her into him for another kiss. His hands moved over her, kneading her ass and thighs, then roaming up to her breasts, trailing fire wherever they touched. He yanked at the shoulder of her dress but stopped when he heard a ripping sound.

"Take off your clothes now before I rip everything off." Dorsey's voice was hoarse and low.

Liza took that as her opportunity to take off her clothing as slowly as possible. Watching him squirm and his cock jump could become her new favorite pastime. She threw her bra out toward him and slipped her panties off. She stood naked save for her twinkling, five-inch heels.

His bedroom was a vast stage for his four-poster California king-size bed. It stood on a raised dais and dominated the relatively compact space. When Dorsey moved toward her, she stopped him. She needed to get to that bed. To have his dark eyes eat her up.

"Stay right there," Liza demanded, climbing into his huge bed.

Her naked skin was so silky on his soft duvet. She lay on her belly, then placed her head on his cool pillow and pushed her ass in the air. She slipped her finger between her slick folds. "The night after the nap pods, I would touch myself and call your name, Dorsey."

"I wanted to fuck you over my desk in that snowstorm," he said, stroking himself.

Liza turned over and lay on her back with her legs high. Her glittery heels twinkled in the moonlight.

God, she loved the way he watched her. The moonlight illuminated his skin, and he looked glorious.

Her slim legs made an elegant upright V in his king-size bed, and his eyes rested on her glistening center. Dorsey raced toward her with fierce urgency, but her high-heeled foot on his shoulder stopped him.

"Funny way of showing it." Liza's eyes never left his. "I think I might have let you."

"Funny way of showing it," he said. Their mutual desire was a living, breathing thing that stalked around the room.

He kissed her ankles and moved them aside and settled between her thighs. Liza sighed as he covered her with his body. He was so hard everywhere, and Liza loved the feel of the weight of him on top of her.

She didn't want to rush this. Who knew if they would have another moment like this? But she wanted him inside her now. His mouth covered her nipple, and she arched her back. She was done thinking. He sucked greedily at her breasts while his deft fingers slipped inside her swollen, aching cleft.

The feel of his rough tongue against her slippery nipples combined with his fingers drumming rhythmically on her slick clit was too much, and Liza bucked and purred. Now it was her turn to beg. "Please, Dorsey."

"Please what?"

"Fill me up."

"You want me to fill you up, Liza?" He taunted her, while he fitted a condom.

"Do it." Liza moaned.

And he did. Thick and throbbing, he slid partway into her, and her body clenched around him. It had been too long.

"Am I hurting you?" His muscles locked with restraint. She didn't want his restraint; she wanted him thundering inside her.

"No."

He sank into her with a throaty groan.

"Take it all then," he demanded. He pulled out and Liza reflexively wrapped her legs around him.

"Take it." He pushed deeper until he was seated to the hilt. "All."

"Fu . . ." a dizzying burst of white-hot pleasure shot through her.

"So damned deep," he murmured against her ear. Then he began to move. Liza held him tight, not allowing him any escape from her embrace. She heard the gentle slaps of her body against his and his deep moans. For a while, they just moved together, looking each other deep in the eye. The intense eye contact was sending Liza over some invisible cliff. She had never made love like this—they were one soul passing between two bodies. He bent down to taste her mouth again, and Liza tightened around every inch of him, making him whisper her name into the hollow of her neck.

"Oh, Liza!" He moved like he had been inside her his whole life. Slow, deep strokes gave way to powerful, grinding pumps. They were a closed circuit, and the power flowed between them until Liza's body shook with it. She was losing control, and she drove with Dorsey toward a powerful release. At the crest of her orgasm, she cried out.

"I love you! God, Dorsey, I love you so much. Don't ever go."

He kissed her deeply, tasting her salty tears and swallowing her "I love yous."

Grabbing her high on his hips, he pounded the words back into her, hard strokes that made Liza grip the black sheets and arch herself up like a bow. Waves and waves of extraordinary pleasure cracked her completely open.

His orgasm rocketed behind hers, and he collapsed on top of her. He didn't go. He just nuzzled her neck and cooed in her ear. Emotion overwhelmed her, and she sobbed. Not cute little cries but deep, racking sobs that shook the bed and alarmed Dorsey.

"Are you . . . Did I hurt you, Liza?" Dorsey's face was horrified, and Liza's embarrassment tripled. That was it. The very last of her dignity. He wrapped his arms around her, and her cries softened. Why had he not said it back? Why couldn't he just put her out of her misery and say *I love you too?* His arms around her *felt* like it. His soft murmurings against her ear *felt* like it. But it would be a long time until she completely trusted her knee-jerk feelings again. *Just say it, Dorsey.*

"I know this great way to get to sleep. I like to think about all the kinds of cloud formations," Dorsey said, still trying to calm her. Liza nodded into his arms.

"Mammatus clouds. Those are my favorite because they look like boobs."

Liza chuckled in his arms. Maybe if he thought of boob clouds, he would forget her horrifying declarations—or return them.

"Shelf clouds roll in with thunderstorms. Lenticular clouds . . ." Liza drifted off on his warm chest.

She woke up sometime later and found his body in the pitch dark. They made love again—this time slowly, with searing intensity and without speaking. They moved together powerfully until their cries shattered the silence. Liza was unsure if the wetness against her face was from her tears or Dorsey's.

LIZA AWOKE TO THE SMELL OF FRIED EGGS AND COFFEE. She went to the bathroom, then grabbed one of Dorsey's shirts from the closet and padded down the stairs.

She saw him smiling at her as she approached. He looked damned good in the morning. She touched her head. Oh lord, she had gone to sleep without a bonnet. Her ponytail was definitely tilting to the side.

"You look good in my shirts. How do you like your coffee?"

"Ton of cream, no sugar." With the sun streaming into the

windows and the warm mug in her hands, it would have been a perfect morning. But there was a twinge of awkwardness due to that desperate declaration of love and endless sobbing shit she did last night. She came here telling herself to be breezy, and she had ended the night like a telenovela.

"Liza, I think we should talk about how we want to move forward." Dorsey's voice was stern. *Oh, here we go.* Stiff posture, formal speech. He was about to reiterate that he did not want a relationship. If he was going to come at her with some long list of side-chick rules, he could save it.

"No, Dorsey, I—" She was stopped by a hard pounding on the door. This type of knocking wasn't a request. Dorsey rushed to open the door, and Liza saw Gigi pushing her way through. She held out her phone like it was a hot sack of manure.

"Liza, is this your sister?" Gigi blurted out.

"Oh, I don't think you—"

"I kind of Instagram-stalk you, so that wasn't a question. This looks like Deya, right?" Gigi asked.

Liza took the phone and looked at an Instagram account called conscious_melanated_mind.

Then she heard LeDeya's voice. "I'm tripling my money today! With my fifty-six thousand, I've invested in my future, and you can too." The camera panned to three striking Black women all made up with distinct touches Liza recognized. "Contribute to the cause. Invest in yourself and watch your blessings triple!"

Liza's heart drummed. Where had Deya gotten such a precise sum of fifty-six thousand dollars? If she added up the last time she'd made a deposit in Granny's savings and her mother's bank account . . .

Gigi nodded toward the phone. "Liza, Isaiah is there. I heard his voice."

Liza's knees went weak.

Deya had taken Bev's and Granny's savings and given them to WIC.

That girl.

It could ruin them.

Liza pressed the bridge of her nose with her thumb and forefinger.

"Why is she even at an event like this? Isn't she, like, fifteen?" Dorsey asked.

Shit.

Shit.

Shit.

Liza stomped her foot, then looked at another video on the same account. LeDeya was there again—makeup immaculate, silk scarf wrapped around her head.

"My mother taught me to be independent. Let's build a community based on our principles. Donate now."

"These people will never see their investments again," Dorsey said.

"I think she has my granny's and my mother's savings. I . . . I think she invested it with WIC," Liza whispered. A terrible thought flashed into her mind. "Have you known him to abuse women sexually as well?" Liza asked Gigi.

"No—well, at least not yet. He has one love, and it's sports betting."

Liza nodded. She had written that huge proposal and leveraged her social media followers to add credence to his cause. Now little LeDeya was in such a rush to be useful and important that she'd sold away her family's life savings.

"How much did Deya take?" Dorsey asked.

"Fifty-six thousand."

Dorsey and Gigi looked at each other. They had the in-sync mannerisms of twins. She could practically hear the unspoken *so what.*

"I know it's vacation money to *you*, but my granny worked for fifty-three years to save that money up, and she has to live for the rest of her life on it." She was trying not to be defensive, but their look made the money seem so trivial. Liza could feel panic hammering in her chest. "I need to get her," Liza said. "Shit, Jersey is a four-and-a-half-hour drive, and I have no actual idea where she is."

When had WIC gotten his hooks into Deya? How could she have been so self-centered as to leave her baby sister unprotected?

Dorsey's cool hand rested on Liza's shoulder. He nodded to his sister and guided Liza silently up the loft stairs. Gigi came running behind them with her day bag and dropped it on the dresser. She took a quick survey of the room turned upside down but did not comment.

"I know what you're doing." Dorsey placed her gold heels together at her feet. "You are running scenarios in your mind, berating yourself for how you could have missed your youngest sister being groomed for a scam. Believe me when I tell you I have fucking been there. You need to stop spinning and get her now."

"All she wanted was our attention . . ." Liza stammered. Dorsey moved over the covers and found her panties, then rummaged through Gigi's small bag with jeweled handles, pulling out a pair of elegant striped linen slacks.

"These are my sister's. You can keep my shirt unless you want to get to Jersey in that dress from last night. There's not much of it left." He spoke in a matter-of-fact tone, like he made love like that every night.

He went into the bathroom, then emerged only ten seconds

later fully clothed. Was his bathroom a Superman booth? Liza dressed quickly, trying to shake the confusion and guilt fogging her head. Dorsey picked up her hand. "I'm arranging a flight for you on our plane. You'll be there in forty-five minutes. You need to find out from Deya where they are before they move. Keep it casual, so she suspects nothing. Then call New Jersey PD."

Liza pursed her lips. For Liza, the cops had always been more like the thing they needed rescuing from.

"Your sister is underage and you need to call the cops if anything . . ." Dorsey trailed off as they came down the stairs.

"I want to go with you," Gigi said as soon as she saw them emerge downstairs.

"No," Dorsey said. "She needs her brother."

Liza's face twisted in surprise. "Why on earth would I take Maurice?"

"Liza, your brother understands how to speak and presents himself with a particular type of posture. He's going to get a lot further than you can with Isaiah. I know it sounds sexist, but I promise you it will work. Maurice is very perceptive. You should give him more credit. Call him and tell him the car will pick him up on the way to the airport."

Liza did not know how Maurice had ever made that kind of impression on Dorsey. She rarely thought of her little brother as anything but a bore. Maybe Dorsey *didn't* think the worst of her family.

"Okay, I'll call him." She was actually grateful to have direction, to occupy her mind and body with action instead of anxious hand-wringing. "Dorsey, I—" Liza started.

"The car's ready. Liza, you need to go." Dorsey was turned away from her, on the phone, probably already filing away last night as a mistake.

TROJAN HORSE

LIZA DRUMMED HER FINGERS ON THE DINING TABLE (dining table!) in the Fitzgerald Airbus ACJ319 corporate jet. The jet interior was fully loaded with faux skylights and even a fake crackling fireplace. Warm creams, gold accents, and honey-toned wood veneers created a luxurious and comfortable interior. Maurice buzzed around the jet, opening every compartment and tasting everything on the serving trays. He would be too drunk to talk to Isaiah if he kept up at this rate. Liza couldn't seem to make herself comfortable despite the environment demanding it. She opened one of the many newspapers from around the country because they were the only thing on the plane to read save the safety instructions. A *Wall Street Journal* article caught her eye.

UPHEAVAL IN THE DEVELOPMENT WORLD

A major disagreement between Pemberley's (PMBY) board and the C-suite sparked the abrupt departure of acting CEO, Dorsey Fitzgerald. The move's announcement came from Robert Bradley, who is the chairman of Pemberley's board. Bradley said the board and senior management "disagreed on strategy" about the company's reorganization efforts. They have begun the search for an interim CEO.

Dorsey had lost his job. He had spoken so hopefully about revitalizing his mother's charitable organization. And now he had lost it all. Could she dare to think it was for her? Had he been slow to act and slow to crush her protests? He had the resources to hurt her—no, bury her. But her movement grew in visibility. Now they would hire someone less squeamish about what it took to do business. They would plow right through the citizens' protest and spit them out into homeless shelters.

Liza suddenly understood the enormity of what she and Dorsey were up against. How stupid they had both been to think they could have each other and sacrifice nothing. She took a deep breath. Maurice looked confused but rubbed his sister's shoulder anyway.

"Sis, she's not dead, just caught up in a scam. We'll get her. We all should have been more vigilant."

Liza said nothing but held his hand on her shoulder. Her little brother was growing up.

Liza absently stared out the jet window. She was irrevocably and deeply in love with Dorsey Fitzgerald. So in love that she could not allow him to sacrifice his mother's legacy and his sister's future for her. An unemployed wannabe who couldn't effect real change if it came to bite her in the ass. Her family would always need rescuing. She would always be a liability to him and his mother's legacy. She could see now that he wanted to live up to her work. His good work would always be overshadowed by the latest Bennett scandal.

Those moments dancing with Dorsey at the embassy made him seem different; august arrogance seemed replaced by shy reticence. Then the shyness boiled away again into a generous and powerful lover. Liza groaned at the memory of the way she had sobbed in his arms and screamed from the rooftops that she loved him.

He hadn't responded.

And she had seen that signature cold facade snap back into place right before she left. They just didn't make sense. She could see the gears turning as he rushed her out of his loft. She'd give it a month before the realization of what he'd sacrificed for her would start to feel like too much. That was the road to resentment and pain.

Liza sighed. She would remember the way he moved inside her for the rest of her life. Her body still buzzed pleasantly in the afterglow of their lovemaking. It hollowed her out without him, but they cost each other too much.

Maurice shoved a handful of grapes in her face. "You need to eat."

"If I eat, it won't be from your gross fingers," Liza said. Maurice then catapulted grapes at Liza's head. *Did I just actually think he was maturing?*

"So I asked around about our boy, WIC. Turns out he used to be a member of the Nation of Islam, and before that he was an Orthodox Mormon out in Idaho. He got over three hundred thousand dollars in donations, mostly from the pretty women he kept around him. Both communities kicked him out for constant gambling, excessive debt, misuse of funds, misuse of labor, and finally multiple complaints from his illegal wives. This dude has dotted around the country squeezing money out of any kind of believer."

"I didn't see any of this on Google," Liza said weakly. Using her sixteen-year-old sister to run a scam was low. She just hoped he had not taken advantage of LeDeya in any other way.

"You are not going to find it on Google. I told you I worked my networks." Maurice thumped his chest.

"Have you ever thought of being a cop, Maurice?" Liza asked.

"Nope, but maybe a detective once or twice. Anyway, this guy lies low because he has a lot of people looking for him, looking for their money. I think there is a way we can scam the scammer. But we need Janae to meet us in Jersey. Remember she was on that banking scam task force. She knows how to move money quietly," Maurice said. He stood up and pantomimed making a layup with a grape, which landed in Liza's water glass.

"Little brother, you may be on to something," Liza said. "I'll call Janae when we land." The plane began its descent. Liza cleaned up her face and attempted to control her demeanor. She called her sister as the plane touched down.

"Any news?" Janae asked.

"Maurice has a plan, but we need you to come with a laptop."

"*Maurice* has a plan?" Janae repeated. "Well, sit down, because this gets worse."

"How?"

"Granny and Mom called in a panic. They know the money's gone."

"Oh no." Liza's heart drummed in her throat. "We have to find them. I'm gonna kill him, then turn around and kill her."

"What do you need me to do?"

"Can you meet us at Teterboro Airport in Jersey?"

"Liza, that's a private hangar. How am I supposed to get in? Wait, how are *you* there?"

"We . . . may have taken a private jet," Liza hedged.

"I am so confused right now."

"Just get here, Janae, and I'll fill you in."

Half an hour later, Janae stepped into the jet. She snatched off her sunglasses and looked around the luxurious appointments.

"Liza, holy shit, how did you score this ride to New Jersey?" Either New York had already started affecting her or Janae came dressed for a caper in a black fitted jumpsuit.

"Dorsey F. and his sister bending over backward for her," Maurice said. He rolled grapes like dice in his hands and popped them into his mouth.

Janae surveyed her sister. Liza knew what she was looking for—all the little things that women, and especially sisters, see. She watched her sister piece it together. Her mascara was ruined. Her weave ponytail was askew. She was in a man's shirt and fine linen pants Janae had never seen. But Janae gracefully kept silent.

"What's the plan, little brother?" Janae asked, getting down to business.

"Okay, Liza's going to find out where they are. Then I'll go meet up with Isaiah and finagle myself into the room and tell him I heard Deya's going to double her money and I want in. They usually have these types of things separated by gender, so I'm probably the only one who could get in and get close to WIC." Maurice paused to swig red wine from the bottle, then continued. "Janae, I need you to fabricate a wire transfer. Hold some money there in his account for no more than fifteen minutes, then snatch Mom and Granny's money while you're in there."

"Ah, a Trojan horse scam. That's pretty sophisticated, but I think I can pull it off. Make sure he gives you all of his financial info. Tell him you can only wire it securely with all of his information."

"What if he doesn't fall for this? How would Maurice get that kind of money to wire to him?" Liza asked, trying not to panic.

"Liza." Maurice stood up in what Liza recognized as his pontificating posture. "Most fraud involves two willing parties. The first is the fraudster. The second is the greedy, willing participant—in this case, WIC. This participant has to believe that a bargain any rational person would believe is too good to be true is *actually* true. I'm betting that WIC is more greedy than shrewd. We need to promise a ton of money, no questions asked."

Liza and Janae looked at each other. A small acknowledgment passed between them. It would have to work.

Liza dialed Deya.

"Hey, Deya, I just wanted to say that I'm sorry for how I acted. This is a really cool opportunity for you to learn how to be an entrepreneur. I saw your Insta story. It's really well done. Who are you going to chat with?" Liza asked, breathing deeply to control her temper.

"Um . . ." LeDeya's voice was shaky. "They haven't really let me sit down with anyone yet. I'm waiting for my turn. I just have to do a few *other* things before I can really get into the learning portion."

"What other things do they have you doing?"

"I'm practicing my entrepreneurial skill by putting small sums here and there," Deya answered quickly.

Liza brightened up her voice. "Are you in a fancy hotel?"

"Liza, of course, we're doing it big over here. We have about four hotel rooms. But the women are just sitting around. The men are investing the money. I just thought I would get a chance to do some investing by now."

"Is your hotel dope?"

"I mean, it's nothing like the place we stayed at in Philly. It's just a regular Marriott by the airport."

"Do you all have a penthouse?"

"No, I told you we didn't ball all out like we did in Philly. We're, like, on the third floor, but the place has free breakfast!" LeDeya laughed. "Liza, if what I plan here works out, though, we can live like Philly every day."

"Wow, Deya. I hope it works out for you." Liza was actually grinding her teeth, but she hoped like hell it sounded like a smile.

After hanging up, she turned to Maurice. "All I got was that they're on the third floor at the airport Marriott."

"That's plenty."

"Maurice, leave your video call on and put it in your front pocket so we can see and hear everything. We'll be recording just in case we have to turn this over to the cops." Janae fussed with his jacket, and Maurice squirmed impatiently.

"I'm going. Do I have everything?" Maurice asked.

"If we can stop somewhere first, I can get some rope and some stuff to make chloroform. What do you have?"

"Liza, what the fuck? I was just asking about IDs." Maurice looked appalled. "What are you trying to do?"

LIZA AND JANAE CROUCHED OVER JANAE'S PHONE WHILE Maurice went up to the third floor of the hotel. When the elevator doors opened, they were able to immediately make out WIC's face half-covered behind Maurice's lapel and hear him greet people. "Welcome, young investors. The party is about to get started. Let's invest in our people."

The phone bounced as Maurice walked out of the elevator. Then they heard, "Hey, I know you. You're Liza's brother, right?" Liza could hear the wariness in WIC's voice.

"Hey, man. I've recently come into a bit of money; Deya told me you know a little about flipping cash?"

Maurice adjusted his jacket, and Liza and Janae could see WIC's face crack open in a wide smile.

"For a friend like you, I can set something up with you immediately. Let's get you to the money room, where the men are." They walked and chatted, mostly stuff that the mic didn't pick up because WIC was too far in front of him.

"Catch up, Maurice," Janae whispered.

Liza could see the predatory gleam in WIC's eyes. "How much are you thinking of investing? If I'm using my personal account, it can't be for peanuts."

"Does . . . one hundred thousand dollars sound like peanuts?"

Janae's eyes bugged out, and she dropped the phone and pushed Liza to the bathroom of the jet. "Liza, I can't move that kind of money! That number's way too big!"

"Does it have to be real money?" Liza asked.

"So now I have to make up money and put that fake money into his account? That will take days." Janae paced. It was just then that Liza noticed the glint of a ring on Janae's finger.

"Janae, what the heck is that on your finger?"

"Oh . . . this." Janae looked away. "I told you I would tell you if anything changes with David and I and . . . things changed."

"Okay, we're in a crisis here, so we're going to talk about this later and make sure this is a good idea. But you could pawn that ring now and get us halfway there."

Janae crossed her arms. "Liza, you have a lot of nerve . . ."

"Okay, okay. We obviously have a lot to talk about, but right now we need a hundred K in ten minutes."

"Well, Dorsey is richer than God. Why haven't you called him? He probably has this kind of money in a billfold."

"Janae, I can't. It's not like that."

"Um, you're flying in your sworn enemy's private jet and wearing his shirt. What *is* it like?"

"Dorsey is not some kind of sugar—" Liza's phone rang, and Liza quickly picked it up to silence it. Any sounds would disrupt the video call they were on. "It's Dorsey."

"Just in time. Let's ask him."

"Janae, I really don't want to do that."

"Fine, you don't have to." Janae plucked the phone from her hand and walked back to the bathroom. Liza was going to be sick. How could Dorsey even stand to look at her after today? She took and took. She waited for Janae, who padded back from the bathroom with a suspicious look in her eye.

"What?"

"It'll be in my account in two minutes." Liza's stomach dropped. *Maurice's plan had better work.* "Liza, he didn't even pause. Oh, you have a *whole* bunch of explaining to do. That was not booty call concern."

They picked up the conversation with Maurice and an increasingly impatient WIC.

"Nah, I'm still not seeing it, bro."

"What is wrong with the internet here? Should we go down to the lobby? I think the Wi-Fi may be stronger down there."

"Nah, I have a room full of curious potential investors, and I should really get back. Hit me up when your money is right, though."

"Look!" Maurice almost screamed. "Th-there it is, a hundred grand, just like I said. Right in your account."

"It looks like maybe we can do business. Tell me, do you want to play it safe with this money? If I put you on the advance plan, we're talking triple, quadruple the returns."

He's such a slimeball. Liza looked at Janae's face, forehead wrinkled in concentration. She was tapping furiously on her laptop. "Janae, can you actually do it? Can you take all of our money out?"

Janae didn't answer, too focused on the numbers on the screen.

"I want to decide with my sister. Where is she again?" they heard Maurice ask.

"Oh, she's out with the women. Let's get you out with the VIP investors. She is quite the little entrepreneur. Her online campaigns have already netted me about three hundred K in three days! She's a little moneymaker. And also, a daughter of Zion," WIC rushed to say. "She'll make someone an excellent Proverbs 31 wife."

Liza heard some muffled sounds.

"Where is LeDeya?" Maurice was more insistent now.

"Why don't you let her finish her little campaign for the day, and you can see her when she's done?" WIC said. Liza tensed. She could see WIC smile. *He thinks he's won.* "I know what you're doing, and it will not work, my brother. She's going to make the money she said she can make. And then she's totally free to go." Then the world turned sideways.

"No!" Liza cried.

Maurice had presumably tried to lunge toward WIC and throw a punch. But WIC was too strong, and despite the shaking of the phone, she could see that he had overpowered her brother.

"Reece!" Janae looked up from the laptop.

"No, you keep typing. Get all of our money! I'll go get Maurice."

MISTER

From: EliteEvents
To: dorsey@yourmail.com

Wow! That's a tall order. But if money is not an object, we are the team that can get that done ASAP. We've added fire extinguishers every 100 yards, so this thing is nice and safe. Will you also need a dance floor?

At your service,
Tom, Elite Events

Dorsey paced in his loft. He thought of nothing else but Liza. *Dorsey, I love you so much! Don't ever go.* She had cried out.

He was hers and there was no way around it for him. They had set the sheets on fire last night, and he wanted her like that for the rest of his life. He had never been held so tight. She was the family he had found.

They worked.

But if Liza's granny lost her life savings, he would feel personally responsible. Dorsey should have told Liza about WIC as soon as he began to circle around her like a vulture.

Gigi watched him pace. "Dorsey, are you sure this will work?"

"I trust her. Janae told me what they're trying to do, and I think it's the only way to catch a crook like that."

"I mean, are you sure this will work to get Liza back?"

"Gigi, she told me she loved me."

"Oh my god, Dorsey." Gigi covered her mouth with both her hands.

"But it was kind of heat-of-the-moment talk, and it terrified me that she would take it back, so I tried to close the deal this morning. But—"

"Oh, and then I interrupted, so her mind is elsewhere." Gigi nodded.

"Yeah, Gigi, I think this is it. She's *it*."

Gigi rolled her eyes. "Yeah, welcome to the moment, Dorsey. I've known this for, like, a year."

"I don't want to leave any open loops or questions about how I feel about her."

"How are you going to do that?"

"I plan to go big."

<hr/>

IT WAS A FULL TWENTY MINUTES LATER BY THE TIME LIZA got to the hotel. She was remarkably calm about what she knew she had to do. She tried to channel more of Dorsey's cool energy. What would he do? He would have called ahead and reserved a room so he didn't waste time shooting the breeze with the concierge. He would scope out the exits and have a quick way to leave.

"I can pay you extra in cash if you can wait here for an hour," she told the cab driver. He nodded and turned up the basketball

game. When she got out of the cab, she walked right in and reserved a room on the fifth floor, just in case they needed to get
lost really quick. Now, how was she going to get close enough to
Maurice and LeDeya without WIC seeing her? She didn't know
yet, but she was damn sure she'd figure it out. She pressed three
in the empty elevator, and suddenly she didn't have to figure it
out. WIC stood in front of the elevator doors as they opened to
the third floor.

"Greetings, future entrepreneurs—"

Liza pulled him in by both arms and forced the elevator
doors closed. His phone bounced and cracked on the elevator
floor.

"What the fuck?"

Impatiently she pressed the button for the fifth floor. She
needed to buy enough time for Janae to move the money. "We're
going to my hotel room."

WIC's eyes twinkled. "Well, Liza, I'm flattered but—"

"Don't be. Tell me where LeDeya is."

The elevator doors chimed open.

WIC made no move to get out of the elevator. "What is
wrong with y'all? Swooping in one by one. Deya is a grown
woman and she can do what she wants."

Liza pressed the elevator hold button. Holy shit. Liza blinked.
WIC was an idiot. A plan unfurled in her mind. "I have a cop waiting in my room upstairs. Deya is sixteen and traveled across
state lines."

WIC froze. "Fuck no, she's not. Her ID says she's twenty-one."

"The scar on Beverly Bennett's abdomen says different."

"Liza. Please. This ain't my style. I don't fuck with children.
I make money. That's all I do."

"You use young women and only care about how useful they

are to you. Do these women know about your wives in Idaho?" Liza's voice shook with emotion.

The stupid look of shock on his face collapsed into pleading. He was going through the five stages of grief in ten minutes. "Liza, look, I have a problem. I started picking my mother's lottery numbers at six years old. When I'm hot, I've won hundreds of thousands of dollars. I could live like your boy Dorsey for a day. But it takes so much to keep up."

"WIC, my *baby* sister? You stole money from a child. You're the worst kind of user."

WIC's nostrils flared. He was cycling through emotions wildly. Liza suddenly wished she had packed a weapon. He sneered, "And what are you, a saint? You're the worst kind of wannabe. Wannabe an activist, you got memed. Wannabe a voice in the community, you got fired. Wanna snatch Dorsey fucking Fitzgerald—impossible even for a much better-looking woman—and you got side-chicked."

Liza blinked back in astonishment. It was everything she had told herself—everything Bev had ever told her, right here in her face. She had to decide whether she would always believe that small, mean voice inside her head. Men like him were experts at exploiting vulnerabilities. It was precisely how they kept their partners docile and dependent. *That* was the thing he had seen in her before and what he saw in Deya now—a desperation to be seen and heard.

"I got memed. I got fired. Maybe I even got side-chicked. But I can't go to jail for life for any of that. Harboring an underage girl across state lines, however . . . different story."

His voice wobbled. It was his turn to feel panic and uncertainty. "I am telling you I did not know."

Liza let go of the hold button. "That's not my problem."

"Liza, you can ruin me forever with this kind of charge. And you know it's not true."

"I don't know *what's* true. I never have with you." Her voice had taken on a Bev quality that she quite liked. She felt like Angela Bassett setting fire to her husband's car in *Waiting to Exhale.*

"Liza. Anything. I will give you anything," WIC pleaded. Spit collected at the corners of his mouth. Liza shuddered at the fact that she used to find him attractive.

"Tell me where she is," Liza said. The elevator doors pulled open again on the third floor.

WIC's gigantic eyes actually looked earnest. "She's in Room 351."

"Those were our granny's and mother's life savings," Liza said. She prayed that Janae had time to take that money out.

WIC bowed his head. Men like this were experts at feigning remorse. She brushed past him—no longer interested in being his audience.

She shot straight for Room 351 and nearly cried out in relief when she saw Maurice limping down the hallway, dragging LeDeya behind him.

LeDeya was trying to pull away from Maurice. Her eyes rounded when she saw Liza. "Why are all of you here?"

"Let's move," Liza snapped with the authority of a drill sergeant. LeDeya, for once, did not give her any bull.

The car ride back to the airport was stonily silent. Every time LeDeya opened her mouth, Liza gave her a look that would curdle milk, and her mouth immediately closed again.

They climbed aboard the private jet in the same fashion, LeDeya forced into silence by the power of Liza's and Maurice's fury. Janae met them at the door.

"Janae, did you do it?" Liza asked, searching her sister's eyes.

"Yes! One hundred fifty-six thousand dollars!" Janae sounded surprised at herself. "I just wired the one hundred right back to Dorsey."

"Oh, Janae." She squeezed her sister, but Janae turned around and grabbed LeDeya.

"And you! How dare you take Granny's money? How dare you take Mom's money? What on earth did you think you were doing?" Janae shouted. It was the angriest any of them had ever seen their sister, and LeDeya crumpled underneath Janae's anger.

"No one is letting me talk!" she cried. "I just liked the stuff he was saying about being a proper lady. He called me Queen. He said I was a genius. None of you ever see how smart I am. I wanted to prove I could do something big for the family. After you got fired from the radio station—"

"Laid off," Liza corrected.

"When the radio station let you go, I knew we were about to have all of those same arguments about money. I just wanted to help."

"He is a swindler, LeDeya. Why do you think I stopped talking to him?"

"You *always* stop talking to guys that like you. He didn't seem to be different!" LeDeya was sobbing.

"He had no plans to pay you. No plans to ever return Granny's money," Maurice said. Liza winced at the gravelly sound of his voice.

"I started to kind of figure that out. I changed the graphic on one of the Instagram videos so that the number was blurred. I thought the money would bounce away and not be deposited. No use anyone else getting scammed like I did."

"Oh, Deya," Liza said, softening her voice.

"WIC wouldn't let me eat. He just kept saying stay a little longer."

"Did he try any—" Maurice started.

"I promise you, all that dude sees are dollar signs." She said this wistfully, as if perhaps she had tried. "Wait, Janae, is that an engagement ring?"

Trust LeDeya to take the heat off herself.

"Oh. Yes. Um, David and I are engaged," Janae said shyly.

"He completely ditched you," Liza and LeDeya said at the same time.

"You're right, and he was wrong for that, but Jennifer embellished his relationship with Gigi a lot, and she was pretty active in keeping him occupied. His father was dying, and he closed up. He got really afraid, you know, and he said he didn't know how I felt about him, and he chickened out." Janae looked down. "He said he was also afraid I had an alcohol problem."

"Why didn't he just ask you?" Liza was not so willing to let that little weak-chinned scoundrel off the hook.

"I love how ride-or-die you are, Liza, but that's a two-way street. I didn't tell him anything about my past. I couldn't tell him I loved him. I had his information. I just didn't call."

Liza was shocked. "Janae, you never called that man?"

"Okay, Liza! Don't drag me, honestly! A man not calling has literally never happened to me."

"Get out of here with your beauty queen problems," Liza teased.

"I told him everything about my past and about my son, and my struggle with alcohol, and how I chickened out on him too," Janae whispered.

"Oh, Janae, I can't believe you told him," Liza said. "How did he take it?"

"He was amazing. I went to see his dad. He told me he wanted his father to see"—Janae paused, getting teary—"the woman he's going to marry."

"Did you tell Ma?" Maurice asked.

"Oh god no. Let *me* enjoy it for a minute."

"You know that she's going to be the happiest woman alive for all of the wrong reasons?" Liza said.

"Can we get her in some woke classes?" Maurice asked.

"I think it's too late for her. Save yourself, Reece," Liza shot back.

They laughed, and Janae asked the attendant if there was a speaker system. They played Janae's favorite Go-Go from the Backyard Band over the airplane speakers as they touched down in DC.

JOHN WAYNE

From: DBrad@yourmail.com
To: dorsey@yourmail.com
Subject: RE: I thought you should know

Dorsey, I almost fell over in my chair! You sneaky bastard!
Was Liza the mezcal girl? One of the No Women? I'm so
happy you came to your senses. I got a weird feeling
about you two during the snowstorm. Janae and I even
talked about it. You two just couldn't stop circling each
other! But you shot yourself in the foot so bad when you
first met we thought there was no coming back from it.
Ha! That's the real story! We are going to have epic
double dates!

David

Dorsey saw Liza on the tarmac first, her ivory and blue high-
waisted linen pants blowing in the wind and his shirt still tied
at the waist. Did she know how many women would kill to look
so effortlessly elegant?

Gigi whistled. "She can have those pants. Who was I kidding? I can never do justice to them again."

Dorsey privately agreed. The pants obeyed the lines of Liza's body, and they looked tailored to her. Her family looked mostly intact as they tumbled out of the plane, perhaps a bit less gracefully. Maurice looked like he'd taken a beating, and LeDeya looked like she'd taken a tongue lashing. Their bags and pockets were full to bursting with the gourmet snacks from the jet.

They had all rallied to protect their family. Fifty-six thousand dollars was such a small sum to be anyone's life savings, but they had done everything in their power to retrieve it. If his family were still intact, he liked to think they would do the same.

LeDeya had made a mistake that young, naïve, idealistic people make. But like Gigi's mistake had, it would make her better. There was no one savvier than Gigi, and over time LeDeya would be a formidable entrepreneur. Maurice was brave and perceptive, and Janae was kind and intelligent. He quite liked this batch of Bennetts.

Bev would be . . . a challenge, but he suspected actions spoke louder than words to a woman like her.

All four of them had a strange look in their eyes when they reached Dorsey, and before he could process what was happening, he was being swallowed by simultaneous hugs. Their thanks and exclamations all ran together, and he couldn't make sense of any one thread of conversation. He looked only at Liza. A single tear slid down her cheek and he would have given anything to wipe it away. This big, messy family wanted him—without wishing he were different. A grape crushed against his shoulder and a bag of snacks popped against his rib. Okay, this hug was just about over.

"Okay," he said after a beat, trying to signal the end of this multiparty suffocation. "Okay, okay," he said again, though the beginnings of a smile worked on his face. They let go and looked around for their car. Liza walked behind everyone and bumped Dorsey's shoulder silently as they walked toward the town car. Town cars were now forever combined with the memory of the night she had let him taste her. She must have been thinking the same thing, because her heated eyes met his.

During the car ride, the Bennetts retold in raucous detail the events of the day. LeDeya was sullen for most of the trip and scrolled through her phone while they all told the story. It wasn't until the end, when they mentioned Liza trapping WIC in the elevator, that LeDeya laughed. Tears rolled down her cheeks as she laughed nearly all the way home.

When her family filed out of the car, Liza nodded to them and closed the car door. She buckled herself back in, and Dorsey smiled.

"You need to get some sleep," he said.

"I can't sleep. I have an idea." She paused. "To get your job back."

"What if I don't want my job back?" he said.

"You want your parents' legacy intact, don't you?" Liza said it like it wasn't a question. "And I have a way that might work."

"Liza, I appreciate that, but I don't need—"

"Dorsey, you're not the only one who gets to swoop in and save someone. Money fixes a ton of problems, but ideas still count for something. And I have an *idea*."

Gigi's elbow nudged him in the ribs. Her huge grin told him everything. *Marry her, or I will.*

"Let's scare up that senator from Virginia. He's dying to get in your pants." Liza's eyes twinkled. Here was John Wayne again. The swaggering bravado of this woman! It was really endearing for her to think she could change anything about the situation with the board. But he had failed spectacularly, and now he would have to take his medicine. He supposed there was no harm in calling the senator to listen to Liza's idea, though.

AN HOUR LATER, THEY WERE HUDDLED TOGETHER IN Dorsey's kitchen. Dorsey kept eyeing the loft. He couldn't remember if the cleaning service had been here today. Would the bed be made? Would Liza's dress still be crumpled on the floor? Liza opened a laptop, and Dorsey realized she was speaking to him.

"Of course, you want to balance your desire to provide affordable units with the need to turn a profit, or at least not lose money."

"Right."

"Okay, so in doing my research for writing this proposal, I found out that the Department of Housing and Urban Development allocates low-income housing tax credits. The developers then offer the tax credits to investors. The IRS allows developers to deduct one dollar from their tax liability for each LIHTC they purchase."

Dorsey nodded. He saw where she was going with this. It could be a win-win. Convert Netherfield Court to low-income housing units.

"The board is very adamant about wanting to build a relationship with the federal government. This is a shortcut," Dorsey said. "Shit, Liza. I think it could work."

The senator shook his head on the video call. "Why don't you call me when you have a real plan." His eyes followed the movement of Dorsey's hand swiping Liza's bangs out of her eye. "Is it true what everyone is saying? People saw you coming out of his apartment?"

Dorsey looked over to Liza, unsure of what he should say. "Senator, I don't see how that's relevant."

"Because you're obstinate and hardheaded. I told you two to do this months ago. This plays much better to those cautious council members. This is a *feel*-good story," he said mostly to himself, "but investors usually claim LIHTCs over a ten-year period. Pemberley is going to need cash up front to bring a project to fruition." He wanted to shut them down. But Dorsey could tell he was still thinking. Liza had sparked an idea in him. They were a perfect team. She had the vision; he had the money. He would make anything happen for her if she asked.

Dorsey tapped his bottom lip. "You can offer the credits through a syndicator who puts together a group of investors. The syndicate sells the rights to future credits for immediate funding."

"Okay, this just may work, but federal LIHTCs don't always cover the whole cost of developing low-income housing. We're still in the hole," Gigi said.

Liza stood up. She was in full swagger. "I'm so glad you mentioned that, Gigi, because HUD offers a little-known funding program known as HOME that can be combined with LIHTCs that would give you a respectable twenty percent profit margin. It's hella tricky, and we'll definitely need a housing attorney, but we can convert Netherfield Court into all low-income housing and turn a nice profit." Liza clapped her hands.

Dorsey looked at her in awe. His capable Liza had a solid plan to save his mother's foundation. *My Lady of Perpetual Help.* He was completely hers. She had to know that.

After arranging a plan to meet with the board the next week, Dorsey closed the call with the senator and ushered Gigi out, then turned to Liza, who looked exhilarated but exhausted.

"Liza, you should go get some rest." He motioned toward the bedroom upstairs.

"My mother's going to have a fit. I should go home."

Dorsey's brow creased. *Foolish of you to think she was yours too.* "Oh of course. I'll drive you."

"Dorsey, you have a lot to figure out here."

Dorsey held Liza's shoulders. "There's not a lot to figure out."

She raised an eyebrow.

"We're going to run this by Finance and Legal. Put a finer point on some of the numbers. It's a damned good idea." He needed her here. *Doesn't she see that?*

"I should really go," she said.

"Let me call my driver."

As he watched her drive off, her words echoed in his head: *You have a lot to figure out.*

MAKE WAY FOR THE *NEW* QUEEN OF SOCIAL MEDIA! There's a new Bennett in town. And I'm not here to bore you about social issues unless it affects my makeup tutorials!" LeDeya bounced on the bed as Liza held the phone at what LeDeya called *her best angle*. Liza mouthed the words "watch it" to her sister, and LeDeya cleared her throat.

"Now, before I review this life-changing eyebrow stamp, I have a small announcement. For any of you that donated to the Netherfield cause, here's a hotline set up by Pemberley Development to help get your funds replaced up to a thousand dollars. I want to apologize for my part in that. Y'all trusted me, and I led you astray. I was legit fooled. But you better believe it won't ever happen again." Deya winked into the camera, and Liza's arm flopped down. "Hey, I wasn't done!" Deya protested.

Liza put her hands on her hips. *"I'm* done. My arms hurt. And I'm tired."

"When did you get so old?" Deya shouted down the hallway.

IT WAS NEARLY SEVEN O'CLOCK THE NEXT MORNING WHEN
Liza woke up. The sun reflected off the decorated windows of
her room. Her mother coughed, and Liza's eyes flew open.
Granny, Bev, Janae, Maurice, and LeDeya sat in patient repose
at the foot of her bed.

Liza blinked in confusion. "What is everyone doing here?"

"When were you gonna tell us?" Janae asked.

"What?"

"I thought Dorsey wasn't your type." LeDeya folded her
arms in accusation.

"Don't be silly. Money is everyone's type," Bev asserted.

"I knew the whole time," Maurice boasted, and everyone
booed him. Even Janae threw a pillow at him.

"The hell you did." Bev laughed.

"I did! Dorsey came by all the time, y'all. We hung out,"
Maurice said. This elicited a laugh from everyone in the room.

"Okay, what purpose does it serve to lie, Reece?" Deya
laughed. "Like you and Dorsey are cool."

"I don't need you half-wits to believe me. I knew. But my
question is, when did it start? I can't think of a time when you
two were hanging out," Maurice wondered.

"The snowstorm," Janae said. "Something happened in that
nap pod. Y'all didn't come out till noon."

"Nah, it was the gala," Maurice argued. "The entire world
could see it at the gala."

"That Instagram post of you making food with his BFF,"
LeDeya guessed, as she scrolled back through her phone. "You got
an insane amount of likes and look! @DFitz commented the same
night with a Heart plus Rice Bowl and Smiley-Face-Tongue-Out!

Oh my god." Deya looked like she was melting onto the bed. "Y'all were stuntin' on us for months!"

"When he brought you that tree?" Granny suggested. "Don't look at me like that, girl. I know how babies are made. He was on you like white on rice."

"Granny!" Liza and Janae said in unison.

"David told me Dorsey was mooning over some mezcal mystery girl. Was that you?" Janae looked astonished.

Bev shook her head. "All of y'all are wrong. It was last year, the night of the meme. I've never seen Liza so out of sorts about a man turning her down. That's why Colin didn't do it for you. You don't like a man running after you."

Liza laughed. "All of you are wrong *and* right. It was death by a thousand little cuts. I was bleeding before I realized I was injured." Liza smiled weakly. "But he has a lot on his plate and—"

"Do you love him?" Granny asked bluntly. "Not do you like his money—do you *love* him?"

"Granny, I am *completely* in love with him." Liza did not hide the catch in her voice.

"He let you ride in the jet?" Bev asked.

"Ma, we all rode," Maurice told her.

"Did y'all . . ." Beverly put her index finger through a hole made by the thumb and index finger on the other hand.

"Ew, Momma!" Liza laughed despite herself.

"Bev, she left a few nights ago with that barely there dress on and didn't come back for two days. Any man would know what to do with that dress," Granny explained.

"I didn't know he would be there!" Liza defended herself.

"I hope Bev didn't get inside your head, child. Running after a man so uppity and stiff."

"Granny, he is the kindest man I've ever known."

"He's certainly the richest," Maurice offered.

"Shut up, Maurice," all the women said in unison.

Bev and Granny wanted to hear the story of rescuing LeDeya all over again.

Every time they got to the part of LeDeya sending WIC the money, Bev rolled her eyes dramatically.

"If I've taught you girls anything, it's never, ever, ever hand a man your *own* money. What on earth was this child thinking?" *This* was the lesson Bev wanted her girls to remember? Don't hand over money? Not "Don't fall for a liar"? "Don't betray your family's trust"?

LeDeya's sheepish look gave way to curiosity. "Does Dorsey love you too?"

Sorry I misunderstood our relationship. It won't happen again. Liza was about to say she didn't know, but Janae cut her off.

"Actions speak louder than words. He gave me a hundred K to move around, no questions asked. He met us at the tarmac and looked at Liza like she was Audrey Hepburn. If I were judging, I would say yes."

"No, Janae. Words mean something." Liza shook her head. "He came close one time, and I"—Liza took a small breath in—"I had the wrong idea of him."

"Well, he's gotten over that." Janae handed Liza her phone. "I don't know what you did, but that man lost his damned mind."

"What?" There was nothing amiss on her sister's Instagram account.

"Scroll," Janae instructed. She did, and she saw an ad:

"Hey DC, it's Dorsey Fitzgerald. You may remember me from this meme." A video popped out of their Netherfield Must Go meme. "Or this one." He pointed to the gala image of them dancing. "Because of Liza Bennett, this area will have one hundred and seventy-five new, state-of-the-art affordable units. I think we can show her a little appreciation. Meet me at sunset on the Frederick Douglass Memorial Bridge at Anacostia Park."

Liza's phone buzzed and beeped.

"He bought, like, all the damn ad space for this region on Instagram," Deya told her. "He's everywhere."

Liza's phone buzzed, rang, dinged, and chirped. Gigi had shared an article of an interview with Dorsey from the *Washington Post*:

DC City Council Approves Six-Story Affordable Housing Unit in Merrytown Neighborhood in Public/Private Partnership with Pemberley Development

Liza had to get to the park tonight.

A HARD KNOCK ON THE DOOR STARTLED LIZA OUT OF HER mirror stare. Janae had done her hair in the most intricate box braids she'd ever had. The baby hair was immaculate. LeDeya had polished and plucked and powdered her face until she looked . . . well, beautiful. She wore a cream maxi dress in gauzy woven chiffon. The ruffled short sleeves swept into a plunging V-neckline and a matching V-back. When she moved, the cascading maxi skirt showed off cinnamon brown thighs through a high front slit.

Janae clucked her tongue. "No one could say no to you tonight, Liza." When she stepped out of her room, the silence told her everything. When even Bev didn't criticize her for too much or too little of something, she counted herself lucky. She had now seen Dorsey's Instagram ad seventeen times, and it was trending in DC, Maryland, Virginia, New York, and Philadelphia.

In the Lyft, her palms itched, and her heart pushed against

her chest like it wanted out. What on earth was he thinking? He must be nervous himself. Now that she knew him, she knew crowds exhausted him.

The ride was quick, but since the entire family piled up in one car to save money, Janae insisted on bringing her battery-operated steamer to straighten out the folds in Liza's dress. Her sister fussed behind her until Liza slapped her hand away. LeDeya shoved a fist-sized puff into her face, and silicate power momentarily clouded Liza's vision.

"For the shine," she said, absently chewing gum and adding gloss to Liza's lips. "You look good, sis."

Maurice massaged her shoulders like a corner man in a boxing match. "Sis, the local news is out here. Don't do that thing with your face in the pictures. The RBF is real."

The white bridge overlooking the Anacostia River was positively teeming with people. Liza wondered how she would ever find Dorsey. So many people stopped to take photos with her. She was getting dizzy, whirling around and smiling.

Bev took Liza's hand. For a moment, with her eyes misting over, it looked like her mother was about to say something beautiful.

"You better get pregnant. Fast." Bev wiped a tear from her cheek. This was (Liza knew) the best she could expect.

Then she saw him. Walking with such purpose, separating the crowd like the prow of a ship, his sister behind him. He wore slim black chinos that stopped at the ankle with a simple white button-down that defined his broad shoulders and slim hips. His black Chelsea boots matched the belt low on his waist. His raven hair was tied back in a messy bun and shaved close on the sides and back. He looked impossibly chic, like he belonged in a villa in Italy. His face wore a worried expression, and he scanned the crowd every few seconds. She raised her hands and waved. He caught her gaze and made his way to her. His smile was so bright and boyish that if she wasn't in love with him already, that smile would have sealed the deal.

"Make sure you get your lanterns," Dorsey said to Liza's family. Gigi introduced herself to them and walked them toward the lanterns. Dorsey turned back to Liza. "When I was in the Philippines around Christmastime, San Fernando would host these huge lantern festivals." He slipped his big, warm hand into hers. It was only the second time they had held hands, and it seemed like the entire city shuttered their cameras at the sight. "I wanted to bring a little of that magic here to say thank you."

"I should thank you."

"The board was in love with the proposal and even wanted to hand me my old job back."

"Dorsey, that's great!"

"I said no."

"Wait, what? Why?"

"Meet the new executive director of WCO Foundation."

"Oh, Dorsey." Liza's joy flowed up. "That's a perfect fit."

"It is. We're also looking for a director for a new division we're spinning up. They would work closely with foreign countries' ministries of culture to highlight and amplify the needs of the respective communities."

Liza smiled. "This person would work *with* the community, not speak for them, right?"

His fingers traced the slope of her neck. "Oh, that's essential." His voice had gone husky, and Liza shivered under the graze of his fingertips.

"We won't be plastering our name all over projects well underway in other countries?" Liza loved looking into his eyes and seeing something soft and yielding in them, instead of the unreadable, flinty onyx she had come to associate with him.

"Never," he said.

"Well, this seems like a great opportunity. Do you know anyone I can speak to about my candidacy?" Liza asked.

"Oh, I heard the interview there is tough. Their executive director for one is a real asshole."

"Dorsey. You're not an asshole. Honestly, you're one of the kindest people I know. The jet, one hundred thousand dollars, no questions asked. You saved my family."

"That only proves my point, Liza. You have to know that I didn't do this because I'm a kind person. I did it for you. To be seen by you, valued by you. I'm *so* in love with you, Liza."

Liza recognized this jittery, chatty, confessional Dorsey, and she wanted him to stop before he said something he'd regret. She opened her mouth to speak, but he shook his head. "I tried to tell you this before, but I did everything wrong. And when you came to the embassy . . ." Dorsey's voice thickened. "When you told me you loved me, I thought it was said in the throes of passion and that you'd want to take it back."

Liza shook her head. She *had* wanted to take it back—not because it was untrue, but because she had been so afraid that he wouldn't return it to her. Dorsey's eyes were red-rimmed and wet, but focused solely on her. It was stone-cold fear of LeDeya, Janae, and Bev's collective fury that kept her from ruining her mascara and crying. Her chin wobbled anyway.

"Do you love me, Liza?" Dorsey searched her eyes. "Or do you still feel the way you did that morning in Alexandria?"

"Oh god, Dorsey!" Liza's exclamation came out breathless. She fanned her eyes. Where had all the air in her lungs gone?

"You had to know that night at the embassy that I loved you back. I was so wrong about you."

"So was I, which is why I invited you here."

"What exactly is here?" Liza looked around. "And how did you pull all of this off so fast?" No traffic, so many balloons they could lift the bridge, the same DJ from the first event—the detail was amazing.

"It's kind of a formal Fuck-It ceremony. And money can move mountains."

A harried-looking woman in black buzzed around them. "The Bird and the Bee have been located," she spoke into a walkie-talkie. "Five and a half minutes to sundown. You two should take your places."

"What places?" Liza asked. Dorsey led Liza toward the middle of the bridge. "Dorsey, what on earth are you planning?" Liza's eyes widened. The sun split into reddish-pink streaks across the sky that seemed to set the river on fire. It reminded Liza of their first night of drinks at the hotel bar. Someone shoved a mic in Dorsey's hand, and Liza could see the tremor there.

The last burst of light streaked across the sky, and Dorsey exhaled a slow breath. "Thank you all for coming tonight!" he said to the crowd. "I asked you here to celebrate someone you already know. The only DJ who gives a jam, Liza Bennett!" The crown erupted in cheers. "By now, you should all have your bamboo lantern or your candle on a banana leaf. By lighting them, I invite us to let go of what has been weighing us down, all of our fears. Tonight I want us to light our lanterns to"—his voice shook—"new beginnings." Dorsey's eyes met hers. "Liza, I love you. I, Blank Datu-Ramos, love you, Alizé Bennett!" The crowd roared.

Liza grabbed the mic. "Just Liza is fine," she told the crowd. Dorsey turned the mic off and handed it to an attendant.

"I want to ask you question number 37 privately," Dorsey said.

"There are only thirty-six questions in the app, Dorsey," Liza reminded him.

He smiled and took a deep breath. "Liza, will you marry me?"

Liza could barely breathe. Hundreds of small, glowing floats made from banana leaves were placed in the water. The Anacostia River was positively ablaze with everyone's hopes and dreams. Over her head, hundreds of candlelit lanterns of various sizes made from a thin gossamer fabric stretched and floated into the sky.

"You don't have to answer now." Dorsey took their huge lantern and scribbled out a note. Liza made out the words *Netherfield Must Go* in print. She wrote *First Impressions* on her own right before she lit the base. The lantern gently floated up and met the others in the sky. In the dark of night, the floating lanterns took on a filtered sodium glow, and it looked like they were at the bottom of a champagne glass. Above her and below her, the shimmering points of light blazed. She put her old mistakes away, and when she looked up at Dorsey, her heart was ready to walk fearlessly into her new purpose.

"Yes."

Dorsey's hands clasped hers, and his slightly sweaty palms trembled. She turned to look at him, and he was already drawing near her. When his mouth met hers, the shutters clicked, and the murmuring fell away. He was all there was and all there would ever be.

EPILOGUE

THE BASEMENT AT MOUNT TABERNACLE AFRICAN
Methodist Episcopal Church was at fire hazard capacity.
Liza looked down at her feet, vivid and glittering green against
the garish red carpet, and tried to imagine them swollen. She
held a fresh bouquet her mother had strong-armed a florist for.
Janae pulled at her peacock-feather shawl. Her sister hated feathers, a fussy holdover from her pageant days, but Bev had insisted.
Now all the women stood around her looking like the Supremes
as the pastor recited his third (and counting) vow.

The fold-out tables on the far-left wall overflowed with foil
trays of chicken, macaroni and cheese, greens, yams, and ribs.
Well-wishers squeezed tilting cakes in Tupperware cases next
to punch dispensers with floating citrus slices. Green cloths covered all the tables, giving the reception a decidedly Christmasy
feel despite the warm weather.

Her mother stood in the middle of the aisle in a lovely egg-
shell brocaded dress she had painstakingly sewn herself. Bev
was a bride. The reverend had finally come around. And god
help them, Bev was insufferable.

HOURS LATER, BEV HOBBLED TO HER CHILDREN'S TABLE, breathing heavily, undoubtedly from the unholy amount of booty shaking she was doing in a church basement. The last of the well-wishers filed out of the room, and Bev finally sat down.

She gestured. "See this, girls? Look around. This is a *real* Christian wedding."

Liza would not take the bait. "Congratulations on your wedding, Ma."

Bev pulled her heels off and pointed the toe of one shoe at Liza. "*You* flew us all out to the end of the world."

"Mom, South Africa is actually not the end of the world." Liza's tone was flat.

Bev shrugged. "Where is it on a map? It just sounds made up."

Deya elbowed Bev. "Ma, it's on a map. It's a famous country. Nelson Mandela's from there."

Maurice put a firm hand at his sister's back. "Liza, Mom has a point. Cape of Good Hope looked like the edge of the world. But that's what was so dope about it. I'm going back."

Bev huffed and gestured to the table overflowing with wrapped gifts and presents. "And you didn't even get any wedding gifts. You just had all of those rich-ass people there donate to the school? Child, I haven't taught you anything."

"Ma, you cried like a baby when that little girl gave you a hug after you donated those schoolbooks," Liza said. The table rumbled with laughter at the memory.

Bev looked only slightly chagrined. "Well, that's just human nature, Liza. I've always been a giver, but you shouldn't put people to work at your wedding."

Liza squeezed Dorsey's thigh under the table. He gave her a

lopsided smile. *None of this matters*, he seemed to say. "As always, sorry to disappoint, Ma."

"It's not worse than your sister—had us flying to a farm in Maine. Maine! Some states don't have Black people on purpose."

"I liked it," LeDeya said. "I've never been horseback riding before." She posted a picture of herself making a funny face. Deya was a social media powerhouse by now. At twenty she had eschewed college and began building a social media empire propped up solely on makeup influencer drama.

"But picking apples? They really had all those Black folks out there picking fruit?"

Janae passed her wiggling infant girl over to David, who kissed her forehead. "It was a weekend of activities. Everyone could choose what they wanted to do. You didn't *have* to go pick apples."

"Oh right, just so I can be the mom sitting everything out?"

Janae expertly steered her mother away from this topic. "The reception is beautiful, Ma."

David shook his head enthusiastically. "The food is fantastic. Seems like everybody took a plate."

"Damn right. I haven't even had a chance to eat. Brides never eat at their wedding, they say."

Dorsey's cool voice made everyone at the table turn. "Are you happy, Beverly?"

"That's First Lady Beverly Bennett Jones now." She smiled.

"I think your mother would have been very proud of you." The table stilled. Everybody loved their grandmother, but Liza had *really* loved her grandmother and had taken her death hard.

"Thank you, Dorsey," Bev said.

Never one to sit too long in sadness, she clapped her hands briskly. "And my first job as First Lady is to get this basement clean before Bible study tonight. Up! Up, all of you. Maurice, you take those chairs! Liza, you fold these tables!"

Dorsey came behind Liza. "Whoa, whoa. What do you think you're doing?"

"It's not going to hurt me to fold some tables."

"What if one of these tables fell over and crushed you?"

Maurice sidled up and pointed to his sister's stomach. "You sure you want to be handling those tables, big sis?" Maurice was astute. She had never given him his due.

"How did you know?" Liza asked.

"You've just been unconsciously touching your stomach a lot. Kind of protective. And Mom had to let out the dress she made for you just three months ago."

Dorsey raised an eyebrow. "I see those private investigator courses have paid off."

"Yeah, I'm saving up money to open a storefront in PG County. I'm going to call it Ear to the Street Detective Agency, or E2S—'When you don't trust the cops but you got to get answers.'" He said the last part wistfully. Dorsey nodded approvingly and Liza clapped him on the shoulders.

"You're going to do well, bro."

Dorsey pulled her away from the tables toward the pews on the perimeter of the room. Sitting her on his lap, he wrapped his arm around her, closing his warm hand over her gently rounding belly. Liza's heart quickened at the feel of his hands. *Will I ever be immune to his touch?* She had traveled the world with him. She'd seen him build a women's hospital in Malaysia, lay bricks in the Congo, and crash on a motorbike in Vietnam. He'd seen her haggle with a cloth maker in Lagos, sob into the night when a mother she had helped almost died in childbirth in Brazil, and order soap, *jabón*, instead of ham, *jamón*, in Ecuador. Liza thought they had seen every aspect of each other.

But now they would get to know each other as mother and father.

Liza interlaced their fingers. "What do you think of Datu for a boy?"

Dorsey grunted noncommittally. "It's a last name. What do you think of Evie for a girl?"

Evelyn had been her granny's name. Liza fanned her eyes and felt a lump rise in her throat. Her granny would have loved to see her pregnant.

Janae swept her feet playfully. "Liza's avoiding cleaning, as always."

Liza looked around the dimly lit basement. She had started this journey with Dorsey on her way to being jaded. Janae had been in a downward spiral of depression. Deya had been lost in attention seeking, and Maurice had been struggling with his identity. But they would be okay. Liza felt ready to focus on her *new* growing family. Her hand moved over Dorsey's on her belly and she leaned into him, letting out a contented sigh. The Bennetts would be okay.

ACKNOWLEDGMENTS

I am so lucky to have been surrounded by wonderful, trustworthy, and competent people throughout the time I have been at work on this novel. To my agent, Kim "the Lion" (made up) Lionetti, thank you so much for your advocacy and belief in me. Me! Thank you to my amazing editor, Cindy "the Hammer" (invented) Hwang, at Berkley. The number of neurotic emails and texts these women have fielded should be in a museum. I am consistently amazed at the level of care and engagement I have received from the Berkley team—folks like Angela Kim, who is patient and understanding.

Thank you to my husband, Heath, who, when we were at our poorest, nearly maxed out his credit card to send me to a writing conference. It was an investment that continues to pay dividends. Thank you for your unfailing support. We're doing it, Pooh! Further, I am deeply indebted to my sister-in-law, Zaneta, for her love and generosity, and I am sustained by the love of my mother-in-law and the memory of my father-in-law, who taught me lessons of perseverance.

I owe a special thanks to all my English teachers, whom I still remember by name and face, every single one of them. To Ms. Biggs, who calmly taught us Toni Morrison's *Beloved* while Texan parents were up in arms. To Dr. Fox and Dr. Graham at Sam Houston State University, who sat me down and told me I should go to graduate school for literature. I went for anthropology instead (you know, the big bucks).

This book is about family. I was raised by a coven of wise women: Aunt Donna who taught me how to use a library and who fed my love of reading; my mother, Bridget, who taught me to *never* fucking stop trying; and my aunt Nita, who taught me to do everything with heart. To my amazing sisters, Darcy and Tasha, and my dope-ass brother, Douglas, for letting me be the feeble nerd I needed to be, even when our environment demanded so much from us all. I owe an immeasurable debt to Nani (you know which one), my first audience member, my baby cousin, and captive audience. I also want to thank my cousin Shvonda, who had to endure my storytelling in the form of elaborate, soapy, Barbie, dramatic play iterations. (You should know that there is a lock-in scene in this book.) I'm going to get it right, dammit!

I owe a special thanks to the Jane Austen community, who have welcomed me with open arms. Bianca Hernandez and Abigail Reynolds represent the best of the JAFF community. I also want to thank the first readers of this novel: Sarah at Lopt and Cropt editing services, Lauryl, Libby, Lindsey, and Laura. I commend you. It was bad. But because of you all, it got better.

I would not have been as fully able to articulate what made this book so successful if not for the guidance of some of the most important mentors I've ever had along the way. Sam Tschida and Carly Bloom, you are my people. You are in my heart.

You introduced me to craft and an amazing space—my Tuesday-night class with Smut University. Grace, Christine, Rhya, Mary, Tam, Marie, Molly—your fingerprints are all over this book. I am grateful to Pitch Wars for affording me the opportunity to build a community of amazing writers: Regina, Maggie, Sarah, Ella, and Courtney. I have relied on you every step of the way and your love and generosity are powerful testaments to the magic of a writing group.

Finally, my acknowledgments would not be complete without special thanks to the people who are so dear to me and have supported me while I wrote this book. In addition to my husband and my children, Zonë, Nahj, and Xiva; my friends Torria, Charlene, Destinnie, Sabrina, and Eric have been faithful cheerleaders and encouragers throughout the years this book has been in progress. I'm so grateful for the steadfast, caring, ready ear of my friends. It takes so many people to push an idea like this across the finish line. Please charge it to my head and not my heart if I have missed anyone along the way. I'm indebted to those who joined me on this journey—taken like I was by the vision of Jane Austen, in color.

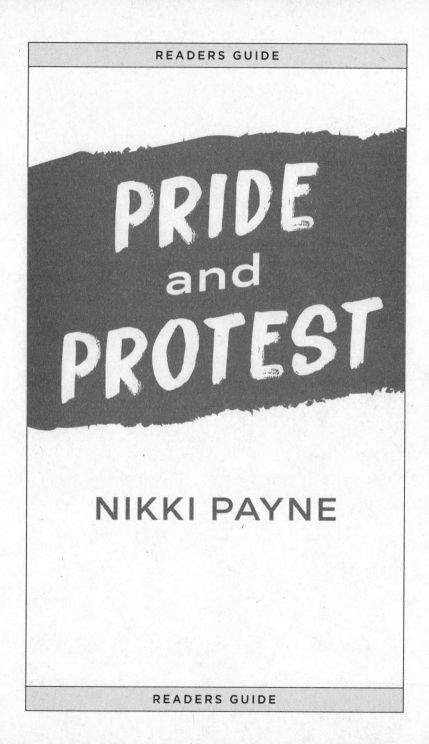

PRIDE and PROTEST

NIKKI PAYNE

DISCUSSION QUESTIONS

1. A large theme in the book revolves around each character growing to become the person that they want to be. Why is Liza a DJ? Is it a job she loves? Similarly, why is Dorsey a CEO? Is it a job he enjoys?

2. Mother-daughter relationships are fraught with so much tension and expectation. What is at the heart of Bev and Liza's discord?

3. Why did Liza mistake Dorsey for waitstaff? What does it say about her own views of the world?

4. Dorsey seems to field many microaggressions from people around him. Why was Liza's mistake particularly egregious?

5. Why doesn't Dorsey correct Liza when he has the opportunity to do so?

6. Considering her past, why do you think Janae drank at the office?

7. At the Hotel Washington, why is Dorsey so cynical about Liza's methodology?

8. In Philadelphia, Liza was excited to see WIC, and then something soured. Was it her deeper connection with Dorsey or WIC's own behavior that made Liza wary?

9. Another major theme of the book revolves around surface understandings and deeper truth, and how one could look like the other. Social media makes this false reality even easier to believe. What were the differences in Liza's and Dorsey's approaches to managing the truth?

10. Why did Liza love the gift in the Tiffany box so much? What does it say about the way Dorsey fulfills her needs? Compare that to the gifts she receives from WIC.

11. Why doesn't Liza tell anyone about her love for Dorsey?

12. What is Dorsey looking for when he roams Liza's neighborhood? Does he find it?

13. Why does Liza believe it is still over between them even after they shared a passionate night?

14. At the embassy, the next time Liza and Dorsey meet, what has changed?

15. Do you think Bev and Liza's relationship will ever change?

Keep reading for an excerpt of the next
Jane Austen–inspired romantic comedy by Nikki Payne

SEX, LIES AND SENSIBILITY

Coming soon from Berkley Romance!

TL;DR

WHAT DID IT SAY ABOUT THE SAD STATE OF HER LIFE that she was at her father's funeral and all she could think about was her sex tape? Yes, she knew it wasn't a "tape" but an infinite network of links that popped up *right* when potential employers were searching her presence online. *Nasty Nora* had made the rounds for about two years after her boyfriend posted it. But what really immortalized her was the freeze-frame shot of her grimace after her boyfriend asked if she'd "finished."

People attached her face to all kinds of dubious truth.

Did you remember to defrost the chicken? *Nora's Face.*
Does this dress look okay? *Nora's Face.*

Her mentions would subside until someone rediscovered the origin of the meme, then the video would trend again. This had been going on for about eight years now. It was all calming down until HBO did an explosive expose on the adult film industry and highlighted her video in the rise of amateur "disruptors." It was exhausting, and why she had to get out of this dangerous crush of people.

This was a sizable crowd for such a private man. The enormous poster of him, positioned on an easel, looked more like a shrine to seasonings. A garland of thyme and baby's breath draped elegantly around the photo. He'd founded Dash of Love Seafood Seasoning right here in Maryland, so it fit that they would memorialize him with mountains of Old Bay, crab hammers, and hot sauce crammed like Tetris pieces on a slick wooden table. Nora searched her bag and huffed in victory when she found salt and pepper packets from a month ago. She moved through the line and solemnly added it to the teetering tower. She swore she saw her dad's eyes twinkle. He looked a lot like her little sister Yanne in this picture. With his sandy skin, smooth hair gelled back, and even the myopic greenish-brown eyes that kept her younger sister in prescription glasses since she was five. Nora should be more broken up. In fact, she should be throwing herself over the coffin and screaming "Take me instead!" or "Not my daddy!" but in truth he'd been a hard man to know, and a part of her felt like that was on purpose.

Her phone buzzed in her hand.

Finally.

"I've been calling you for hours, Yanne." Nora tried not to make her voice pleading, "Mom's acting real . . . strange and this place is weird." The funeral home looked like the inside of Scarlett O'Hara's home, right down to the velvet green drapes. Her mom was teary-eyed and deferential to everyone she met, as if she wasn't the love of her father's life. She had insisted on sunglasses and a scarf even inside.

Her sister sighed over the phone. "Nora, chill. Remember what your therapist says 'Don't shrink. Stand your sacred ground.' I'm with a drummer. He just finished my tarot—Three of Swords, Nora. He predicted I was going to do some heavy shit today,"

"Except *you're* not doing heavy shit, Yanne, you're with a drummer. *I'm* doing heavy shit. You're late."

"Late for what, exactly? His embalming ceremony? His spirit is no longer with us."

Nora deployed her favorite weapon. Dead silence.

She could *hear* her sister squirm.

"The man was barely there for us when he was alive, Nora, and now he expects our punctuality for this pretense?" She pronounced it PreTONSE. If she was over-enunciating, there was a crowd.

"That is not the point. You said you would be here on time. You're not here on time. Sexing up a drummer is what you are doing." Her tone was too imperious, she knew. She couldn't help it with Yanne.

"You need to talk to someone about your sex thing. Your mind is like a sieve that only keeps the dirty stuff."

"You're late and that's not sexy."

"Time is a circle, Nora, not a line." She hung up.

Late. Late. *Like I knew she would be.* Yanne had an infuriating habit of never being there when Nora needed her. There was always some poetry reading or love of her life or social injustice that took precedence over everyone and everything else in her life.

Slipping her phone down into her purse, Nora made a note of all the exits. Then took an inventory of the bathrooms. Did she imagine all the glances? She smoothed the pleated crepe of her dress. It was the most expensive thing she owned. Her father had bought it for her in France and yes, it was yellow, but it was also gorgeous and reminded her of him. But it was too much, the glances told her so. There was a time when she would have been used to the looks. Back when she was semifamous for her athleticism and record-breaking 500-meter races. She had even graced the cover of *Track and Field* magazine. That was back when her whole life was ahead of her.

But at her father's funeral? No one would think to approach her here. Right? All of these eyes—it was probably the dress. Daddy always bought her yellow dresses "because it makes your dark skin shine." Nora had thought, even today, he might like to see her in yellow.

She didn't frequent a ton of funerals, but this one was particularly strange. For one, everyone looked so damn good. Everyone here, at least, the high society of the DMV, treated the event like Easter Sunday—decked out in their best black, exchanging cards, and speculating on the price of someone's new Potomac property. She even saw The Beverly Bennett. Her mother's gossipy over-the-top girlfriend who screamed her daughters' net worth to the rooftops. In her fifties, she was still a knockout, dressed in a tight black number that made men half her age whistle. She acted like it was such a miracle that not one but *two* of her drop-dead gorgeous daughters (she had at least seven of them) had catapulted themselves into the stratosphere.

Guess how?

The sheer power of being drop-dead gorgeous. *It's not news, Bev!* She wasn't bitter. She wished Liza and Janae well, but she just wanted to stop hearing about them. Nora would never stop traffic like the Bennetts, but she had been popular in the past. She had good skin and strong straight teeth. Some would even call her lovely in a soft light, but she wouldn't ever have a serious relationship. The video had assured that.

Beverly Bennett patted her mother's back, and a ring the size of Mt. Vesuvius glinted on her finger. It added to Nora's mounting off-kilter feeling to think the relatively well-off Dashes used to buy hand-sewn dresses from those "poor Bennetts" out of pity.

The funeral itself was *off.* Somebody's nephew was playing an up-tempo high school marching band rendition of "When the Saints Go Marching In." Nora decided right then that there would be no upbeat numbers at her funeral. *I want that shit sad.* Not jazzy and vaguely sexy like this one. Even stranger, she and her mother, the chief mourners, if you will, were being completely ignored. No bereaved aunties and uncles tapped her shoulders. No one gave them their thoughts and prayers or handed them lukewarm potato salad. She knew her mother was not on good terms with her father's family, but this was downright cruel.

Nora felt a light tap on her shoulder and jumped a bit too high. She was terrified of that tap. That someone in a crowded room was going to squint their eyes and walk toward her. Maybe a man sucking his teeth would say, "You look so familiar. Have I seen you somewhere before?" And of course the question was rhetorical.

Of course they had seen me. All of me.

Every tiny little action Nora engaged in always, *always* had outsized consequences. Which is why she liked to minimize her *mistake footprint* all together. It was simple. No risky decisions equaled no traumatic mistakes. She was the poor kid in those *If you Give a Mouse a Cookie* books, and she could prove it. Here is what is bound to happen re: making a hot sex tape with your college boyfriend:

1. First, do *not* make a hot sex tape with your college boyfriend. He will be your boyfriend for three more months. Tops.
   - And if you are incredibly ridiculous and say yes, don't try to be the super cool girlfriend when he suggests you put it online.
   - Don't say "Yeah, it's cool. It'll be funny."
   - It *won't* be funny. It will only make you infamous in Maryland, Virginia, and DC for an excruciatingly long time.
2. You'll lose your track scholarship (you loved track more than you loved your boyfriend) because of the morality clause.
3. You'll get a nickname like Nasty Nora
4. You'll drop out of college nine credits shy of your degree.
5. And instead of being a hot PE teacher at a progressive artsy elementary school, you'll be lucky to get a job as a pharmacy tech at a big chain grocery store.

TL;DR. See Point One.

Another tap on the shoulder, this time more insistent.

"Are you Shenora and Maryanne Dash?" A twitchy, round-faced white man held out a thick cream card to her. *An estate lawyer. This should be interesting.*

"I'm Shenora and this is my mother, Flora. My sister hasn't arrived yet."

"Mrs. Dash would like to speak to you in the offices upstairs."

———

THE PLUMP, BROWN-SKINNED WOMAN'S UPTURNED MOUTH dropped like a stone when she saw Nora walk into the office. She sat at the head of the table like a mafia don. Fur coat, thick gold rings, soft cotton halo of shoe polish black hair. When she spoke, Nora could see that she had teeth long and white as piano keys.

"You have a lot of nerve showing up here, Flora," the woman hissed at Nora's mother.

"Excuse me?" Nora asked. *Sure, they weren't married, but what was this—the 1950s?*

Mom rolled her shoulders. "It's not about me. It's about my girls. They have the right to pay their respects."

Nora couldn't seem to stop blinking. "Mother, don't respond to that. Of course we do."

Mom didn't meet her eyes. "Nora, please."

Nora, please? Why was she allowing this woman to talk to her like this? Mom looked behind her at the door. "Nora, this is Mrs. Dash."

So what? Why was some auntie allowed to talk to her mother this way? Nora locked arms with her mother and moved to push past the threshold when her mother froze.

"Mrs. Dash is your father's wife of thirty-five years."

Your father's wife. Three words and Nora couldn't push enough air out of her lungs to speak. Everything rolled over her in slow motion. She gasped and stumbled, like she had missed a step on an invisible stairwell. Thick tongues slid over yellowed teeth. Eyes matted with liner and mascara blinked and watered as they stared out vacantly at her. She felt streaks of hot and cold panic roll around inside of her.

My father's current wife?

Of thirty-five years?

Her stomach threatened to spill the ham sandwich she'd chosen for lunch. Her hands shook with impossible tremors. *My mother was a mistress? Didn't you have to be sexy and mysterious to be a mistress? Did mistresses bake pies?* These panic attacks had gotten worse in the past year. She could feel them coming but was powerless to stop the crippling panic from washing over her. They were all looking. So many eyes.

He never belonged to us.

Her father, already a hazy, distant man, was coloring himself even farther out of the picture like a finger smudge on a poor charcoal rendering. He'd been obscure, mercurial, chronically late, and impossibly charming. He winked after telling a bawdy joke and never made it to a single sporting event she was in. *Her* father, on top of being all of those things, wasn't even her own.

The constriction of Nora's throat intensified. Maybe she would suffocate to death right here at her sexy mistress mother's feet.

"Nora! Have some water. Have a seat. Nora!" She heard their distant alarm, but couldn't reach out to them. She just stood there, compulsively swallowing and sweating through her lovely yellow dress.

Oh, she forgot one. Another reason not to make a sex tape with your college boyfriend:

6. You'll develop an inconvenient panic disorder
   that makes even the smallest tasks seem impossible.

Thank goodness she'd cultivated a calm and predictable life, minimizing ridiculous surprises . . .

Just then, Mrs. Dash slapped the table commanding the attention of everyone in the room. "Honey, if you need smelling salts after that bit of old news you'll need a stretcher by the end of this meeting."

Author photo by Frank W Images

By day, **Nikki Payne** is a curious tech anthropologist who asks the right questions to deliver better digital services. By night, she dreams of ways to subvert canon literature. She's a member of Smut U, a premium feminist writing collective, and is a cat lady with no cats.

CONNECT ONLINE

NikkiPayneBooks.com

🐦 NikkiPayne14